By KATHY LYONS

WERE-GEEKS SAVE THE WORLD
Were-Geeks Save Wisconsin
Were-Geeks Save Lake Wacka Wacka

Published by DREAMSPINNER PRESS
www.dreampsinnerpress.com

WERE-GEEKS SAVE LAKE WACKA WACKA

KATHY LYONS

DREAMSPINNER PRESS

Published by
DREAMSPINNER PRESS

5032 Capital Circle SW, Suite 2, PMB# 279,
Tallahassee, FL 32305-7886 USA
www.dreamspinnerpress.com

This is a work of fiction. Names, characters, places, and incidents either are the product of author imagination or are used fictitiously, and any resemblance to actual persons, living or dead, business establishments, events, or locales is entirely coincidental.

Mass Market Paperback ISBN: 978-1-64108-177-1
Trade Paperback ISBN: 978-1-64405-312-6
Digital ISBN: 978-1-64405-311-9
Library of Congress Control Number: 2020937830
Mass Market Paperback published January 2021

Printed in the United States of America
∞
This paper meets the requirements of
ANSI/NISO Z39.48-1992 (Permanence of Paper).

Sometimes it feels like stories are created through magic. There's a strange alchemy in words that generate laughter, paint pictures, and make me feel so much that I'm crying as the words flow through my fingertips. I'd like to claim the experience as my own, but it's not. Without the dedication and support of every person at Dreamspinner, I wouldn't have attempted this series, much less seen it to fruition. Every time another person touched the manuscript, the story got better.

My gratitude overflows. Thank you, Elizabeth, Lynn, Brenda, Gin, Amelia, Anne, Julianne, Katie, Polly, Camiele, Mara, Ariel, and all the others who have toiled so hard to make me look good. Thank you for your vision that gave me the opportunity. Thank you for staying true when so many try to tear you down. Thank you.

Signed with love,
Kathy

Chapter 1

THE DAY LADDIN GOT RECRUITED
(Eight weeks before Lake Wacka Wacka becomes a problem)

"YOU WANT me to put wallpaper on the teahouse wall," Laddin Holt said. Though he didn't phrase it as a question, his tone all but screamed, *Are you serious?*

Bing Wen Hao nodded. The man was producer and lead actor for the *Red Wolf: Origin* movie. He was also a stickler for detail and Laddin's boss. "China invented wallpaper. This room would have a textile-type wallpaper."

"But the wall is only seen when it gets blown up. It's on screen for ten seconds at most."

Bing Wen Hao merely looked at him, his face an impassive mask. But Laddin had been working shoulder to shoulder with the guy for two months now. He could read Bing's opinion in the smallest shift of his chin, and on this point, Bing was being irrationally stubborn.

"It will take me hours," Laddin said, still hoping to reach some sane part in his boss's brain. "I have a dozen other things to do today."

No-go. Bing was overwhelmed with anxiety because some Chinese bigwig was coming this afternoon. And when the boss got anxious, everybody suffered.

"Details matter," Bing stressed.

Laddin knew that. He was the king of details, which was why he'd gotten the job of assistant director on this indie kung fu movie. It was quite a step up from being the explosives guy on five failed action shows. He was in charge of everything that wasn't acting or camera placement. That meant the entire set design was his department, and he refused to fail now just because his boss was being irrational.

"Perhaps we could try different lighting—" he suggested, but Bing wasn't going to let that pass.

"If you cannot do it, perhaps someone else will be able to."

Laddin ground his teeth. Those words—or versions of it—had plagued him his entire life. His right hand was deformed, with his middle and fourth finger never growing beyond infant size. The docs had never given a good explanation of why. They suspected a growth plate break or a congenital birth defect. Didn't change that his hand looked deformed. At first he'd hated himself for his handicap. But thanks to his mother, he realized it didn't limit his ability to do anything he wanted to do. And yet, other people always questioned his capabilities.

"I can have it done by noon," he snapped. "But you hired me to tell you when something doesn't make sense. This doesn't make sense. Not for ten seconds of screen time."

He waited in silence as Bing stared at him. His boss's expression was blank, but there was a whole lot of something going on inside his head. It was excruciating, standing there waiting, but patience was one of Laddin's strengths, and eventually he was rewarded.

"You are correct," Bing finally said. "Continue with your assigned tasks."

Score one for the underling with nerves of steel. And then, to show Bing he wasn't an asshole, Laddin offered a compromise. "I can roll a faint design onto the wall that will make it look like faded wallpaper. Shouldn't take more than a half hour."

Bing gave him a nod—his version of "thank you"—and then moved off to do his own work.

Though Laddin was annoyed by the man's obsessive attention to a detail, he couldn't fault Bing's work ethic. The guy lived on the set night and day, working to make this movie as spectacular as possible on a very tiny budget.

And that meant Laddin had to start painting ASAP. He'd just grabbed the roller brush when his morning call from his grandmother came through.

"Hello, Grandmama. I'm still alive."

"Oh, you poor baby. It still hasn't happened."

He chuckled because really, what else could he do? "Most grandmothers would be happy that their only grandchild is still around."

"You're not going to die, Laddin. How many times do I have to tell you that?" Her voice settled into her performance tone. Grandmama was a psychic by profession, and sometimes—most times—she needed to put on a show. "The day we realized your hand was different, I had a vision. The great Angel Charoum whispered to me that in your twenty-eighth year, you would transform into something magic—"

"I'm really busy right now. We're supposed to start filming tomorrow, and everyone's on edge." He knew his grandmother hated being interrupted, and usually he'd let her prattle on, but he didn't have the time today.

"Don't despair, Laddin. It will happen for you. I know it will. There are still two months left before your birthday. You remember who Charoum is, yes?"

"He's the Angel of Silence." Of course he knew. Charoum's prediction had been the topic of discussion for nearly every day of his twenty-eight years.

"Exactly! And when the Angel of Silence speaks, it's very important to listen."

"Yes, Grandmama." And he had listened his whole life as everyone speculated on what the vision could mean. Most thought he would die, but Grandmama had insisted he'd transform into a magical being.

For the past ten months, his mother and grandmother had called every day to make sure he still breathed. Laddin just wanted it to be over. Death, rebirth, or becoming a crazed leprechaun—it didn't matter to him so long as *something* happened, because at this point, he was pretty sure he'd spent his entire life anticipating an event that his grandmama had imagined to add excitement to her only grandson's birth. And if it created endless speculation about his twenty-eighth year, then so much the better for her.

Him, not so much.

He was about to invent an excuse to get off the phone, but then it vibrated in his hand. A quick look had him rolling his eyes, but he knew he had to answer it. "I'm sorry, Grandmama. Mom's calling. I have to tell her I'm still breathing."

"Of course, Laddin. Don't worry. It'll happen soon."

"I'm sure it will," he lied. Then he clicked over to his mother. "Hi, Mom. I'm still alive."

SEVEN LONG hours later, most of the day's to-do list was finished, the Chinese bigwig was here and wasting everyone's time, and Laddin was taking a much-needed break, sitting in his work area and going through the special effects for tomorrow's scenes.

Suddenly a deep voice said, "Aladdin Holt?"

"Don't touch anything," he grumbled. It was what he always said when someone walked into his work area. He didn't look up until he was done with the C-4, but when he finally did, he wished he hadn't.

Two guys stood in his work area. One wore stripper pants; the other had on some sort of Doctor Strange outfit. "You want the set next door. They're doing that *Game of Thrones* wannabe thing."

Doctor Strange grinned. "We know. Where do you think we got these outfits?"

The stripper—whose torso was movie-worthy—shook his head. "He's joking. They had way better stuff than this crap. Still, these getups allowed us to fit in while we found you."

Well, that changed their category in Laddin's mind from "thieves" to "groupies." They were both beautiful enough to be actors, but neither of them had the charm. Which meant they were hangers-on who looked for odd jobs so they could participate in the movie magic.

Laddin pulled a business card out of his pocket and handed it over. "Here's my email address. Send me your résumés and I'll look them over." It wouldn't help them, though. He'd never work with a guy who wore stripper pants, and Doctor Strange was already poking into things on the electrical bench. "I asked you not to touch anything."

The guy raised his hands and wiggled them in the air. "Not touching. Just sniffing." Then he gestured at the *Quit Slackin' and Make It Happen* poster taped to the back of Laddin's door. "It's like a Successories warehouse exploded in here. Tell us, Mr. Holt, do you find moviemaking a little lacking in magic these days? If so, we've got a deal for you!"

There was a dryness to his tone that set Laddin's hackles on edge. What did this asshole care if he found expecting to die hard to take? "You need to leave here now," he said, his patience exhausted. He advanced. He was small compared to the guy in stripper pants, but he was fast, and he had some frustration to work out.

Fortunately Stripper Pants held up his hands in a placating gesture. "Ignore Wiz. He's an ass. My name's Nero, and we're here to offer you a job. It's rewarding work, saving the world. That's not an exaggeration, by the way. You'd be doing good for a lot of innocent people."

God, could they get any more annoying? Every asshole in Hollywood thought their movie idea would change the world. "I've already got a job, and even if I didn't, this"—he flicked his fingers at the guy's clothes—"doesn't impress me."

Wiz grinned. "Didn't think it would. But how about we try this?" The guy whipped out a three-ring binder and started chanting cheesy fantasy crap.

Laddin had absolutely no time for this nonsense. He grabbed stripper boy's arm and yanked him around into a choke hold.

Or he tried to. Normally people underestimated his strength, given that he was a small guy among the tall, dark, and handsome actors in Hollywood. But when he got a hold of a guy's arm, he held on with a death grip that usually took everyone by surprise.

Not this time. Sure, he managed a quick grab, but Nero was more than a match for him. The guy probably spent all his time in the gym, because Laddin's best wrestling moves did nothing. Hell, the guy didn't even bend. Which left Laddin standing there, holding on to the big guy's wrist and thinking, *WTF?*

Then Wiz finished whatever the hell he was saying with a grand flourish, and both men froze as if waiting for something to happen.

Laddin waited too. It was force of habit. Grandmama often said things with a flourish, and it was only polite to wait for the dramatic results. But he didn't have any patience left today.

"I'm calling security," he said as he pulled the walkie-talkie off his hip.

Nero grabbed his hand and held him firm, but turned to look at Wiz. "What the hell happened?"

Wiz was frowning as he looked down at his binder in confusion. "I don't know. I said it right."

"Damn it!" Nero growled. "Call Gelpack!"

"I am!" Wiz said as he started texting one-handed.

Laddin had had enough. He broke the grip on his wrist and pulled up the walkie-talkie. He had one hand on the button, then suddenly stopped, his eyes widening in shock.

Goo oozed around and under the door to his work area. It moved fast and with purpose. Laddin had spent his entire career on a Hollywood set, but this was something he'd never, *ever*, seen before. Hell, it was worthy of *The Shining*. He gasped and shrank back, the gesture bumping him into Nero, who took the opportunity to grab the walkie-talkie with one hand and restrain Laddin with the other.

"Don't worry. He's with us," Nero said as the goo formed into the vague shape of a human.

"What is it?" Laddin gasped, but no one answered. They were too busy talking to each other.

"Why didn't it work?" Nero demanded.

"I said it exactly right," Wiz said, his tone defensive.

"Unless it's him?" Nero said, looking back at Laddin.

"You think it's the wrong spell?" Wiz asked.

There was an edge of controlled panic to both their voices, as if they were worried but used to working things out on the fly. And all the while, Laddin just stared at the goo as it turned to look at him. It didn't even have eyes but the vague impression of orb indents, and yet Laddin would swear it was staring straight at him.

"What are your feelings at this moment?" the gel-like thing warbled.

Nero groaned. "Not now."

"I cannot understand his emotions. I will fix the spell if he explains."

"Later—" Nero grumbled, but the gel thing paid him no heed. It advanced on Laddin with steps like a man's, though it appeared more like a mold that had been filled with water—fluid, liquid. If he'd seen it on the big screen, he'd have called it cheesy. But in real life, it made the hair on the back of his head stand up in terror.

And then the truth hit him full force.

Today was the day. He either died or transformed into…. "Magic," he breathed, seeing his grandmother's prophesy play out before him. Then he laughed, though the sound had a hysterical edge to it. "It's today!"

"Um, yeah, this is magic," Nero said, confusion in his tone. "Well, the spell was. He's—"

"Magic!"

"—alien."

Laddin shrugged. Either one worked for him. "I'm not going to die," he said as he started taking deep, relieved breaths. His grandmother's prophesy was coming true, and it didn't involve him coming to a painful end. Relief sent waves of giddiness through him.

"Not intentionally. It could still happen by accident," Wiz muttered. Then he peered at Laddin. "Are you okay? Maybe the spell did do something. Maybe—"

"The spell was ineffective," the transparent creature said. "You did not say it with clear intent."

"The hell I didn't!" Wiz huffed. "I intend for this guy to become a werewolf. I intend to get it over with so we can move on to the next guy. I intend to get myself a really stiff drink after this is all—"

Laddin's head snapped up. "A werewolf? Really?" The idea was exciting in a terrifying kind of way.

Nero twisted him around. "You believe in weres?"

Behind him, Wiz snorted. "This is Hollywood. People here believe everything."

"We do not!" Laddin snapped, the reaction automatic. It was his grandmama who believed everything. And had taught it to him.

The gel thing addressed him. "I do not understand your emotions. Most people are frightened." He raised his hand and extended it toward Laddin, who immediately choked on his giddiness. Except it wasn't giddiness anymore. The sight of that clear ooze coming close to his face was terrifying, and he squeaked in alarm.

"That is better," the thing said. "The spell should work now. His pattern has settled into fear." The head spun toward Wiz. Not the body, not the shoulders, just the head—*Exorcist*-style. "Fear will make it stronger, to be sure."

Nero blew out a heavy breath. "We were trying to do this nicely. Without trauma!"

"That was never going to happen," Wiz grumbled.

"Shut up and do the spell again. With intent this time!"

Wiz started speaking, his words a mesmerizing mix of nonsense and real words. Laddin focused on it rather than the gel-like horror before him. Nothing here was odd, he told himself. In fact, he'd been waiting his entire life for this very moment. He felt his shoulders relax and his breath steady.

"He is not frightened enough," the alien said. "His mind appears to be unusually accepting. Are you sure this is the right man?"

"Yes!" Nero snapped. "It's Hollywood, for God's sake. Who knows what people here think is true? For all we know, you're not his first alien."

"That is most unusual," the thing said, and there was interest in his warbled voice. "I should like to probe this further."

Laddin had no idea if it was intentional or not, but the word *probe* exploded in his mind and tightened areas of his body into hard knots of terror.

"Much better," the alien said as he turned toward Wiz. "You may finish now."

Wiz did. His voice rose with an impressive crescendo while his free hand danced in the air. Then there was a boom. Not an audible boom but a vibration that affected Laddin more than the biggest car explosion he'd ever pulled off.

His muscles quivered and his bones rattled with the power of it. His throat closed off and his shoulders hunched. But inside, he was still caught up in Grandmama's prediction. Finally, the batty old woman had been proven right, and that made him happy. She may have plagued his childhood with one wacky idea after another, but in this, she was 100 percent right.

"Do not be so calm," the alien warbled. "Otherwise you will die."

The line was so stupid that it actually made Laddin loosen up even more. His cells were bathed in an electric current that was almost fun as it coursed through his body in erratic and uncertain patterns. But before he could fully relax, a sound filled the room—a guttural roar like that of a beast. It was harsh and terrified, but the fury in the roar spiked Laddin's adrenaline. That was the sound of a creature about to attack. And from the depth of the noise, he knew it wasn't a small animal.

In fact, it sounded like a very pissed-off wolf.

The others must have had the same thought. Wiz and Nero stared at each other in shock. The alien, however, seemed to settle more firmly into its form as he warbled.

"Much better. You will survive now." Then he looked at the other men. "The other one will die without help."

"What other one?" Nero demanded. Then he waved off an answer, pointing hard at Wiz. "You watch this one. Gelpack, you're with me. At least you can get a leg ripped off without dying."

The alien oozed toward the door. "It is hard to stabilize a werewolf while being dismembered, but I will try."

Laddin turned to help. After all, this was his set, his workplace. But his body moved strangely. His head was tilted too far forward, and his vision was different—more side to side, less in front. His balance was off because his hands were taking weight.

He looked down and saw fur and paws, and when he gasped, his tongue was too long and his nose… mamma mia, the scents! He could smell everything! He started spinning, stumbling as he tried to maneuver. His backside was wiggling, and he kept trying to stand up to see better, but he was a wolf. He couldn't stand like a man.

He was a wolf! The joy of that flooded his body, and he yipped in excitement. There was so much to explore. Not just his body, but everything in his office was new. Dust bunnies and spilled soda, cracker crumbs and gunpowder. He couldn't decide what to smell first.

"Settle down!" Wiz exclaimed as he knelt down with his arms wide. "You're going to break something! And in here, who knows what you'll set off."

That sank in. His office was filled with explosive charges and delicate electronics for special effects. He'd spent hours organizing things in the most logical and safe manner. The last thing he wanted was to mess that up. So he stilled, though not quite frozen. His backside was wiggling back and forth. It took him a moment to realize that it was his tail whipping around behind him. And with that knowledge came the need to see, so he twisted around to could look. But then his ass turned as well, and he was spinning like a top.

Wiz groaned. "They always have to see their tail. Hold still! I'll grab it so you can see it. I've never seen a happier wolf in my life."

There was a sharp tug on his butt, hard enough to make him yip in surprise, and then he lunged forward to bite. It wasn't a conscious movement. Hell, nothing he did right now was conscious. It was all instinct. The more he thought about moving anything, the less he was able to do it. But he lunged and nearly took a hunk out of Wiz's hand.

Fortunately the guy was fast. One second his hand was right there, the next it was gripping Laddin's muzzle tight.

"There'll be none of that!" he snapped. "But now that I've got you…."

Something sharp stabbed him hard in the neck. A hypodermic needle, he realized as Wiz abruptly stood holding the thing high. Laddin growled in annoyance, but Wiz just shook his head.

"You're a new pup. We need to get you into a safe environment. Then you can chase your tail all you want."

Lethargy was growing fast. It was becoming harder and harder to stay standing, and damn it, his head was dropping too. He whined, high-pitched and mournful, but that was all the sound he got out before he flopped onto the floor. He could see his paws spread out before him, but he couldn't move them. And pretty soon his head lolled to the side. He tried to keep his eyes open. If nothing else, there was so much to see from this angle. And the smells….

Too late. He was going under.

But the good news still echoed through his heart, and his last conscious thoughts were joyous.

Grandmama had been right! He'd transformed into something magic! And being a werewolf was fun, fun, fun!

Chapter 2

SIX WEEKS LATER, BRUCE DISCOVERS WEREWOLVES AND FAIRIES, OH MY!

BRUCE COLLIER had been nine when his father had first told him Bruce's uncle and younger brother, Josh, were monsters. He'd laughed because he was nine, but it hadn't taken him long to realize that his father was serious. The older man had shown him police images of bodies ripped apart, blood everywhere, and a black-and-white TV covered in gore. That was the impression that had burned into his nine-year-old brain. An old TV, front and center in a family living room, just like where he and his brother and sister often sat and played video games. It was smashed and covered in things that made his stomach lurch.

"Your uncle did that, and Josh carries the same curse. It's buried right now and we're going to keep it that way. We're going to keep him weak and frightened so it never comes out." Then his father squatted down so that they were eye to eye. When he spoke, Bruce could smell the acrid scent of whiskey and tobacco on his father's breath. "But if something goes wrong, if Josh does change, then I'm going to need you to protect your mother and sister. I'll take care of Josh, but you need to be strong enough to fight for them. Can you do that? Can you fight for your mother and sister?"

Bruce nodded because that was what a boy did when his father asked such things. And that was also when the lessons in violence began. His father punched him, and he learned to punch back. His father shoved his face into furniture, and he learned to grab whatever was at hand to hit him back. His father beat him, grappled with him... and ultimately lost to him. But only after years of daily battle out in the back shed where no one—especially not Josh—could see them.

And every day his father would point out how the beatings helped him. He was strong and could punch like a Mack Truck. That made him a valuable member of the football team. He watched people carefully for signs of evil and created a strong pack of loyal friends. That served him well as a college quarterback. He learned to protect his mother and sister against any foes—even though no enemy ever appeared—and that was what drove him to firefighting.

All good things.

Except now that he was a mature man heading toward thirty, he realized he'd been a brute to his little brother. His pack of loyal friends in high school were more a gang of thugs than harmless kids hanging out after school. And though he had saved lives as a fire medic—a firefighter/EMT—he had never once seen signs of evil in his little brother.

Until today.

Today, when Josh had shown up unexpectedly at their parents' house for Sunday dinner. He'd buffed out and had a handler, who was definitely spouting bullshit. Josh had not been in a hospital, as his parents had been told. And he certainly hadn't been recuperating from stress, as that huge asshole Nero had said. No, his little brother was clearly *still* under enormous stress, and it was breaking him. Hell, he'd even blurted out that he was gay in an attempt to turn the conversation away from where he'd disappeared to for the past six weeks.

That alone had been bad enough, but then Josh demanded his father make a weird outfit out of Volcax—a heat-resistant fabric so secret Josh could be jailed for having it without approval from the Pentagon.

Bruce had no idea why his father agreed to make the clothing for his brother, but he understood the hard look his dad gave him on the way out the door. It said, without words, that Bruce was to protect his mother and sister. That his father was going to take care of Josh, one way or another.

That might have worked on Bruce if he'd still been nine years old. Only he wasn't. He was twenty-nine, a firefighter, and old enough to decide for himself if his brother was evil.

Besides, his sister was just back from deployment with the Army. She had way more combat training than he did. So for the first time in his life, he decided to protect his brother instead.

He followed them. He saw Josh and his father go into the warehouse, presumably to make whatever weird outfit Josh needed. Bruce snuck in and waited, listening to their conversation and hoping to get Josh alone. It never happened.

Then he followed Josh to a hotel where Nero was waiting. He tried to catch his brother, but Josh went straight to Nero's room while Bruce was still parking his car. Stupid, stupid. He was a firefighter, damn it, not a cop. What the hell did he know about deprogramming someone from a cult? He'd been trying the gentle approach. He wanted to talk to his brother as a friend. Now he was thinking about busting in and abducting the guy. But given his brother's new size, Bruce wasn't sure he could take him unwillingly, and he didn't think Nero would let Josh escape without a fight.

Which left him sitting in the hotel parking lot and fuming at his own incompetence.

"Sucks, doesn't it?" a voice abruptly said from his right. "You're trying to be a good guy for the first time in your life, but you haven't the foggiest idea how. I can relate."

Bruce spun in his seat, fumbling as he grabbed for the heavy flashlight that he kept close. It was his only weapon against the… ventriloquist dummy? Circus clown? Weird short guy covered in leafy greens who suddenly sat in his front seat. The guy had bright eyes and a hard cut to his jaw… and was also about three feet tall and wearing curly elf shoes on his tiny feet.

"How did you get in my car?" Bruce demanded. The question wasn't at the top of his list of worries, but somehow it was the first stupid thing that came out.

The small person's brows rose and lowered in an obvious taunt. "Figure out who I am and that'll answer all your questions." His voice was musical and laced with humor. And as Bruce stared, his hair turned from spinach green to tomato red. Oh shit. He was hallucinating! He always knew the chemicals in his father's factories would fuck with his brain eventually.

Bruce looked around frantically, half searching for any other threats, half checking to see if his vision had gone wonky everywhere.

Nope. Everything looked just the same in this brightly lit parking lot. Everything except the hallucination sitting in his front seat. Only this didn't seem like a hallucination so much as a clown dream gone bad.

"Okay," he said, faking calm as best he could. "Who are you?"

"My name's Jonas Bitterroot, and I'm the fairy indirectly responsible for your brother's situation."

"And what situation is that?"

"He's a werewolf, and he's about to risk his life trying to kill a demon. Only it's the wrong timeline for him, even though it's right for Nero."

Not one single word of that made sense, except maybe one. "Werewolf." His father had never explained the evil curse that was inside Josh. Not even when Bruce had been a stubborn teen who'd demanded real training in a dojo and not the daily beatings his father had given him. But he remembered his dad often saying, "Pretend you're fighting a werewolf, a bigass dog with smarts. How would you defeat that?" Not once had he said *vampire* or *ghoul* or *creature from the black lagoon*. It was always a werewolf, and then he'd show Bruce those police photos again. The one with the claw and teeth marks through the bodies.

"You already knew," the hallucination said with a smirk. "If you know that, then it's a short, obvious hop to what I am." He grinned as he wiggled his curly toed shoes.

"Bullshit," Bruce fumed. "My brother is not a werewolf, and you aren't some demented Christmas elf."

"Elf!" the guy cried as he straightened up to his full half-pint size. "I am a fairy prince, and the only reason I look like this is because you lack imagination. This is the only image of a fae that exists in your limited thoughts, and so here I am." He gestured disdainfully at himself. "And wearing salad!" He pulled off a leaf and chomped on it with an angry grumble. "Did you get hit with a head of lettuce when you were a kid or something? Who dresses like this? Even in your imagination?"

That's when Bruce remembered the Christmas decorations at his mother's favorite restaurant. Every year they put elves in the salad bar. His sister had thought they were adorable, especially the ones wearing leaves for clothing and fake cherry tomatoes for hats. He looked at the so-called prince beside him and yes, his hair did indeed look like half a cherry tomato.

"This isn't real," he said out loud. "I've hit my head. I'm dreaming. I'm—"

"You're a moron, that's what you are." The elf dropped his head back against the seat. "My mother told me to stay away from humans. They're all stupid and have rigid minds. They self-destruct and take everything else with them. But even she said they make really good ale. So I had to find out. One day I went to a human bar, and sure enough, the ale was spectacular. But then a bar fight erupted, all because I started gifting the idiots with better looks according to *their imagination*. Was it my fault one of them was a Shakespeare scholar? One donkey head later, and suddenly I was about to die. Nero saved my life, and wham, now I'm stuck in a cheap car wearing iceberg lettuce with big brother Bozo beside me."

If this was a hallucination, it was damned persistent. Bruce tried to ride it out. He tried to count his breaths, calm his heart rate, silence his thoughts—all that meditation stuff that did absolutely no good at all.

The fairy prince was still there when he finished counting to ten.

He sighed. "What do you want from me?"

"What do I want?" the fairy taunted. "I want this thing to be over. I'm tired of you mortals screwing up every plan I make." He leaned in close enough that Bruce could see the bright red radicchio leaves that made up his undershirt. "And I want you to pay for the problems you've caused me." The threat was delivered in a chilling way that would have been terrifying… if it hadn't been said by a salad elf.

Bruce rolled his eyes, pretending to be unimpressed when, in fact, he was completely freaked-out. "You get that line out of a bad movie?"

The fairy held his gaze for a moment, then another, but Bruce was an old hand at intimidation games. This didn't faze him in the least. In the end, the hallucination broke first. He sighed and held up an old dime novel. "Wisconsin short story. Author never made it big except locally, and now his creation is eating up the entire state."

Bruce rolled his eyes. "Either start making sense or get out of my car."

The fairy glared at him in disgust. "Have you heard about the big black hole in Wisconsin that used to be a lake? It's expanding into a death zone that will kill the planet in a matter of months. Any of that sound familiar?"

Of course it did. It had filled the news for weeks now. But what did that have to do with him or his brother?

The fairy tucked the book away beneath the layers of lettuce. "That's what your brother and Nero are trying to fight—a demon created in a bad short story that became legendary enough to end the world. Don't tell me it doesn't make sense. You mortals create all sorts of nonsense, not us. We just...." He wiggled his fingers at Bruce's face, and his skin suddenly felt like it had seven pounds of makeup on it. "Play with what you imagine."

"Get this shit off my face," Bruce growled. He didn't want to look in the mirror, but he couldn't help himself. Hell. Now he was a salad elf too, and his face was made up of sunflower seeds.

"Why should I?" the fairy taunted.

Bruce couldn't think of a damned reason, so he gripped the steering wheel tight in celery-stalk hands and tried to tell himself he'd simply have to ride out the hallucination.

"This is real," the elf said.

"You're a real ass, you know that?"

"And you're so jealous of your brother, you don't know a fairy gift when it's being offered to you."

Bruce's eyes shot open. "What the hell are you talking about?" Then he saw it—bright red and on his dash. A glowing cherry. It appeared to be a nor-mal piece of fruit, the kind he'd find in any grocery store, but he knew it wasn't. He could *see* how much it wasn't. It was too perfect, it glowed with unearthly light, and most telling? He wanted it like he'd never wanted anything before in his life.

"You want what your brother has?" the elf said. "Eat that."

"Hell no. You think I'd touch anything from you?"

The fairy snapped his fingers, and suddenly every-thing was normal again. Bruce wore the same clothes as before, his face was made of flesh, not sunflower seeds, and even his reflection showed the normal bags under his eyes. Everything was the same... except for the salad fairy sitting beside him and the glowing cherry on his dash.

"Your brother has found his power."

"Says you."

"Says him, if you bothered to ask."

He had tried, in a roundabout kind of way. He'd invited his brother out for a beer, said they should catch up. He'd extended an olive branch, and it might have worked if that asshole of a handler hadn't whisked him away.

"Stop being jealous of him. Eat that and find what he has."

"I'm not jealous of my dweeb of a little brother!" he snapped, though even he heard the childishness in the statement. Because he did envy his brother. Josh was smart, as in PhD in chemistry smart. He had true friends like Savannah, who was worth a dozen of the dumbass jerks Bruce had surrounded himself with in high school. And yes, Bruce had found a team in his fellow firefighters, but they all had their own lives. Sure, they had his back in a fire, but at the end of the day, they went home to their families, whereas Bruce just went home.

"Why are you doing this?" Bruce asked.

"Why do fairies do anything? Because we're bored. And in this case, I'm waiting for dawn over White River State Park, when your brother and his lover fix my problem and become my slaves forever." He grinned in a truly malevolent way. "Why are *you* doing this?"

Bruce dropped his voice as dread slid through his body. "What do you mean 'slaves forever'?"

The fairy waved a single carrot-stick finger at him. "That's need-to-know only, brother. And you don't need to know." He waggled the sliced onion that served as his eyebrows. "Unless, of course, you want to be what he is. Then all you have to do is pop the cherry into your mouth."

"And become your slave forever?"

"Nope. That there"—he pointed to the cherry—"that's a freebie. Eat it and you'll get exactly what your brother has—no more, no less. You'll be stronger than you ever have been before. Faster too. Think what a difference that would make at work."

Bruce did think about it. He thought about all the times he'd been too slow or too weak to save people in trouble. A boy had died because Bruce hadn't been able to carry both him and his sister at the same time. A floor had collapsed, breaking his best friend's back, because Bruce hadn't been fast enough with the axe to get them both free. What would it mean to be better at work than he'd ever been before? Who could he save if he ate that beautiful little cherry?

But the fairy prince wasn't done. While Bruce was still feeling the desperate pull of temptation, the creature waved his hand over the dash. Suddenly next to the cherry there was an apple, as big and beautiful as the one that had tempted Snow White. The color showed like a dark ruby, and its scent filled the interior of the car with the smell of warm apple pie. It filtered into his thoughts and his darkest desires. Bruce was already reaching for it when he stopped short.

"What is that?" he demanded as he forced his hand down.

"That, my friend, is going to cost you. Eat the little fruit, and you get the same thing as your brother. Same wolf nature, same wolf power, same wolf needs." He hesitated for a moment on that last word, and Bruce was smart enough to note that it was significant. But he didn't have time to ask, because the fairy kept talking.

"But eat the other one and you get more. More power. More strength."

"More needs?"

"Hell yes," the guy said with a grin. Then he shrugged. "Look, if you don't want it, don't take it. I'm not forcing anything on you."

"Just offering me a gift horse, and I'm not supposed to look into its mouth."

"It's shaped like an apple, so it doesn't have a mouth."

He was trading witty words with a salad elf. And he wasn't even drunk. Best to focus on what he cared about. "How—exactly—is my brother enslaved to you?"

The elf shrugged. "He's not yet, but I'll get him. He's one little fairy promise away from taking orders from me."

The elf's confidence was annoying, but it didn't seem misplaced. Josh couldn't resist diving into weird shit. He was a nerd, a geek, and a freak, all rolled into one gullible package. If anyone would take what this fairy offered—hook, line, and sinker—it was Josh. Which meant that if Bruce wanted to be a good big brother and not an asshole, he had to do whatever it took to save Josh from himself.

But he wasn't going to do it by eating fairy fruit.

He was going to talk to his brother, even if it meant facing off with Nero. So without another word—and only a single last glance at the cherry—Bruce opened his car door. Or he tried. There wasn't a door latch. He fumbled around trying to feel for where it should be, but all he got was smooth paneling.

"I can't let you interrupt him right now," the fairy said cheerfully. "First off, what they're doing now—nobody wants you to see that. Second, there are rules to a fairy offer. You don't go getting cherries without popping somebody's cork somehow."

"What?"

"Mixed metaphor?" the fairy asked. "Human language is so hard to understand sometimes."

Bruce shook his head. He'd started this day after a long night shift, and now it was well past one. That was probably the real reason he was talking to a salad fairy. He'd fallen asleep in his car and was dreaming. "Let me out of my car."

"I can't let you interfere with tomorrow's events. There's too much at stake for both our worlds. It's too dangerous."

"But you will if I eat the cherry."

"Pop the cherry! Isn't that the expression? Don't you want to pop it?"

"Answer the fucking question. If I eat the cherry, do I become immortal?"

"Hell no. You become a werewolf, just like your brother. He's not immortal. He's optionally hairy and somewhat immortal under the right conditions." He grinned. "Like when he starts working for me."

An immortality enslaved to this asshole? "Over my dead body." None of this made sense except for that. This fairy prince meant his brother harm. Ergo, Bruce was going to protect him.

The fairy snorted. "You can't stop me if you don't play." He wiggled his fingers at the apple.

"Watch me." Bruce reached behind his seat and grabbed the brick he kept in his car in case he had to break a window... or a fairy face. It would hurt him to smash up his car, but his brother was worth it. Assuming he could talk sense into the guy. Which was pretty funny considering he was the one talking to a salad fairy.

"Are you sure you don't want to go for the fruit? It's not a bad deal."

"No," Bruce said firmly. "Now let me out of my car."

"Fine, fine," the fairy said with a smile. "But it's pretty late. Don't you think it's time for a nap?"

Bruce knew he was in trouble the moment the words left the fairy's mouth. Because the words had power. Bruce's eyelids started drooping, and the brick fell from his lax fingers. He fought the suggestion. Hell, he fought it with everything he had, but it wasn't enough.

The world went dark.

HE WOKE when the sun burned into his retinas.

"Fuck. Fuck. Fucking hell!"

It was morning, and the cherry and the apple still sat on his dash, looking as perfect as they had the night before. More perfect, even, because they were now in sunlight. His mouth watered just looking at them. But rather than take a bite, he grabbed them both and dropped them into his jacket pocket. No way was he touching them any more than he had to. The temptation was too strong.

He started the car and headed as fast as he could to White River State Park. He hadn't missed it when Bitter-ass had dropped the location of whatever was supposed to go down. Plus, his brother was never on time for anything, so Bruce still had hope that he'd be able to stop any enslavement from happening.

He found Nero's car after seven long frustrating minutes of searching. And then it was quick work to follow the trail up to a wood-enclosed glen. He saw clothing and a backpack stacked neatly beneath a tree, but before he could get there, Mr. Salad Fairy appeared, only this time he was tall, dark, and sneering. But the attitude was the same, as was the way he plucked the fruit out of Bruce's pocket.

"Looking for these?" he taunted.

"No. Looking for my brother."

"Well, you're in luck. He'll show up here in a moment."

"As your slave?"

"Not this time." The asshole waggled his very dark, very sculpted brows. "But I'll get him eventually." He waved the apple in front of Bruce's eyes. "Unless you want to play?"

"No, thanks."

"Suit yourself. But you can give them a message for me, can't you?" He plucked a green piece of parchment seemingly from the air and handed it to Bruce. With it came the cherry, which seemed to hum in the palm of his hand. "That's the freebie," he said. "It's so you can have what he has, Even Steven." Then he held the apple in the sunlight, where it shimmered and glowed as if it had come from the Garden of Eden. "This gives you *more*." He stressed the last word like he was offering up Eve's temptation. "Call out my name three times. Do you remember it?"

He did. Jonas Bitterroot. But that's not what he said. "I'm not calling you. I just want to talk to my brother."

The asshole shrugged. "Suit yourself. I got a more interesting slave this time. But your brother is still on my radar, and I do like the way he thinks."

"Buzz off," Bruce growled. "Or blink out. Or do whatever the hell you…." His words trailed away. He was alone in the clearing. "Asshole," he muttered.

Then he read the note.

When you're ready, call me. I will have five shields, hoodies, and a magic bullet available for your use. No charge except for the dragons.

The words didn't make any sense, but he supposed that was the point. If he wanted to understand, he needed to play. Pop the magic cherry, swallow the red pill, or walk the yellow brick road. It was all an invitation to danger where fairies could change appearances and mess with his head at will. It didn't sound remotely safe, and his little brother was smack-dab in the middle of it.

He held out the cherry and felt it pulse right there in his palm. It would be so easy to pop it down, but then what would happen?

He didn't get the chance to answer as sounds came from the clearing. His brother's voice. And Nero's response.

"So it's done? We're… free?"

"I think so."

There was more talk that Bruce didn't follow. He got closer and saw that Nero was naked and Josh was wrapped in his arms. He wanted to sneer at that. He wanted to make some sort of sound to at least make them jolt apart, but he couldn't. He was too busy seeing how completely devoted they were to each other. Happy, sad, laughing, and crying, all at once. They were in love, damn it. And that made him shrink back into the shadows, feeling like he was spying on a honeymooning couple. Whatever Josh had found, it was making him happy.

But was it real?

He didn't know. He did believe that Bitterroot was still watching Josh, which meant he was still in danger. And if Bruce wanted to protect Josh, then he had to stick around. Even more important, he had to understand what was going on.

There was only one way to do that, and it was pulsing in the palm of his hand.

"Congratulations, little brother. Looks like you found love," he said.

Josh and Nero jerked apart, but it was Josh who spoke. "Bruce, what are you doing here?"

"Following you. *Watching* you."

He saw his brother's eyes widen in horror. "Look, I know it seems strange, but—"

"It seems like you're both werewolves who make fairy deals."

Nero tensed and his eyes narrowed. "What makes you say that?" he asked in a too-casual tone.

"The freaking fairy told me."

"What?" Nero exploded.

"The short one who acts like we're all idiots." He didn't want to say Bitterroot's name out loud.

Josh jolted forward. "You didn't make a deal with him, did you? You didn't—"

"All I did was listen and agree to hand you this." He passed the message over to Josh, who shared it with Nero. They cuddled together to read it. He knew they didn't mean to look so cozy together, but that didn't change the way they fitted each other perfectly.

Meanwhile, Nero frowned. "What the hell does that mean? We already killed…."

Josh groaned. The sound was thick and deep, and he slapped his palm against his forehead for emphasis.

"We're back in this timeline. In *my* timeline, where I was recruited to find a way around the fire blast."

Nero nodded. "Yeah, I know."

Josh held up the parchment. "Don't you see? In this timeline, the demon is still killing Wisconsin."

"What? No, we…." Nero's voice trailed into a loud groan. "We risk our lives, and he gets dragons." He crumpled the paper in his fist. "Did I tell you that he's the one who told us about the demon in the first place? He's the one who sent us on this hunt. Unbelievable."

Josh looked at his brother. "Did you read this?"

Bruce snorted. "Of course I read it. He *wanted* me to read it. Otherwise he would have put it in an envelope."

Nero was staring at Bruce. His eyes were laser focused, and his stance shifted so he could quickly step in front of Josh if needed. Damn it, the man was *protecting* Josh in the way Bruce should have been doing as the older brother. In the way that Bruce had wanted someone to protect him for most of his life. And now Josh had it in a huge brute of a werewolf lover.

"What else?" Nero demanded, proving he wasn't as stupid as he looked. "Fairies don't give up information for free. What else did he offer you?"

Bruce held out his other hand. Nestled in his palm lay that dark red cherry. He lifted it up to the sunlight, and all three of them were temporarily mesmerized by the beauty of the simple fruit.

"He said if I want what you've got, I just have to eat this. And I do. I want it." Bruce had been staring at the fruit, feeling the pull of desire. He was going to resist, but then he looked at his brother and Nero. Josh had certainly fallen head over heels in love, but Bruce didn't trust Nero as far as he could throw him. The man wielded too much power over Josh, and that spelled disaster for his little brother.

But he couldn't protect Josh unless he played. And the only way to do that was to eat the cherry.

So he tossed the thing in his mouth. And out of the corner of his eye, he saw a butterfly burst up from a leaf and fly off.

"No!" Josh cried out, but it was too late. Bruce chewed quickly and swallowed after spitting the pit into a nearby bush. All three waited in tense silence, prepared for something dramatic to happen.

Nothing.

Wasn't that the way? Even in fairy magic, his brother had all the luck. Nero sighed and slapped his car keys into Josh's open palm. "Go get my phone from the glove compartment and call in. Tell them that we've got another recruit."

"But why?" Josh asked. "Nothing's happened."

"Yet."

Bruce felt the heavy pressure of disappointment. That cherry was a big fat zero of—

Heat burned through his body. And since he'd been waiting for something, he noticed the tiny increments that built in his gut before expanding through his nerves. It felt like a small fire burning low, except that the base of his spine fired with a kind of electric pulse. Each beat shot up his spine, pounding in increasing strength. Up his spine, down his legs.... His muscles contracted in response. His back arched, his arms went wide, and his head jerked backward as he tried to scream.

It reached his brain faster than he expected, and once it was there, his mind whited out, although he felt the glow of a thousand suns right in the center. And once he saw that, felt that, knew it as something gloriously special, it all collapsed. The heat, the power, the joy—everything inside him fell apart. And when it reformed, he stood on four legs. His face was reshaped, and his backside moved as never before.

"Crap," Nero said from somewhere above. "I hope he fits in my car."

He wasn't going into any car. He was going to run and bound and smell things. He was in the woods as a wolf, and the power in his body was glorious. So he tensed his muscles—

And collapsed.

He stood and leaped away, except only his back legs moved. His front went lax and he dropped his nose into the dirt. He focused all his attention on what muscles worked how, and he completely failed.

And that was how Nero and Josh got him to the car. And then some movie-star gorgeous guy looked him in the eyes and told him to sleep.

Chapter 3

MEANWHILE IN MICHIGAN, LADDIN QUITS WULF, INC.

"YOU CAN'T be serious. They were just rabbits."

Laddin looked up from where he'd been staring out the window at the Michigan woods. He was in Captain M's office, delivering the bad news in the firmest possible way. "It wasn't just the rabbits," he protested, but she cut him off.

"You can't leave Wulf, Inc. because you ate a bunch of rabbits. The woods would be lousy with furbies if we didn't keep the population down." The woman was his trainer and also the administrator in charge of all the combat packs at Wulf, Inc. She'd been with him from the moment he'd been brought into headquarters as a werewolf, and she'd wasted no time in making use of his talents. Not just his ability to blow things up, but also his tendency toward OCD. Everything in its place, and all that. She'd set him to organizing her office workflow, and he'd taken to it like a duck to water.

Oh hell—that was another creature he'd eaten the last time the moon shone bright. Apparently he was the kind of werewolf that lost its mind every full moon and ate anything that ran, flew, or hopped.

"You have to get past this, Laddin. You're a predator now. And predators—"

"Eat bunnies?"

"Yes."

"No."

She shook her head. "It's hard going through life hating yourself for what you are."

Been there, done that. He used to hate himself for his deformed hand—a birth defect that becoming magical hadn't fixed. But he'd made peace with it, so he had to believe he'd find a way to survive without eating living meat.

"Look, it's not just the rabbits. Nobody asked me if I wanted to be made into a werewolf."

She shifted uncomfortably in her seat. This was a major problem with Wulf, Inc. They couldn't tell people they had the werewolf gene before they activated it. The Paranormal Accords said as much. And so Wulf activated the gene and then hoped the person would sign up with the organization afterward. It was ass-backward, and everyone knew it.

"Even if we could have asked you—and you know we're not allowed—you wouldn't have believed a word of it."

That was probably true, but it didn't matter. "Do you know why I worked in Hollywood?"

She frowned. "I'll bite. Why?"

"Because I liked pretending to be part of the action without actually being in it. I'm a couch superhero. I'll cheer on Captain America, but I sure as hell don't want to actually fight the Nazis. I don't schlep through the jungle in search of Dr. Doom, and I sure as hell don't want to go face-to-face with any demon. I'm sorry, Captain M, but you activated the wrong guy."

She leaned forward. "This doesn't make sense. Two weeks ago you were jonesing to go out into the field. What happened?"

He'd eaten a bunny and realized it tasted *delicious*. And if that hadn't been bad enough, he'd been the one responsible for packing up the belongings of Nero's dead teammates. That had been a major eye-opener. He'd seen their entire lives in their things. They'd been cut off from their families because they couldn't talk about the paranormal, they lived in the daily practice of violence, and at the end of it all, so few people remembered them. Not the ones they'd saved, who didn't know what had happened, and not their families, who hadn't spoken to them for years. Only the organization mourned—for a few weeks—before it restructured, activated new recruits, and created new combat packs with the survivors.

"I don't want to be a killer, even of bunnies."

"We're protecting the world. You don't have to be on the front lines."

He nodded. "I love the work you're doing." Wulf, Inc. took out genuine baddies, and he had no problem with that. But it was still "eviscerate this" and "disembowel that" everywhere he looked, which made his wolf side want to roll around in the blood too. But he was a man first, and he didn't want to split open anyone's gut. Not when he could buy plastic-wrapped chicken breasts at the grocery store. "I just don't want to be part of it."

Captain M stared at him, her nose twitching as she thought. "There's something more."

"Yes." And now he came to the real sticking point. "I'm not going to disappear from my family's lives. I won't." Because that's what people at Wulf, Inc. had to do. The paranormal had its place, and it wasn't with the vanilla normals.

He saw her absorb his statement, her expression going grim, but there was understanding in her eyes. Not every werewolf worked in Wulf, Inc. Many had regular lives, assuming they could keep their natures under complete control.

"So the only reason you're still here is because you're trying to figure out how to control the moon madness."

It wasn't a question, but he answered it anyway with a nod. Not every werewolf went psycho with the full moon, but he'd drawn the short straw and would have to work extra hard to control himself. Good thing he was used to overcoming obstacles.

"The next full moon isn't for another few weeks. Do you mind helping us out until then? It won't involve you killing anything."

"What have you got?" he asked, investing his voice with a perkiness he didn't feel.

"Josh's brother ate a fairy fruit—"

"What? Why?" He'd been reading up on magic, and nothing was more unpredictable and guaranteed to bite you in the ass than fairy magic.

Captain M shrugged. "Because he's an idiot? Because he wanted to play in the weird pool too?"

Laddin shook his head. "No. I mean, what was he promised?"

"Well, that's what I'd like you to figure out. The rest of the team is going up to run support for the bigwigs. They're still trying to find the demon that is poisoning the lake and Wisconsin in general. The problem—other than the obvious—is that the paranormal energy is so thick around the lake that it's attracting every paranormal wackadoodle in the world. They can't find the demon if they're constantly fighting ghouls and goblins gone wild."

"I'm to run support?" he asked.

"You can coordinate with me, but mostly I need you to handle Bruce. That's Josh's brother." She held up her hand before he could object. "I know you're a puppy yourself, but there isn't anyone else. The others will be around to help if needed, but they can't take out a nest of angry pixies if they're babysitting a fairy werewolf."

He nodded, though the idea of taking out a fairy nest made him sad. He knew that the little fae were usually a menace, but they were also just having fun. There had to be a way to work with the tiny fluffs of magic without killing them. But it was a losing battle. After all, cockroaches weren't evil either, but that didn't stop anyone from fumigating their house.

"Come on, Laddin. Don't bail on me yet. Give me a chance to prove that there's a place here for you."

He nodded, because he'd been trained since birth to respect a powerful woman's wishes, but she also had to respect his choice. "I'll help out now, but after this, I need to go back to my family."

"We're family too, if you want us."

He knew it was true, but he didn't want to give up one family for another. He wasn't built that way.

It didn't take long for him to pack up. After all, he'd come here with nothing, not even his clothes. Before long he was on a short eight-hour drive to a pizza farm in a tiny town in Wisconsin. How did they farm pizza, anyway?

The signs along the road explained it—the place used its own locally sourced ingredients for its five-star pizza. Great. Except business must be crap since the owner, Mary, had rented out her entire home to the Wulf, Inc. crew.

There wasn't time to ponder pizza farm economics as he pulled into a big barn designed for farm equipment but being used as a garage. He saw Nero's car next to a Wulf, Inc. van that had seen better days. And it obviously hadn't been washed since its time in the swamp, because boy, did that thing stink!

He got out as Wiz and Stratos, another member of the team, arrived. Like him, they turned up their noses at the stench from the van.

"What the hell is that?" Stratos demanded as she covered her nose with her tee.

Yordan—a big guy with a loud mouth and a fondness for putting them through calisthenics—pointed at Laddin. "That's his problem. The new wolf is asleep in the back. He's probably hungry and has to go potty, but don't let him do that as a wolf. The first task is to get him to switch back to a human."

Laddin nodded. He'd been briefed.

Bing hopped out of the other side of the van, his expression set in that same bland mask he'd had on the set. Laddin had been surprised to find out that his boss had also turned werewolf, but in the end they'd settled into the same trainee level. They'd both been yanked from their lives, had to learn how to live as a werewolf, and eventually they'd both have to decide what to do about it. "Listen up," Nero boomed using his alpha voice. "We've found a way to kill the demon that's poisoning Wisconsin. It's a complicated maneuver, and there's no room for new recruits. You all are here to help keep the nasties away while Josh and I do what needs to be done."

Wiz folded his arms. "Have we *found* the demon that's killing Wisconsin?"

Nero winced. "Not yet. We'll report to Wulfric, tell him what we know, and he'll decide how and where to use us."

Josh's head snapped up. "Wulfric as in the immortal founder of Wulf, Inc.? That—"

"Yes! That Wulfric. The one who only comes out when the world is about to end. So get your gear. Yordan and Bing are with me and Josh." He gestured to his car. "Stratos and Wiz, follow behind. Let's do what we're here to do."

The others did as they were told—all except Laddin, who stood there feeling very left out. Then Yordan, Bing's trainer, slapped the keys to the van into his hand and gave him a hard look. "For the record, I'm against this. You don't know shit about training a new recruit."

It was 100 percent true, but Laddin had seen the Wulf, Inc. assignment roster. Thanks to the demon, they were severely short on staff. "I'm the only option there is," he said.

"Don't baby him," Yordan continued. "He may or may not know who he is and what has happened. Keep him in the cage unless he's human."

Laddin shook his head. "I'm not keeping him caged! Do you know how traumatizing that is?"

"Less traumatizing than getting your own throat ripped out. Believe me, I know." And he did—just a few weeks ago, he'd lost control of Bing and nearly died in that exact way.

Which meant that Laddin had no room to argue. Instead, he ducked around Yordan to talk to Josh, who was already inside the car and buckling his seat belt. The guy looked both harassed and happy, which was a strange combination. His blond hair was mussed, his customary who-cares attitude seemed frayed, but whenever he looked at Nero, there was this intense burst of something from him. Lust? Love? It was hard to tell, but Laddin knew it was rooted in happiness. Because right then, the guy wore a sloppy smile on his face as he watched Nero climb into the driver's seat.

Sadly, that smile faded the second Laddin knocked on the car window.

Josh was quick to lower the window, his expression neutral. "Don't trust him, Laddin. He's got a cruel edge."

"Your brother?" Weren't brothers supposed to be one for all and all for one? Or at least, not hate each other?

"Yes, my brother!"

Obviously it was different for these two. "Do you have any idea why he did it? What exactly—?"

"He did it because he has to ruin everything I have. That's what he does. He sticks his nose into my life and destroys it."

Laddin took a slight step back. "How does him becoming a werewolf destroy your life?"

Josh blew out an angry breath. "He'll find a way. He always does."

By that point Nero had settled into the driver's seat. He reached out to squeeze Josh's thigh. "He can't ruin this. It's not possible."

Laddin watched as Josh's expression softened. Then he covered Nero's hand with his own. "He'll try, though. I don't know if it's jealousy or just a neurotic need to be the best at everything. He had everything when we were kids. He was the big man in high school, my dad adored him, and even my sister looked up to him. But he still had to make sure I was shit."

Nero shook his head. "He can't make you any-thing—we already know who you are."

Josh nodded as he looked to Laddin. "I sound cra-zy, but I'm not wrong. And we can't afford to have him meddle in what we're doing. That demon will destroy the planet if we don't get this right."

"He won't interfere," Laddin promised.

"Exactly," Nero said in a distracted kind of way. "Laddin's got this, right?"

"Of course I do," he lied. "I've handled lots of brothers who eat fairy fruit and turn hairy."

Nero turned his attention to Laddin and grinned. And wasn't that a sight to see? Laddin didn't think he'd ever seen the guy so happy before. "That's what I thought," Nero said. Then he shifted the car into Re-verse and hit the gas. Laddin had no choice but to hop out of the way.

Seconds later the others followed Nero, leav-ing Laddin alone with the big van and the mysterious brother inside.

No time like the present.

He unlocked the van door and hauled it open. Sun-light streamed in from the barn opening and illuminat-ed the mess inside. Trash and supplies littered the floor in a haphazard fashion that irritated his sense of order. But all that faded into nothing as he got a look at the wolf in the cage.

OMG, he was beautiful. At first all Laddin saw was the fur, a rich dark brown with a cherry-red undertone that seemed to glow in the sunshine. He wanted to sink his hands into it. But as he maneuvered around, he saw an animal resting on his side, his breath steady and even. But there was power in his form—thick muscles beneath the fur and sharp claws. And though the mouth was closed, Laddin had no trouble imagining the teeth inside the long, sweet muzzle.

"Hey, Bruce," he said, his voice soft with awe. "Time to wake up, buddy."

Unable to resist touching the creature, Laddin unlocked the cage and swung the door wide. Then he sat on the van floor and reached inside to stroke the wolf's fur. It was as soft as it was magnificent. Laddin's skin tingled where his fingers were buried in the ruff, and even though his arm was perilously close to the animal's mouth, Laddin slipped his fingers beneath the shock collar someone had put around the thick neck.

"Come on, Bruce. Wake up."

He shook Bruce's ruff hard.

"I'm sure you need to talk about something. Like why you felt the need to eat fruit given to you by a dangerous fairy?"

A single eye slitted open. It was yellow with burned edges, like crème brûlée, which was Laddin's favorite dessert. And it focused unerringly on him.

"We don't have to talk about that right now," Laddin said, pitching his voice to make it as soothing as possible. "Tell me about yourself. What do you do for a living? Josh ran out of here so fast, I didn't get a chance to ask."

There was a flicker of movement at Josh's name, but Laddin had no idea if that was good or bad. Then the wolf bared his teeth while a low, rumbling growl shook his body.

"Don't be like that. He's your brother, you're supposed to love each other. But tell you what. How about you switch back to being a human and I'll listen to how he did you wrong, okay?"

Bruce lifted his head and shook it. Not in a denial, but in the way of a creature just waking up. Then he pushed up on his paws and tried to stand. Except the cage wasn't quite big enough for him to rise to his full height, so he nosed forward, trying to get out.

"No-go, Bruce," Laddin said. "You've got to change back to a human first." Then he grabbed the wolf's head and turned it so they were looking eye-to-eye. "Shift back to being human. Then you can do whatever you want."

In response, the wolf raised his back leg and pissed all over the van. Some of it got Laddin, but he was quick on his feet as he jumped back.

"Ew! That was so not cool," he said as he swiped at the splash on his jeans. But then he realized his mistake. While he was jumping backward, the wolf had leaped forward, out of his cage, to stand in the middle of the barn.

Damn, Bruce looked stunning in an intimidating way. He was a big wolf, larger even than Nero, and he stood there poised, his eyes taking in the entire place. Then he started leaning left and right on his paws as if testing out his weight and balance. He was figuring out how to manage a wolf body. Laddin smiled in recognition. After all, he'd done the same thing not so long ago.

"Fun, huh? It's like you get to learn everything all over again, but you're faster and stronger than ever before. Like toddler Thor or something."

The wolf eyed him and bared his teeth.

"Bullshit," he answered, though he didn't know what he was responding to. "I'm your trainer, and you're going to listen to me. Those are the rules, and frankly, this is not a safe place for you. You've been a wolf for long enough, Bruce. It's time to change back to a human."

The wolf turned his head away, and Laddin eyed the open barn door. Why hadn't he thought to close the thing first?

"You need to stay inside, Bruce."

Laddin knew he was in deep shit. If Bruce took off here, Laddin would have no way to control him. And without a human talking to him and reminding him who he was, Bruce was likely to remain a wolf forever. That wasn't so bad a fate, except the human mind didn't go quietly into oblivion. It asserted itself, it got angry, and that overwhelmed the wolf until the creature went crazy and killed everything in sight.

"Change back to who you are, Bruce. You're a human man first, wolf second." That wasn't exactly the way Captain M had described it, but she wasn't here.

Bruce ignored him. He started moving around, slowly at first, but quickly learning how to walk. The guy was coordinated, that was for sure. It had taken Laddin hours to figure out the basics of walking without his back legs tripping him up.

"Come on, Bruce," Laddin said. "Shift back." Even he could hear the edge of panic creeping into his voice. "You're my responsibility, and I really don't want to screw up on my first mission." Against his better judgment, he reached back into the van and picked up the remote for the shock collar. He didn't want to use it. Hell, he didn't want to touch it, but if he didn't get the barn door closed, that was going to be the only way to keep Bruce in sight.

Meanwhile, the wolf began to trot. Not walking forward and back like he had been doing, but a trot that headed toward the back of the barn. Great. While Bruce went to the back, Laddin headed for the door. He could shut it while—

Shit! Some instincts were normal to all lupines, and Laddin knew how much fun it was to chase things—like *him* as he ran for the barn door.

Bruce pivoted and leaped forward. He moved with grace—at first—but then his front legs couldn't keep up the pace. It was that whole arm/leg thing. The human mind forgot to use the arms while the back legs were still working, and that usually led to a nose in the dirt.

Yup. Nose plow. Laddin was ready. He jumped forward and grabbed the shock collar. Then he held Bruce's head down in the dirt like Yordan had done to him not so long ago. It was a dominance move. Then again, even as a human, Yordan had had the muscles to take Laddin down.

Laddin, not so much.

It was like holding on to a bucking bronco, and a life in LA had no way prepared him for the spinning, twisting, biting nightmare that was wolf Bruce. Laddin's arms were jerked nearly out of their sockets, and his wrist wasn't going to be able to take the strain much longer. He'd grabbed on with one hand, but he managed to haul his arms together enough to latch on with his second. He kept waiting for Bruce's body to betray him. The guy hadn't learned how to move fully as a wolf yet. Shouldn't he be face-planting about now?

Or now?

Or now?

Laddin gasped as he was jerked left and right. Keep hold! Keep hold! He did, even when Bruce flopped sideways, rolling over him in an effort to dislodge him. Laddin's head banged painfully on the dirt, and he lost his breath as 180 pounds of wolf muscle crushed his ribs. But he held on.

He felt a finger snap, and he cried out in pain but didn't let go.

Then Bruce righted himself and started lunging for the barn door, though it wasn't so easy, given that he had to drag Laddin along. Words and curses flew through Laddin's mind, but he didn't have the breath to voice them. All he had was a steady determination to hold on. *Hold on!*

And then Bruce planted his feet and twisted sideways. He bared his teeth, then bit down hard on Laddin's leg. Pain shot through Laddin's nervous system, and he screamed. His hands loosened, but he didn't let his grip slip until the wolf bucked again.

He couldn't hold on. Not when he was afraid he was about to lose his leg. Damn, damn, damn. He gathered the energy to shift. It was the only way to make sure he didn't bleed out.

The change was familiar now, and he dove into the sensations. Heat, then a shocking energy that tipped into pain. Next step, he would dissolve into joy, only to reform on four legs.

But he never made it that far. Just when his body was about to dissolve, Bruce hit him broadside, knocking him over and completely disrupting Laddin's focus. He lost the change energy and remained completely, vulnerably human. Even more so when Bruce closed in for the kill, putting his mouth to Laddin's throat.

Panic burned hot and hard. His heart raced, and his mind scrambled to find a solution even as it refused to focus on anything but the teeth at his throat. There was no time to try to shift again, no way to break free, and the blood from where he'd been bitten was soaking his jeans. What to do? What to do?

His wolf mind answered while his human brain was still stewing in panic. He had to submit. It was the only way to soothe the wolf in Bruce. And though neither the wolf part of Laddin nor the human side wanted to do that, he realized it was the only way.

So he lay there, absolutely frozen. His breath was short and tight, and his body rigid with fear. He felt the saliva drip from Bruce's mouth roll down his neck. Did Bruce understand that Laddin was submitting? He sure hoped so. One good chomp and Laddin was dead.

But the wolf wasn't biting down. Instead, Laddin lay there, feeling Bruce's breath hot against his neck, doing his best to remain calm. Why the hell wasn't the animal doing something? "I'm submitting," he whispered. "You're the boss."

Nothing.

Then a weird sense of déjà vu hit him. This was just like before, when Nero and Wiz had first turned him into a werewolf. It was as if every moment of his life had been leading him to right here, right now. It didn't make sense. Sure, his becoming a werewolf had been predicted ever since he was born. But this moment hadn't been foretold by anyone. And yet the inevitability of it settled onto his shoulders and into his very heart.

He relaxed. What would happen would happen. And if this was the end of his very short life, then so be it. His breath eased out, his head fell to the side, and his belly remained open and vulnerable. And though he knew better than to look directly into Bruce's wolf eyes, he was vividly aware of the wolf's piercing yellow gaze.

"I submit to you, Bruce. I'll follow you wherever you lead."

He didn't know if the man inside the wolf understood his words. It didn't matter. The wolf must have felt something, because he slowly released Laddin's neck. Then he took a step back.

Laddin exhaled and tried to move, but dizziness swamped his awareness. Shit. He'd lost too much blood. He needed to shift *now*. So with a slow hand, he unbuttoned and unzipped his jeans. It was all he could do. Then he threw himself into his change.

He was well practiced at it now. The heat, the tingling excitement, and the joy as his body dissolved in an electric fizzle, then reformed as wolf. He moved his leg and arm—now wolf legs—feeling them healthy and strong. Then he shimmied out of his bloody jeans and shook as he maneuvered onto all fours. It was annoying to still have his shirt on, but it didn't get in the way.

His vision sharpened, and his world became a kaleidoscope of tastes and smells. But the most important thing he saw was Bruce's wolf slowly backing away from him.

Now came the difficult part. Bruce hadn't killed Laddin, but that didn't mean he'd accepted him either.

Laddin walked slowly forward, keeping his head down in submission. He sniffed the air, noting the burned-cherry smell of the other wolf. Odd, but he liked it. And still he crept closer, trying to invite a friendship.

It only took a few seconds, but to Laddin it felt like an eternity. Eventually Bruce lowered his head, his nose twitching as he too sniffed—nose to nose at first, with Laddin's head sunk below Bruce's. Then Laddin kept walking, sniffing along Bruce's flank and around his tail. The first time he'd done this with Josh, he'd been repulsed by the idea of sniffing someone's ass. But there was so much to learn down there. And he wanted to know everything about Bruce.

Beneath the burned-cherry smell, he scented Bruce's family connection with Josh. He knew Bruce was healthy, though there was an acrid tang to the air that meant something. He had no idea what, but it was unique to Bruce. And he knew when Bruce finally relaxed enough to rub against him.

Friends.

The word had never felt so sweet. And then Bruce turned, obviously to head out the barn door.

Shit! He couldn't let that happen, though the scents out there were really tempting. Well, if he couldn't talk Bruce into staying, he would have to try playing. And there was nothing Laddin's wolf liked better than play. So when Bruce was almost out the barn door, Laddin leaped in front of him.

He kept his head down low and his tail wagging high. He moved left and right and then even spun around once, just to see if he could get Bruce into the mood.

The larger wolf watched him, his ears cocked with what might have been curiosity. Did he understand what Laddin wanted? Maybe. Bruce's tail swished back and forth a bit, and his mouth opened in what Laddin hoped was a wolfish smile.

Laddin lunged forward, nipping without intent. Bruce shied backward, but then he bit back. Not hard. A quick clamp of his jaws before he danced forward. He wasn't as smooth on his feet as Laddin, but then again, he was brand-new to his lupine body. By the looks of things, though, he'd be a quick study, Laddin thought as Bruce leaped sideways and didn't stumble. It had taken Laddin a week to master that.

Laddin pressed forward again, closer this time, and Bruce played back. Laddin went left and right, trying to get his mouth on Bruce's neck. He never came close, though, as Bruce adjusted and fought. He was making a rumbling sound, not a growl, and Laddin wondered if that was his play sound. If so, it was pretty angry, but he'd take it. Especially since he was moving Bruce steadily deeper into the barn.

It was a losing game. He knew that. Eventually Bruce would tire of the game and Laddin would have to think of something else. He needed to get those barn doors closed, and he couldn't do that as a wolf.

He was still scrambling for options when he ran out of time. Bruce jumped past him, tail held high, and headed for the door. It was an invitation to follow him outdoors, and Laddin even considered it. But the more time Bruce spent as a wolf, the less likely he was to ever come back to his human form. In short, playtime was over. Laddin had to get serious about setting down the rules.

But he really, really didn't want to.

He dashed forward. He might be small for a were-wolf, but he made up for it in speed. He got between Bruce and the door, then shifted back to human. He did it quickly, returning to his body on all fours, T-shirt still on but naked ass waving in the wind.

"See how easy it is?" he said to Bruce. "Come back to human."

He straightened up onto his knees. He'd chosen this location specifically because his discarded pants were in reach. And while Bruce watched him with those burnt-yellow eyes, Laddin was able to grab the shock collar remote where it had fallen to the ground. Then he slowly stood up.

The collar was just in case. His real goal was to get
to the barn doors. Unfortunately, the damn things were
huge. He would have to slide two heavy doors together,
and Bruce could easily slip outside while he was clos-
ing them. But he had to give it a try.

"Think about what you want to do, Bruce. Are you
hungry? We could grill some burgers. Are you a coffee drinker? You've got to be jonesing for a cup. God
knows I am. Do you have a girl? You can't call her if
you're only going to howl through the phone."

Bruce was listening to him, his head cocked to one
side as Laddin talked. Then he saw the solution. Hallelujah! The doors were electric. All he'd have to do was
distract Bruce while the things closed on their own.

He found the button quickly and kept talking as
he moved toward it. "I had a girlfriend once in high
school. She was sweet, a mathlete, and smoking hot. I
did all the things I was supposed to with her. I treated
her well, I bought her flowers, and I listened when she
talked. Good things. But I didn't get into kissing her,
you know? I'm freaky enough with this hand." He held
up his weird hand while tapping the barn door remote
with his elbow. "I didn't want to be gay too."

The door rumble was loud—too damn loud. They
both jumped at the sound. Laddin had hoped the noise
would make Bruce shy backward from the doors, and
he'd been right—for about half a second. And then
Bruce leaped forward, trying to escape before the frus-
tratingly slow doors closed.

Laddin jumped too, right in front of the wolf. He
sure as hell didn't want to have a repeat of their last
human/wolf tumble. He couldn't shift again so soon,
so a bite would definitely kill him. He tried to be extra

careful as he caught Bruce around the middle while still trying to grip the shock collar remote in his good hand.

They tumbled sideways. Laddin wrapped both arms around Bruce's middle as they rolled. This was a "grind your teeth and squeeze as if your life depended on it" moment, and yet part of Laddin still noticed how soft Bruce's fur was. And that burned-cherry smell was stronger up close. Even his human nose picked it up.

Nice.

Oh shit. Suddenly it wasn't so nice as Bruce wiggled and twisted, his growl going through his entire body into Laddin's. Why wouldn't the guy quit? Laddin squeezed his eyes and his arms as tight as possible and held on.

One more moment. One more moment.

They were almost closed. Almost....

Then Bruce head-butted him. Laddin had no idea if the move had been intentional, but it was damned effective. Stars exploded in his vision as his temple took the brunt of the wolf's skull. His grip loosened for a split second, but that was all it took. Bruce broke free with a hard jerk. Then he was on his feet and headed toward the door before the last few inches closed.

He was going to escape. Which meant he'd never return to human.

Damn it! Laddin had no choice now. He didn't want to do it, but there was no other option. Even though he was still reeling, he managed to pull the shock collar trigger. He just prayed it would be enough to slow Bruce down.

It did. But what he saw would haunt his dreams. Bruce—that magnificent wolf—abruptly stiffened. His body jerked awkwardly in different directions, and his legs failed to support him as his back arched. But worst of all was Bruce's yip, a high note cut off midsound. It was awful, and Laddin had to blink back tears at the sound.

"I'm sorry," he said as he crawled forward. "I'm so sorry."

Bruce's eyes were fixed, his body still arched in apparent agony. He lay on his side, and his legs were curled awkwardly. Horribly.

It took a moment for Laddin to realize the truth. Holy shit. The collar was still frying him!

"No! No!" Laddin fumbled with the remote, looking for an off switch. There wasn't one. He stabbed it again, but it didn't seem to have any effect. The electric sound kept going. "Stop!"

It did—finally—though each moment felt like forever to Laddin. And that was nothing compared to what Bruce must have endured. Laddin rushed forward, dropping the horrible remote as he moved.

"I'm sorry, I'm sorry," he kept saying as the last of the sunlight was cut off. The doors had finally closed, but that didn't make a damn bit of difference if he'd killed Bruce.

The wolf was lying there twitching. His legs were rigid, his spine arched in horrible flexion, and his burnt-yellow eyes were glazed.

"Bruce, no. God, no. I'm so sorry."

Laddin stroked the fur, his hands tingling painfully wherever he touched Bruce. Holy hell, this was not normal. He wanted to feel for a pulse, but where was the pulse on a wolf? He couldn't find it, not through his tingling fingers. He couldn't hear any breath either, not through the pounding of his own heartbeat. And he couldn't stare into those accusing yellow eyes anymore either.

He tried to close the wolf's eyes, but that was a lot harder than it looked like on TV. You didn't just brush your hands over them and bam, the eyes closed. So he attempted to straighten out Bruce's spine, trying to get the legs to release. The muscles were still twitching at random, in horrible spasms that wouldn't end.

"I'm sorry," Laddin breathed. "I'm so sorry."

He continued to stroke through the fur, wondering if his hands were becoming numb to the tingles or if the electricity was fading. Time ceased to have meaning. Life narrowed down to the brush of his hand through fur and the desperate search for breath. He couldn't feel if Bruce's chest rose and lowered, not through the general twitching. And he couldn't hear anything above his own pounding heart.

Was that a blink? Had Bruce's eye closed and opened on its own?

Maybe? He didn't dare hope. Except he did hope, and plead, and pray, all while staring into angry yellow eyes.

Blink! It was a blink. Bruce was alive!

"Thank God," he breathed as his head collapsed down to rest against Bruce's wolf chest. "Thank God."

And now, with his head right there, he could hear the rapid beat of Bruce's heart. It mixed with the steady pounding of his own, and he was grateful, so damned grateful, that he pressed kisses to the fur.

He felt the tingles under his ear and thought they were due to more electricity. But then the air turned cold, and sweat dried on his skin enough to make him lift his head and stare. His mouth dropped open as he saw the golden tingles expand across the wolf's body. Bruce wasn't dying, as he at first thought, but shifting.

He was coming back to human!

Laddin rocked back on his heels, relief making his entire body weak. And he watched with awe as the wolf body dissolved into a light that burst through his retinas. And then it drew back together, coalescing into flesh and blood. The skin was flushed with health, the bones strong, and the muscles lean with a ropy strength. Bruce was alive and strong.

And gorgeous.

Laddin was used to looking at sexy actors with sculpted bodies and pretty-boy manscaping. But there was something different about Bruce. His body wasn't built for show. He'd earned his heavily muscled torso with hard work. His chest hair was thick, his dick was hard, and his thighs were corded powerhouses. That was when he remembered that Bruce was a firefighter. That involved heavy, sweaty, daily *work*. And wow, did that ring Laddin's bell.

While Laddin was caught up in his very inappropriate moment of lust, Bruce straightened out his body. He rolled fully onto his back, stretched out his legs, and used his hands to easily release the catch on his collar. And when he pulled it off, he stared at it and slowly, carefully crushed the thing into crumpled electronic parts.

Okay, that was impressive.

Laddin didn't want to look into Bruce's eyes, but he couldn't avoid it either. He had to say how sorry he was, but Bruce found his voice first.

"I am going to fucking kill you."

Chapter 4

BRUCE LEARNS EUPHEMISMS

RAGE.

It burned through Bruce's body—not in a physical way, but the memory of agony was there. As was the certainty that he'd been betrayed. Pain and betrayal were inextricably linked in his mind, and he had no room in his rage to analyze it. All he had was a target—a man with slender shoulders, bright brown eyes, and dark hair that kept flopping into them.

"You did it! You turned back into yourself!" the guy crowed.

Bruce sat up, his lips curling. "I was always me," he said, and his voice sounded weird to him. Deeper, hoarser, and with a rumble that moved like a wave through his cells, as if making a roll call. And every part responded, *I'm here, awake, and pissed off.*

"Okay, yeah, but you're not a wolf anymore." The guy's mouth curved into a bright smile, and he threw up his hands in happiness. "Yay!"

Bruce narrowed his eyes. The man seemed to be stretching here, putting on a false cheer in the hope that Bruce would play along.

He didn't. He rolled over to his knees, feeling his body settle into smooth motion. Arms, legs, torso—all seemed to vibrate with power despite the vivid memory of a fiery electric pain and the desperate minutes where he lay powerless in a twitching lump.

The guy moved with him, then hopped up onto his feet. Bouncy much? And though Bruce was feeling out his own body, he was still watching his environment, which was why he jolted in surprise. The man wore a T-shirt and nothing else. And since Bruce was still on the ground, he got an eyeful of the guy's junk. It was thick, ruddy, and bobbed way too close to his face. Bruce had the urge to grab it and squeeze, but that wasn't his style, so he surged to his feet instead.

Bruce towered over the smaller man as a way to establish control of the situation. Much easier to intimidate someone from a higher position. Only this guy didn't freeze, and he sure as hell didn't act intimidated.

"You're moving well," he said, inspecting Bruce from top to bottom.

Truth. Every part of him felt fluid. There was no pain, no ache. He couldn't remember the last time his back had moved without catching, or his knees had bent without popping. Even his neck didn't crack. The life of a firefighter often meant body aches, if not from an injury on the job, then from the constant training. He'd been living with that background noise of pain for so long, this was startlingly unfamiliar.

"I don't see any swelling or red spots." The man was walking in a slow circle around Bruce. "Nothing out of whack. Sometimes people don't come back quite right, but you're good. I'd hoped that shifting would fix this"—he held up his right hand to show two infant-sized middle fingers—"but I'm as I always was." His eyes narrowed as he moved behind Bruce. "I don't see any scars. Did you have any? If so, they're gone now."

The man chattered on, his tone bright, and he moved like a puppy discovering a new toy. Up, down, sideways. He even squatted down for a moment as he peered at the back of Bruce's leg.

"There's a burn scar here. It looks nasty. How long have you had it? I bet it hurt like a bitch when it happened."

It had. Bruce had gotten it on one of his first calls as a firefighter. It had been a bad house fire, with kids trapped upstairs—two unconscious teenagers. He couldn't carry both, so he'd picked up the girl, thinking he could carry her faster and then come back for the boy.

There hadn't been time. He'd gotten the burn when the floor had collapsed beneath his foot, and he'd had to fight to get it out while the flames ate at his flesh. His partner had managed to grab the girl while he worked himself free, but the agony alone had nearly killed him. He'd awoken in the hospital to the sound of a woman crying. It was his own mother at his bedside, but in his mind, he always confused it with the other mother. The one who'd lost her son because he hadn't been strong enough to get both of her children out.

"You're not talking," the man continued. "Strong, silent type. I get that, but you're going to have to talk to me sooner or later." God, the image of an overeager puppy wouldn't go away. He reminded Bruce of Josh on Christmas morning, when the kid had been hopped up on sugar and excitement.

And because that image was so strong, Bruce reacted as he always had with his little brother—he wrapped his arm around the guy's neck and put him on the floor. Not because he didn't like happy people, but because in his home, bouncy, excited puppies got kicked. "You need to calm the fuck down."

He expected a struggle. Josh had always squirmed and twisted while Bruce slowly, inevitably pressed him into the floor. There were usually obscenities and sometimes tears, but this guy was too perky for that. Sure, he squirmed, but he was no match for Bruce's skill. And he never stopped talking.

"Oh! Oh! I know that voice. That's the 'you need coffee' voice. I bet you like thick-as-tar coffee with like eight teaspoons of sugar."

"You are really freaking annoying, you know that?"

He snorted. "You think you're the first person to tell me that?" Then he pushed on Bruce's arm. "Come on. Let me up. It would be undignified if I was found like this, with my ass waving in the wind."

Yes, it was, though it was a very cute ass. Bruce eventually let him go; then he smiled as the man scrambled to his feet and tugged down his shirt as if he was trying to cover the important bits. He didn't.

"Have you gotten over your grumpy mood?" the man asked as he walked over to a nearby car. "I'm really sorry about the shock collar. I had no idea it would do that to you. But I had to, you know?"

Bruce felt his humor fade. How many times had he heard that pathetic excuse? It was what his father had always said after a particularly brutal "training" session.

Sorry about punching you, Bruce, but you have to learn how to take it and keep fighting.

Sorry your ankle's too jacked up for football, but I'm teaching you how to keep going, even when you're hurt.

Sorry I turned you into a bastard to your only brother, but I thought he was a monster.

That was the hell of it. Bruce was only now realizing that his father somehow knew Josh was a werewolf. He kept calling Josh a monster, and then he taught Bruce to keep Josh meek. It had taken moving away from home—and years of self-reflection—for Bruce to realize that it had been his father who was the monster, and Josh the innocent victim.

Until Bruce discovered that Josh was a werewolf. Now he didn't know what to think.

"Who the hell are you?" he said, his voice low and threatening.

The guy looked up from the trunk of the car. "Still grumpy, huh? Okay, I can work with that." He popped it open without breaking eye contact. "My name's Laddin. That's short for Aladdin 'cause my grandmama said I was magical. I know it doesn't make sense because Aladdin's lamp was magical, not him, but whatever. Mom was hopped up on painkillers at the time."

Bruce stared at him. "Do you ever shut up?"

Laddin blinked. "You asked me a question." He leaned against the car bumper. "Look, I can take grouchiness, but you're just being illogical." Then he reached into the trunk and unzipped a bag. A moment later he'd pulled out sweatpants, which he tossed straight at Bruce's face.

Bruce punched them aside with a swift stab of his fist, only belatedly realizing what they were.

Laddin watched him with an expressive eye roll. "They're clothes, Bruce. So you don't have to stand here in your birthday suit." Then he reached inside and pulled out another pair and yanked them on with swift movements. "And in case you're wondering, my ass is bare because you bit through my jeans and had me spurting arterial blood everywhere."

Bruce's breath caught at that, but he had only the vaguest memory of what had happened more than five minutes ago. It was fuzzy, confusing, and he didn't like thinking about it. And he *really* didn't like the idea that he'd bitten through this guy's leg, whoever the hell he was. To cover his confusion, he grabbed the sweatpants and tried to pull them on with his usual efficiency.

The moment he bent down, his head started to spin. And though he grabbed on to the sweatpants with a solid grip, that did nothing to keep him upright. He stumbled for balance. He knew this feeling—he was a firefighter and a paramedic, for God's sake. He should have recognized the symptoms of low blood sugar and dehydration long ago. But no, here he was, about to faint and hurl at the same time.

"I got ya, big guy. Come over here and sit down."

For such a small guy, Laddin had strong arms. And though it was humiliating, Bruce had seen too many macho men take a header, so he allowed Laddin to guide him over to an old blanket draped across a straw bale. He half sat, half collapsed, down. And when a barn cat hissed at him and dashed off, he barely had the strength to give it an annoyed glare.

"Don't be like that," Laddin said, and it took Bruce a moment to realize he was talking to the cat. "Drink this."

Again, Bruce didn't know who Laddin was talking to until a warm sports drink was shoved into his hand. When he stared at it, Laddin unscrewed the top and guided the bottle to his mouth.

"Drink," Laddin ordered. "Shifting takes a lot of energy, and you were cooped up in the van for a long time."

Not to mention the day Bruce had spent shadow-
ing Josh, then taking a fairy-induced nap. He mentally
scrolled back in his mind as he tried to make sense of
what was happening. His first clear memory was of Sunday dinner with his family—he had no idea how long
ago—when Josh and Nero had shown up to get some
specialty fabric from his dad's company. The rest of his
family had been blind to what was going on, but Bruce
had seen right away that his brother was under Nero's
spell—as in cult-level brainwashing. He'd tailed his
brother and done everything he could to get Josh alone,
but he hadn't been able to make it happen.

At the time, he hadn't realized they were werewolves. That had come later. In the end, he'd realized
the only way to save his brother was to join him and
somehow create the opportunity to drag his brother's
ass to safety. So he'd popped a fairy cherry and ended
up naked in a barn with werewolf Aladdin.

While he was ruminating on that, he drank the sports
drink and waited for his lightheadedness to clear.

Then Laddin settled in next to him. Bruce hadn't
even realized how chilly it was until he felt Laddin's
arm around his naked shoulders and the heat as their
thighs pressed against each other.

"You're cold," Laddin said as he disentangled the
sweatpants from Bruce's grip, then draped them across
Bruce's legs. It wasn't enough to cover him, but it helped,
especially as Laddin pressed his cheek to Bruce's shoulder as he adjusted the makeshift blanket.

Then they sat there while Bruce slowly sipped
his drink. He wanted to chug it down, but his stomach
was churning, and queasiness dogged every breath. He
sipped while Laddin squeezed his shoulder with one
hand and made cooing sounds at the hissing barn cat.

"Come here, puss. I won't hurt you. I just want to pet you."

"It probably has fleas," Bruce grumbled.

"For all you know, *you* could have fleas," Laddin countered in a teasing tone.

The cat sniffed at Laddin for a moment, then turned on its tail and stalked away. Laddin sighed in disappointment, and Bruce couldn't help but remember all the times his sister, Ivy, had begged for a cat. She'd never gotten to keep one, but that hadn't stopped her from trying to get one, including bringing a kitten home from a neighbor as a Christmas gift.

That had not gone well for anyone—especially the kitten. Bruce shuddered at the memory of his sister's tearstained cheeks as she watched their father toss the tiny cat out into the snow. Bruce had managed to sneak out and rescue it a half hour later, quietly taking it back to the neighbor, but that had been a long, awful thirty minutes for everyone. And the beating he'd earned from his father afterward hadn't been fun either.

Now, Laddin leaned his head back against the straw bale. "The cats probably know we're werewolves. They probably have some sort of instinct to keep away from us."

Bruce didn't comment. He was still waiting on his blood sugar to stabilize, while being ridiculously mesmerized by the feeling of having Laddin's arm across his shoulders and the idle way that Laddin stroked a couple of fingers through his hair. It didn't feel sexual. Well, not much. It was more like the way a kid would pet a cat. Since the feline had run away, Laddin was petting Bruce instead. Normally he'd hate it, but he wasn't feeling so great, and the caress was soothing. And when Laddin's fingers touched the back of his neck, he shivered in delight. That really ought to have set off all sorts of alarms in his thoughts, but honestly, it just felt nice.

He closed his eyes and let his head drop forward, giving Laddin better access to his neck and shoulders. There was lots of skin there to caress, and the guy seemed all too willing to touch him.

"I've got good news and bad news," Laddin said, his voice slightly breathless. "Which do you want first?"

Neither, but it didn't sound like he had a choice. "Hit me with the bad stuff."

Laddin nodded, but instead of speaking, he twisted around such that he was half hugging Bruce. He dropped his chin on Bruce's shoulder, and his free landed gently on Bruce's thigh. It was warm and squeezed down hard enough to be felt through the thick sweatpants. And damn if the nearness of that pressure didn't make certain other parts of him perk up.

Hell. He was getting a boner. He couldn't possibly be that hard up. Sure, Mr. Sunshine was attractive. And the man made him smile—inside—and that was more anybody ever had. But still….

Rather than dwell on those thoughts, he shifted to look Laddin in the eye. "You're not talking."

"I hate giving bad news."

"You'd rather give it after, then, and kill the happy one?"

Laddin's lips curved. "I usually solve the problem first, then say I've fixed it. In this case, I have some ideas, but I'm not absolutely sure. Do you want to know what 'the problem' is?"

"Yes."

Laddin blew out a breath that skated across Bruce's chin and heated him enough that his nipples tightened.

Bruce didn't move. It would draw too much attention to it if he covered up. But damn if his chest didn't tingle in a really embarrassing way.

"Your body isn't handling coming back to being human very well." Then, before Bruce could ask, Laddin rushed on to reassure him. "Overall you're doing great. I mean, there's a one-in-three survival rate for new recruits, so by that standard, you're doing amazing."

"One in three?" he echoed, the idea terrifying.

"Yeah. But the odds get worse when you count the ones who can't come back to human well."

"Like me."

Laddin winced. "Maybe like you. I'm still hoping the electrolytes will help. Gelpack could probably stabilize you, but he isn't here." He slanted Bruce a sidelong look. "We weren't expecting you."

Because he'd gone the fairy-fruit route. "Who's Gelpack?"

"You'll meet him later, but be careful. He's kind of like a clown. You'll either like him or he'll haunt your nightmares." Then Laddin brightened up. "I like him."

Bruce would lay odds that Laddin liked just about everyone. He had one of those eternally bright personalities Bruce usually hated. "So back to me...."

Laddin sobered. "Yeah. Your brother had a real problem grounding back into his body. That's the good news."

"Josh's problem is good news?"

"Yup, because I paid attention. I know how to help you, but you aren't going to like it." He grinned. "Unless you love it. Josh ended up loving it, so there's no telling—"

"Get to the point!"

"I am!" Laddin huffed as his hand brushed across Bruce's chest.

Fire spun through Bruce's body, totally out of proportion to what that simple contact should have created, and he gasped as much in embarrassment as delight.

"Do you think I drape myself all over the first hot stranger I meet?"

Bruce was still in the grips of reaction, his cock suddenly throbbing beneath the sweatpants. "Maybe. I don't know you," he growled.

"Well, I don't. But Josh was all about touch. In the beginning, it was the only way to get him back into his body. Then, later…." Laddin shrugged, his torso rubbing erotically against Bruce's arm. "Well, he did it by enthusiastic choice afterward."

Bruce closed his eyes, trying to get a grip on his whirling thoughts. "What are you talking about?"

Laddin tilted his head so that his temple was on Bruce's shoulder and his mouth was perilously close to Bruce's jaw. "You need to have an orgasm," he said. "It's the fastest way to get into your body. It's also pretty damn fun, so all in all, it's not such a bad thing."

Horror shuddered through Bruce's body. "You are not going to jerk me off, you perv."

Laddin reared back. "As if! Mamma mia, I don't want to touch you any more than you want me to."

That would have been reassuring, except his dick was screaming, *Yes, yes, yes!* And if he didn't miss his guess, Laddin's sweatpants were tenting, though he'd adjusted his hips to try to hide it.

Meanwhile, Laddin continued to stroke Bruce's shoulders, the touch growing firmer until it felt more like a massage. And damn it all, Bruce really wanted to close his eyes and feel.

"You need to have a personal moment," Laddin said gently. "I get that it's awkward and embarrassing.

Believe me, I feel the same way. But you need it, and I can't leave you alone until you do it."

"This is bullshit," Bruce said, though he couldn't deny the temptation to touch his own dick. "I was fine a few minutes ago. This is just low blood sugar."

"Uh-huh. Believe me, I was thinking the same thing at first. But it's been fifteen minutes since you started drinking. Five since you finished the bottle. Feel any more connected to your body?"

No. If anything, he felt more lightheaded. He could imagine his entire body floating off into a hazy sleep except for the places where Laddin heated his skin. Those spots were warm, happy, and begging for more.

"Something happened to put you into your head. One minute you were all grouchy bear, and suddenly you're dizzy and can barely lift your arms. Care to tell me what it was?"

He hadn't a clue.

"Never mind. You need to get on with polishing your knob."

"Are you twelve?"

"You don't like that phrase? I've got others. 'Choke the chicken.' 'Go fly fishing.' 'Liquidate the inventory.'"

"You are a child."

"And you need to get busy."

Hell no.

"How about 'celebrating palm Sunday'? 'Digital penile oscillation'? 'Give yourself a low five'?"

"Holy hell, how many of those have you got?"

"You kidding? I went through the LA public school system. I'm just getting started. Like you need to," he said, pinching Bruce's taut nipple. And while Bruce bucked in reaction, Laddin kept talking. "You must

have done it with your friends when you were a kid.
Didn't all eleven-year-old boys go into a back room
and spit-shine their water pump? Yank on the crank and
whack the weasel?"

Yeah, so there had been some of that when he'd
been young and randy. "We called it 'visiting Miss
Michigan.'" He held up a hand with his fingers together. "Because the state is shaped like a hand."

"And the UP has that very pointed shape."

Bruce hadn't thought about it that deeply, but
he supposed it applied. "I had a friend who called it
'teaching Cyclops the lambada.'"

Laddin tilted his head. "Not bad. Gives it a bit of
an international flavor."

Bruce chuckled. "I think it's a global phenomenon."

Laddin grinned as he straightened, moving away
from Bruce's shoulder. "How ya feeling now?"

It took a moment for Bruce to check himself. He
remembered the protocol he used to go through as a
paramedic, checking a patient's vitals and doing a head-
to-toe inventory. He used it now and was disappointed
to realize he felt good. His heartbeat was steady, his
breath was even, and his legs and even his toes had
heated up.

He shook his head to clear it. There had to be a
reason he was suddenly feeling better. The electrolytes
in the sports drink he'd finished had probably kicked in.
That was it. It couldn't possibly be because Laddin had
snuggled up tight to his side.

"Better," he said quietly. "More solid."

"You grounded into your body, and all it took
was a little raunchy talk." He gave Bruce's shoulders
a squeeze. "See? Now you don't need to shuck your
corn." Then he waggled his eyebrows. "Good one,

right? Didn't think I'd know that one, did you? Since I'm city-born and -raised."

"I grew up in Indianapolis. That's not exactly Mayberry."

Laddin drew back, taking his arm and his heat with him. "Where?"

"It's from a TV show my mom used to love. We'd watch the reruns together." He let his head drop back onto the straw bale. "It was filmed in black and white."

"Ugh. You guys in the Midwest are living in the Dark Ages. You know that, right?"

"Not me. My mom. And yes, we know." Although in his mother's case, it was more like the Denial Ages. But rather than think about that, he shifted against the straw bale, feeling strength come back into his body. His hard-on was still hungry, and he really missed Laddin's touch, but it didn't seem like his only lifeline anymore.

He watched as Laddin jumped up from the floor, brushing off his pants with quick swipes of his hand. Bruce took his time pulling on the sweatpants, doing his best not to gasp when the fabric skimmed over his dick. It made no sense. He was hard and horny, and he was watching Laddin as if the guy were the newest *Playboy* centerfold. Bruce had always noticed cute guys before, but he'd never had such an overwhelming reaction to one.

"You said my brother was like… that he needed…."

Laddin dug into the trunk again and pulled out a T-shirt with a wolf emblem on the front. The thing was all wavy hair as the creature howled to the moon, and beneath it were the words *Wulf, Inc.* "A blow job after every shift?"

Bruce's eyes widened. "Seriously?"

Laddin laughed as he threw the T-shirt at Bruce. "Not after the first few times. That didn't stop him from wanting one, though."

Bruce couldn't imagine his brother as one of the crass crew—the guys who talked nonstop about sex with bad jokes, crude references, and stupid double entendres. His brother had never been that lame, and the idea that Josh had turned into some beast that needed to rut all the time just reinforced his need to get his brother out of here.

"It's the Nero guy, isn't it?"

Laddin smiled, his expression growing wistful. "They're cute together, aren't they?"

Cute wasn't the word he'd use. What he'd seen was a lot bigger and much more dangerous. They were consumed by each other, trapped in each other's spheres and unable to break free. He had no doubt that Josh thought he loved Nero. His brother was naïve that way. When he fell, he fell hard and gave his all. As a kid, Josh had always obsessed over things, while Bruce had scrambled to keep their father completely unaware of the fallout. Josh's first dive into chemistry had been when he tried to recreate the experiment that created the Flash. That had cost Josh all his hair and all Bruce's allowance as he tried to hide the damage to the basement. As time wore on, Josh's experiments had gotten more sophisticated, but his habit of completely immersing into whatever—or whomever—was still there.

Bruce, on the other hand, knew better than to trust the first kindhearted guy who showed up. Sure, Nero pretended to cherish and protect his brother, and the sex was probably off the charts. But he'd also turned Josh into a werewolf, talked him into risking his life, doing

God only knew what, and most telling, he'd destroyed Josh's relationship with his family.

Or he'd tried to. Bruce was still here for Josh, and he was going to do what he should have done from the very beginning: protect his little brother. And if that meant diving into Josh's nightmare world of werewolves and other monsters, then that was what he was going to do.

But first he needed to learn the lay of the land. He leaned back against the straw bale, consciously relaxing his pose, as if all he needed was a beer and a plate of nachos. "Give it to me straight. What exactly does it mean to be a werewolf?"

Laddin echoed his pose, only he settled onto the fender of the car as he stretched out his legs. "It means you can turn into a wolf."

Yeah, that part he'd already figured out. "But how?" He leaned forward. "I need details."

"I could give you a ton of them, but it won't matter. You are a fairy-fruit werewolf. None of the rules apply to you."

"And those rules are…."

"Individual."

Sounded like a recipe for disaster. Or the standard bullshit con artists used to cover their dirty deeds. He just couldn't figure out if Laddin was one of the brainwashing cult leaders or another guy caught in someone else's charismatic orbit. He certainly seemed nice enough, but Bruce would need a lot more to go on before he could trust Laddin.

"Fine," he said. "Let's start with Josh, then. How did he join your ranks—?"

They both looked up as the barn doors started rolling open. Someone was coming, and Bruce didn't want to be sitting here half-naked when he met whatever

foe decided to stroll in. Plus, it was cold outside, so he
pulled on the wolf T-shirt and jumped to his feet.

Laddin was much more casual. He tilted his head
to look through the growing crack in the door; then he
smiled at Bruce. "Why don't you ask him yourself?
That's the team coming back. We'll get your assignment from them."

Bruce frowned. "*My* assignment? I didn't join your
team." It was a knee-jerk response. He never joined
anything without triple-checking the small print and
doing an exhaustive internet search for scams. His father had drilled distrust into him from the day he was
born. Unfortunately, Laddin was smart enough to point
out the flaw in his statement.

"You ate the fruit, you joined the team. Wulf, Inc.
is responsible for all the lupine shifters in the world,
and the bite marks on my jeans prove you qualify. Ergo,
you get assignments from us."

"Is that so?" he challenged. "I have to obey you.
No loophole, no way around it, no—"

Laddin cut him off with a wave of his hand. "Of
course there are workarounds. We're magical creatures.
The only rule about us is that there are no rules unless
we make them." Then he leaned forward. "Which we
do, because it makes everyone safe, including you."

That was bullshit of the first order. Only abusive
people spouted, *We make the rules, and you have to
obey for your own good.* But he didn't say that. Instead,
he turned toward the car just now heading inside, and
blew out a relieved breath. Josh sat in the front passen-
ger seat, alive and apparently whole.

Good. His brother was alive.

Now came the hard part—rescuing him from this
whacked-out cult.

Chapter 5

EVERYBODY LOVES WULFRIC

LADDIN WATCHED as Bruce tried to straighten up, something that was hard to do in slouchy sweatpants and a too-tight T-shirt. The guy was big, that was for sure. He had shoulders that could lift a car and probably had, given that he was a firefighter. But he was also a grouchy sourpuss who tended to look on the dark side of life.

Laddin knew the type. Bruce had probably been disappointed too many times by people who had promised something and failed to deliver. Welcome to the club, buddy. But going through life with a growl was just a waste of energy, and Laddin had no time for people who wasted anything that could be put to better use. His mother had taught him that the first time he'd whined about his messed-up hand. Every time he grumbled, she made him do chores until he discovered that he could do twice as much as people with two normal hands, simply because he didn't waste time complaining.

"Your clothes are in there," he said to Bruce as he gestured inside the van. Then he did his own bit of getting ready.

He checked his cell for messages from Captain M (none), reported via voicemail on Bruce's progress (wolf back to human), and then prepared to meet the most awesome man in Wulf, Inc. history. Because the car that was pulling into the barn had Nero and Josh in the front seat and Wulfric, the two-hundred-year-old founder of Wulf, Inc., in the back.

Laddin didn't know much about Wulfric except that he was incredibly reclusive, everyone wanted to be his friend, and he only came out when the world was ending. He and his witch mother had deployed to Wisconsin when the lake had turned to poison, but he'd been as ineffective as everyone else at finding the demon. And now Laddin was going to get a chance to meet him, all because he was at the pizza farm along with the other members of Wulf, Inc.

It wasn't until Nero had thrown the car into Park that Laddin realized Wulfric, the man of shifter legend, looked like he'd been chewed on by an ogre. Half his face was swollen, and the other half was ripped into shreds. There was blood everywhere, and he'd slumped sideways in the car with his mangled face pressed up against the window.

Laddin rushed forward, intending to open the car door, but stopped, realizing the guy would fall onto the ground. So he stood there looking awkward, his hands hovering uselessly near the door handle. Meanwhile, Nero and Josh both got out. A closer look showed that they too were worse for wear. Or at least their clothes were, given the tears and blood splatter. They, on the other hand, appeared completely healthy despite their anxious expressions.

"What happened?" Laddin asked.

"Hellhounds," Josh said as he opened the back door and gently reached inside. "Don't trust your eyes with him. He's got a fairy glamour that makes him appear beautiful."

Laddin frowned. Wulfric looked anything but beautiful right then. More like a special effects monster gone bad.

"We got Wiz to dispel the magic for now," Josh continued. "But if he suddenly looks like the picture of health, it's an illusion."

Got it. "Why didn't Wulfric shift?" That was the fastest way to heal.

"Too exhausted," Nero answered. "He should be in a hospital, but they're overrun with regular human casualties right now. Besides, he's better off resting here and waiting for one of the clerics to magic him better."

Laddin swallowed. Wulfric the Legend looked like he was about to lose his lunch as Josh gently shook him awake. "How long will that take?"

Nero's expression turned grim as Josh helped Wulfric straighten up and move away from the window. "He's got a freaking death wish. He ran in front of the entire hellhound pack—as a damned human—to buy time for people to get away. And before you ask, no, I don't know why there were hellhounds running around the lake. They were probably attracted by the mystical shitshow we've got going. Wulfric was there doing some sort of seeking spell for the demon. Luckily, we were looking for *him*. If we'd been a few minutes later, he'd have been lunch meat." Nero rubbed a hand over the back of his head, and his eyes were haunted. "It's a mess up there, Laddin. Everyone is trying to figure out why Lake Wacka Wacka is poison. We got military, scientists, reporters, and the paranormal everywhere. It's a real fucking apocalypse." He added those last words in an agonized whisper as he bent to help Wulfric out of the car.

"Don't open that door!" Bruce snapped as he moved around the car. "Josh, get out of my way."

Nero's head snapped up. "You don't issue the orders around here."

"I'm a paramedic. Hate me all you want, but I'm your best shot of keeping him alive." He grimaced as he looked inside the car. "Short of a hospital."

Josh backed out of the way, his expression completely locked down. "He's really important, Bruce."

"They're all really important. Now get me a med kit. Whatever you've got."

Laddin leaped to obey, but Nero was closer. He got to the van first and peered inside, but he obviously didn't remember where everything was. So Laddin elbowed him out of the way, grabbed Bruce's empty cage and passed it to Nero, then crawled inside to grab the kit. And while he was maneuvering, Nero grumbled a question at him.

"Is he stable?"

It took a moment for Laddin to realize he was referring to Bruce, not Wulfric.

"Good job getting him human and all," Nero continued. "But how freaked is he?"

"Not freaked at all," Laddin said as he passed the basic kit over to Nero. He still had to grab the defibrillator and anything else that might be useful. "He chose this, remember?"

"Which makes him really untrustworthy," Nero said before he rushed back to the car with the kit.

Laddin couldn't disagree. No one chose to become a werewolf without having ulterior motives, and in Bruce's case, there was a fairy involved. That always made things dicey. But there hadn't been time to ferret out any of that information. Still, Bruce was a paramedic and a firefighter. That had to count for something.

Bruce was working on the greatest werewolf of all time, asking him questions like, *Where does it hurt?* and *Can you follow my finger?* As Laddin came closer, he had to admit that Bruce looked more than competent. He worked on Wulfric with a businesslike efficiency, not seeming to be distracted by his patient's fame as he opened up kits, put in an IV, and gently probed for deeper wounds.

"I can clean out these cuts," he said to Wulfric, "and put on bandages. But you'll need a plastic surgeon or it'll scar—"

"No, he won't," Nero said from Bruce's opposite shoulder. "Wounds only make him more beautiful."

Wulfric's swollen lips curved. "True."

Bruce grunted. "If so, then you're going to be gorgeous."

"Gorgeous is a step down for him," Nero said. His tone was light, but his expression was worried. "What about internal injuries? Brain bleeds? Arrhythmias or spinal stuff?"

"You get those terms off *Grey's Anatomy*?" Bruce asked. "You'd have to be at a hospital to find out. And then you'd have to ask the doctors."

Wulfric shook his head. "My mother can—"

"She can't," Nero interrupted. "She wandered off. That's why we came looking for you."

Wulfric sighed and closed his unswollen eye. "She's looking for the demon."

That was obvious. *Everybody* in the paranormal world was looking for the damned demon poisoning Wisconsin. And the vanilla humans were looking for everything else, from a microscopic black hole to radioactive algae.

"All right," Bruce said as he stepped back from the car. "I'd prefer to put you on a backboard and carry you to a hospital, but failing that—"

"I've got the backboard here," Laddin said.

Nero frowned. "The van had a backboard?"

Laddin didn't bother answering. He already knew that the field wolves never read their emails or paid any attention to the recommended organization of the van.

Bruce was all business as he grabbed a blanket to set underneath Wulfric. Laddin could see the plan without asking. He was going to help Wulfric roll onto the fabric and then they could ease him out of the car. "Great. So where do we carry him?"

"He's got a room here," Nero said. "We just need to get him there."

"I can walk," Wulfric said.

"Maybe you can," Bruce said, "but no one looks macho passing out. And I don't think your face could take another hit."

"My face has seen a lot worse," Wulfric answered, but he gestured his acquiescence. "I am at your mercy."

It took time and coordination to move Wulfric out of the car and onto the backboard, then carry him inside to the guest area of the main house. The pizza farm was also a quaint B&B that had been completely rented out by Wulf, Inc. Wulfric's room was the first on the right, and they gently set him down on the bed.

"Thank you," Wulfric said, his voice melodic. Lying there on the bed in his bloody clothes, he looked small and vulnerable. Then he looked at Josh, Laddin, and Bruce in turn. "Welcome to Wulf, Inc. Mother and I are grateful for your work."

He spoke with old-world charm that should have seemed strange, but it still managed to touch Laddin's heart. He didn't mention that none of them had fully signed on yet, especially Bruce. Or that Laddin intended to leave after the next moon.

Exhaustion seemed to kick in, and Wulfric's eyes drifted shut. Bruce set down the heavy field medical kit and looked to Nero. "I'll stay here until the… whomever arrives. He shouldn't be left alone."

Nero dropped his hands on his hips and looked Bruce over from head to toe. "Josh, stay with Wulfric for now. Your brother and I are going to have a little chat."

Bruce rocked back on his heels, set his jaw, then turned to Josh. "Never thought I'd see the day you blindly took orders from anyone."

Oh shit. There was that grumpy guy taunt. Obviously Bruce didn't like anyone ordering his brother around. But instead of facing off with Nero, he had to poke Josh—probably to get Josh to fight for himself. But whether Bruce realized it or not, Nero was in charge. So as Josh's face grew ruddy and his jaw jutted forward, Laddin quickly stepped in to interrupt the fight before it started.

"Yes, Josh will obey," he said. "Because Nero's his trainer and the alpha. That means Josh has to take orders until Wulf, Inc. decides he's safe to go free."

Bruce's jaw tightened and a muscle over his eye twitched in anger. Well, he'd better buckle up, because it was about to get worse.

"And furthermore," Laddin said as he rounded on Nero, "Mr. Paramedic is my problem, so if there's anything to *get straight*, I'll be the one to do it." That was a dicey position to take because technically Nero was the highest-ranking person in the room except for the unconscious Wulfric. But new recruits were always touchy. That was why they had one person in charge of each new puppy. And though Laddin had zero experience training a newbie, he was still the only one who should be disciplining Bruce. Those were the rules, after all. But would Nero abide by them?

He and Nero engaged in a heavy stare down, but eventually Nero dipped his chin. Thank God, because Laddin had been sweating.

"Fine," Nero growled. "You get him under control. And then get him back to base. He's a liability here."

"Yeah, because you're overrun with medical knowledge," Bruce taunted. "What are you going to do if he goes into arrhythmia, has a brain bleed, or spinal stuff happens?"

Nero flushed as his own words were flung back at him, and Josh came around the far edge of the bed to face off with his brother.

"You don't know jack shit here, Bruce, so shut up and listen."

This was ridiculous. They were having a "who's in charge" argument in a sickroom. So Laddin—who was arguably the shortest and smallest one there—jumped in front of Bruce and pointed his finger straight at his nose.

"Not a word. Outside."

Bruce stiffened, and it looked like he was going to argue. But he was a firefighter, which meant he understood the chain of command. Laddin watched as he swallowed down whatever he wanted to say, gave a mocking bow, then sauntered out the door.

Laddin didn't wait for it to close before spinning around to glare at Nero. "Get your puppy in line or mine is going to kill him."

Nero and Josh answered at the exact same moment, "He could try."

Maybe it took an only child to see the obvious, but Nero was being head-up-his-ass stupid. "You don't think sibling shit is powerful? That it can cut deep and dig up the most awful stuff at the worst fucking moment? What happens if Bruce goes off the rails?" He stared at Nero. "What happens *to Josh* if we have to kill his own brother in front of him? Or worse, if Josh is the one who has to take him down?"

Laddin watched as his words hit both men. They blanched and swallowed, looking appropriately chagrined. Meanwhile, a low chuckle came from the bed. *Apparently Wulfric wasn't unconscious after all.*

"Never underestimate the little ones," he said. "We have to be smarter."

Laddin felt his lips twitch. Yes, by werewolf standards, he was below average in size, but that didn't make him *little*. Still, he couldn't deny that being included in a "we" with Wulfric made his inner child do a happy dance. "I'm the fastest too," he said. Josh started to object because—honestly—the guy's long-legged body was built for speed, but Laddin interrupted. "I'm fast because I know where everything is stored. Like the backboard and my laptop."

He had them both there. Josh had indeed misplaced his laptop dozens of times in the lab.

And with that parting shot, Laddin stepped outside to confront Bruce. The man was leaning against the wall, a smirk on his face.

"Obviously you heard every word."

"You guys weren't quiet."

"Actually we were, but your werewolf hearing has kicked in."

That startled Bruce enough that he paused. Good—because Laddin wasn't finished.

"And just as obviously, you didn't hear the message." He paused long enough to make Bruce think, but not let him speak. "And that message was… *they can and will kill you.*"

Bruce smiled and echoed the other weres' words. "They can try."

"Mamma mia, you big guys are idiots. First off, there would be two against one. That alone ought to make sense to you. But Josh has been training for weeks now. Nero's been the alpha of an elite combat pack for three years. Any of that give you pause? Josh has been around the block, Nero's been around the world, and you've taken one step. Catch a clue or die. Those are the werewolf ways."

Bruce didn't respond as his expression tightened into a hard mask. But it was a respectful mask, so that gave Laddin hope. As did the knowledge that Bruce was a firefighter. He was no stranger to harsh training. Laddin was counting on him responding to a drill-sergeant tone.

"Second off, thank you for helping Wulfric. He's important to us, and we appreciate the help."

It took a moment for those words to sink in, and Bruce's eyes widened in surprise. He obviously hadn't expected gratitude.

"It's my job." He delivered the words in a flat tone, but they told Laddin that Bruce was always a first responder, no matter whether he was getting paid for it. His role as a firefighter/paramedic was his identity, and that scored points in Laddin's mind.

"You're not on the paramedic clock here," he said. "You don't have to help if you don't want to."

He waited for Bruce to say something, but no words came out. If Laddin was a good judge of expressions—and he usually was—then Bruce himself was feeling conflicted about everything. And that didn't jibe with the fact that he'd willingly become a werewolf.

"Third, I need to know why you did it."

Bruce's eyes narrowed. "I'm a paramedic. I can't not help."

"I'm not talking about Wulfric. Why'd you eat the fruit? Why are you here in the first place?"

He was just posing the questions. He didn't really expect any answers, but then Bruce's gaze hopped to the closed bedroom door. "I'm here for my brother."

"Josh is doing fine."

Bruce's mouth flattened into a thin line. He didn't respond, but his silence spoke volumes.

"You're a 'see it to believe it' kind of guy. I get that. So why are you taunting Josh instead of talking to him?"

Bull's-eye! Bruce flushed the same ruddy color that his brother did.

"I haven't had the chance." His gaze shot back to Laddin, and it was dark with challenge. "You want to thank me for taking care of Wulfric? Let me talk to my brother *alone*."

"Josh doesn't answer to me."

Bruce shrugged. "Find a way."

Laddin nodded as if he were considering the difficult challenge. He even rubbed his chin for good measure. Then he grabbed the door and opened it enough to whisper inside. "Josh. Your brother wants to talk to you alone. You up for that?"

A chair scraped back, and Josh appeared in the doorway. "Sure. Am I allowed to beat the shit out of him?"

"No."

"Bummer. I guess I'll just have to think of something more devious."

Out of the corner of his eye, Laddin saw Bruce wince. Probably because Josh was a scientific genius and had likely put his brother through a lot when they were kids. But to his credit, Bruce didn't back down. He stood there, tall and stern, as if he were facing a firing squad.

Ugh. Laddin made a mental note to thank his mother for not having any more kids. This sibling shit was annoying.

"Keep it quiet," he ordered, "and keep it right here." That way Nero would be on hand if the shit hit the fan. "I'm going to see about our rooms." He'd only been a trainer for a few hours, and already he was exhausted. God only knew how bad it would get after a couple of days. Maybe, if he was lucky, the big black lake of doom would kill them all first.

Chapter 6

BRUCE TRIES TO MAKE AMENDS

BRUCE HAD been heading for this moment for a few years now. The realization that he'd been a monster to his brother had led him, step by step, to right now, when he could finally apologize. If he did it right, he and Josh could start again without their history coming between them. Except now that he was here, he had no idea what to say.

So he started at the beginning.

"I was an ass to you, and I'm sorry."

Josh jerked backward a half step. Clearly he hadn't expected an apology, and his eyes narrowed in suspicion. "O-kaaaay," he said, drawing out the word. "Care to be more specific?"

Not really, but Bruce supposed beggars couldn't be choosers. "I was a horrible big brother. I was supposed to look out for you. Instead, I hurt you every chance I could." He wanted to give excuses. He wanted to explain about what their father had said about Josh, that he was a monster and it was up to Bruce to keep his brother weak and off-balance. But that didn't change the facts. "I'm sorry," he stressed, wondering if Josh knew how hard it was for him to say those words.

"I heard that. I just don't believe it."

In all the times that this moment had played out in his head, it had never occurred to him that he might hear those words from Josh—that his brother wouldn't see, wouldn't feel how genuinely sorry he was. Josh had always felt things. He teared up at those "save the animals" commercials, and he used to do a happy dance whenever he made their mother smile.

"I…," Bruce protested. "How can I convince you?"

"Start by admitting the real reason you ate that cherry."

Shit. "If you don't believe I'm sorry, then you're not going to believe I did it to protect you."

"Bull. That was all about getting power. You saw that I had something, and you wanted to get in on it."

"I saw that you'd joined a cult and the only way to get you out was to go in myself."

"Do you even hear how ridiculous that sounds? I'm doing important things here. I'm trying to save the fucking planet."

"And I'm just trying to save you," Bruce said, leaning in so he could speak quietly. "That fairy bastard still has his eyes on you. He said so."

"I can handle Bitter. And even if I can't, how could you possibly help me? You don't know jack about anything."

"I'm a fast learner."

"No, you're not."

That stung. Maybe he wasn't a mega-brain like Josh, but he was smart and resourceful. And becoming a paramedic wasn't exactly chump work. But he'd never win in a verbal war with his brother. He took a breath and blew it out slowly. "I'm here to help—to be the brother I wasn't when we were kids."

Josh threw up his hands. "Oh wow! How nice. Except you're ten years too late. I don't need a brother, and if I did, it sure as hell wouldn't be someone like you."

Bruce set his jaw and shoved his fists deep into his sweatpants pockets. He would not revert to acting like the kid he'd been, who would have punched Josh by now. "Lots of people value someone like me."

"Not me," Josh said in a hard tone. "I was recruited, Bruce. They need brains, not brawn. You're just another meathead."

"Really? Because it looks to me like I'm the only medical skill you've got."

That was a true hit, and Josh knew it. His eyes narrowed and his jaw worked, but he didn't lash out like he'd done when they were kids. Instead, he rocked back on his heels and spoke with the cold authority of someone who knew what the hell he was talking about.

"Yes, you are," he said. "And that's the only reason you're still here." He lifted his chin, and his words came out like tiny stones that *hurt*. "I'm the one who figured out how to defeat the demon. I'm the one who negotiated with a fairy prince and came out ahead. All you've done is piss in your own cage."

Bruce felt his face heat. How many times had he had to slap down a new firefighter who thought he knew more than everyone else, just because he'd finished fire training? The newbies were always high on arrogance and low on real knowledge. He'd taken great pleasure in knocking some reality into their thick heads before they got themselves or someone else hurt.

Josh was right. All he'd managed to do so far was to come back to human. He hadn't a clue about being a werewolf, much less fighting a demon. But he'd come in hot to save his brother. When he'd heard the menace in Bitterroot's voice, he'd felt like he had no choice. Josh was in over his head. So even though it might take some time before Bruce figured out his head from his tail, he was here to watch his brother's back. And that was always a good thing, even if all he did was give Josh the chance to fight back.

"I'm here to help," he said, because all those other words weren't going to come out right.

"You're here because you're jealous of me." And then Josh's eyes widened in surprise, his expression softened, and his lips curved. "Holy shit. You're jealous of me." He let his head drop back as he looked at the ceiling. "Why didn't I see that before? All those times you beat me up. All those things you did to make me feel small. It was because you're jealous." He grinned as he looked back at Bruce. "I'm smarter than you. I'm going to earn a hell of a lot more money than you. And now I'm happy. Do you hear that?" He leaned forward as if shoving something shiny into Bruce's face. "I'm happy, and there's nothing you can do about it."

And then he looked over Bruce's shoulder to where Laddin was leaning against the wall, listening to every word.

"We've had our private chat. Now keep your puppy the hell away from me," Josh said, then spun around and went back into Wulfric's room.

Meanwhile, Bruce stood there, feeling raw. In his imagination, they'd had the conversation in a bar over beers. They'd talk about sports and Josh's chemistry stuff. Then Bruce's apology would have landed on softer ground. Never in his wildest dreams had it gone this badly. And now he was smarting from the pain of being so wrong.

"Is it true?" Laddin asked. "Are you jealous?" His voice was calm, but there was an edge to it. Enough to let Bruce know he had to answer.

"No."

"He's got a lot to be jealous of. He's brilliant, a ton of fun, and has a bright future with a guy who loves him."

Bruce turned to stare hard at Laddin. "Sounds like you're jealous."

Laddin's lips curved. "I gave up jealousy the day I quit peewee football." He held up his hand with the shortened fingers. "Even with this, I could catch and throw. And since I was fast, I was an asset to the team."

"What does that have to do with anything?" Bruce tried—and failed—to keep the annoyance out of his tone.

"I hated football. It's just a bunch of guys beating up on each other. But it made me realize that I needed to go for what *I* wanted, not what everyone else had."

"Football is about a lot more than simply beating each other up."

Laddin shrugged. "Maybe, but I had much more fun blowing shit up. A little C-4 made my life Nirvana. Pretty soon I was working on movie sets for real money, and I wasn't risking brain damage to do it."

"You sure? Post-concussion syndrome happens with explosives too."

"Clever," Laddin said as he pushed off the wall. "Turn the questions around to me and put it straight into your area of expertise. The thing is, I'm not playing. We're talking about you now. About why you chose to rescue a brother who doesn't need or want your help."

Damn, he'd underestimated Laddin. Not only did he have the guts to face down Nero in Wulfric's bedroom, but he was smart too. That earned Bruce's respect... and an honest answer. "That fairy meant business. He was talking about *enslaving* Josh."

"And you could have told Josh that. But instead, you pop a cherry into your mouth and become just like him. Sounds like jealousy to me."

"It's not! I was trying to protect him!"

"Because you know all about fairies and werewolves and stuff like that."

Bruce shut his mouth. This was a rehash of the exact argument he'd had with Josh, and he didn't feel like doing it again. He buttoned his lip and moved into an at-attention stance. If he was going to get chewed out, then fine. It wouldn't be his first time. But he'd be damned if he discussed his fucked-up brotherly relationship with anyone.

Except Laddin didn't chew him out. He stood there and watched him, his gaze heavy and his body weirdly still. In the short time that Bruce had known Laddin, the guy had never stopped moving. This sudden stillness was unnerving. Which—he supposed—was exactly the point. But he'd lay odds that he could outlast Mr. Hyperactive any day. He stood still too... and waited.

Laddin lasted about two minutes.

"What are you doing?" Laddin asked.

"I'm waiting for my orders." He had to stop himself from adding "sir!"

"Right. Because this is the military... not."

Now it was Bruce's turn to be confused. "Aren't you, though? Fighting demons and fairies and whatnot?"

Laddin nodded. "Yeah, but we're different. We're werewolves. We create packs."

"Isn't there a hierarchy within the pack?"

"Well, yes. Nero's the pack leader, unless Yordan's there putting us through calisthenics. Then there's Captain M, who is my trainer. She's higher up than the rest of us, but she's not technically in our pack. Actually, we haven't really been named a pack yet. Everyone calls us the geeks, though that's not a real pack name, just a description of who we are." Laddin frowned. "Wow. We are a mess."

He said it. And the guy's frown of consternation made Bruce smile. "Let me help you out. You're my trainer, right? You're in charge of me."

"Yes."

"Should I go back in there where I'm needed?" He gestured to Wulfric's bedroom door. "Or are you going to poke me with more useless questions?" The answer was obvious. He needed to go back and stay with Wulfric. He relaxed back on his heels and waited for Laddin to say just that.

He didn't. Instead, Laddin cracked Wulfric's bedroom door open and poked his head in.

"Any change?" Laddin asked Nero.

"His supernatural healing is kicking in. He'll be fine. And even prettier for it."

Bruce didn't believe it, so he quickly stepped around Laddin and pushed into the room. Sure enough, the hamburger that had been Wulfric's face was already sealing shut. Bruce snatched up the stethoscope and listened to Wulfric's heart. He even gently prodded the man's body to see if anything had manifested that needed immediate attention.

Nothing. Wulfric was indeed healing fast and healing well. Bruce looked up at Laddin. "Is this normal for a werewolf? Do all of us knit together so quickly?"

Everyone in the room shook their head, including Josh, but Nero was the one who spoke. "This is special to Wulfric and maybe a couple of his other descendants." He eyed Josh, who abruptly gasped.

"Wulfric is my ancestor?" Josh asked.

Nero nodded, and Bruce had yet one more thing to process. Because if Wulfric was Josh's ancestor, then he was Bruce's as well. Now *that* was something to think about.

He flashed a grin at his brother, hoping for a moment of family camaraderie. No-go. Josh wouldn't even look at him.

Bruce set aside his stethoscope and studied Wulfric, who was in some sort of meditative trance, his body relaxed and his eyes shut. If he crossed his hands on his chest, he'd look like a vampire in his coffin, but his arms lay lax with the palms upward by his sides.

Laddin came close. "Wulfric's good? Nothing urgent right now?"

Bruce shrugged. "Nothing I can see, but there's plenty I can't see—"

"Good," Laddin interrupted. "I guess that means we go with option two."

Bruce frowned, not remembering any options.

"I'm going to poke you with useless questions, and you're going to answer them all."

Oh goody. "Somehow I thought becoming a werewolf would be way cooler," he drawled.

Laddin snorted. "Didn't we all."

Chapter 7

LADDIN LEARNS THE FIRST RULE OF A FIREFIGHTER
BRUCE LEARNS THE FIRST RULE OF A WEREWOLF

LADDIN SMILED as Mr. Grumpy followed him away from Wulfric's room. Bruce might not want to talk, but he needed a break from Josh, as well as the family drama brewing between them. Because whether he knew it or not, Bruce was wiped. His shoulders drooped every time he forgot to stand at parade rest, and though his jaw remained tight, his head would occasionally tilt one way or another as fatigue nailed him.

Laddin's goal was to get the man to rest, even though Mr. Macho would probably take a nail gun to his hands rather than admit it.

They swung by the kitchen on the way out the door and grabbed a couple of thermoses he'd set on the counter earlier. After popping his, he took a long swing of coffee, letting the caffeine penetrate his cells. It didn't happen that fast, but he pretended it did even when he was drinking decaf.

Bruce must have smelled the brew, because he immediately perked up. "That other one for me?" he asked.

"Yup." He passed it over, trying to hide his smile as Bruce popped the top and started chugging. He was definitely a caffeine addict. Then Laddin grinned as Bruce started gagging. "Spit it out and I'll force you to drink another one."

Bruce gave him a dark look, but he did swallow. "What is this?"

"Bone broth. I grabbed it the minute I found out you were Josh's brother. It was the only thing he could keep down for the first few days."

Bruce grimaced as he sniffed the thermos. "There's other stuff in there."

"They're called vegetables. You're a paramedic. Surely they covered those in one of your classes."

"Must have missed that day," he said, but he took another sip.

"You can have coffee later. Right now you need to replenish." He opened the front door and gestured Bruce outside. They both squinted at the bright sunlight.

"First rule of a firefighter. Coffee never comes later."

"First rule of a werewolf. Food comes first. The rest is ketchup."

Bruce snorted as they walked. Laddin didn't have any particular destination in mind—he only wanted to find a pleasant place to sit and chat. His job as a trainer was to get Bruce in control of his werewolf nature, but no one could do that while half a breath away from exhaustion.

"Let's start easy," Laddin said. "When was the last time you slept?"

"In that fucking cage."

Oh yeah. "By the way, you're going to have to clean that up. Pissing in there was just peevish."

"I was feeling peevish." Then he frowned. "Whatever that means."

"It was one of my grandmother's words. She used it when I was being especially annoying."

Bruce grunted as he finished off the last of the bone broth. As a reward, Laddin passed him the rest of his coffee. Bruce gratefully took a big swig, then grimaced again. "You like a little coffee in there with your sugar?"

"My charm comes naturally. I have to work for my sweetness."

Bruce slanted him an amused looked, then finished off the coffee with big gulps. That completed the nutrition portion of the afternoon. Fortunately they'd come upon a bench that looked out over fields of recently tilled ground. The land looked rich and fertile, and off in the distance, they could see the farmer on his tractor churning under the debris from the winter.

It was a picturesque scene, and Laddin would have loved it if the temperature had been above freeze-your-balls. He wasn't going to last long out here. Then he remembered he was supposed to be looking out for his trainee too, so he turned as Bruce dropped onto the bench. "You cold?" Bruce was wearing sweats and a T-shirt. And he'd found his shoes in the van, so at least his feet were covered.

"No," Bruce said, surprise in his voice. "Why aren't I cold? It's like fifty degrees out here."

"Werewolf metabolism."

Bruce nodded as if that made sense. But then he looked at Laddin. "So why are you shivering?"

"Because you drank the rest of my coffee."

"My bad." He didn't sound like he was apologiz-
ing, but he did look back at the house. "Want to go back
inside?"

No, he really didn't. Bruce needed the respite. "I
can take it if you can."

"Now who's being macho?"

He was. He plopped down on the bench next to
Bruce. That helped some because the big guy blocked
the wind. What helped even more was the heat rolling
off Bruce's body. Wow. Bruce was a furnace.

"Except for the last two months, I've lived my entire life in Southern California," he said. "Why would
anyone ever live out here?"

"Because it's so great in a place that has earth-
quakes, devastating fires, and smog? Not to mention
the price of real estate there?"

"But we've got Hollywood."

Bruce arched a brow at Laddin. "You say that like
it's a good thing."

"It is. I've worked explosives for movies since I
was fourteen. Some kids play with Play-Doh. I got to
shape C-4."

Bruce seemed to mull that over for a bit. "You
don't seem like an explosives expert."

"I'm a neat freak. I need things put in their place."

"So do firefighters."

Laddin grinned. It sounded like he was getting a
little respect from the new recruit. He counted that as
excellent progress. "I've been hyperorganized since I
was little, and let's face it, what boy doesn't like things
that go boom? Mama had a friend in the business, and
she got me on as an assistant. I've been in Hollywood
ever since... until seven weeks ago."

Bruce turned to him, his expression curious, which on the usually grumpy guy was akin to a grin. "What happened seven weeks ago?"

"I became a werewolf."

Bruce looked at him a moment, his expression shifting to surprise. "So you're new. I didn't know." And then he leaned back on the bench. "Cool."

What did that mean? "I'm still fully capable of training you," he said, mentally praying it was true.

Bruce turned to him with a frown. "I'm not doubting you," he said. "I actually like that you're new. It makes you less indoctrinated."

Laddin stiffened. "We're not a cult. There is no indoctrination. We're—"

"Werewolves. Yeah. I got that."

His words sounded agreeable enough, but Laddin could tell Bruce was still skeptical. And truthfully, he had a point. Wulf, Inc. had all the benchmarks of cult—isolation from others, a charismatic leader, and an enforced period of captivity at the beginning while new wolves learned to control themselves. But there was a major difference. "We're allowed to leave," he said. "I'm quitting the moment I get the moon madness under control."

Bruce straightened in surprise. "Really? Do they know that?"

"I've told Captain M. If it wasn't for the disaster at the lake, we'd all be moving on one way or another. Once you prove you've got your wolf nature under control, everybody chooses what they want. I want to go back to LA and my family."

Bruce arched a brow. "Family? You got a wife and kids?"

Laddin snorted. "No wife—I'm gay. No kids ei-ther." Then he held his breath as he slanted a look at Bruce. Being gay in Hollywood was no big deal, but Bruce was from Indiana. Who knew what he'd think? The last thing Laddin wanted was to add homophobia to their dynamic.

But far from being weirded out, Bruce actually seemed to relax. "What about a boyfriend?"

"I wish. I've been working 24/7 on Bing's mov-ie." He exhaled in relief. It was nice here, talking ca-sually to Bruce. "Bing's a werewolf too. He got turned the same day I did. You'll meet him eventually. He's a TV star in China, an incredible martial artist, and has freaky mind control powers."

"He the one who put me to sleep?"

"Yeah, probably. He got turned into a werewolf on the same day I did. That means his movie is kaput now, so I'm out of a job." He was sad about that. Working as Bing's DP had been a step up for him. But there would be other jobs. "All I've got is a meddlesome mother and grandmother, but they're important to me. I'm not cutting them out of my life."

"Good for you." Bruce flashed him a smile. It was a relaxed look, and suddenly Laddin's insides went liq-uid. The firefighter wasn't just ripped, he was rugged-ly handsome when he smiled. He'd never make it as a movie star, but when the skin around his eyes crinkled and his teeth flashed white, Laddin couldn't help but see all that potential beauty. Assuming he stayed away from the grumpy side of life.

"But I've got to get control of the moon madness first. Then everything can go back to normal." After he finished training Bruce, that is, and after they caught the demon and saved Wisconsin.

It was quite the to-do list, but Laddin had faith that someone would figure it out. His job was to take care of Bruce, and that meant getting the man to relax. So he stretched out his legs before him while they both sat quietly staring at the tilled field—pastoral beauty at its finest. Laddin knew he would get really bored soon, but at the moment he was content to let his gaze meander over the field.

Then something caught his eye, and he squinted. There it was again! Off in the distance, a yellowy-or-ange puff of something exploded. Laddin frowned. He couldn't have seen that right. But then another one went off.

"Did you see that?" Laddin asked.

"Hmm?" Bruce murmured.

"Over there." He pointed and looked back at his trainee. Bruce wasn't looking. He didn't even have his eyes open. Then Bruce let out a big yawn and slouched even deeper against the backrest.

Yup. Bruce was exhausted, and Laddin wasn't go-ing to wake him because he was seeing things out in this freezing wasteland. So he settled back against the bench, unable to resist sinking into Bruce's hot side. And he was hot, not just temperature-wise, but in every sexy inch of the grumpy bear.

Laddin had no idea why that was so attractive to him, but something about getting a crabby man to smile was a major turn-on for him. Especially when the sourpuss was a good guy underneath. He believed that Bruce wanted to look out for his younger brother and was trying to make amends for whatever had hap-pened when they were kids. He also saw that being a first responder was something burned into the core of his being, so that made Bruce extra appealing. But what really made Laddin's dick sit up and take notice was the easy way they spoke to each other. Bruce wasn't awkward with him and didn't stare at his hand. Those were small things, but they added up to a huge win for Laddin.

And yes, there were obviously deep things going on in that grumpy head of his, but Bruce didn't take it out on anyone else. He growled when he was annoyed, was silent when he wasn't, and then bantered back when he felt safe. He was easy to understand, easy to navigate. And fun, fun, fun to make smile.

Bruce's jaw had gone slack, and his head dropped sideways onto Laddin's shoulder. It was a comfortable weight, and Laddin enjoyed the feeling of supporting him. He never got to cuddle with anyone anymore. His last relationship had ended over a year ago for the same reason he didn't have a pet. He was never around because he worked 24/7 on the set of whatever project he was on. And if he didn't have a job, he was too restless, too needy.

At least that's what his ex had said.

Laddin had ditched the ex, but he missed the skin-to-skin contact he'd had with a lover. He ached for someone to touch while they were watching TV. And he needed someone to banter with when the long days became even longer nights. They didn't have to be deep discussions. Even a conversation about the Lakers was special when it happened with someone he cared about.

He sat there on the bench, enjoying the moment while his mind wandered. Naturally, it went to sex, something that was bound to happen when he was snuggled against a hot firefighter. Laddin didn't get the impression that Bruce was into men, so in a backward kind of way, that gave him the freedom to fantasize about all sorts of dirty things with him. They'd never happen, and Bruce would never know, so why not indulge in some very adult make-believe?

If he'd been alone, he'd probably rub one out. Hell, his cock was already throbbing at the pictures in his head, but he could show restraint. He could close his eyes and imagine this big warrior arching in need as Laddin sucked him off. He could feel the sharp bite of penetration as he impaled himself on Bruce's cock. And best of all, he could imagine slowly, gently bending Bruce over as he spread the man's iron cheeks and thrust inside. It would feel like being surrounded in muscle. And then he'd reach around to grip Bruce's thick cock and hold on for the ride.

God, he wanted that. And those images were so graphic that he nearly came in his pants. He didn't, but his very next shower would be extra special.

So he sat, and when he opened his eyes, he let his gaze wander over the dark field. Odd how there was no sign of the slow death of the state here. It wasn't surprising, he guessed, since Lake Wacka Wacka was fifty miles away. It was the closest they could get and still stay under the radar. They didn't have any official standing as scientists, military, or reporters, so they did what they could from here. And when they couldn't, they found a way to sneak in, either in their wolf forms or with an invisibility spell.

Puff. Puff-puff.

There it was again. Laddin narrowed his eyes as he tried to see clearly. Orange puffs of smoke exploded right next to an oak tree. There was a little bit of greenery dividing the fields. Low bushes, that one large oak tree, and—there they were again. Puffs of orange smoke. What the hell was that?

He had to know. And sitting here with Bruce was getting him so horny—he had to do something or burst. With careful hands, he eased Bruce's head onto the back of the bench. Then he touched the man's face, trying to judge if his skin was cool. Nope. Still Mr. Furnace, so he'd be okay for a bit longer. Better yet, Laddin spied a plastic trunk next to the house. Opening it, he found thick afghans, probably meant for this purpose. He grabbed two and draped the first around Bruce, then wrapped the second around himself.

Then he took off to find out what was exploding like cheese powder between two wheat fields.

It took him a while to get there—it was a lot farther away than he expected—but something kept drawing him closer. It was the oddness of the puffs. Sometimes they were small and splintered into three. Sometimes they were slow in the air but had a big explosion. He was an expert in demolitions, but he couldn't figure out what kind of charge would make those booms. And they were booms. Not very loud ones, but they were definitely there according to his werewolf ears.

If anything, it reminded him of the Angry Birds game that so many of the crew played between takes. And as he got closer, he could see the different-colored bombs flying up in the air, sometimes high, sometimes low, sometimes splintering, and sometimes bouncing in ways only possible in a video game.

About a hundred yards out, the smell hit. If he hadn't been so intrigued by the explosions, he would have stopped in his tracks. But he didn't, though the stench grew increasingly vile. It was like the worst kind of foot odor gone nuclear, or something forgotten in a refrigerator for years. At first it just made his stomach rebel, but as he got closer, his eyes began to water and he had to cover his nose with the heavy blanket. He was starting to think the explosions were stink bombs the wind carried straight at him.

He was sure it was paranormal. Nothing natural could smell this horrible—not without someone noticing much earlier. He would have to text Nero to let the team know something dicey was happening out here, but he wanted to have more information first. Smelly exploding lights weren't enough to go on. Plus, he was just a few feet away from seeing....

Laddin stopped walking and blinked a half dozen times. There were little pieces of cheese all over the field! He noticed several slices of American cheese, but he also glimpsed blue cheese, gorgonzola, brie, and cheddar. The only reason he recognized them was because his mother had once dated a cheese snob, and she and Laddin had learned all the different kinds as a way to impress the guy.

Except normal cheeses didn't have little legs and arms, and didn't jump around like....

Pixies! He was watching little pixies shaped like cheese launching themselves into the air with a slingshot like in the Angry Birds game. Oh my God, the sight blew his mind. And it also explained the smell, because honestly, some of those cheeses were like a fart from a warthog.

He grinned as he decided to spy on the cute little fairies. He knew he should be careful. The fae in any form were dangerous, so he had to stay out of sight. But they were pixies, all shaped like cheeses. And wasn't that the most adorable sight ever?

He needed to take pictures. No way could he explain this to Nero without evidence. He silently pulled out his cell phone as he tried to make sense of what they were doing.

Simply put, they were playing Angry Birds. The pixies were loading a slingshot full of cheddar cheese bombs and launching it at a knee-high structure made of rocks and sticks. In the game, there would be a pig in the makeshift structure, and he could see something inside it, but he couldn't tell what. And now he knew what those puffs of orange were. They came from little cheddar cheese bombs exploding against the stick structure.

Totally precious! He was so captivated that he forgot that the air smelled incredibly foul, especially after one of those cheese bombs exploded. He made the mistake of inhaling.

Oh hell. There was no way to stop the sneeze. He tried, but everything he did just made more noise before a truly loud, from-the-gut sneeze ripped through his nostrils.

When his watering eyes finally cleared, he saw that every single cheese was staring at him. And pointing. And screaming one word in unison.

"Attack!"

Chapter 8

BRUCE DISCOVERS FAIRY CHEESE

BRUCE FELT safe, which was weird because nothing in his life was safe. Not his job, not his parents, not even his little brother. The only one he felt reasonably confident about was his little sister, Ivy, but that was because she'd finished her deployment and was home. No suicide bombers likely to get her in Indiana.

And yet life had never felt more relaxed than it did when he stretched out on a bench with Laddin. Normally hyperactive guys like Laddin drove him nuts. Squirrels were less animated than his trainer. And yet the man made him laugh. Even better, he respected Laddin's intelligence, which made him feel like he wasn't alone against a whole lot of crazy. Apparently that relaxed him enough to fall asleep right there on the bench when he really ought to be finding out what it meant to be a werewolf.

He knew he should force himself to wake up, but every firefighter knew the value of a good nap. He'd doze for five more minutes, then start asking questions.

It went exactly as he planned. Five minutes into sleep, he started asking questions. Only he just wasn't talking to Laddin. No, Mr. Salad Elf appeared right in front of him, his tomato hat slipping to the left so that a tomato seed dangled from his ear like an earring.

"Really?" Bitterroot said, gesturing at his outfit. "Can't you think of something else? My clothing comes from your memoires."

"Nope," Bruce answered, happy to torture the fairy any way possible, if only in this dream.

The dream prince snorted in disgust, then spent a long minute studying him. Finally Bruce gave up waiting.

"What do you want?"

"It's not about me, Bruce. What do you want?"

"I don't want anything from you."

"Are you sure?" He held up the glowing apple, his expression making him look like the snake in the Garden of Eden. Bruce didn't have to look twice to recognize it as the same apple he'd been offered before. The one that would give him *more*, whatever that meant. As far as he was concerned, it was all bullshit.

Bruce waved his hand, knocking the thing aside. But of course, this was a dream—that was the only way to explain the fact that he was sitting on a bench made of celery—so the apple stayed right where it was, pulsing with temptation.

"Things didn't go so well with Josh, did they?"

"What do you care?"

"Well, think about it. You want to protect your baby brother, right?"

Bruce grunted his agreement. He didn't mean to, but the sound reverberated through the dreamscape anyway.

"That cherry you ate made you his equal," Bitter-root continued. "He's got just as much magic as you do. So you can't protect him from anything he can't handle himself. What kind of a big brother is that?"

"It's the kind he's got. Besides," Bruce drawled, "it's not the size of the wand that matters—"

"But the magic within it," Bitterroot finished for him. "And you have a cherry's worth of magic. I'd say that's small potatoes, but what you ate was tinier than even that."

Bruce winced but didn't push. Yeah, the apple was all bright and beautiful. He knew it would taste like the best apple ever made. Hell, his taste buds were still yearning for another cherry, but he knew this apple would be even better.

But he didn't move. His issues with Josh wouldn't be solved by a bigger magical dick, so he looked away. Except... he couldn't look away, so he forced his eyes shut. Only they were already shut, because this was a dream.

In the end, he fuzzed out his thoughts. "If that's all you've got," he murmured, "I was taking a nap."

"Are you so sure about that?" the fairy taunted. "I think your partner might prefer you to be awake."

At first his mind flashed to his partner at the fire-house, but Joey was doing fine. Last he'd heard, the fireman was on a Disney vacation with his sister's kids and probably rocking it out with Mickey. Mean-while, Mr. Salad Elf huffed out a crouton and threw it at Bruce's head.

"Not that partner, idiot. *That one*." The landscape around them zeroed in on Laddin screaming as he flailed at... at... flying Cheetos? Bruce couldn't see clearly, and the more he blinked and focused, the less he could make out.

Then he saw Laddin's face. He'd gone pale, and his skin showed sweat. He was flailing at something and maybe screaming. Bruce couldn't hear, but the panic was clear—Laddin's and his own. His heart had started racing, and he lurched forward to try to get to the guy.

Then everything disappeared. The whole landscape was replaced by the obnoxious fairy and his damned glowing apple.

"Where is he? Where's Laddin?"

Bitterroot held up the apple. "Care to make a purchase? It won't cost much," he offered. "I swear."

"Fuck you," Bruce snapped. Then he focused as hard as he could on waking up.

He jolted awake, gasping as he half rolled off the bench. His arms got tangled in a heavy blanket, and he threw it off him with a curse. Then he searched around frantically for Laddin, but he couldn't see him. Just an endless landscape of newly turned field. Hell, he could be anywhere!

Bruce did a slow circle, searching for a clue. All he saw was the fairy leaning against a tree while eating an apple. For a split second Bruce had a moment of panic. Was that *his* apple? Had he taken too long to decide? Was the bastard even now eating—?

No. It wasn't his apple, and the fairy wanted him to say yes. Plus, he didn't intend to eat the inventory anyway. This was a ruse to get him to panic and say yes in desperation. But it wasn't going to happen. He had to think of a better way of finding Laddin.

"You'd find him immediately if you took me up on my offer."

"I don't even know that what you showed me is real."

Bitterroot gave him a wounded look. "Everything I say is true. You have my solemn oath on that."

"Unless you're lying about that."

The fairy polished off the last off the apple with a disgusted grunt. Then he shook his head and spat a single word. "Mortals."

Bruce didn't bother with the obviously response of "Fairies." Instead, he closed his eyes and tried to remember the details of the images he'd seen of Laddin. What did the environment look like? Were there any trees, buildings, clues, anything?

"You're not going to find him that way."

Bruce opened his eyes and glared at the fairy. The prince was gone, but the apple was hanging from a branch in an oak tree just this side of the field. Bruce resolutely turned away from it. Or he started to, when he saw something far in the distance. A flash of light? A trick of the apple? Hell, he didn't know. Maybe his eyes were screwing with him and he'd have to use his other senses, but….

Smell. He had a keen sense of smell, but not as a human. Which meant, hell, he had to shift to a wolf, and he didn't know how.

His gaze slid back to the apple. Last time he'd eaten the cherry and bam, five minutes later, he'd been a wolf. The apple would likely do the same thing. But no, no, no! God, the temptation was killing him. He had to close his eyes, smell as a human, and pick a direction. If he was wrong….

His gut clenched in fear. What if he was too late? What if he chose wrong? What if someone died because he wasn't enough again?

He couldn't think like that. Indecision was definitely the wrong choice, so he had to pick. He'd seen
something beyond the apple, so he'd go in that direction. He hoped it wasn't a distraction set up by Bitterroot. If it was, that meant he ought to go in the opposite
direction.

But he'd already started jogging, zipping around
the apple that was so close he could easily grab it. He
didn't. He kicked it up from a jog to a run, and if this
was the wrong direction, then so be it. Rather than let
his stomach clench tighter in fear, he pushed himself to
run faster while his eyes burned from the wind. Pretty
soon his breath was sawing in hard gasps and his side
was killing him. But the fear for Laddin grew expo-
nentially stronger the farther he went. He still didn't
see anything, but he heard... was that screaming? Did
someone call for help? Damn it, he couldn't hear over
his own breath.

It didn't matter. He would run until he dropped. He
focused on the ground, the way they'd taught him in
firefighter school. The flashing something or other had
been near another tree, far across the field. He'd head
there. He put everything he had into setting one foot in
front of the other. That was his destination. He kept his
senses alert for anything else, but he was going there.

He *ran*. And he was going faster than he'd ever
thought he could before. Plus the smells were sharper,
and he could even taste the air. It wasn't until he could
smell something awful that he realized he was running
on all fours.

He was a wolf. He'd done it! He'd shifted, and the
joy of that gave him an extra spurt of energy. Unfortunately, it also had him inhaling deeply of something

that smelled like moldy cheese. Moldy, fermenting, back-of-his-garage, something-died-in-it cheese.

He blinked as his eyes watered, and he breathed through his mouth rather than his nose. Then he saw bright things bouncing up and down, while white rope stretched along behind the bouncing things. Except it looked more like string cheese than rope. And Laddin was batting the things away as he fought from his knees.

Laddin! I'm coming!

He thought the words but had no breath to voice them. Meanwhile, tiny wedges with legs were swarming all over Laddin, who grabbed a rolled-up orange thing with his fist and squeezed. Unfortunately, the orange stuff oozed out through is fingers and apparently sealed his hands shut. Laddin was now swinging big orange-covered fists and batting things away with his forehead.

"Stop it!" Laddin boomed. "I don't want to hurt you."

But it sure looked like they wanted to hurt him. They were swarming him, and wherever they touched him, they flattened out and hardened. Whole areas of Laddin were covered in that stuff and seemed completely stiff. Pretty soon the guy wouldn't be able to move. And if one of the flat squares covered his nose and mouth, Laddin would suffocate.

Bruce rushed into the mix. He didn't have hands, but he had his body, his mouth, and even his tail. It took a frustrating amount of time to figure that out. His back end was definitely a hindrance, but it didn't matter. He needed to bat the things away from Laddin. It was a losing game because every… were they really tiny cheeses? Whatever. Every cheese that he batted away came back again, and he couldn't knock them all aside. He had to figure out something else.

Then he realized he'd made a mistake. Oh hell. He'd been snapping at the things with his jaws. And rather than have them seal his mouth shut, he'd swallowed what was definitely cheese.

He tasted American cheese, which was the most recognizable to his palate. Blue cheese, brie, cheddar. Those filtered across his taste buds as well. The other ones—the harder, almost crunchy bits—were simply weird. But if they flattened on Laddin like concrete, what the hell were they going to do to Bruce's insides?

Then another thought ripped through his mind, mostly because his belly was beginning to rebel. It was stupid and not something he thought about often. But sometimes his body reminded him that it was real.

He was lactose intolerant. He'd never admit to his fellow firefighters that pizza gave him gas, but this was different. He'd swallowed a ton of magical cheese, and his gut wanted to toss it back out. Fine with him. He'd love to vomit the crap out, but it wasn't going that direction.

And all the while, things were going worse for Laddin. He'd been on his knees because his ankles were wrapped together. Now his arms were trapped because the string cheese had bound his wrists like handcuffs. Laddin was making furious sounds as he toppled over. Why the hell didn't he shift to wolf? Then they could both run away.

Meanwhile, Bruce's gut wasn't handling the cheese well. He knew the feeling of bloating, but this was like a bomb was building inside, and he was going to let it loose like a flame thrower. There was no choice. It was the only way to get it out.

So he did. He lifted his tail high and let it rip. Gas burst from him like a valve release, and good God, the smell was enough to make him gasp. A loud bell-like tinkling filled the air, and part of him realized it was laughter. The cheese was laughing at him. If he hadn't been in the middle of magical fairy gas, he would have smashed the cheddar bits with rocks.

But he didn't have the strength or the coordination. In fact, thanks to his burning ass and the roiling in his gut, he lost his footing, tripping and falling face-first into a pile of sticks and rocks. Ow. Ow. Ow! One of the sticks poked straight into his gums, and another caught his snout. He flinched away, but that only made it worse... which was hard, given his general state of misery.

But he couldn't stop fighting. He had to keep the things off himself and Laddin. He struggled to his feet. If nothing else, he could body-block the things from attacking Laddin. Except as he searched for a target, he realized that all the cheese had fallen back. And when he really looked hard, he saw that they seemed to be cheering.

Cheering?

He turned to try to help Laddin, who had fallen onto his side in the fetal position. But while Bruce stared, the cheese manacles on his wrists popped open and their tiny hands were clapping together. The squeezed American cheese between Laddin's fingers solidified back into squares and hopped up and down in celebration. His ankles released too, and all the string cheeses around his torso and legs were doing backflips of joy.

WTF?

Bruce started to yip a question, but another disaster was building in his gut. He was back on his feet, and he danced around, crashing into the stick construction again. The pieces went everywhere as he accidentally destroyed whatever the structure had been, and the bell-like cheers got even louder.

He would have stopped to wonder, but he didn't have time. Tail-up time.

He released another long, loud fart of magical gas, and this time Laddin made a sound—a snort mixed with a chuckle that quickly turned to laughter that blended in with the high-pitched cheering from the fairies.

Hell. Bruce was never, ever going to eat cheese again.

Chapter 9

PROMISES, PROMISES

OF ALL the memorable sights in Laddin's life, nothing topped the sight of Bruce shooting fairy cheeses out of his lupine ass. And even funnier? The pixies seemed to love it. After tumbling, rolling, and flailing through the air from the explosive release, they gathered together and dashed back at Bruce's mouth, obviously hoping he'd eat them again.

He didn't.

He growled and backed up. And though he looked like he was going to explode—again—he didn't chomp down on a single fairy. What he did do was glower in frustration at Laddin, who couldn't stop his hysterical laughter—"hysterical" being the key word, because he was losing it big-time.

The past two minutes had been the most terrifying experience of his life. He'd been slowly encased in cheese that hardened into something like concrete. First a knee, then his chest. Next his hands had become boulders of rock. As soon as he understood what was happening, he realized he had to duck down to protect his nose and mouth. He needed to breathe, but that didn't stop him from feeling like he was being encased in stone.

He'd kicked, he'd rolled, and he'd hyperventilated with horror, but nothing stopped the steady assault of the cheese. He was going to die, and nothing could stop that.

Until it *did* all stop. Suddenly he could move again. His lungs dragged in air, his hands opened, and his ankles released. He didn't know why, and he didn't care. He could breathe easily again! He could move! And for long moments, that was all he focused on. But eventually he looked up, and what he saw was so ridiculous that hysteria bubbled up and came out as side-splitting laughs that had everything to do with the joy of being alive.

He was alive, and Bruce was shooting fairy farts.

Eventually Bruce lost patience. It couldn't be comfortable pushing out those explosive little fae. And though he couldn't speak as a wolf, he *could* get into Laddin's face and growl with menace. He had a good growl, one that made the hairs on Laddin's neck leap to attention, and it was enough to ground Laddin back into the present and calm the hysteria that still careened around inside him.

He held up his hands in surrender. "I don't know, Bruce. Truly, I've got no idea."

Then a tiny voice cleared his throat. It was hard to tell what got their attention first, the sound or the abruptly rank air. But either way, both man and wolf turned to look at a tiny clump of white lumps that smelled like dairy gone very, very bad.

"We greet you, friend of the True Cheeses," it said with a very deep bow.

Laddin narrowed his gaze until he could make out a face with dark eyes that looked like mold on the cheese body.

"I am Grand Master Cheesy, the great Fetid Feta. We ask you, Hero of the Bottom Air, is this human friend or foe? If friend, we will cheer his place as your second. If foe, we will destroy him with fermentation bombs and diabolical string mozzarella. What say you, Sir Bottom Air?"

The words didn't make sense. Bruce first stared at the fairy, then turned to Laddin, his wolf expression managing to be both grumpy and baffled. Laddin wasn't any help at all. It took all his resources just to hold back the panic. Then Bruce shook himself as if trying to clear his vision.

"They're pixies," Laddin said. "Or a fairy of some sort." He looked at the Grand Master. "Right? You're pixies?"

The Grand Master did not answer Laddin. His attention was all on Bruce. "Friend?" he repeated. Then he brandished a tiny, moldy fist. "Or foe?"

All around Laddin, the string cheese was getting ready to attack again. He saw them squat like a spring about to release, and panic set all his cells to screaming. "Friend!" Laddin cried out. "Bruce, tell them I'm your friend!"

Bruce didn't speak because—damn it—he was still a wolf. He probably didn't remember how to shift back. And now cheddar cheese boulders were starting to combine into larger ones. Shit. Laddin knew from experience that they were hard as rocks.

"Come on, Bruce. Tell them I'm your friend," Laddin said.

Bruce yipped once, then sidled up right next to Laddin, twisted his backside, and let fly with another rancid fart. Laddin thought he was making a statement, but the wind from his body was strong enough to send the string cheese rolling away. Tumbling alongside them were bits of parmesan that had come from places best left unmentioned.

And while those cheeses were laughing with great cheer, Laddin was quick to make everything clear to the Grand Cheesy. "That means we're friends. Great friends!" he said as he wrapped his arms around Bruce's wolf neck.

Fortunately Bruce dipped his chin in agreement. And then he turned and licked Laddin from chin to temple with a big wet tongue.

"Ew!" Laddin mumbled as he wiped away the slobber. "Cheese breath." But given all the smells around here, that was probably one of the better ones.

They both turned to look again at Fetid Feta. The fairy was watching them with narrowed eyes, but the in the end, he bowed deeply before speaking again.

"Then we greet you, Cheese Breath, and welcome you to our great holy war."

"No, I'm not…." Laddin stopped himself. Obviously the fairy thought he'd been introducing himself as Cheese Breath, but it wasn't worth correcting. Especially when there was something more interesting to pursue. "Um, what great holy war, exactly?"

"The one against our mortal enemy! You destroyed her structure and have therefore declared us the winner in this battle. Behold the enemy prisoner before she departs." He made a great gesture to the pile of sticks and stones, and there, sitting and sulking, was a tiny fairy who looked relatively normal compared to all the cheese around her. She wore a dress made of flowers that did not go with her furious expression as she pushed to her feet, kicked at a loose pebble, then gave them a middle-finger salute before puffing out of existence.

In response, all the cheese fairies pointed their middle fingers sideways and made a farting noise before pointing at Bruce and dissolving into laughter. Honest to God, it was a funny, funny sight, and Laddin couldn't help but snort in laughter. Or maybe it was hysteria still. Hard to tell.

Bruce looked at him with a wounded expression, but he didn't really seem hurt. If anything, the poor guy looked bewildered. Laddin dropped his forehead into Bruce's fur and took a deep breath. The wolf definitely smelled better than anything else around here. And while he took comfort from the wolf's solid presence, he whispered into the fur, knowing that Bruce would hear him clearly enough.

"We have to get out of here," he whispered. The fae were capricious, and no mortal was safe around them.

Bruce woofed softly in agreement, and so Laddin straightened to his feet with a smile. His knees were weak and he kept a hand deep in Bruce's ruff, but he made sure his voice was strong. "Well, Grand Master Cheesy, Great Fetid Feta, we thank you for this experience. Sadly, we must be leaving." He was very pleased with himself for remembering the details of the leader's name.

Except Feta didn't seem so pleased. He leaped forward and dropped his hands on his crumbly hips. "You cannot leave! You have declared yourself our friend and therefore cannot leave until our grand mission is accomplished!"

Laddin narrowed his eyes. "And what is that grand mission, exactly?"

Feta looked like he was shocked that Laddin didn't know. His mouth gaped open, and then a puff of mold came out before he turned to all the assembled cheeses, lifted his arms high, and began to shout. All the other True Cheeses joined in until the field rang like it was filled with wind chimes.

"Fairyland! Fairyland! Fairyland!"

Laddin looked at Bruce, who shifted his front legs as if he were shrugging. And still the cry continued until Laddin felt dizzy. He held up his hand to stop Feta, who quieted immediately and with him all the other fairies. Suddenly Laddin's ears all but rang with the quiet.

"What about Fairyland?"

"Fairyland! Fairyland! Fairyland!"

The entire group began cheering again until Laddin clapped his hands over his ears. Bruce too dipped his head and whimpered, not that Laddin could hear it. He felt it through the press of Bruce's wolf body against his.

Finally Feta silenced everyone and Laddin dared to drop his hands from his ears. "Is the place in danger?" He had no wish to name it aloud again.

Feta shook his head solemnly. "We are barred from the holy land, blocked by those who will not dress as cheese."

Now he understood. "You cannot get to the holy land, and you want to go home."

"Yes," Feta intoned. "So we wage our war."

"But how are they stopping you?"

Feta shook his head sadly. "We don't know. We only know that much from the words of the prophet." He gestured to a wedge of cheese beneath a tree. "Smoked Gouda has so said."

Laddin blinked. Dark smoke appeared to waft off the fairy wedge of cheese.

"Maybe we can help," he offered, and suddenly everyone took an excited step forward. "I said maybe," he quickly clarified. "Do you remember how you got here? How did you leave the holy land?"

A low voice spoke, and Laddin didn't have to look to know that it was Gouda. "Always here, never there," he intoned.

Right. In short, they had no idea. "I, um, I need to do some research, then, to see if I can find you an answer—"

"Sir Bottom Air knows! He comes from the holy land. We can ride on his wind straight to Fairyland!"

Apparently, Bruce had been upgraded from Hero to Knight of the Bottom Air. "Okay, but—"

"Fairyland! Fairyland! Fairyland!"

"Stop!" Laddin snapped, his patience wearing thin. This had been a hell of a day already, and the charm of working with a bunch of cheeses was wearing off. "Look, Bruce doesn't know anything. He's brand-new to this—"

"Not Bruce! Sir Bottom Air!"

"Er, right. Sir Bottom Air doesn't know his head from his, um, bottom right now. He doesn't know how to take you back. He's just learning…." Laddin's voice trailed away at the stern look from Feta. Worse, he had the sinking feeling that he was the one talking out of his ass because Bruce was a werewolf, thanks to fairy fruit. And perhaps the guy knew a whole lot more about fairies than he was letting on. Laddin looked down into Bruce's eyes. "Do you know what they're talking about?"

The wolf's head dipped low and he shook his head no.

"See," he said to Fetid Feta. "He hasn't any idea—"

"We will ride him!" the mozzarella cried. They'd been creeping closer and now abruptly jumped up on

Bruce's back. The wolf shied sideways, but there were too many cheeses there, and all of them tried to leap on his back. Mozzarella, camembert, ricotta, all sorts of cheeses that jumped, sprang, or tumbled into the air while Bruce shook himself to keep them away. They landed anyway, but with every shake, the fairies went tumbling out of his fur with more tinkling laughter.

They all thought this was a game, except Laddin knew it wasn't. Fairies were immortal. He'd learned that in his basic training through Wulf, Inc. They could be squashed, sliced in half, even consumed, but they came back in a puff of light and laughter. Humans weren't so lucky, and mortals often died when they participated in anything having to do with fairies. That had been drilled into them.

Laddin wished he'd paid more attention to that fifteen minutes ago.

"Sir Bottom Air says no," Laddin declared forcefully. And before Feta could get angry, he held up his hand. "I swear we'll look into getting you home. Sir Bottom Air and I will do what we can for you."

Feta looked up, hope shining on his pale face. "You swear? On behalf of all pixies for the True Cheese?"

"Um… er… yeah. I swear."

Feta hopped off the rock and came to stand right before Bruce's eyes. "And you, Sir Bottom Air? Do you so swear?"

Bruce stared at the fairy so long without moving. He didn't so much as blink. And when Laddin started to squeeze the wolf's back, the animal turned to look directly at Laddin and slowly, firmly shook his head no.

Crap. "What do you mean, no? Bruce, swear to them!"

Again, a steady, firm shake of his head no.

"Sir Bottom Air does not pledge himself!" Fetid screamed. "Attack!"

Laddin cursed, and Bruce let out a woof of anger.

They had no choice now—they'd have to run for it.

So they did, as hard and fast as they could go, which for Bruce was a whole hell of a lot faster. But it didn't help. No matter how quickly they moved, the pixie cheeses were faster. They leaped, they tumbled, and they exploded into noxious plumes of fermentation, making Laddin choke. And the moment he slowed, the string cheese bound his feet and the American cheese wrapped his hands into solid balls of yellow.

No! No! He couldn't go through that again! But here he was tumbling to his knees, though he still had breath to bargain.

"Wait! Wait! I have pledged myself to you, right? Aren't I enough?"

Up ahead, Bruce whirled around, his nostrils flaring but his mouth resolutely shut. The cheese near him quickly surrounded him, but they didn't move to attack.

Meanwhile Feta bounced up to Laddin. "Are you enough? Can you get us to Fairyland?"

"I don't know. But I have pledged to help."

"Standard forfeit?"

Laddin was pulling at the string cheese around his ankles. Damn, the shit was like iron.

"Standard forfeit?" Feta repeated.

Stall for time. "Um, what's the standard forfeit?"

"Firstborn child."

Laddin recoiled. "Absolutely not!" The very idea horrified him. How the hell had he gotten himself into this situation? All he'd done was investigate some weird lights, and now suddenly he was talking about the life of his future offspring. "I promised to help you find a way to your holy land. That's what I'll do. I'll search our... um... holy records and tell you what answer I find there."

"You must open the pathway or make him do it!" Feta pointed to Bruce.

"I can't promise that!" Laddin snapped back. "I'm just going to do research. That's all I can do!"

Feta frowned, taking a long moment to think. Then he turned toward the other cheeses. "Research," he said as he looked at his fellow cheeses. "Research?"

There was a moment of silence as all the cheeses looked at one another. And then, on the far side of Bruce, came a tinkling cry.

"Research! Research!"

The others took it up. In fact, the string cheese that bound his ankles abruptly unrolled and clapped its hands. "Research! Research!"

Laddin took a moment to breathe, but it did nothing to calm his racing heart. "So, we're agreed, right?" he asked. "I promise to do research."

"You promised to give us answers."

"Answers?" he echoed. Fine. He'd give them answers. They might not like what he found out, but that's what he'd give them. "Agreed." Whatever it took to get the hell out of here.

"Agreed," Feta said, and there was weight behind the word unequal to the stature of the tiny fey. In fact, the impact of that single word hit him as hard as if he'd taken a blow to the sternum from a sledge hammer. "Report back in seven minutes."

"What?" Laddin gasped. "No! That's not enough time."

"It is the standard time frame."

"Bullshit. It's usually a day or a year. Didn't Rumpelstiltskin give the miller's daughter overnight to do that straw-into-gold thing?"

Behind him, Bruce snorted his disgust. Laddin couldn't blame him—he didn't think he got that fairytale even remotely right either. But it didn't matter. Feta stomped his foot and created a noxious cloud.

"Agreed. Report here at dawn with your answers."

Laddin didn't like it, but his mind was frazzled, his heart beat a zillion times a minute, and he was clammy with sweat. At that moment, he'd agree to give over whatever answers they wanted, as long as it got them out of there without another damned piece of cheese attaching itself to his body. So he nodded. "Fine. Tomorrow at dawn, right back here."

"Agreed!" Feta cried as he stomped his foot.

Laddin pushed to his feet, his knees barely strong enough to support him. He was shaking, he now realized, but as he took a tentative step, Bruce came to his side and used his large wolf body to brace him.

Thank God.

They began to walk away. They plodded steadily, carefully. It was a long way back to the house, and they both glanced behind often. Every time, the cheeses waved cheerily at them, but they didn't follow and were soon lost to view.

If only the feeling of dread climbing into Laddin's chest could disappear so easily. He hadn't read the full history of Wulf, Inc. Hell, he hadn't even read half. But he had read the parts where the message was always and forever, *Never Bargain with Fairies*. It was like a corporate motto or something. In fact, it had been etched into stone at Wulfric's first home in America.

So what had Laddin done on his very first solo mission? He'd bargained with fairies.

"I think I screwed up," Laddin finally said as the house came into view. "I don't know how yet, but I have this lousy feeling that tells me I'm in trouble."

Bruce responded with a snort that sounded very much like "Duh."

Chapter 10

SITTING ON THE PORCH SINGING THE WEREWOLF BLUES

LADDIN WAS screwed. Bruce knew very little about all this fairy werewolf magic stuff, but he did know people. He knew that as much as Bitterroot tried to make nice with him, the fairy was trying to trap him. He could smell the stink of manipulation flowing off the elf. He could also tell that the little pixies were funny mischief-makers, but there was a real agenda behind their actions. It was like a fighting a fire. The element wasn't evil, but it was implacable. And those damned pixies had an agenda and wouldn't rest until they consumed everything in their path on their way to whatever goal they had.

Unfortunately, Laddin had landed himself smackdab in the center of their crusade. And as much as Bruce wanted to tell the man to wise up, his wolf mouth wasn't forming the words. So he padded along beside Laddin and tried every way he could think of to become human again.

No-go.

The best he could do was lean against the man's leg, trying to tell him in an animal way that he would do what he could to help. But he was a big wolf, and Laddin wasn't large enough to take his weight without stumbling. Worse, Laddin thought Bruce was the one who needed comfort.

"Easy there, Bruce. I know that was scary." He squatted down right there in the field and wrapped his arms around Bruce's neck. "I've got you. It's okay. You'll be fine."

Bruce huffed out a breath in frustration. Wasn't that the fucking truth of his entire life? He tried to help, and it went sideways. He tried to show support, and it was completely misinterpreted. That was one of the many things he admired about his brother. The guy's thoughts and intentions were always crystal clear. There was no misinterpreting the big middle finger he got from his little brother. Josh communicated. Laddin did too, because Bruce sure as shit knew that nearly dying there had shaken the guy. But when it came time to express his thoughts, all Bruce could do was fuck it up. So he stood strong and let Laddin comfort him because— maybe—Laddin got some strength from the hug too.

Then Laddin shivered. Whereas Bruce was covered in thick fur, Laddin was only wearing sweatpants and a T-shirt.

"Sun's going down, and I lost the blanket somewhere back there," Laddin said against his fur. "Let's get inside before I freeze to death."

Bruce rumbled agreement, and Laddin pulled back.

"Was that a growl? You want to stay outside?"

Fucking hell. He shook his head no.

"Inside, then?"

He nodded his head. And then for good measure, he licked Laddin's chin. That was the only way he could think of to express his concern. Laddin laughed. Of course he did. Nothing kept his happiness down for long. But he did wipe his face off.

"Ew!" he teased. Then he straightened up. "Inside it is. We can play catch or something later."

Catch? *Catch!* Did he seriously think that Bruce wanted to run around after a stupid ball? He was not a dog! He was a man trapped in this wolf body who couldn't fucking talk right then. The best he could do was snort his disgust.

"You don't want to wait? Well, okay." He leaned down and picked up a stick, which he tossed ahead of them. Then he grinned as he looked down at Bruce. "Go on! Go get it!"

Bruce snorted and looked away. He was so not going to chase that stick. Except some sort of instinct kicked in the moment the stick flew through the air. His body tensed and he nearly leaped after it, even though he was not a fucking dog.

"Don't be like that," Laddin said. Then he stopped and squatted down in front of Bruce. "I know you've got a human mind in there. I know you're not a dog. But a part of you is a wolf, and wolves like chasing things. So do it. Let yourself be a wolf right now. You'll get back to human soon enough, but there's something really joyous about chasing a stupid stick. It gives the mind a break." He blew out a breath. "That's something I think we could both use right now."

It was the last part that got to him. Not the "be the wolf" mantra shit, but that Laddin needed the simplicity of throwing a stick for Bruce. Laddin thought he was helping Bruce, and that gave Laddin something to focus on—something other than what they'd just been through.

So fine. He could be the wolf for Laddin. And not because his lupine mind latched on to the next stick that Laddin launched into the air. He saw it soar and he took off after it like it was the answer to world peace. Or to fixing things up with his brother. Or to giving Laddin a reason to laugh.

He caught the stick after the first bounce. He snatched that stupid stick up and hauled ass back to Laddin, who was indeed grinning from ear to ear.

"Better?" he asked as Bruce dropped the stick at his feet.

Bruce didn't answer, not because he couldn't but because, yeah, maybe it had been fun to run like a rocket and he didn't want to admit it. Laddin must have known, because he picked up the stick and launched it with a powerful stroke. Damn, he could throw.

Bruce took off, determined to catch the thing before it hit the ground. He didn't come close, but he got the stick and was back before Laddin's laughter faded.

They kept going like that, making steady progress back to the house. And as a bonus, the movement seemed to keep Laddin from getting too cold. But pretty soon the guy was shivering. It was time to pick up the pace. So the next time Laddin launched the stick into the air, Bruce didn't follow it. Instead, he trotted behind Laddin and nipped at the man's legs.

"Hey! What was that for?"

To get him running. But since he didn't have words, he nipped at Laddin's heels again, forcing him to jump forward.

"What are you—?"

Bruce woofed. It was a deep, short sound, echoing with command—the exact tone of voice he used
with new firefighters with more strength than smarts.
And when Laddin turned and dropped his hands on his
hips in annoyance, Bruce woofed again. The man's lips
were blue, and his shoulders were up almost to his ears.
He needed to start running now.

Woof, woof! Then he nipped at Laddin's knees. And
he kept nipping until Laddin started jogging backward.

That wasn't exactly the plan, but at least it got
Laddin moving. Bruce trotted beside Laddin, easily keeping pace. And then Laddin finally understood.
He groaned, but he flipped around and started jogging
steadily forward.

"You're going to love Yordan," Laddin muttered.
Since Bruce didn't have a mouth to ask the question, he
simply head-butted Laddin's rear end to make the guy
move faster.

They made it to the house soon after that. Though
Laddin didn't seem too concerned, Bruce didn't see
any signs of sweat on the man, even after the run. That
told him Laddin had been in dangerously cold territory,
and he was grateful they'd finally made it inside. But
once there, they had to slow down to take in the situation in front of them.

A woman in tight-fitting black leather was hunched
over a man who currently resembled Two-Face. Half
his features were stunningly gorgeous. The other
looked like hamburger meat. Bruce recognized him as
Bing, the one who had made him fall asleep in the van
way back when.

A large guy Bruce didn't know hovered nearby. His
hands shook and his body was covered in dark goo as

he harassed the woman. The big man didn't look hurt, per se, but it was hard to tell, given all the crap on him.

"Can you fix his face? He's an actor, you know. His face is important. I mean, he's important, but he's not going to die, right? But he's going to want to die when he realizes his face is…." He swallowed as he looked down at the man stretched out on the couch. "Actually, Bing, it's not so bad," he said, though the lie was obvious to anyone with a brain. "You'll be fine." His gaze hopped back to the woman. "Right? He'll be fine."

Bruce had seen it before—the shock a person felt after a disaster. It left people muttering about the most ridiculous stuff to cover how terrified they were. Yes, Bing's face was important, but mostly the big one just wanted his friend to live. Fortunately, the woman was obviously a seasoned first responder. She didn't speak, and Bruce doubted she heard much of anything as she clutched something in her hand and muttered. Her eyes were shut and one hand rested gently on Bing's chest.

Meanwhile, Laddin jolted forward. "What happened?" There was no response. Big Guy was staring at Bing, but Laddin moved quickly to the counter, where he grabbed a washcloth from a bowl of water. Then he crossed back to dab at the big man's goo-covered lip, which, now that Bruce looked closer, was definitely swollen.

It wasn't exactly the first choice in health-care assessment. Bruce would be taking vitals and getting the man to talk about what hurt and what didn't. But Laddin wasn't a paramedic. But he wasn't stupid either as he spoke in a sharp tone.

"Yordan! Where do you hurt?"

The man jolted and glared at Laddin. "I'm fine," he snapped. "It's Bing—" His voice broke on the word.

"You're not fine," Laddin said. "What happened?"

"Bing tried to hypnotize a lich."

"A zombie sorcerer? Seriously?"

"We thought that since the undead asshole used to be human, Bing'd be able to woo-woo the thing into submission." He swallowed, and his gaze grew haunted. "I should have known that he couldn't do it with the undead. I should have kept him back."

"He wouldn't have listened," Laddin said as he continued to wash the black stuff off Yordan's face. Then he jerked his head toward the woman. "Is she the cleric?"

Yordan nodded. "She was here for Wulfric and…." He swallowed. "Well, we came to find her."

Bruce turned to study the woman more closely. In that form-fitting leather, she looked like a biker babe fantasy. Though he could smell smoke, blood, and any number of other disaster stinks on her, she seemed calm as she held something in her hand and exhaled in steady breaths.

That totally pissed him off. She should be putting compresses on Bing's face. She should be checking his vitals. She should be doing any one of a zillion other things instead of just bowing her head and… what? Praying? Of all the ridiculous, useless, stupid—

His thoughts trailed away as Bing's face began to knit. The burns smoothed, and though the blood didn't disappear, the skin beneath it grew upward from raw muscle to pale gray, then flushed pink skin. It made Bruce gasp, but no more than everyone else. Bing took a deep breath, the kind one takes when the painkillers finally kick in. Except he hadn't been given any drugs. And his face was healed.

Once Bing took that breath, Yordan's head snapped up. His expression flooded with gratitude deep enough to spark tears, which he wiped away with unsteady hands. Laddin exhaled too as he patted Yordan's massive shoulder.

"See. All better."

"Yeah," Yordan breathed. "Yeah."

Meanwhile, the woman looked up, her expression serene. "He'll be fine, but he needs to rest. Now what about you?" she asked as she looked at Yordan.

"I'm good. Really. Save your prayers for someone who needs them."

She snorted as she put her necklace back on. That was what she'd been holding in her hand—a silver crucifix that looked dainty nestled against all that dark leather. "I'm fresh out anyway. I was going to see if you needed a hospital." Then she looked at Laddin. "Hi, I'm Cara, mystical healer. Are you the paramedic?"

Laddin shook his head. "Not me. Him," he said, pointing to Bruce.

Everyone looked at him, and he straightened up to his full height. Except he was a wolf, which meant he stood there looking stupid. And that was exactly the look she gave him.

"Well?" she prompted. "You planning to lick the wounds better?"

He flushed. Or he would have, if he'd been human. Only he wasn't.

He tried. He really tried to switch back to being a man. He visualized himself standing up to his impressive height. He thought of all the times he'd been needed out in the field. The car accident victims he'd treated, the house fires he'd help put out. Hell, he'd delivered three babies over his career and held them against his own chest to keep them warm. All of those memories flashed through his mind. He was damned good in a crisis, and yet all he could do right now was stand there with his tongue hanging out.

Fucking hell!

Meanwhile, Laddin shuffled his feet. "He's new. He hasn't gotten the hang of switching back and forth yet."

Cara straightened up, and Bruce heard the crackle of her knees. He knew that sound. Knew the soft grunt when a body kept functioning long after it needed to rest. He could help her. As a paramedic, he could take some of the load off, if only he was a man. And yet try as he might, he remained exactly where he was: on four paws.

"Typical man," she groused. "When you need his help, he's a dumb animal."

Bruce growled in response—dark and ugly, and mostly directed at himself. What the fuck? He was a man.

"Don't growl at me," she snapped. "Either get it together or get out of my way."

How many times had he said the exact same thing to a new firefighter? Either help or get out of the way. He was trying!

"Don't bother" came a voice from behind him.

Josh. Bruce whipped around to see his little brother dropping a backpack onto the floor so he could lace up his boots. He was wearing a field uniform, and damn if that didn't look good on him. But it had obviously never been worn before, which told Bruce that Josh was new to the first responder game, and that was terrifying. Because his brother didn't have that kind of skill. He thought things through too well. Fieldwork was all about gut reaction, and his brother lived in his head.

But though Bruce took a step toward the guy, Josh was already dismissing him.

"Bruce won't help unless there's some glory in it." Then he glanced up at Cara. "Or he's trying to get laid."

That wasn't true! He hadn't been about the glory or the sex in years—if ever. Even firefighter groupies got old when the tragedies became real. He was a fireman because he was good at it. He saved lives. But none of those words made it to his mouth.

Meanwhile Cara snorted. "One of those, huh?"

No!

"Yeah," Josh said as he looked him dead in the eye. "And obviously useless as a werewolf."

She chuckled as she looked back at Bruce with pitying eyes. "Don't sweat it, puppy. Some of us aren't cut out for this kind of work."

The dismissive look cut deep. He'd said those words before to kids who'd never made it as a firefighter. Don't worry, kid. It happens. Not everyone is cut out to be a firefighter. Go find something that you're good at, because you sure as hell aren't one of us.

But he *was* cut out for it. He'd been on the front lines for years—far longer than his brother, who was right then offering Cara an earpiece. He had another for Nero, who grabbed it out of the backpack and popped it in like a pro. Because they were pros.

"What the hell is that stink?" Nero asked as he looked around. "It smells like rancid dog."

"Fairy cheese," Laddin said. "Pixies."

Nero cursed. "Of course. Why wouldn't there be pixies that smell like rotten cheese?"

Cara grabbed a heavy mace from the corner and dropped it on her shoulder. She handled it like it was a designer purse, but it looked like it weighed a ton. "All the magical whatsits are showing up. We think they're drawn to the dead zone."

"Are the fairies an imminent threat?" Nero asked Laddin.

Tell him about your promise. Tell him you made a deal with them.

"I'm handling them."

No! No, you're not!

"Good. Look, I know it's not your job, but we need someone here to coordinate with the home office, to keep them up to date on Wulfric's progress and a few other things, at least until Bing and Yordan are back up. Do you mind helping out?"

"Of course not," said Laddin.

Nero nodded his thanks and handed over a small tablet. "Wulfric and his mother are there and there." He pointed to two bedrooms. "Bing and Yordan." He pointed at two more. "Stratos and Wiz are going to stay by the lake because we've got other wounded wolves taking their rooms. That means you'll have to bunk in the barn."

"What? Why?"

"Because you stink, and they're sick."

Josh looked up from a tablet he'd pulled from his backpack. "It's really bad, Laddin. The stench is—"

"I know." Laddin sighed. "It's in his fur."

"Then get him to shift or get outside." That came from Nero, but everyone was looking at Bruce as if he were a dirty toddler who'd messed his pants.

Bruce looked back. With every fiber of his being, he wished himself human. He'd been trying before, but this was like a wish to live, a need to breathe, a hunger for power or respect or any fucking thing he'd ever wanted in his entire life all rolled together in one desperate plea. *I'm a man!*

But he wasn't. He remained a stinky, useless, mute dog.

The woman snorted. "Typical." Then she lifted her phone up and snapped a picture.

Bruce bristled. Did she think he was a show dog? Would she pass his picture around to her friends and laugh at the wolf who smelled like fairy cheese?

"Did you just catch a Pokémon?" Josh asked as he looked over her shoulder at her cell.

"Don't judge," she said as she pocketed her cell. "It's the only way I get my mother out of the house. I won't trade with her unless she catches a few of her own."

"I'm not judging," Josh answered, his voice filled with admiration. "I wish I'd thought to do the same. Anything cool out here in Wisconsin?"

"I just got a Gyarados. What have you got?"

They wandered off together, talking Pokémon in the same way Bruce and the other firefighters talked about sports. Nero followed behind, grumbling good-naturedly about geeks and their games. Meanwhile, Laddin was on his phone, doing his job coordinating with someone. Yordan and Bing were shuffling off together to their beds, though it was more like Bing was walking and Yordan was shuffling.

And Bruce stood there, completely ignored. Hell, he wasn't even cutting it as amusement. Cara had been playing Pokémon Go, not taking his picture. Never in his life had he been so completely dismissed. As a kid, he'd been big and could fight. As an adult, he had valuable skills and an imposing presence.

But what was he now? A stinking dog.

The humiliation of it all burned in his gut and came out as a low whine. Laddin heard it, of course, but he was on the phone. All he could do was turn and give Bruce a sympathetic smile—the kind given to kids and very frail elders. *Sorry you're helpless, but please be quiet while the useful people work. We'll get to you as soon as we can.*

He'd never hated himself more.

No! God damn it, he was not going to drop into self-pity or self-loathing. That was not his style. Maybe he didn't have hands or instruments, but he could see and smell. There was a ton of stuff he could notice with those two senses. And if there was a problem, he could bark.

That was what he'd do. He'd be useful with the ability he had. So he padded away from Laddin, who was busy on the phone.

The first thing he did was look in on Yordan and Bing. Yordan looked pale and exhausted, but he was waving away a healthy Bing with a weak hand. "Lie down yourself. Magical healing is still exhausting. You may be pretty again, but I'll bet you're dreaming about taking a nap."

"If you do the same," Bing answered. Then he turned and wrinkled his sharply etched nose at Bruce. "God, it's true. You Americans stink."

"It's not me," grumbled Yordan as he collapsed on a bed. "Get out of here, mutt."

Then, before Bruce could muscle his way in just to prove he could, Bing shut the bedroom door right on his nose.

Fine. They didn't look like they needed anything other than rest. He'd make himself useful with Wulfric.

It was hard turning the doorknob with his paws—in fact, he couldn't do it at all, so he tried with his mouth. All he managed to do was to slobber all over the thing. He was about to ram the door in frustration when someone opened it from the inside.

He hopped back only to stare at the most ethereal beauty he'd ever seen. She was a pale brunet with dark mahogany eyes, small bones, and fair white skin. She said something in a language he didn't understand, and damned if she didn't look like an elven queen as she held her hand to her nose and waved him back.

He tried to muscle past her, but he didn't want to hurt her, and she wasn't budging. She seemed to have a vein of steel inside her, for all that she looked light enough to ride a stiff wind. And then came the ultimate insult, as she backed him up enough to shut the bedroom door behind her. Damn it, there was no way he could check on Wulfric now. He needed hands!

"You belong outside," she said firmly. "You're going to make everyone sick with that stink and—" She abruptly quieted as Wulfric coughed from inside the bedroom. She waited in tense silence to see if it would repeat. It didn't, so she turned back to him. "My son needs his rest, and you're only making things worse."

So this was Wulfric's mother. Wow. She looked even younger than Wulfric. And they were both supposed to be more than two hundred years old? Way cool, except he was a paramedic. He needed to check on Wulfric. He yipped at her, irritation in the sound.

"Yes, I know you're a werewolf," she said. "But you're a problem with that smell, and we need solutions." Then she grabbed him by the ruff in a vise-like grip. He tried to shake her off, but he didn't want to hurt her. That meant that biting was out too. And hell, she was strong as she dragged him to the front door.

He tried to dig his heels in, but he had paws on a hard floor, and he slid despite all his efforts.

Then Laddin looked up from his phone. His eyes widened at the sight, and Bruce had a moment of satisfaction. Laddin, at least, would explain. He'd tell this woman Bruce was a paramedic and—

Laddin opened the front door for the woman, and Bruce was unceremoniously shoved outside. The moment his ruff was released, he turned back. Now he was really pissed and frustrated. He'd be damned if he sat outside like—

"You want to help?" the woman said. "Talk to your fairy benefactor. Find out where the demon is and then you'll be of some use. But until then…."

She didn't finish that sentence with words. She shut the door in his face. Which sucked.

He could paw at the door. He could howl and growl and maybe even knock the damn thing down, but what would that accomplish? Nothing. He couldn't even call Bitterroot like this. He could only snort and plop down on his useless paws as he stared out—

"Feeling rejected? Oh, poor baby." Bruce's head snapped up, and there was the fairy, standing there with his tomato hat on and a smarmy look on his face. Bitterroot tugged on his lettuce lapels as he twirled around. "I'm beginning to like this outfit. I'm so handsome that I make even this look good."

Bruce didn't answer. He didn't have a human mouth to say anything, though he did wonder if the creature could read his thoughts. Just in case, he thought something really loud.

You look like I could cut you in half with one bite.

The fairy stopped admiring himself and arched a brow. "You could try," he said, challenge in his tone and posture.

Okay, so the guy could read his thoughts. That was disconcerting.

"Only the really loud ones. You're buried in Oh poor me. I'm mute. I'm ugly. Nobody loves me."

He hadn't been thinking any of that. It had been more of a *fuck you* to everyone and the world. But either way, maybe he could find a way to turn this to his advantage.

Do you know where the demon is? The one that everyone's looking for?

"The one that's killing the world?"

Well, it was just Wisconsin at the moment, but yeah, the whole world was going to tumble pretty soon after that.

Bitterroot offered up that shiny red apple. "Take a bite," he said. "Maybe you'll be the hero everyone needs."

Bruce turned his paw over and tried really hard to raise his middle finger. Damn it, he couldn't even give the guy a one-fingered salute. He dropped his head down on his paws and closed his eyes. Problem was, the fairy was still there, clear as day, though his eyes were closed.

Asshole.

"You can do it, you know. Be the hero everyone needs. My people have seen that much, but first you have to take the apple."

Bruce rolled onto his side, stretching out his legs. Every drug dealer promised the same thing. *Take this and you'll feel better. You'll be happy and everyone will love you.* It was all lies.

"I don't lie, remember?"

Said every liar throughout time.

"Listen to me, you idiot! We've seen it. I'm a fairy prince, and we want Earth to survive just as much as you do. I went to our seers, and they said that if you eat the apple, you can save the world."

Bruce cracked an eye. He had to admit the picture Salad Guy painted was appealing. Except for the details. *How do I save the world?*

"That's for you to figure out."

In other words, the fairy was lying. What Bruce had to figure out was how to become human again. And useful.

"Here's a hint. Eat the apple."

Eating the cherry fucked me over. At least before I had a purpose. Now all I can do is sit on the porch and stink like limburger cheese. Why would I go for the apple?

"Because we've—"

Seen it. So you've said. But until you can give me details, I'm not interested. Unless…. He lifted his head and stared straight at the fairy's bright carrot tufts of hair. Unless you can tell me where the demon is hiding. That was what everybody wanted to know. That was how he'd be the hero.

Bitterroot shook his head and held up the apple. It still pulsed with that bright red temptation, the shine so bright it was hard to look at it and even harder to look away. But Bruce was a paramedic—he'd seen plenty of burned-out junkies and the disasters they left behind. Bitterroot was the same as every pusher on Earth, hoping to hook Bruce into something he didn't understand and couldn't control. So even though Bruce had taken the cherry, he was not going for more. *No.*

Then he closed his eyes, and this time, there was no fairy tempting him in the darkness. No fairy, but the apple still hovered there, looking bright and beautiful. Even better, the smell of hot apple cider masked the cheese scent, but only barely. And though he lay on the porch doing nothing, he knew that all he had to do was think the word *yes* and it would be in his hand, in his mouth, and in his body.

It was right there. And as long as he stared at it, he couldn't think of anything else. He couldn't rest. And he sure as hell couldn't figure out how to shift back to human.

Get it out of my sight, you fucking fairy!

"It'll disappear the moment you truly want it gone."

And that was the worst possible truth. Because really, what did he have to lose? His life was already fucked-up. What would it hurt to try for more?

No! No! No!

Except the more he denied it, the larger the apple got in his mind. This entire magical world was fucked-up madness. And all he could do about it was lie on the porch and endure.

Chapter 11

MOON MADNESS ISN'T THE ONLY THING THAT MAKES LADDIN CRAZY

IT WAS dark by the time Laddin made it outside to the porch. Bruce was still there, stinking to high heaven, and though he lay down in a relaxed pose, the wolf was licking his lips while his tail twitched in irritation.

"Oh shit, you're probably starving. You should have howled or something."

Bruce gave him a dark, angry scowl, which, on a wolf face, was a bit intimidating.

"You know, pride never fed anyone. You're hungry, you should have said something." He opened the door to the house. "I'll just be a second. Wait here."

Laddin grabbed a couple of the new plant-based burgers from the refrigerator. Bruce's stomach probably wasn't up to meat yet, so he quickly microwaved them, grabbed some condiments, and slopped them on a plate. His hand hovered over the slices of American cheese before he backed off with a shudder. The memory of being suffocated by cheese wasn't fading, and he couldn't bring himself to touch the slices—even if they weren't pixies... as far as he was aware.

Then he turned back to the door, only to find Bruce standing half in and half out of the house. Obviously the guy was really hungry, which made Laddin feel all the more guilty. He was Bruce's trainer. And sure, he'd been busy coordinating casualties and bed space for the Wulf, Inc. crews, but Bruce should have been his first priority, and he'd completely neglected the man's needs.

He held up the plate of burgers. "You want ketch-up? Mustard?" Nods each time. Then he gestured weakly toward the cheese. He didn't even have to ask. Bruce was wildly shaking his head. "We're in agreement there," Laddin said as he set the plate down.

Bruce had no problem figuring out how to eat as a wolf. He gobbled down the burgers in the time it took for Laddin to get a bowl of water out. "I know it's not how you're used to drinking, but you're a wolf now too. You need to learn...." His voice trailed away as Bruce lapped up the water without so much as a pause.

Okay, so Bruce was practical and not into the nice-ties of food consumption. In that, he did better than Laddin, who'd refused at first to put his face into food instead of eating with a fork and knife. "Captain M wouldn't let me eat for a week unless I did it as a wolf. But my mama drilled polite table manners into me. She said proper table manners were a sign of civilization, and if I complained because of this"—he held up his deformed hand—"she ate one-handed, too."

Bruce looked at Laddin's hand and face, then gave the wolf equivalent of a shrug.

Laddin grinned. It had been a long time since he'd felt like he had a handicap, but it was sure nice to be around someone who didn't seem to notice it at all.

He supposed it was only natural for people to see his hand and get awkward. They didn't know whether to ask about it or ignore it. But Bruce didn't seem to care one way or another.

He abruptly wrapped his arm around Bruce's furry neck and gave him an impulsive hug. Of the many awful things going on right now, Bruce felt like a warm blanket at the end of a hard day. "I know things are fucked-up for you right now," he said against Bruce's neck, "but I'm grateful to have someone to talk to."

Bruce nuzzled back, which was pure delight. Laddin doubted the guy would have done so as a human—he wasn't the touchy-feely type—but right now, Laddin needed a warm body to hug.

They stayed that way for a moment, but eventually Bruce got restless. Laddin released him with a happy sigh, then looked out the open front door. "You probably need to go out. It was a while before I figured out exactly how to use the outdoor facilities, so to speak...." His voice trailed away.

Only Bruce wasn't headed back out the door. Instead, his nose was twitching as he walked down the hallway.

"We're sleeping in the barn, remember? Every room here is full with wounded wolves." He stood up and joined Bruce. "So here's the situation. There's a big lake about fifty miles from here. We call it Lake Wacka Wacka. Anyway, it's full of poison that is seeping into the land and expanding across Wisconsin. Nobody outside of Wulf, Inc. knows why. We do, because Nero saw it happen. A demon dropped into the lake and suddenly, bang, everything started dying."

He took a breath and tried to keep his voice calm, but he'd been talking to people all day, hearing the stories of what was going on, and it had shaken him. He needed to share, and right now Bruce was the best person to talk to.

"The demon is somewhere around there, poisoning the lake and the land. We know it's getting stronger because the dead zone is growing. But we can't find the damn thing. And the scientists, the military, and the reporters aren't finding it either. Having all those humans around is bad enough, but suddenly mystical baddies are showing up too. They're probably drawn to the possibility of the world ending."

He dug his fingers into Bruce's fur, feeling grounded with every shift of muscle and fur. Even the way Bruce breathed eased his own breath.

"You saw what happened to Bing's face, right? That was from a lich—a big undead magical guy. I also heard there was a mated pair of chupacabra. Think Bigfoot without hair and with evil teeth. They're not supposed to mate, but everything's gone wonky around the lake. That's what demon energy does. It screws up the natural order. And if you think responding to a human domestic violence call is dangerous, try to get in between a pair of emotional chupacabras." A shudder ran through him, but he took a deep breath and regained control. "So we're in a bit of a bind. No one can find the demon because we're all busy keeping the paranormal weirdoes away from the vanilla scientists. And the journalists are everywhere. Be careful where you shift, because somebody's going to snap a picture if they can."

If Bruce was listening, he gave no sign of it. Instead, he pressed his nose to the first bedroom door, then looked expectantly back at Laddin.

"You want to check on the patients, don't you? Even though you're in your wolf form and can't do anything if there's a problem."

Bruce nodded, then cocked his head at Laddin until he eventually gave in.

"Okay, okay. You can tell me if there's a problem. But be quiet, and don't take long, because you still stink."

Laddin opened the door as quietly as possible, and Bruce padded inside. Laddin watched as the wolf inspected the patient, sniffed the wounds—though how he could smell anything over the bad cheese odor was beyond Laddin—and then cocked his head and pressed his ear to the man's chest. The patient was so exhausted that he didn't so much as twitch. That might have worried Laddin, but Bruce turned back to the door and nodded with a slight dip of his chin.

"All good?"

Another nod.

"Then I guess we're on to the next one." And so they went, from one room to the next.

Several of the patients woke up holding their noses as they complained about the smell. Laddin made them wait as Bruce performed his tasks. Tasks that—incidentally—no one asked him to do but Laddin respected nonetheless. Wulf, Inc. was hard up for medical personnel, so no one bitched too much about having a smelly wolf come sniff their aches and pains.

Eventually the task was done, and they went together out to the barn. Laddin pulled out a couple of bedrolls even though he knew Bruce would likely stay a wolf for the night. It was way more comfortable in a cold barn. He'd do it himself, but he knew that it was better to reserve his shifting strength for when he really needed it.

Bruce busied himself sniffing around the barn. Laddin remembered finding every little smell fascinating. Disgusting or sweet, it made no difference. He actually longed to do it with Bruce now. There was nothing like moving around in a pack, asking in lupine ways, *Did you smell that? Cool, huh? What about this? What do you think this is?* They never used human words, but everyone knew what the other was saying. Wolves were simple that way.

He stretched out on his bedroll and looked out the window at the three-quarter moon. "Do you see that, Bruce?" he asked as he pointed at the night sky. "She's beautiful, isn't she? Cold, remote, and she still plays havoc with my life. And yet, I look at her and I'm in love."

Bruce padded over, his gaze on the dark sky before returning to Laddin.

"I'm one of those weres who is affected by the moon. I don't go rampaging about like a movie werewolf, but yeah, I feel the power in her. It's like an electric wire in my bloodstream. The stronger her light, the hotter the buzz. And during a full moon, I get hit with Moon Madness. It makes me want to kill everything in sight." He dropped his head back and stared up at the dark ceiling. "Sometimes I feel like I'm up there, lost in all that endless black. Even before this werewolf thing, I felt different. And it wasn't just my hand." He held it up so that it was a dark silhouette over the bright moon. With the three-quarter shape, his hand didn't seem so weird. "I can't really connect with people the way I want. I see them. I see what they want and who they are, but they never seem to look at me."

He rubbed a hand over his face.

"God, I'm tired. I only get poetic when I'm wiped out. But I don't want to go to sleep, ya know? I'm afraid I'll be suffocated by cheese the moment I close my eyes."

He snorted at the image. It was funny, but only because he didn't want to feel the horror of it again—of that white stuff binding his arms and legs, of the dark cheddar bits pelting his body or the feel of an American slice covering his nose and mouth. Twice a slice had flattened over his mouth, and twice he'd been able to bite through it while magic tingled on his lips and tongue. He hadn't had the explosive farts Bruce had let loose, but he'd felt the pixie magic in him all day, and it hadn't been pleasant—kind of like sparks of energy bursting through his belly. It had taken hours before the magic had come out the other end, and the memory still made him queasy. He had no idea if that was normal, and with everyone fighting monsters near the lake, it seemed too trivial to mention.

A cold wet nose pressed against his cheek, and Laddin smiled. He burrowed his good hand into Bruce's ruff and scratched through the thick pelt. It was comfort, pure and simple, and he relished every second of it.

"Do you know what the best part about being a werewolf is?" he asked. "It's this right here. You'll see. The pack will do things together as wolves. We all have to practice hunting so we know what it's like and can control the urge when it's inappropriate. And wolves hunt in packs. We'll do this whole chase thing. I don't take down any deer. And I won't eat the meat either." He shifted to allow Bruce room to stretch out beside him. "I'm not vegetarian or anything. I just can't get past eating Bambi." He gave another shudder. "Then afterwards, we all tumble together and sleep. A big ol' puppy pile, everyone touching, everyone happy. We've usually had a hard run and everyone's got full bellies. A lot of us do a romp through the stream to get clean, and then we shake the water off on each other before snoozing in the sun." If he closed his eyes and didn't inhale too deep, he could pretend he was back in Michigan by the streambed with everyone else. "It's like having family that doesn't drive you crazy," he murmured. "And if they do, it's okay to bite."

The wet nose lifted from his neck to his cheek. And then he felt a lick against his five-o'clock shadow, a soft tongue against the roughness of his skin. Sweet. Gentle. He smiled as he turned into the kiss.

And then, quite suddenly, it *was* a kiss. A man's mouth touching his. Exploratory lips. Hardness of teeth. And deepening to more as he opened up to the thrust and parry of their tongues.

It was so natural, he didn't question it. His hand was no longer burrowing into fur but kneading the back of a man's neck. And the weight against his side was now man-shaped—no longer soft with fur, but hard with bone, muscle, and a thick erection that was impossible to miss. And extra special, no more rancid cheese smell. Just hot, sexy man.

Until that man stiffened in shock and pulled back.

Bruce was naked and looked so appalled that Laddin felt a wash of shame. But then he bristled internally. He hadn't asked for the kiss. He'd just gone with it when it came. Whatever was going on in Bruce's horrified mind, it wasn't Laddin's fault. And after everything that had happened today, Laddin didn't have the mental bandwidth to deal with any more drama. Besides, this particular problem was 100 percent Bruce's issue. Let the big firefighter figure it out.

And that was exactly what happened when the guy spoke about ten seconds later.

"I'm straight," Bruce said.

The massive erection against Laddin's thigh said differently, but he didn't respond.

"Really, I am. I can't tell you the number of women I've bedded. A different one every night."

Laddin nodded. "I believe you."

Then Bruce looked down at Laddin's mouth, and he bit his lower lip. It was an endearing sight, like a child seeing a sweet and dreaming about licking it.

"I'm not into men," Bruce said.

"Are you sure? You never looked at a fellow firefighter and thought interesting things?"

Bruce's gaze slid away, and when he spoke, his words were low. "You don't understand. Gay wasn't okay in the firehouse."

"We're not in your firehouse. We're not even in Indiana." Laddin smiled and gave his best come-hither look. "Things change."

"But I've never...." Bruce swallowed, and his gaze roved over Laddin's face. Down below, Laddin felt Bruce's dick twitch against his thigh. He gently took Bruce's hand and pulled it to stroke down Laddin's chest, over his tight nipple, and across his quivering abs. It was a slow stroke with Laddin guiding while Bruce followed the motion with his eyes. Laddin had burrowed into the bedroll in shorts and a T-shirt, but now he guided Bruce's hand beneath the fabric and back up over his chest. He couldn't stop the gasp when the calluses on Bruce's fingers rubbed against his nipple. The sensation was electric, and it made Laddin's toes curl in delight.

It had been so long since someone had done that to him. God, how he'd missed it. Then Bruce did it again without prompting, pulling the rough edge of his nail across Laddin's tight nipple. And he continued as Laddin's hips thrust upward and his erection throbbed hungrily.

"Can fairy fruit turn me gay?" Bruce asked, his words heavy with confusion.

"You think I know?"

"He said it would give me what my brother had."

Laddin shrugged. "Josh is definitely gay. But I'd bet you already had thoughts every now and then. Lots of people are bi-curious."

Bruce's eyes widened, but he didn't speak. And for a werewolf, he looked a lot like a deer in headlights.

Laddin sighed. He was too tired to deal with sibling crap or fairy-fruit crap or even sexual-identity crap. He was hard as a rock now, and horny as hell. Bruce was a good kisser and had a physique that rang Laddin's bell big-time. But he didn't need any extra complications in an already complicated life.

He was about to say something about going to sleep, but then Bruce abruptly kissed him again. The move was quick and almost brutal, but Laddin didn't mind. Especially since their mouths devoured each other in aggressive thrusts. It was as if Bruce was angry he wanted to kiss Laddin, and yet he couldn't stop himself.

And that, naturally, turned Laddin on even more. There was nothing like being wanted with a hunger that defied reason. Need pulsed through his blood, and he clutched Bruce's shoulder in a tight fist.

And then Bruce drew back. His breathing was rapid, his eyes dazed, and he licked his lips like he wanted to go back.

Laddin flashed him a teasing grin. "Thought you weren't into men."

"I wasn't. Except apparently, right now, I am." He cocked a brow at Laddin. "You got a problem with that?"

"Hell no." Lust was pounding hard in his blood, and he wanted to pin Bruce down and thrust into those tight asscheeks. But sex was never simple unless the rules were stated clearly. "You ever been with a man before?"

Bruce shook his head.

"Then I'm in charge, got it?"

Bruce's nostrils flared at that. He was a dominant male, and he obviously didn't like ceding control. Laddin could respect that, but this was about safety.

"You tell me what you want, and I'll give it to you. But when someone says stop, we stop. Got it?"

"I won't want to stop."

"Too fucking bad. You have to control yourself. You're a lot stronger than you used to be and your needs are—"

"That's not what I meant," Bruce interrupted. "I mean… I want this. I want to fuck you, and I'm not going to change my mind."

Oh. Suddenly all those lascivious fantasies he'd had outside rolled back through his mind. He couldn't believe that he'd get to act out one of them. Only one. But then, Laddin was too hot to be picky.

"Okay, then. I'm going to take you on a ride like you've never had before." He reached out and gripped Bruce's erection. Damn, the man was huge, just the way he liked them. And his hips bucked with power as Laddin grabbed hold. But he didn't stroke him. He simply squeezed and held still.

"One more thing."

Bruce looked up. "Yeah?"

"I'm doing this 'cause I'm lonely. It's been a long time for me, and you look good naked."

Bruce grinned. "I can accept that."

"So why are you doing it?"

Bruce's eyes widened, and Laddin could see he'd hit the bull's-eye. Bruce was a guy who relied on his instincts. He was practical by nature and decisive in a crisis. And he probably didn't spend a lot of time figuring out why he did the things he did.

"Maybe I'm lonely too," Bruce said, his voice rough with challenge.

"When were you with your last girl?"

Bruce swallowed. "A couple weeks ago."

"So it's not a loneliness problem. You probably get laid whenever you want. Firefighter groupies, if I had to guess."

Bruce nodded.

"So what's riding you now?"

Panic filtered across Bruce's expression. He didn't want to look into his motives, and he sure as hell didn't want to think he was suddenly gay or bi or whatever. He was going with the flow, and Laddin had to decide if that was what he wanted. A quick fuck with a hot guy who needed the distraction. Was that enough for him?

Tonight? Yes. On a night when he was likely to have cheese nightmares, a hot fuck was the perfect distraction.

"I don't need an answer," he said as he began stroking his fist up and down Bruce's shaft. Bruce's breath caught and his eyes shuttered to half-mast. "But you'll need to figure it out for yourself tomorrow."

"It's just a fast fuck," Bruce whispered.

"Nothing's going to be fast, boy," he said, making his voice rough as he challenged the alpha guy. After all, Bruce was the young one here, in terms of being a werewolf and of gay sex.

Sure enough, Bruce stiffened at the term. And his expression sharpened in response. "You promised me a ride, *boy*." He shoved his hips upward as he punctuated the sentence. "That's what I want. And that's what you're going to give me."

Laddin grinned. The mood was established, the terms clear. A hard fuck with no consequences. He could work with that. Hell, he was going to love that. But Bruce was going to get a whole lot more than he bargained for.

"Then let's get started."

Chapter 12

LADDIN SPEAKS HIS MIND AND BRUCE LOSES HIS

BRUCE HAD no idea how he managed to turn back to human. One second he was trying to comfort Laddin with a doggie nuzzle. The next second he was kissing the guy. But never in his life had he been more grateful to be a man.

Laddin pushed him backward and began devouring his mouth. The kiss was simple, thorough, and wholly exciting. And though Bruce pushed back—he thrust into Laddin's mouth and ground against him—it was Laddin who was in control and Bruce who opened. And that threw Bruce so badly, he had no choice but to give way completely.

Before, he'd always been the dominant partner in sex. He picked the woman, he carefully pursued her. If she said yes, he felt wanted in the most primal of ways, and that eased the guilt he carried for being such an asshole when he was younger. But always he chose the woman, he gave what he wanted and no more, and he was driven by his own needs.

Not this time.

For the first time in his life, he didn't have a clue what he needed or why. Except that Laddin kissed him as if he wanted to own Bruce. Not as a slave, but as a favorite toy to play with, to enjoy, to bang against the floor and tear open to see how the insides worked. And Bruce wanted that too, because he didn't know who he was anymore. If Laddin could find that out, Bruce would give him anything he wanted. And maybe together they'd be able to figure out the parts that made up the man. Or the wolf. Or whatever he was now.

So when Laddin started kissing down his chest, he let his head flop back and closed his eyes in surrender. His dick was thrusting upward, searching for more, but Bruce didn't even try to control it. He let it do as it wanted and waited for whatever Laddin chose to do.

Laddin was patient in ways that Bruce had never been. The way he kissed Bruce was steady, thorough, and methodical. Each rib was nipped in careful exploration. His nipples were worked in precise ways. Tongue first, teeth next, and then a pinch that had his hips bucking like a bronco.

And all the while, Laddin kept one hand wrapped firmly around Bruce's cock, as if he was holding the reins in a hard fist. He let Bruce thrust and squirm, but he flowed with the movements, never giving Bruce the friction he wanted. If Bruce pushed up, Laddin's fist went with him. If Bruce drew back or shifted his hips or even pulsed with need, Laddin simply rode with the angle and occasionally squeezed. Laddin's grip stopped any possible release and kept Bruce's hot pulses of hunger from overflowing.

Bruce was exhaling hot bellows of need, but they didn't change Laddin's thorough exploration of his nipples, then belly. Then, finally—mercifully—he brought his mouth to Bruce's dick.

Bruce waited with breath suspended for Laddin's grip to ease. His entire focus was centered on that fist and the moment it would let him slide up and down.

But it didn't move. Instead, Laddin licked at his tip—a tiny brush that echoed through his whole body. And again. That slow lollipop lick felt like a tongue laving every part of his flesh. Somehow the tip of his dick had become everything he was. And when Laddin's fist slipped lower and his mouth teased across the entire head, Bruce shook with the sensations. No part of him remained untouched. Then, when Laddin began to suck, his mouth moving with glacier-like progress, Bruce felt himself wholly engulfed.

Wet. Heavy. Inevitable. Unstoppable.

He surrendered to Laddin's weight. He let it crush him with need, obliterate all his thoughts. His orgasm was only part of the process. He was so blown apart that when he released, the bliss merged with the annihilation.

Suddenly he felt free.

Boneless, mindless, released, and erased into bliss.

And then Laddin rolled him over.

"On your knees," he ordered.

Bruce obeyed.

"You think you're done, don't you," he said.

He did.

"There's more, but you have to stay exactly like this. You have to be relaxed."

Not a problem.

He waited while Laddin got something from the truck. He didn't move—hell, he barely breathed as Laddin returned. Then he felt hands on his asscheeks, spreading them open, and an invasion that was like everything else Laddin did—slow, steady, and completely thorough. A finger wet with lube. His mind told him that, but his body didn't care.

He was open. He was empty. And Laddin was going to fill him up.

The finger moved in and out. There seemed to be no rush, just a push that went progressively deeper. Over and over. And then there was a wiggle somewhere deep inside. A place that had him drawing a deep breath in surprise.

"Don't tense. Ride it."

He wasn't tensing. He was *feeling*. But in order to do that, he had to open up wider. He had to let Laddin press and rub wherever *that* was.

Laddin didn't. He gently removed his finger only to replace it with two, offering stretches and pokes that weren't getting there but were coming steadily closer.

Bruce whimpered. He'd never made that sound in his life, but he did now. He wanted, but he had no ability to demand. The words wouldn't form; the force wouldn't come. He was a creature of open need.

He waited.

Eventually a hard, blunt tip pressed at his opening. And like before, the thrust was steady, patient, and inescapable. A little deeper each time. A little wider with every thrust. And while the burn added to the sensations, Bruce didn't resist. He was too open and too needy.

He simply existed while pleasure spiraled outward from the point of penetration. And while the thrill built with each invasion, Bruce didn't move with it. He didn't buck, and he sure as hell didn't bear down. Not until Laddin was fully vested. Not until the heat of his body added to the burn of expansion.

Then Laddin leaned down over Bruce's back. Bruce felt the heat of his breath across his shoulders and the weight of his body on his spine. He bore it easily. He was a big guy, and he wanted this. Then Laddin grabbed hold of his dick in a grip of iron, just like before.

"Now you move," he ordered. "Whatever you want."

The words didn't compute. What he wanted? He'd been emptied of wants. And yet his body knew exactly what to do.

His hips thrust into Laddin's fist. Sensation burst through his consciousness from two places. Every thrust had his dick weeping with pleasure. And every shift had Laddin rubbing against that place deep inside him. It was incredible. He tried to control his movements. He tried to measure the pleasure as it built inside him. But it was too much to process, too big to absorb, and he ended up squirming and thrusting in a wild ride of everything at once.

Only it wasn't enough.

He cried out in frustration. No words, just sound and need and—

"My turn," Laddin rasped. "My. Fucking. Turn."

With each word, he thrust hard. And at the deepest point of penetration, he banged that spot. Bruce arched and tried to open up wider, deeper. He wanted to be split apart, and as Laddin grunted against him, he was.

Split wide. Torn open.

Exposed. Pleasured.

Orgasm in a white-out of sensation.

Absolute, unending bliss.

BRUCE CAME back to himself in darkness. He felt gentle adjustments as Laddin spooned against him, then covered them both with a heavy blanket. The warmth was welcome, but the gentle press of lips between his shoulder blades was sheer delight.

"I've never had sex like that before," Bruce said into the darkness.

"Yeah, I know." There was humor in the tone, but it was also kind.

"I don't mean it like that," Bruce said. "I told you I've never been with a man before. I mean…." What did he mean? "You're good at that."

A low chuckle vibrated from Laddin's chest to Bruce's spine. "Yeah," he repeated. "I know."

"Cocky bastard," he said without heat.

"Yeah," Laddin said again, "I know." And this time he added a thrust from his hips. Laddin's cock was thick and heavy against Bruce's backside, but it wasn't demanding anything—just hanging out—and that made Bruce smile.

Bruce exhaled, feeling a pleasant burn in his body, like exhaustion after a good workout. It felt good, but it wasn't quieting his thoughts. If anything, they were ramping up. Words began to crowd his mind, and eventually the pressure had him speaking them aloud.

"He offered me an apple," he said into the darkness. "I can't not see it, even when I close my eyes. All I have to do is reach out and I can have it."

He felt Laddin's body tighten. His arm was stretched across Bruce's middle, and the fingers stopped brushing gently against his chest hair. Bruce hadn't even noticed the caress until it stopped. And then Laddin spoke, his voice quiet.

"Who's making the offer?"

He didn't want to say Bitterroot's name aloud, so he found another way. "Same asshole who gave me the cherry."

"That turned you into a werewolf?"

"Yes."

"And now he wants to turn you into what?"

Bruce shrugged, the movement sparking sensations along his backside where they were pressed together. "He says I'll be more."

"More what?"

Might was well confess it all. "More than Josh."

Laddin blew out a heavy breath. "Thank you, Mama, for keeping me an only child."

Bruce shook his head. "It's not like that. It's not rivalry."

"You sure about that?"

Yes. No. Maybe. "Josh doesn't need me like I am. I need something to offer him."

"How about friendship? Brotherly love? All that relationship stuff."

"He's already rejected that."

"And you think becoming bigger and badder than him is going to change anything?"

Bruce shook his head. "It'll give me a way to stick around. If he needs my protection, then I can work on all the other stuff. In time, he'll see that I've changed. That I'm trying to help."

Laddin dropped his head down onto the bedroll. He must have been keeping it raised, because the heat of his breath moved to the back of Bruce's neck. The blast of air that parted his hair was a measure of Laddin's frustration. He didn't approve—that much was clear. So Bruce tried to explain.

"I was a dick to Josh when we were kids. A real asshole in so many ways. I'm trying to make up for that."

"This isn't the way. Fairy magic always comes back to bite you."

He'd guessed as much. Becoming a werewolf hadn't done anything but make him feel like an idiot. "I want to be able to protect Josh—the way I didn't when we were kids." He'd never expected to be on the front lines—or near the front lines—of the world ending in Wisconsin. But here he was, and he couldn't even use the medical skills he had because he had no control over his werewolf nature. "If I was more capable, if I had more to offer, I could help Josh. I need to be there for him."

"You can't even shift at will. What makes you think having more ability will accomplish anything but land your ass in disaster?"

Nothing. "I'm not seeing any other options right now. Josh won't even talk to me."

"Then you're not looking hard enough." Laddin abruptly shoved upright and pulled Bruce over onto his back so that they could look eye to eye. It was hard to see in the darkness, and yet Laddin's light brown eyes still seemed to bore into him. "Going for the apple isn't the way. It will only repeat the first mistake—only the mistake will be bigger this time."

"And the first mistake was?"

"Did that cherry help you in any way? Do you feel like you're on your feet and soaring to bigger and better things?"

No. And yet…. "I just had the best sex of my life. That ought to count for something."

Laddin blew out a breath. "We could have done that any time. You didn't have to eat a cherry to do it."

Except they never would have met without the cherry.

"I don't know if you can fix things with Josh, but I promise you, that fairy apple isn't going to do it for you."

Bruce firmed his chin and glared at Laddin. "I'm not giving up on my brother."

"Your brother is doing fine. It's you you're worried about. I'd look there first."

That statement hit uncomfortably close to something Bruce couldn't even name. "There's nothing here to look at. Nothing at all."

Laddin touched his face. The fingers were thick with calluses, but his caress was gentle, and the combination of the two set Bruce's skin to burning. "Do you really think that? That you're nothing?"

Hell no. He was much worse than nothing. He was the monster his father had claimed Josh was. But he wasn't going to talk about that—not to a guy he'd just met, no matter how good he fucked. So he shook his head. "I've got red in my ledger. I'm trying to wipe it clean."

He didn't think Laddin would get the Black Widow reference. He wouldn't know it except that Marvel comics were one of the few things he and Josh had shared. At least they had, before sports, girls, and their father had gotten between them. But Laddin was smart, and he obviously followed the pop culture reference just fine.

"Don't give me that movie shit. If you wanted to save the world, you'd become a doctor or a—"

"A fire medic?"

Laddin grimaced. "You really based your life on a Black Widow comic?"

He shrugged. This was the most introspection he'd done in years. It wasn't his strong suit. But maybe that was a side effect of becoming a werewolf. He started thinking in ways he'd never done before. He started thinking about *himself* in ways that made him question his entire life up until now. Was everything he was, everything he'd done, all about making up for being an asshole older brother?

He thought for a moment. He remembered all the things he'd done to his brother when they were kids. Things that would get a parent arrested. Verbal and physical abuse were only the beginning. He'd been mean because his father had taught him to be mean, and the older man had praised him the more vicious he got.

The memories made him feel sick, and he flopped back onto the bedroll with a grunt. "I want to make up for being a shit older brother. That's all."

"Have you tried saying 'I'm sorry'?"

Those two words seemed so lame. And when he'd actually used them, he'd been too late. Josh had blown him off with surprising strength. "This apology thing," he said in the darkness. "It's a new thought for me."

Laddin didn't respond except to grunt. Bruce knew what the sound meant. It was the universal noise of "whatever." It meant that Laddin was done talking. He'd given his opinion and wasn't going to belabor the point. That was both comforting and thoroughly frustrating, because Bruce needed to sort this out. He needed to find a way to connect with Josh. And he needed that damned fairy apple to leave his thoughts. Because the more he thought about it, the more it hung in the air right behind his closed eyelids. If he focused on it even a little, he could smell it and feel the tingle of its magic against his tongue.

"Let it go for tonight," Laddin said as he tucked his arm around Bruce's chest. Then he dropped his head against Bruce's arm and inhaled a long, deep breath. "You don't smell like cheese anymore."

"Thank God for small favors." But then he remembered that in the midst of mulling over his own problems, he'd forgotten all about Laddin's. "You have to talk to the pixies tomorrow morning."

"Yeah. I know."

"Have you set an alarm?"

"Yeah. But I don't know what I'm going to say to them. I spent half the day searching for answers and found nothing helpful."

"I'll go with you. No matter what, we'll figure it out."

"Thanks."

"No problem." He didn't know if it was the sex or the fact that they'd nearly died together this afternoon, but at some point Laddin had changed from being Bruce's trainer to his comrade in arms. Bruce wasn't about to leave him hanging without backup against killer cheese fairies. That thought was so ridiculously silly, it made him snort. "I'm there for you, man. We'll confront the limburger together."

"Grand Master Cheesy, Great Fetid Feta."

Bruce felt himself relax, the tension from thinking about things that made him uncomfortable easing because he was focused on Laddin. "I can't believe you can say that with a straight face."

"Hey, I'm not just a pretty face. I can tell my Fetid Feta from Smoked Gouda any day."

"And here I thought you were just a great lay."

He felt Laddin smile against his back. "I'm a man of many talents."

They bantered back and forth for a bit, settling into a rhythm of chuckles and quiet breaths. Eventually Laddin drifted off, his soft snores making Bruce think of the atmosphere in the firehouse late at night. He wondered if this was what being in a werewolf pack was like. Did firefighters and werewolves share that sense of family? The idea comforted him and allowed his mind to quiet into sleep.

Rest was beautiful and so welcome.

So the last thing he expected when he woke hours later was to find a fairy army practicing maneuvers on his chest. It wasn't a dream, and holy fuck, what the hell were they about to do to his dick?

Chapter 13

FAIRY FIRECRACKERS ARE NOT AS FUN AS THEY SEEM

LADDIN WOKE with a start when he heard a strangled cry from Bruce. Their bodies were intertwined, and though he lifted his head, he couldn't seem to move away from him.

WTF?

Holy shit, he was tied down!

The memory of being suffocated by fairy cheese had him straining in real panic. His head started pounding, his breath heaved, and he fought, fought, fought like a demon possessed.

"Ow! Laddin! Shit!" The words were punctuated with grunts, and somewhere from the edge of his vision, he saw bright yellow lights tumbling and spiraling away. He didn't care. He needed to get free, and it was working. First a shoulder, then a foot. And then he was grabbing and ripping at whatever the hell was on top of him. Which—now that he was mostly free—turned out to be his bedroll.

He blinked while Bruce took a breath with him. His eyes were dark, his worry clear.

"Can you turn on the light?" Bruce asked, his voice low and quiet.

The light. Right! He'd left a camp light right by the bed. He banged down with his fist to turn it on, and the fury of the motion made him feel better… until he looked around closer and saw the bright yellow lights for what they were.

Pixies.

He rubbed a hand over his face and tried to calm his racing heart. "I told you I'd give you answers at dawn. It's not fucking dawn."

"These aren't the same fairies," Bruce said. His voice was low and filled with tension. Laddin blinked as he focused on his lover, only to see what the problem was.

Bruce was roped down like Gulliver had been by the Lilliputians. Slender stripes of white light lay in even lines across his naked body. Extra layers pinned down his far wrist and ankle, and all of it seemed to sizzle slightly. Oh crap! When Laddin sniffed, he smelled burned flesh. The only part of Bruce's body that was free of the burning white ropes was where Laddin's arm had stretched across Bruce's upper torso and neck. Since Laddin had been in a bedroll, he'd been protected. But Bruce had fallen asleep lying on his back, completely exposed.

Holy shit. He had to get those ropes of light off of Bruce. He reached forward, but Bruce quickly stopped him. "No! Look at your arm."

He looked, and sure enough, there were white lines like string cheese causing a low-level burn that hurt like hell. The only thing that had protected him was the bedroll. He tried to pull off the line from his arm, but the

stuff wouldn't budge, and it burned his thumb and fore-
finger where he grabbed hold.

It didn't matter. He'd freed himself when he
shoved himself upright. There had to be a way to haul
that shit off Bruce. So he grabbed his discarded T-shirt,
wrapped it around his fingers, and tried to pull one of
those ropes off Bruce.

It didn't work, though he kept pulling, even when
his T-shirt disintegrated where it touched the ropes.
Worse, the more he tugged, the brighter and hotter
the ropes became. And hell, the hair on Bruce's chest
and—shit—at his groin was smoldering now. Laddin
patted the flame out, but he doubted that would prevent
the next spark.

Why the hell had he ever thought fairies were cute?

"Get that shit off him now!" he commanded.

"We have beaten the Windy Wolf in fair combat,"
a tiny voice said.

Laddin looked, but he couldn't see the speaker.
What he did see was a dozen lights gathered in a mass
at the far side of Bruce's head. He was trying to sort
out some sense of form from the bright things, but it
was like picking out individual lights in a firecracker
explosion. They moved too fast and were too bright for
him to catch. And then suddenly, a glowing ball soared
through the air and exploded in bright blue color like
a firecracker above Bruce's chest. It was really pretty, except it burst with real force. Two more launched,
and Laddin tried to bat them away. He got the red one
quickly, tossing it up toward the ceiling to burst in brilliant crimson. But he couldn't get to the second one
in time, and it exploded against his hand with vicious
pain. "Stop that!" Laddin ordered.

"We defeat the Windy Wolf!"

And again, more firecrackers launched. Laddin hit them away as fast as he could, but it was a losing game. There seemed to be no end of firecrackers, and he couldn't sit here and play defense the whole time. Especially since he was getting the shit burned out of his hands. Every impact felt like a bee sting, hot and sharp on his palm, but at least they weren't exploding on top of Bruce.

"Stop it!" he yelled again. "Why are you doing this?"

"Acknowledge our win!" the voice said again. "We have beaten the Windy Wolf!"

Finally he found the speaker—a beautiful fairy woman wearing a flower hat larger than her entire body. In fact, it was hard to see her face because she had tilted it so far back to look at him, she should have toppled backward. Except normal physics didn't seem to apply to fairies.

"Sure, sure. You win—"

"No!" Bruce grunted from the floor. "Find out the forfeit first!"

"What?"

Bruce rolled his eyes. "Don't you know any-thing about betting? You can't let someone win with-out knowing what you lose." He blew out a breath. "I thought you went to public school."

Apparently not the same kind of public school as Bruce. He took a breath and tried to focus. God, he needed coffee. Obviously this wasn't a simple barroom bet over favorite teams. This was fairy bargaining, and Bruce was right. He couldn't agree to anything without understanding the terms.

"Stop the… uh… game. We will discuss terms."

"We discuss!" the female fairy said as she grabbed her flower hat and threw it hard onto Bruce's belly.

Bruce groaned as the hat seemed to explode. The resulting welt on his belly grew red and hot right beneath her feet.

"Stop that!" Laddin snapped. He was pissed off now, and damn it, Bruce couldn't take much more of this. And his own hands were already swelling. "What's your name?"

"I am Dollarback Erin Rodger-Dodger! I run back and fall forward, I rush for yards, and I am in charge of the Superest Bowl there is!"

Well, that was a mashup of random football terms. And even he knew that Aaron Rodgers was male. But again, that wasn't the point.

"I hail you, Rodger-Dodger. What are you trying to win?"

"Power! Glory!"

In the background, the fairy lights all jumped up and down and cheered.

"Okay—"

"And passage to Fairyland." She stepped resolutely up Bruce's chest and hopped onto his chin. "The Windy Wolf has lost. He will give us passage."

"He doesn't know how." Then he looked at Bruce. "Why do they think you can?"

"I have no idea!" Bruce grumbled.

Meanwhile, Erin Rodger-Dodger held up a glowing light—another firecracker. If she spiked that down on Bruce's eye, he'd lose it. "We will throw fire until he does," she cried.

Bruce growled in response and strained his head, but those white ropes lay across his chin and neck. His head was pinned down, and the more he strained, the more it burned hot lines into his skin.

"That's enough!" Laddin said, slapping the fairy away. It was surprisingly hard to do, given her tiny size, and the firecracker exploded against his hand, making him clench it in pain. But as long as he was bigger than them, he would break Bruce free if he had to burn the shit out of both his hands.

So that's what he did. First he studied the white lines, looking hard to find where they seemed to be pinned to the ground. If he squinted really hard, he could make out tiny pins. Maybe? It was all he had to go on, but there was no way he could pull those out with his fingernails. He needed…

The toolbox. Good thing he knew exactly where it was in the van. He looked down at Bruce and mouthed, "Hold on." Then, before Bruce had a chance to react, Laddin leaped up and ran straight for the van.

The fairy lights followed him. He knew it because little fireworks explosions kept going off around his head… and because he could smell his own burnt hair. But he didn't let that stop him as he grabbed the box and ran straight back to Bruce. A moment later he had the thing flipped open, grabbed the pliers, and used them on the nearest rope pin. Then he hauled on it with all his might.

The thing was like concrete. While the firecrackers kept going off, Laddin squeezed the pliers hard and used all his back muscles to haul upward. He felt like a young King Arthur pulling on the sword set in stone. Below him, he watched Bruce flinch. His eyes were squeezed tight against sparks, and he looked haggard. But he didn't cry out.

And then—hallelujah—the pin gave way. It came out with what felt like a sudden pop, and Laddin almost lost his grip on the pliers as his arms flew up. The white rope flew to the side as well, coming off Bruce's neck to expose a dark red burn underneath.

Shit, that looked awful. But it didn't matter. Laddin focused on the next pin, this one tied to a rope that restricted Bruce's shoulders. Fortunately, this one didn't take as much work. He wasn't sure why, but that pin came up faster and easier. As did the next and the next.

Finally Bruce was free enough that he could help, and he started by batting away firecrackers. He levered himself upright and hissed as one of the white lines burned into his belly.

"Don't move! You'll cut yourself in half!" Laddin snapped.

Bruce stilled, his abs tight as he held a half sit-up. A quick glance at his eyes told Laddin that he was watching the fairies, ready to knock away any incoming firecrackers. Good. That freed Laddin to go to the next pin. He worked as quickly as he could, pulling pins with steady progression down Bruce's body. But his hands were swollen, and sweat wasn't making it any easier to grip the pliers.

"Goddamn fucking...." Bruce swore as he continued to bat aside fireworks, his bulging muscles only making the remaining ropes burn deeper into his legs.

Eventually, after long eons of agony, Laddin got the last rope unpinned, tossing if off Bruce's right ankle. And when it was done, he whipped around to confront the fairy assholes. Except there wasn't a single fairy in sight. None. The only thing he saw was the flickering flames of a barn fire.

Fucking hell.

Chapter 14

FIGHTING FIRES AND
BUNNY RABBITS ALIKE

BRUCE SMELLED the fire before he saw any
flames. It was a scent he had trained for, and he knew
just what to do. The problem was, he knew what to do
while wearing protective clothing and carrying gear.
Right now he was buck naked and cursing from more
than a dozen burns. His training told him to get out
now. He grabbed a shovel instead.

"Go!" he bellowed at Laddin. "Get help!"

He started shoveling a perimeter around the flames
and dumping the dirt on whatever smoldered. The biggest danger in a barn fire was the dust in the air. That
stuff ignited like kindling and could bring the whole
place down on them in seconds.

Fortunately they'd already had the spring rains, so
there'd been some dampness in the air. It was probably the only reason the whole building wasn't currently
ablaze. That meant his main worry now was the straw.
So he shoveled and stomped in his bare feet, and he

flinched when one of the car alarms started blaring like it was the second coming. The van went off next.

"What the fuck?" he growled as Laddin came running forward with a small fire extinguisher in his hand.

"Getting help," Laddin said as he pulled the pin on the fire extinguisher.

"Get out!"

Laddin ignored him as he started spraying.

"Over there!" Bruce said, pointing to the nearest bale of hay. It didn't look like it was on fire yet, but if it caught, they were screwed. Thankfully, Laddin didn't argue. He went where he was told and sprayed with quick efficiency while Bruce took care of the rest. He even had a moment to notice that Laddin—also stark naked—had some handsome muscle definition and a tight ass. His backside was currently sporting ugly burn welts and that bothered Bruce, but there wasn't time to tend to wounds while he was shoveling dirt onto straw as if he was digging a trench. Which he was.

When he finally looked up, he realized the work was pretty much finished. He and Laddin had done it. And at the very same moment, Josh and Nero opened the barn doors.

"Wait!" he bellowed. The sudden inrush of air could be a problem. He didn't want a breeze stirring any flames back to life. They didn't listen to him, of course. So he stood with his shovel ready as he scanned for flames. Fortunately his nose seemed to work better now that he was a werewolf, so that helped him zero in on the few embers that were left. They were nothing big, but a single spark could set the whole place ablaze.

He stomped over and began shoveling some more while Josh's voice rang clearly over the car alarms.

"Did you set fire to the barn?"

Nero cut him off, proving that he was the more experienced first responder. "What do you need? Where?"

Bruce held up his hand, still searching every nook and cranny. But he didn't see anything, and even better, he didn't smell anything except his own rancid sweat and the dirt he'd been shoveling.

Meanwhile, Laddin turned off a car alarm—thank heaven—and the second abruptly shut off as well. In the pounding silence, Nero barked his question again.

"What do you need?"

Laddin looked at him, and Bruce took a deep breath. "I think it's out. We need to watch for a few minutes just in case, but Laddin needs burn treatment."

"Me?" Laddin snorted. "You look like you were thrown on a griddle and covered with hot coals."

Did he? He really didn't want to look… or feel. Because once the adrenaline wore off, he knew it was going to hurt like hell.

"Can you shift?" Nero asked.

Laddin nodded. "I can, though I was trying to save it."

"Not with that arm. Was someone playing tic-tac-toe on your back?"

"Yeah," Bruce muttered. "Pixie chicks."

Laddin snorted a laugh. "You were waiting to say that, weren't you?"

Bruce shrugged. That pun had slipped out, but it wasn't bad. Meanwhile, Nero snapped his fingers at Laddin. "Get furry." Then he looked at Bruce. "What about you? Got control of your wolf?"

Hell no, and it burned his pride to admit it. "I'll use the burn cream."

Meanwhile, Bing and Yordan appeared, both looking haggard. They were running, and Yordan set a hand on the barn door as he took in deep breaths. "What do you need?" he gasped while Bing surveyed everything with dark, serious eyes.

"Faster responders," Nero muttered while Josh found a switch and flicked it on. The barn was suddenly flooded with electric light, enough to illuminate Laddin, who padded forward as a red wolf with short cinnamon fur and a smile that showed he was fully healed.

Bruce exhaled in relief when he came close and buried his hands in the warm fur. "Can you sniff around? Find anything smoking and let me know."

Laddin nodded and set off to do a tour of the barn. Meanwhile, Nero was watching Yordan.

"You look like shit," he said, and Yordan bristled. He was in shorts and boots, which gave them a good look at his gray skin, where every cut and bruise stood out in livid relief.

"Talk to me after you fight a lich. What happened to you?"

That was a good question. Josh was walking stiffly back from the light switch. His clothing looked good—his skin too—but he looked bone-tired. Nero did too, and one of his eyes was swollen, and there was blood on his pants.

"Phantom kangaroos," Nero said.

"What?" Yordan barked.

"You heard me. We were holding a perimeter while some witches tried a demon locator spell and got attacked by ghost kangaroos."

Josh took up the tale. "It was easier to herd them away than figure out how to kill them, but one got Nero in the face with his tail. I thought he was dead, but he shifted while still in the air. That bruise is from the landing." There was a tremor in his voice that Bruce recognized as true emotion—likely fear and relief mixed with adrenaline letdown. He'd heard it a thousand times, and it was more proof that Nero meant a great deal to Josh. That gave him a twinge of jealousy that was unworthy of him. If his brother had found true love, then good for him.

Assuming Nero returned the emotion.

"It'll heal," Nero said.

Meanwhile, Yordan pushed off the doorframe. "I wasn't questioning you. I want to know why kangaroo ghosts are showing up in Wisconsin."

A female voice answered from the door. "Because the demon wants them here." She spoke in a tone that reminded Bruce of bells, with a haunting melody in every note. But the sound only reflected a fraction of the beauty of the woman. She was small, a brunet, and had skin that glowed beneath the electrical light. Her eyes were mahogany with a strange light behind them. And though her lips and body curved in a way to tempt any man, there was a mystical innocence in the way she moved and in the high tenor of her voice. Bruce remembered her as Wulfric's mother, the same woman who had dragged him outside to sit on the porch all afternoon.

"Lady Kinstead," Nero said as he straightened to attention. "I'm sorry we disturbed you."

"Barn fires are deadly," she said as she looked straight at Bruce. Then her lips curved. "Aren't you a pretty one?"

Bruce flushed, realizing belatedly that he was still standing there in his birthday suit. He moved his hand and shovel to cover the important parts, but a moment later he realized he hadn't needed to. The woman was smiling and talking to wolf Laddin as she stepped around Bruce to pet Laddin's coat and press a kiss to his forehead.

"You're so sweet," she cooed.

Well, that pricked his pride. He couldn't remember a woman preferring a dog to him. Then he realized what a ridiculous thought that was. He crossed to the van to find something to wear. Weren't there extra clothes in there? Even though he knew it wasn't good to cover up his burns—hell, moving was sending bolts of fire across his skin—he wasn't going to stand naked in front of a woman while covered in grime and seeping welts. Especially a woman who preferred a wolf to him.

Except the moment he'd managed to pull on a pair of sweatpants, she left Laddin to look straight at him. He flushed—again—because damn it, at that moment he wanted a shower and some painkillers, not to be the center of attention. And he certainly didn't want to be asked questions he couldn't answer. But that didn't stop her from voicing them.

"What did you learn about the demon?"

What demon? He'd stumbled across evil cheeses and fairies with fruit. Meanwhile, Bing peered at him.

"That was from a demon?" he asked, gesturing to Bruce's wounds.

Nero shook his head. "Pixie chicks."

Yordan's head snapped up. "That a joke?"

Nero shrugged, but Yordan peered at the burns.

"The chickens pecked at you?"

"No," Bruce rasped as he shoved his feet into his sneakers. "Pixies pinned me down with burning ropes. Laddin pulled them off me."

"What does that have to do with chickens?"

Lady Kinstead waved her hand at the men. Bruce had no idea what the gesture meant, but the men fell silent as she stared at him.

"What did you learn?"

That pixies weren't even remotely cute. That if it hadn't been for Laddin, he'd probably be dead or turned into a frog or whatever crazy shit fairies did to uncooperative victims. He didn't learn a damn thing about a demon, but he did figure something else out.

"They want to go to Fairyland."

She laughed in a mystically beautiful and wholly creepy way, because really, that kind of dreamlike sound shouldn't be coming from a body as earthly looking as hers. But it did, and it took him a moment to focus on her words instead of her form. "All earth fairies want to go to Feyland."

He thought it was Fairyland, but whatever. "Why?"

"Don't you want to go to Heaven? To talk to God?"

Uh, yes, he supposed. He hadn't ever really thought about it.

"Feyland is their Heaven. They are created from its magic."

"They want to die?"

She rolled her eyes. "So pretty, but so stupid."

Was she talking about him or the fairies? Probably him, because she continued to explain.

"Fairies don't die like you do. They can only go to Heaven if you take them."

"But I can't take them."

"You can if you eat the apple."

Nero jerked his head around. "What apple? Where?"

"Make it a condition of eating the apple," the woman said.

Bruce couldn't believe she was asking this of him. "I'm not helping a bunch of arsonist fairies get into heaven."

"Not the pixies," she said. "The demon. Demand that Bitterroot tell you where the demon is before the entire world dies. He will agree. He knows Feyland will be hurt too, if the Earth dies."

From the opposite side of the barn, Josh banged his fist against a hay bale. "Fucking perfect. First a cherry, now an apple."

"No!" Bruce snapped. "I am not going to eat more fairy fruit!"

Nero blew out a breath. "You might have to, if it's the only way to find the demon." His expression was grave. "We're facing the end of the world, here. If we can't stop the poison from expanding into Lake Michigan, the whole continent will be contaminated."

"It's not just an apple," Bruce growled. How the hell didn't they know that?

"Of course it's not just an apple," Nero argued. "But we've been looking for weeks and haven't found the demon. According to the science crew, there's only a few days left before the dead zone hits Lake Michigan. If we poison the Great Lakes, we poison Canada, the US, and eventually the world. Everything will die."

Bruce knew that. Fucking hell, it was all over the news, 24/7. They all had this graphic of the lake at the center of an expanding circle. Some drew the circle in red like blood, others in green like poison, as if that made any difference. The point was that everything inside that circle died—slowly at first, but with increasing speed the closer you got to the center of the lake. And that circle was growing every second of every day. Foot by foot, it was expanding, poisoning the land with cyanide and putting some unknown crap into the air that was killing everything on the earth. No one knew exactly how far it had to go until the world ended. But they all agreed that once it touched Lake Michigan, North America was screwed, and the western hemisphere soon after that. The latest projections said they were only days away from that happening. A week at most.

And there was no solution in sight.

But as much as Bruce wanted to be the savior for everyone, he already knew it wouldn't work. "I've asked. Bitter—" He cut his word off. He did not want to call the guy. "He doesn't know where it is."

"He must," Lady Kinstead said. "I have seen it. If you eat the apple, you save the world."

That sounded like a great idea... not. A crazy beauty tells him to eat the apple and whammo, the world is saved. Right. And yet all the people around him seemed to take her seriously. Worse, her words were an exact echo of what Bitterroot had said to him, which was freaky scary. Especially since he did not know how to save the world!

Then Nero started drawing that same map in the dirt with his boot. "That's the dead zone," he said. "That's Lake Michigan. We're right fucking here." He planted his boot at the edge of the line representing Lake Michigan. "A few more feet and we're all dead."

Bruce threw up his hands. "He doesn't know. I already asked. I already offered."

Josh closed his eyes. "Of course you did."

"What the hell is that supposed to mean?" Bruce said as he rounded on his brother. He wasn't really angry at Josh, though the guy was being a prick. He was overwhelmed and in pain—and for most of his life, Josh had been his target whenever he felt like shit.

"It means—" Josh answered, but Nero got there first.

"Don't get into that crap now," Nero snapped at Josh. Then he rounded on Bruce. "You asked him already?"

Bruce nodded. "The fairy prince doesn't know."

The woman crossed her arms in anger. "The fey know," she said. "Why do you think I am here?"

He had no idea.

She stomped her foot. "Eat the apple! Make them tell!"

Nero grimaced. "Do we call him now?"

She pursed her lips and her eyes grew vague. Or bright. Or something. Bruce couldn't even tell what, but her entire face went weird. Then she solidified back to normal. "It must be him," she said, pointing at Bruce.

"I already asked. He didn't know."

"Then why do you still see the apple?"

He hadn't really been seeing it. It hadn't even been in the forefront of his thoughts right then. But at her question, the damned thing appeared before him, all bright and shiny and smelling like the apple pie he loved so much. He would have closed his eyes, but he knew it would remain there behind his eyelids. So instead, he focused on Josh as he gave his answer.

"He wants to enslave Josh. He said so."

Josh and Nero jolted at that, both of them reacting in predictable ways. Josh shook his head, his expression filled with defiance. Nero frowned, clearly thinking hard in the way of a guy used to sorting through military strategy. But neither said a word.

Bruce looked at the woman. "I don't know how I fit into the picture, and I don't know why the bastard picked me to offer the fruit to. But I know he wants my brother, and I'm not going to help him. He won't get Josh through me. Not ever."

Lady Kinstead glared at him. "Then your brother dies along with the entire world. At least a slave is alive."

Nero shook his head. "There has to be another way." He stared hard at the woman. "We have to find another way."

She sniffed. "What do you think we've been trying to do? You even went back in time, and you failed."

"I didn't—" He cut off his words, but Josh finished them for him.

"We did. In this timeline, we haven't changed a thing."

"Yes, we did!" Nero answered. "We know how to kill it now."

"Not if we can't find it."

And that was it—the big question for everyone. Where was the demon that was creating the expanding circle of death?

While everyone mulled over that disastrous question, Bruce chanced a look outside.

Oh fuck. It was a minute or two short of dawn. Laddin had set an alarm, but it had probably been drowned out by all the noise from the cars.

"Laddin!" he said. "You're late!" Laddin had promised to give the cheese pixies some answers at dawn—at the tree that was over a mile away!

"Late for what?" Nero asked.

But there wasn't time to explain. Wolf Laddin looked at the sky, whimpered in fear, and then took off. He was running like the wind as a wolf, and Bruce didn't hesitate to follow him, doing his best to keep up on his human feet. He wasn't nearly as fast, but there

was no way in hell he would let Laddin face those demon cheeses alone.

By the time Bruce rounded the barn and headed
out through the open field, he knew it was hopeless.
They weren't going to make it before dawn. Even Laddin, who was a distant streak of reddish brown in the
distance, wasn't going to get there in time. Bruce was
running like his life—or Laddin's life—depended on it,
but they didn't have a prayer.

"Eat the apple. You can run faster."

Bitterroot was back, hopping through the field
beside him like a damned bunny. He had no problem
keeping up, and Bruce wanted to kick him, just for the
hell of it. But he didn't have the time and he certainly
didn't have the breath. But as it turned out, he didn't
need it to talk to the creep. The bastard could pick his
thoughts right out of his head.

Fuck off! he thought as loud as he could.

Bitterroot ignored him. "Laddin's not going to
make it in time. And in case you haven't noticed, magical creatures are all very angry around here. Wisconsin
is one big knot of hate and fear. It is not going to go
well for your lover."

We're all pissed off. You should be too. We'll all
die if we don't stop that demon. So instead of hopping
like a jackrabbit beside me, tell us where the bastard is!

Then, out of spite, he imagined Bitterroot as an
ugly Peter Cottontail with buck teeth and donkey ears.
And to his shock, the fairy abruptly changed into exactly what he'd pictured—complete with a polka-dot
bow tie and a ratty straw hat. If he'd had the breath, he
would have burst out laughing as Bitterroot stumbled at
the sudden change in his body.

"I am angry, you idiot. And I'm trying to help!"

Bullshit.

"Eat the apple, you fool. Lovina was right. The Seers have all said you will eat it."

And save the world?

"Sometimes. It's not clear."

Great. And because he wasn't stupid, he knew that the two might not be connected at all. He could save the world by entirely different means. Or not save it at all. So this argument was getting them nowhere.

What do you get?

"Other than a saved Earth?"

Yes.

"Standard contract."

Like what? My firstborn child? Wasn't that what all the fairy tales wanted?

"Don't be insulting. We cherish human children. I am the grandchild of a human girl. It is how I am who I am."

An asshole?

"A prince. Listen, I'm offering you a bargain here. I'm hoping that more power will save your world and mine."

Testy, testy, he mocked. Because the guy's tone was aggrieved, as if he really was doing something against his own better interest. Which made Bruce distrust him even more. Anyone who said *This is for your own good* was lying. Still, the offer was getting tempting.

What kind of power would I get?

"I told you. You'll get *more*."

What the hell does that mean?

Bitterroot rolled his eyes. "Whatever you intend to be more." He gestured to Bruce's feet. "You want speed, yes? You would have more speed."

Bruce did want to go faster. He was only three-quarters of the way there, and the sun was already up. He couldn't see Laddin, and his heart squeezed in fear for the guy.

"It's not just speed. If you intend violence, you'll become vicious."

"No," he rasped. "Never."

"Then you'll have more strength to carry children out of fires. And more ecstasy when you ejaculate."

Bruce winced at the graphic image that came to mind. *My ejaculations are fine.*

"But they could be more."

Hell, the guy definitely knew how to tempt him. No one needed more—not in the way the fairy described— but Bruce sure as hell *wanted* it. Big, powerful guys had the advantage in firefighting. It was simple physics. And who didn't want bigger and better O's?

All I care about now is Laddin.

"Then take more power to help him. Because the earth sprites are angry." The bunny eyes narrowed as he gazed into the distance.

What are they doing to Laddin?

"He should have bargained more carefully."

What—?

But it was too late. Prince Hop-Along was gone.

Chapter 15

SMALL PRINT? WHAT SMALL PRINT?

BRUCE TRIPPED on something. The ground was uneven, and he'd been paying attention to Laddin, not where he planted his feet. But he could see Laddin now. The guy was fully human and leaning against the tree that was their destination. Bruce couldn't see the fairies, but he knew they were there. Especially since his last glimpse of Laddin had shown the man talking. That might have been reassuring… if there hadn't been a wildness in his eyes.

Suddenly Bruce face-planted with a grunt, banging up his head, getting dirt in his burns, and making for a very noisy entrance. He couldn't even hear what Laddin was saying over his thundering pulse and his desperate gasps for air. He'd run here full-tilt after fighting a barn fire, and he was done. It was barely five minutes past dawn, and already his adrenaline stores were gone.

He meant to push himself to get up, but instead he breathed in dirt while the apple shimmered just in front of his mouth. All he'd have to do was roll forward and take a big ol' bite.

He didn't, but he was salivating for sure. By the time he got enough energy to push himself to his feet, he was surrounded by angry-looking cheeses.

Great. There was no way he'd be able to leap in and drag Laddin to safety now. Bruce took a moment more to catch his breath and slow his heart rate. And then, finally, he could hear what Laddin was saying.

"...three inches deep. C-4 is the easiest, but raw gunpowder will serve as well. The fuse should be...."

WTF? Bruce pushed forward, barely managing to avoid stepping on a militant-looking provolone. "Why is he talking about explosives?" He directed his question to the Grand Cheesy, whose name he couldn't really remember. The fairy stood in front of Laddin with his arms crossed and his head cocked to the side. And hell, now that Bruce was breathing more normally, the smell hit him. It wasn't a big concern right now, but he didn't want to start gagging at a key moment.

The grand whomever turned and gave him a bow. Laddin was still talking about fuse types in a steady though desperate voice. "I greet you, Farting Friend," said the Cheesy.

"I'm not—" He almost said *a friend* but realized that would be antagonistic, so he quickly adjusted his words. "—farting for you."

"What the hell?" He heard Josh's voice; then his brother stumbled forward. Bruce had been so focused on catching up to Laddin that he hadn't realized he'd been followed. Josh had arrived. His brother could always run fast, though he too was obviously winded. Behind him was Bing, running silently through the field. And much farther back were Yordan and Nero.

Bruce could see they wouldn't be able to help. The fairy cheeses were already marshaling a perimeter. Josh was being cordoned off by string cheese, and though Bing might not see it yet, they were preparing to launch some kind of hard white cheese boulders at him from the slingshot they'd used the day before.

"Stay back," Bruce ordered. "The American slices will suffocate you, the string cheese is like steel, and I think the blue cheese is poisonous."

He watched as Bing nodded and slowed, pointing to his mouth before gesturing back at Yordan and Nero. Bruce guessed his gesture meant he'd tell the other two. Meanwhile Josh was frowning at Laddin. "Why is he talking explosives?"

"—det cord. That's a thin, flexible plastic tube filled with pentaerythritol tetranitrate—"

"Quiet," ordered a voice near Josh. "You do not have leave to speak!" It was a fairy made of crumbly cheese with blue streaks in it, with stilts for legs. As soon as it came near, Josh started gagging on the stench. Bruce held back his choking, but only because he was upwind.

"Stilton!" the Cheesy ordered. "Stand guard!"

"Aye-aye, Cheesy!" the stinky cheese answered with a salute.

Meanwhile, Laddin kept talking while his eyes rolled around in their sockets as if he was searching desperately for something.

Trying to keep his voice calm, Bruce spoke as respectfully as possible. "What have you done to Laddin? Why is he talking like that?"

"He broke our bargain."

Yeah, Bruce already knew, but he tried for logic. "He came here. He was going to tell you what he'd learned."

"He promised answers at dawn. He broke that promise." The Cheesy folded his moldy arms. "So he gives answers now. All of them." The cheese grinned. "Until I say stop."

"And when will you say stop?"

The Cheesy didn't answer, but he didn't have to. Nero had come up behind Josh, and he rasped out the answer. "He won't say stop until the victim dies. No food, no water, no rest. Just endless talking."

Bruce turned around and stared at the cheese. "Until Laddin…." He couldn't say the word *dies*.

"Yes. Unless we negotiate something different."

It took a moment for Bruce to absorb that, but he always thought clearly in a crisis. That meant that *he'd* have to do the negotiating, even though he had no freaking clue how to do it. "Not we," he said to Nero. "Me. I'm their… friend." He turned back to the Cheesy. "Right? You and me, we can discuss this."

Thankfully, no one scoffed at the idea that he could get Laddin out of this. They were all still recovering from the run, while Laddin kept talking as if he was reading out of a detonation manual.

"You can buy det cord at…."

"He failed to keep his promise," Cheesy said. "I win."

"Yes, you do," Bruce soothed. "But what does the win get you? You don't need to know how to set det cord." Or at least he prayed they didn't. "You need to know how to get to your heaven, right?" And when Cheesy just stared at him, Bruce said the word. "To Fairyland. You want to go to—"

"Fairyland! Fairyland! Fairyland!" The cheese chorus kicked up, right on cue.

"That was his first answer," Cheesy said as he looked back at Laddin. "He said we cannot go. But he lied."

At that moment, the fairy chorus changed from screaming "Fairyland" to chanting "lies." That was bad enough, but while Bruce had been talking to the Cheesy, the group setting up the slingshot had redirected their white cheese chunks. They now pointed it at Laddin and took aim. Bruce didn't even notice it until his peripheral vision caught the launch of a big hunk of something that separated into three parts in the air, then nailed Laddin in the face, chest, and belly.

Crap!

At least it wasn't that suffocating American cheese… yet. The boulders landed with heavy thuds, and Laddin cried out in pain. But with his next breath, he continued explaining det cord, though he sagged against the tree.

Now that Bruce looked closer, he realized Laddin wasn't leaning against the tree—he was tied to it by string cheese. And worse, the places on his body pummeled by the cheese were already welting up.

"It wasn't a lie—" Bruce argued, but Stilton had come closer and puffed a cloud of noxious air his way.

"You will take us to Fairyland," the Cheesy said. "Smoked Gouda has seen it."

"Everybody keeps saying that, but I don't know how!" Damn it to hell, this was frustrating. "We spoke with the other fairies. The girl ones with the flower hats."

Cheesy spun around. "They will surrender?"

Bruce shook his head. "They want to go to Fairyland too."

"Fairyland! Fairyland!"

Bruce clenched his hands. He wanted to squash every single fairy here, but damn it, he'd tried that before. He'd flattened them, eaten them, and even farted them, but they'd come back stronger than ever. It was impossible to negotiate with illogical beings who didn't die. Especially when they were perfectly capable of killing every man here.

Maybe if he focused on why they thought he would take them to Fairyland, he'd get some answers. He turned to Smoked Gouda, who was reclining in a dark fog at the base of the tree. "What exactly did you see?"

Gouda opened his eyes to half-mast, puffed out a bunch more smoke like a guy with a pipe, except that his body was the pipe, and then smiled in a dreamy kind of way. "You are the path to Heaven." He closed his eyes again.

Fortunately Bruce had some experience negotiating with stoners, so he knew what to say to that. "I'm the path, right?"

Gouda nodded.

"And this path won't do jack shit for you if you kill his friend."

Gouda did absolutely nothing. Right. He had to talk to the Cheesy.

"Grand Cheesy, according to Smoked Gouda, I'm the path to Fairyland. Well, in order to do that, I need him"—he pointed to Laddin—"healthy, strong, and whole. You've got to release him."

"It is our right—"

"Of course it is. I'm not arguing about that. I'm talking about your ultimate goal." He took a single step forward and invested all his strength in his words. "I need him."

The Cheesy wasn't even listening. "It is our right to have answers."

Bruce was so sick of people who talked about their rights without thinking about the damage they were causing. "How about this? What if I bring a fairy prince to you? Then you can talk to him about getting to Fairy-land, huh? Maybe that's the way to get you over there."

Cheesy turned and gave him a big grin. "You are indeed great, Farting Friend."

He really had to get them to use his real name. "But I won't do it unless you release Laddin. Him and all of us."

"Agreed!"

Really?

Then Cheesy did something truly disturbing. He ripped out one moldy eye and threw it at Laddin. It hit Laddin in the chest with a puff of grossness, but it worked. The string cheese released, Laddin slumped off the tree, and—best of all—he stopped talking.

Hallelujah! Except Laddin was going to fall on his face.

Bruce had fast reflexes, but even so, he barely got there in time. He caught Laddin around the torso and eased him down to the ground. Then he held Laddin tight through the shakes, murmuring all the comfort words he knew.

"I've got you. Just breathe. It'll be okay now. I've got you."

Except the interlude didn't last long. As Laddin's shakes began to quiet, Cheesy stomped in front of them. "Where is this prince?"

Looked like there was no rest for the weary. Fine. He looked up and said the words. "Bitterroot, I call you. Bitterroot, get your ass over here. Bitterroot, come now!" He was pretty sure all he needed to say was the guy's name, but he wanted to sound official.

Right on cue, the fairy appeared, but his expression was a smirk. "Nice try, but I will not speak with them."

"What? Why the fuck not?"

"Because they are earth sprites, and I don't like them."

Bigoted much? "Too bad," Bruce snapped. He pointed straight at Bitterroot's face and spoke to Cheesy. "There he is. Negotiate away."

Except the Cheesy was looking every which way, as was everyone else in the clearing. "Where?" the Cheesy cried. "Where is he?"

"Right there!" Bruce repeated and pointed hard.

Nero groaned. "We can't see him. He's refusing to negotiate, isn't he?"

Cheesy continued to scream, hopping up and down so that chunks fell off him in little tiny puffs of rancidness. "You promised I could speak with the fairy prince. You promised! And if I do not, then you all are forfeit!"

"All of us?" Fucking hell. Were they all about to start spouting meaningless facts until they died?

"That's the deal with fairies," Josh said, his voice tight with anger. "You pulled us into the bargain, so we all pay the price—which they get to pick, by the way, because you didn't specify the forfeit." Then he glared at Bruce as if he was supposed to know this stuff.

Meanwhile, Bitterroot held out the apple to Bruce. "Maybe if you take a bite, you'll figure out the answer. Maybe you just need more brainpower."

"Asshole," Bruce muttered, but he started reaching for the apple because damned if he could figure out a better answer. At least until Nero spoke up.

"Bitterroot, Bitterroot, Bitterroot! Show yourself, you fucker. You owe me!"

The fairy spun around to face Nero, his body and outfit changing to normal-looking elf clothes complete with a human-like body, except for the butterflies clinging to his hair. That was new.

"Not anymore, I don't!" Bitterroot snarled. But in this, he apparently made a mistake, because all around him, the cheese fairies gasped and pointed. Then they mobbed him.

Cheeses from every direction ran, jumped, and tumbled straight for the fairy prince. It was a swarm of fairy cheese, which would have been hysterical if the situation hadn't been so dire. Cheesy was jumping up and down, screaming, "Talk to me! Talk to me!" But all the others were repeating his name over and over, "Bitterroot! Bitterroot! Bitterroot!"

For his part, the fairy prince began fighting as Bruce and Laddin had the day before. He slapped the creatures away. He kicked, flicked, and even bit when they came near his face. In truth, it didn't look like he meant to chomp down. It was more like he was gritting his teeth, but one of the brie was a little too close. Or maybe it squeezed between his lips—it was hard to tell. But it didn't matter. Once it was done, the cheese was inside him.

Bruce knew what came next. He'd lived through it yesterday. But it didn't happen all at once. First, Bitterroot threw his hands down and bellowed, "No!" while a single butterfly flew up from his hair and disappeared.

The word reverberated through the field like an earthquake. Fairies tumbled away like sand thrown up by a storm. The only reason Bruce and Laddin didn't fall was because they were already on the ground, but the others stumbled and went down. All except Bing, who was apparently part cat. And while everyone was recovering, Bitterroot got a horrified expression on his face.

It started out with a grimace, then went to a half-lurch as he apparently tried to burp. Yeah, Bruce knew from experience that wasn't going to work. Then

Bitterroot clutched his stomach and glared. "I hate earth sprites," he growled.

Bruce could relate. He glanced at the others as they pushed to their feet. "I'd back up. He's going to blow."

And sure enough, there was no stopping it. Bitterroot hunched over. His face twisted, and his back arched. And then there came the longest, most appallingly big fart Bruce had ever heard. It went on and on while everyone watched with horrified expressions. The humans scrunched up their faces in disgust and maybe a little sympathy. Because really, this had to suck. But the cheese fairies stepped forward with rapt expressions.

"Bilious Brie," they whispered. They said it over and over again, their voices growing stronger with each repetition.

And similar to what had happened with Bruce, the pixie shot out from Bitterroot's ass. But unlike Bruce's experience, this fairy was not tiny. No, the cheese increased in size the longer Bitterroot farted. Brie started out the size of a finger, then became a hand, then a boy, and still it grew. While everyone watched, Bilious Brie formed into a roly-poly man of more than six feet. But true to the bilious name, the cheese had a greenish-gray cast to it.

"Whee!" he cried as he danced around in a circle of joy.

"Bilious Brie!" the cheese fairies exclaimed. Well, not all of them. The Grand Cheesy was noticeably upset.

"Talk to me! Talk to me!" he screamed, but it was useless.

Bitterroot gave everyone a contemptuous glare before he winked out of sight.

"No!" Cheesy screamed in true despair. And then he whipped around, pointing an angry finger at each man in turn. "He didn't talk to me! He didn't talk to me! You forfeit everything!"

"He spoke," Bruce countered. "He said no."

"And that he hated earth sprites," Josh inserted. Which was true, except that didn't seem to matter to Cheesy.

"That was to you! He spoke to you, not me!"

Unfortunately, that was probably true. And even worse for Cheesy's mood was that all his fellow chees-es were now gathering around Bilious Brie. They leaped up on the guy, hugging him, which left Cheesy in a terrible position. And naturally, Bruce wasted no time in pointing it out.

"You seem to be losing your followers. I think the Grand Cheesy title is about to go to Billy over there."

"I am the Grand Cheesy!" he said, stomping his little foot.

No one seemed to care, least of all his fellow cheeses. Worse, they started echoing Brie's squeals of joy. Every "whee!" had a fairy chorus complete with clapping of hands and stomping of tiny feet.

And that was when the Grand Cheesy got really angry. His face scrunched up and his moldy bits turned black. But he didn't yell at his fellow cheeses. Instead he looked at Bruce, then at Laddin and everyone else in the field.

"You will pay me the forfeit."

"Shit," Yordan mumbled. "This is gonna suck."

"Answers! Now!" He pointed at Bing, who began talking in Chinese. His eyes widened and he apparently struggled to keep silent. It didn't work, and the strain had him dropping to his knees. Yordan dashed to the man but was caught by Cheesy's finger-point next. The big guy managed to make it to Bing's side but then started saying something about someone begatting someone else. Bruce recognized the phrases as *Bible* verses, and Yordan looked completely horrified by the words spilling from his mouth.

Nero was next. He'd been running forward, probably to tackle Cheesy, but Bruce already knew that wouldn't work. Just as he got near enough to slam his fist down, his body lurched as he started listing stats from personnel files. He started with Josh, talking about his academic accomplishments and family tree.

Meanwhile, Laddin started shaking in Bruce's arms. He moaned "no" in such a despairing whisper that it wrenched Bruce's attention away from everyone else. "No," he repeated. Laddin was terrified of repeating what he'd just escaped. His body shook, his eyes were wild, and he rocked back and forth while whispering *no* over and over.

This man, who had been nicknamed Mr. Happy by his teammates, was completely undone. If he started listing more explosive facts, it was going to break him. Bruce knew it as surely as he knew his own name. Even if they found a way out, it would destroy Laddin.

So he made the only decision he could. "Grand Cheesy," he said. "I will bargain again. I'll give you something you really want."

Josh was holding Nero, and he glared at Bruce in fury. "Haven't you done enough?"

Bruce ignored him, though the words hurt. He was doing the best he could. It wasn't like anyone else had better ideas.

"What do you offer?"

"I'll make you big," he said. He pointed at Bilious Brie. "Maybe as big as him."

"You can promise this?" Cheesy asked.

Bruce wanted to say yes right away, but he'd learned that there was always a loophole, always a problem. So he asked the smartest guy he knew if his logic was sound. Looking at Josh, he spoke quickly.

"When the fairies came out of me yesterday, they didn't come back big, but when Brie went through Bitterroot, he came out huge. That's because Bitterroot is made of fairy magic, right? Brie absorbed that magic and became large."

Josh frowned as he thought things through. "Yeah, I guess. But it's hard to say—"

"Good enough for me." He turned back to Cheesy. "I can promise to make you bigger. If I succeed, you will let all of us go and you'll never bother us again. If I screw up and it doesn't work, then you still let them go. You don't fucking touch any of them."

Laddin looked up, his eyes huge. "No, Bruce—"

Bruce kept going. "But you get me as your slave. Whatever you want."

"For a day!" Josh bellowed. "Just for a day."

"For your lifetime," Cheesy said. "Or I stay with what I have." He pointed a finger at Laddin. Jesus, he was going to hit Laddin next.

"Okay!" Bruce screamed. "I agree!" Then he reached out his hand. "You win, Bitterroot!" he bellowed into the air, knowing that the fairy prince was likely listening. "I'll eat it." Then, for extra emphasis, he repeated the asshole's name three times. "Bitterroot, Bitterroot, Bitterroot!"

"What?" Josh gasped. "Don't be an idiot!"

Bruce shot his brother a look of disbelief. Why couldn't Josh see that there weren't any other options? Then Mr. Salad Fairy appeared directly between him and Josh, and Bruce held out his hand for the apple.

"Standard terms?" Bitterroot asked.

"Yes. Fine." He rushed out the words before they could choke him. At this point he didn't care what the terms were. It was worth it if the others went free... if Laddin and Josh stayed safe.

"Done."

The apple plopped into Bruce's hand, and he didn't waste any time. He bit down into the red, juicy fruit, and he loved every damned bite. The tingle, the taste, even the smell was divine. Out of the corner of his eye, he saw a butterfly drift away on the wind, but it was a vague impression drowned out by the feeling of the power that started flooding his system. The *more* that Bitterroot had promised. His body strengthened as exhaustion disappeared. His mind thought ten times faster. A hundred times! He scanned the field and caught details he hadn't noticed before. Stupid things, irrelevant things, but he noticed them nonetheless. He saw that Josh had burn scars on his ankles, that Bilious Brie had a pasty white exterior but that the inside of his mouth was that sickly green color, and that Laddin had finally stopped shaking but was now holding on to Bruce like he had last night, with need mixed with tenderness. That, plus a healthy amount of terror.

And when the apple was all done, Bruce did an experiment. He was supposed to be more of whatever he focused on. He tightened his fist and brought it down on the dirt right next to Cheesy, all the while thinking about how his strength needed to be *more*.

It was. He smashed into the dirt as if he'd used Thor's hammer. Cheesy and the other cheeses didn't even blink, but everyone else did. And Bruce knew that it had worked.

That meant it was time for the yucky part. And it really sucked, because he still had that glorious taste of apple in his mouth. Fuck, he really didn't want to do this.

"Okay," he said to Cheesy. "Come on. Let me eat you."

Everyone else looked disgusted, but no more than Bruce felt. It was Cheesy who brushed a lumpy bit of feta off his arm and said pompously, "That is not dignified for a Grand Cheesy."

Bruce gaped. "Are you fucking kidding me?"

"If you wish to transfer magic to me, you can simply touch me."

Really? Well, thank God, because he didn't want to eat the guy anyway. Especially if it would save him a five-minute fart. So he took a deep breath and focused on giving *more* to Cheesy. More magic, more size, more whatever it was that had made Brie into a six-foot-tall walking nightmare. And he prayed with everything he had that this would work.

It didn't. At first.

There were long agonizing seconds when nothing seemed to change. But then the Grand Cheesy began to swell. Just like Brie, he started out the size of a finger, then quickly expanded. Hand-sized, kid-sized, five foot… five-foot-six….

Bruce stopped.

It was childish of him. He was pretty sure he could have gotten Cheesy up to the same size as Brie. But he was pissed, and he'd only promised *bigger*, not *as big as*. So there. He'd done as he promised. And though Cheesy looked at him and demanded, "More! Bigger!" Bruce flipped his middle finger at him.

"That's all you get. Now release them."

Cheesy looked like he wanted to argue, so Bruce pushed it.

"I did as I promised. You are bigger. Now release them"—he gestured to Nero, Bing, and Yordan—"or I claim you as my slave for the rest of your life." Not a bad choice, given that the fairy was immortal.

Cheesy grimaced and flicked tiny pieces of feta off his body at each of the men. One by one, they stopped speaking and dropped in exhaustion as they breathed in heavy gasps of relief.

Then the large fairy turned to the others and stomped his fetid foot. "I am the Grand Cheesy!" he bellowed.

Bilious Brie stopped spinning, and the other cheeses stopped as well. In fact, all the little cheeses seemed to hover in place, their gazes going back and forth between the two oversize fairies. Apparently they couldn't decide whom to follow, especially as Brie held up his hands and bellowed, "Whee!" But it wasn't in a joyful way. It was more like a challenge.

Cheesy answered with his own raised hands. "Grand Cheesy!"

Bruce swallowed, seeing what was coming. "We need to get out of here before they start wrestling."

Nero nodded. "Copy that." He grabbed Josh, and they hauled each other to their feet. Bruce did the same with Laddin while Bing and Yordan echoed their movements. Then Nero snapped, "Haul ass."

They did. They didn't slow until they were halfway home and the alternating "Whee!" and "Grand Cheesy!" argument had faded. By the time they made it to the barn, everyone was gasping for breath. But they'd made it safely, which was a big win in Bruce's book.

Every fire you walk away from was a win. That was in the firefighter's manual. Problem was, these guys weren't firefighters. So while Bruce was still thanking God they were all alive, Nero grabbed him by the shoulder and slammed him against the barn wall.

"And now, Mr. Apple, we're going to have a little chat."

Great. It was just an hour past dawn, and this day kept getting better and better... not.

Chapter 16

THE MIRACLE OF A HOT SHOWER

LADDIN FELT completely useless. He'd run back to the house as if Satan himself was chasing him, and in Laddin's mind, that wasn't far off. He couldn't shake the horror of speaking compulsively, unable to stop, unable to drink or swallow, just rasp out word after word of non-sense. He'd tried everything, but he'd lost control of the one thing he'd thought was wholly his own: his voice.

He still couldn't believe what he'd said. He'd given a master class on demolitions, and who the hell knew what the pixies would do with that, or if they even cared? But that made it even worse, because he didn't think the magical creatures needed an education on blowing things up. What they'd done to him was out of simple spite. And that filled him with a sick nausea he wasn't sure he'd ever be able to shake. Right now his thoughts and his body felt like stone—inert things that no longer functioned. It was as if he had died back at the tree but was somehow still moving and breathing.

And in the midst of that, Nero had shoved the man who had saved them against the barn wall and demanded to have "a little chat." Then he'd dragged Bruce into the house, threw him into a chair, and was now grilling him as if Nero were Jack Ryan and Bruce the key to a terrorist plot. It was awful, and everyone else let it happen.

Though Laddin still felt like he'd had his insides scooped out, he shouldered his way forward and tried to use his voice for something good. "He saved our lives!"

"He *risked* our lives first—" Nero said.

"No!" Laddin cried, though his voice came out as a heavy rasp. "*I* risked our lives. This was my screwup, and he saved us."

That should have meant something to Nero. The guy was fair-minded, for the most part. But he shook his head at Laddin. "You fucked up, but everybody does when they first meet fairies—"

"Exactly—"

"But I know your motives." His gaze turned dark and angry as he looked at Bruce. "I don't know what's driving him—"

"He came to save my ass—"

"And I know this wasn't his first fairy rodeo."

There was silence as everyone stared at Bruce. He had dropped into the chair and was waiting with a bored expression on his face. Laddin knew him well enough to understand what Bruce was doing. He was pretending not to care when he obviously did. A lot.

"He gave up his firstborn child to Bitterroot," Laddin said softly. "That's the standard fairy deal."

Josh paced around the kitchen island. "And how the fuck could you do that?" Josh exploded. "Give a kid to that asshole?"

Meanwhile Bruce jolted with equal shock. "What? No! I asked him that specifically."

Laddin blew out a breath of relief, but Nero didn't let it go. "And what did he answer—specifically?"

Bruce frowned as he thought back. "He said that they revere human children. Oh shit." He grimaced and glared into space. "Bitterroot, you fucking asshole, what did I promise you?"

Everyone waited for the fairy. He didn't show. Instead, a piece of parchment appeared on the kitchen table. It was the fairy contract, and right there in bold letters it read *In return for More, Bruce Collier will give his firstborn child to Bitterroot*. Simple. Bold. And though there were lots more words, those were the important ones.

Laddin read it and sank onto the floor. The idea of losing a child gutted him, and it wasn't even his. But that was what Bruce had given up for him—to save him and fix his screwup. The knowledge tore at him.

Meanwhile, Bruce leaned back with a sigh. "It's okay," he said out loud. "I don't have a kid."

"Yet," Nero said.

"Never. Dad saw to that when I was sixteen."

Josh whipped around. "Bullshit."

Bruce shrugged, but his eyes were bright with emotion as he looked at Josh. "Remember when Dad caught me making out with Mary Beth Davis? Well, he had me at a doctor the very next day. He said he didn't want to chance me having another you." The hatred inherent in that statement made everyone flinch, Josh most of all. But Bruce didn't stop. "He never said you were a werewolf. I have no idea how he knew what you were. Are. But he chopped my nuts rather than risk me making another one of you. His words, not mine."

Josh stood there, his skin pale, his mouth clenched hard. Nero was shaking his head.

"No clinic is going to cut a sixteen-year-old kid."

Bruce's gaze went to Nero. "It wasn't a clinic. I don't even know if it was a real doctor. All I remember is Dad handing me my usual morning smoothie, then waking up on a table in a place I didn't recognize. I was hurting like hell, and beside me there was a guy explaining that I'd need to ice my balls for a couple days and there'd be no football until Monday."

Josh shook his head. "That doesn't make sense. You're his favorite. It'd be his fucking wet dream for you to make a dozen little Bruces to entertain him in his old age."

"I had it checked a few years ago. I was dating someone, and she wanted kids." Bruce shrugged. "I'm so mangled up with scar tissue that reversing it is out of the question."

Laddin stepped forward. "Not in the normal way of things, maybe. But with magic—"

"It's not reversible," Bruce repeated firmly, his jaw hard. "Because if it was, I'd have to give my kid to that asswipe fairy."

Right. No kids. Ever.

Meanwhile, Josh was still pacing. "He never clipped me. He didn't touch Ivy. Why would he pick you?"

Bruce shrugged. "You ran faster? She's a girl? How the fuck should I know?"

Laddin frowned, looking between the lines. "Did they run faster? Or did you run interference to protect them?" Everything he'd seen of Bruce told him that the guy protected people, even at the cost of his freedom. That had been the forfeit he'd agreed to with the Grand

Cheesy, if things hadn't worked out. Bruce had offered himself up as a slave.

"No," said Josh as he continued to pace. "This is all bullshit. You hated me when we were kids. You *tortured* me."

"Yeah," Bruce said, his voice thick. "I did. I fucking loved hurting you. Because in my head, you were the reason I'd had my balls chopped. I blamed you because I was a stupid kid and because Dad cheered every time I knocked you down." He straightened up in the chair, leaning toward his brother. "But I'm not that dumb kid anymore, and I've been trying to make it up to you. For years. But you wouldn't return my phone calls and never came home so I could talk to you face-to-face."

Josh rounded on his brother. "Why would I? Why would I believe a word you say?"

Bruce didn't have an answer for that. Neither did anyone else. So the silence hung dark and heavy in the kitchen while all Laddin could hear was the rasp of Josh's breath and the hard beating of his own heart.

"He just saved our lives," Laddin inserted into the silence. Why didn't anyone remember that? Why wouldn't anyone *listen* to him?

"And he ate a fairy apple," Nero said softly. Then he reversed a kitchen chair and straddled it. It was a casual pose, but no less intimidating as he faced Bruce. "We need to know everything. From the beginning. What did Bitt—you know who—offer, and why did you take it?"

Bruce nodded, but his gaze was on Josh. "Yeah," he said. "I'll tell you everything."

And he did, starting with a salad fairy offering him a cherry, which he refused until Bitterroot threatened

Josh. Then he explained the cheese fairies, the regular fairies, and the fire, all the way up through this morning when they'd all been there. And he explained that the apple would give him *more*, though he had very little idea what that meant.

By the third time through, Laddin had had enough. "He saved our lives, Nero. All of us. Say thank you and be done with it."

Nero rubbed his hand over his face. "But what is he leaving out? What isn't he telling us that will come back and bite us in the ass?" Then, before Laddin could argue, Nero held up his hand. "I'm not saying he's hiding anything on purpose. But every detail counts with the fae."

"There isn't anything more," Bruce said wearily. "I've told you everything."

"Not by half," Josh said from his place next to the kitchen island. "You didn't tell us why you ate the cherry in the first place."

"I did tell you," Bruce said, irritation finally leaking through his tone. "He said he wants to enslave you. I was trying to stop that."

"And suddenly you're acting like a big brother? Now, when I don't need you at all?"

Laddin saw the impact those words had as they hit Bruce. He didn't know if anyone else saw the guy flinch or notice that his gaze dropped to the floor, but Laddin sure as hell saw the way the man's hands tightened into fists and then slowly, carefully released. So Laddin said what Bruce wouldn't.

"He's still trying to do it, though. Because you're his brother and because he protects people. He's a fireman and a paramedic. And if he can't help his little brother, then who the hell is he?"

"I don't know," Josh answered, his voice bleak. "I don't know who he is at all." And with that, he turned on his heel and walked away.

All Laddin could do was shake his head and murmur what everyone was thinking. "God, what some people do to their kids."

Nero grunted an agreement.

Then a female voice spoke, the tone light and airy.

"The alpha human is often cruel." Lady Kinstead floated into the kitchen and poured herself some coffee. As was typical for her, her clothes were a bit messy—there were even a couple of leaves in her hair—but she looked completely, stunningly beautiful. In fact, she was the embodiment of what Laddin thought a fairy queen would look like. Except according to reports, she was completely human and more than two hundred years old.

Nero cleared his throat. "Lady Kinstead, good morning. How is Wulfric?"

She smiled warmly at him. "Dying. As are we all." Then she turned her ethereal smile to Bruce. "You got your magic!" she said happily. "Where is the demon? We must kill him, you know."

Bruce cleared his throat awkwardly. It was nice to see that he was as affected as everyone else by the woman's aura of vague mystical authority. She was bafflingly mysterious even when she appeared normal. After all, she was only sipping coffee.

"Um, yes," Bruce said. "I know. But I haven't found the demon yet."

"Hmmm," she said, putting her cup down. "Well, do it before Thursday. It'll be too late to fix things after that." Then she waved goodbye before wandering out the back door without shoes or a coat.

Everyone watched her until the door shut. Then they turned their eyes to Bruce, who'd folded his arms across his chest and was glaring.

"No pressure," he quipped.

"No logic," Nero answered. "Unless you're holding back—"

"You seriously think I'd keep it secret if I had the answer to saving the world? That I'd wait until I had fame or money or, fuck, I don't know what."

"I've heard the tales from Josh." Nero spat. "I know what you did to him as boys."

Bruce leaned forward. "And I haven't denied them. But even then, do you think I would hold the entire world hostage as some kind of sick game?"

Nero shook his head. "No," he finally said. "Everything in your file says you're a stand-up guy."

Bruce jolted and his eyes narrowed. "You have a file on me?"

"Of course we have a file." He pointed out the door. "She's your great, great, great... I don't know how many generations grandmother. I even looked at activating you instead of your brother, but you're just a medic. He's the genius."

Well, that had to burn, but Bruce didn't seem hurt by the comparison. In fact, he nodded. "I always knew he'd come out on top," he said softly. "Brains beats brawn all the time if it's given the time to develop."

Laddin stepped forward. "That's what your father wanted you to do, isn't it? Keep Josh down so he never developed into the brainiac everyone saw coming."

Bruce didn't answer in words, but his shrug was eloquent enough. It told Laddin loud and clear that Bruce had no idea what had been in his father's head but that the results were obvious. Josh did develop into a brain.

And now as a werewolf, he had brawn too. Not to mention a boulder-sized issue with his brother.

So Laddin turned to Nero. "You done here? We're both running on fumes. We need showers and a nap. You too, so—"

"Yeah," Nero agreed. "We're done. I've got to kick this up the chain of command, and that'll take time." Then he gestured down the hallway. "The room down there is emptied out if you want it. You'll have to share, but it beats the barn."

Given that the barn smelled of smoke and was open to fairies, Laddin didn't argue—and he wasn't letting Nero change his mind either. He grabbed Bruce's arm and tugged him upright. "Come on. Let's get washed up. You smell like a dumpster fire."

"Ain't that the truth."

They started walking down the hallway to the open bedroom, but Bruce slowed, then turned back to Nero. "What about…." His gaze moved to the window, then returned to Nero. "The pixies? We can't just leave them out there."

Nero grimaced. "We can and we will. I've already texted Captain M about them, and we'll do our best to keep the area cordoned off, but there have been Earth fairies since there's been an earth. We can't kill or bargain with them. At least not easily. And they're only going bad right now because we're so close to the lake and that demon."

"But what if someone else walks by? What if a kid—?"

"Most people can't see or hear them. Only paranormal creatures like us get the show. And we know to give them a wide berth."

Bruce nodded, though he looked like he wanted to argue. Laddin didn't give him the chance. Instead, he tugged him farther down the hallway. "Come on," he said. "You have no idea how much I want a hot shower right now."

"I bet I do," Bruce responded.

Yeah, he probably did. They found the room, and Laddin opened the door. The bedroom was small and had a queen-sized bed that would only fit one of them comfortably. It looked like heaven to Laddin, as long as there were no pixies in the vicinity. Especially since it had an attached bathroom.

Actually, the room was a converted closet, but it had plumbing, and that would do for Laddin. As for Bruce—

"This is great," the guy said, relief heavy in his words. "Better than my first firehouse."

Once the door shut behind them, Bruce let some of his feelings show. His shoulders sagged, his head dropped against the paneling, and his eyes seemed to be drawn to the bed. But he simply stood there for a moment, holding himself back, until he finally said, "The smell of smoke doesn't bother me. If you'd rather be alone, I can stay in the barn—"

"We'll make it work here," Laddin said. "In fact, why don't you take the first shower? I'll go get our gear from the barn." Actually, Laddin would grab *his* gear, because Bruce hadn't come here with anything.

"I can wait—" Bruce offered, but Laddin held up his hand.

"Shower. Take all the time you want. Use up all the hot water too, if you like. I grew up taking cold showers because my mama was greedy that way. It'll make me think I'm back home."

Bruce smiled at that, and it was a measure of the guy's exhaustion that he headed for the tiny bathroom. "If you really don't mind."

"I don't. It's the least I can do since you saved my life." And it had been *his life* that had been saved. Not the others'. Bruce had chosen to sacrifice his firstborn child just to save Laddin.

That meant a lot, and Laddin intended to let Bruce know it. Afterward. After they showered and got some rest. After things settled and they figured out where the demon was. After they saved the world, Laddin would 100 percent find a way to make things up to Bruce. But for the moment, all he could offer the guy was a hot shower.

Fortunately, that seemed to be all Bruce needed.

"Thanks," Bruce said. "And don't worry about the hot water part. We firemen do it quick… and with a big hose."

Laddin snorted. It felt good to banter with Bruce. At first Bruce hadn't seemed like a bantering kind of guy, but in moments when he was too exhausted to maintain his grumpy demeanor, the man was funny and kind. Was this the person he'd be if he wasn't carrying the weight of the things that had happened when he was a kid? Or when he wasn't fighting fairies or fires or whatever he had to handle as a paramedic?

Laddin leaned against the door, waiting a moment before he left to get his things.

Bruce noticed. Of course he noticed. He was hyperaware, as most first responders had to be. "What?"

"Do you joke around with your firefighter pals?"

"What?"

"Make hose jokes and stuff like that? With your fellow firefighters?"

Bruce narrowed his eyes. "Yeah, sometimes, I suppose."

"And now you're doing it with me."

"Yeah. You got a problem with that?"

Laddin smiled. "Hell no. I was just noticing."

Bruce crossed his arms. "I wouldn't read too much into anything right now. I'm not exactly on my game."

"That's when the real Bruce shows through."

Bruce's gaze canted away. "Yeah. Don't look too close. You might not like what you see."

There was a little extra weight behind those words, and it bothered Laddin. The man really didn't like himself. Then again, that wasn't a surprise. He'd all but shown up wearing a hair shirt. "I like what I see just fine," he said. Then he grinned. "It's the smell that's the problem."

Bruce straightened up and gave him a mock salute. "Aye-aye, Captain."

Laddin nodded and waited until he heard the water start. He wasn't worried that Bruce would bail—there was something soothing about the sound of a hot shower. He knew exactly what Bruce would do. He'd do what every person did—exhale in relief and let the water wash everything away.

He listened for a moment, letting the sound do for him what it was doing for Bruce—wash away the memories of this morning. And with that thought in his head, he went into the barn to get his suitcase. Besides, he should probably clean up a bit first. They'd all run straight for the fairy disaster. No one had bothered putting things to rights in the van or....

He opened the barn door and saw the mess inside. The van doors were wide open, the contents inside in complete disarray. The burns were clear, as was the small trench Bruce had made around where they'd been sleeping. And as Laddin looked, he remembered it all. The way they'd fought the pixies as firecracker bombs went off on Bruce's naked body. He remembered the ropes that had cut into his flesh. And then there was the fire.

Everywhere he looked, he saw evidence of what had happened. Not just the horror, but the bedroll mashed into a wad because they'd been wrapped in each other's arms. The trench around that felt like a desecration of sorts. Laddin looked across it all, the memories battering him, but it was all a delay tactic.

This morning's horror was over, but it was going to haunt him. He stared at the bedroll because he didn't want to look out the barn door. He remembered the pixie attack because he didn't want to think about the cheese fairies. About getting pinned to the trunk of a tree and having words forced out of him. He felt violated and weak.

His throat burned, and he wished he'd brought a water bottle out with him. He forced his feet to move to the van. All he needed to do was grab his suitcase; then he could head back inside. Maybe he'd step into the shower with Bruce. Wasn't that a lovely fantasy?

He tried to hold all those things in his head. The image of soaping up with Bruce. Of having the big guy put his wet mouth against him, on him, around him. He tried to think of happy things, sexy things, anything.

But it didn't work, because no matter what he did, he had to look up. He had to step outside. He had to see the open field and remember.

And in the remembering, he broke.

Chapter 17

DISASTERS, SANDWICHES, AND PANTS

BRUCE DIDN'T linger in the shower. He knew Laddin wanted a good soak, and it would be rude to take up all the hot water. But when he came out, the guy wasn't around. Knowing Laddin, he was probably cleaning up the barn, and though Bruce felt guilty for not going to help, he really appreciated the silence. He needed to process what had happened in the past two days.

He stretched out on the bed and stared up at the ceiling while his mind churned. Except the more his mind chewed on what had happened, the more he wanted to turn to Laddin. He wanted to talk to the man, ask questions about this magical world he'd landed in… and discuss the other thing. Whenever the world got too overwhelming for him, he turned to a good hot fuck to clear his mind. It wasn't mature of him, but that had been his habit.

The problem now was that he didn't want a good hot fuck. He wanted Laddin. And even more shocking, the idea of putting Laddin in the same category as any of his hundreds of distraction-of-the-moment girls filled him with disgust. Last night's no-consequences sex aside, his relationship with Laddin had advanced well beyond the for-now category.

He knew what was happening. He'd been in enough serious relationships to recognize what he was feeling. First came friendship. He genuinely liked Laddin, which was hard to believe, given that he usually despised chronically upbeat people. But Laddin made him smile. A lot. And that was rare.

The next step was respect. Laddin had kept his head as he fought alongside Bruce against both sets of fairies, and more significantly, he'd stood up to Nero during that long interrogation. That took balls—anyone could see that Nero was Laddin's superior officer. In addition, Laddin had seen things that no one else understood. He'd said what Bruce could barely articulate about his childhood— that he'd tried to run interference between his father and his younger siblings. Or he had for a while, until the day his father had cut his balls. At that point he became angry and mean. Like father, like son, right?

He flinched away from that thought and forced himself to chew on something else. He'd eaten the fairy apple. What did that mean? Could he really save the planet? Not likely. As a young firefighter, he'd en- visioned himself saving whole buildings of people— imagined a grateful woman dashing into his arms be- cause he'd put out a fire in her house, or rescued her aging parents from who knows what disaster. But even in those fantasies, he'd never saved a planet. He was a paramedic and a firefighter, not a superhero. And he sure as hell wasn't qualified to solve this mystery. That was Josh's territory.

He shook his head, trying to clear his mind. Where the hell was Laddin? Why wasn't he here babbling away about something? The guy was the perfect distraction—a sounding board and comic relief. He was also sexy, honorable, and he made Bruce feel like he wasn't all that bad. The fact that a stand-up guy like Laddin found something to value in Bruce eased a pain inside him that he'd been carrying for a very long time.

And Laddin ought to be back by now.

Bruce got up from the bed. The apple had given him renewed energy. Hell, his brain was going like a hamster on a wheel. If anyone ought to be resting, it was Laddin, who'd had all the work and none of the extra fairy juice to handle it. So Bruce pulled on some clothes, grabbed a couple of sandwiches from the kitchen counter, and headed out to the barn to force the guy to take a break. Or at least to eat. Neither of them had eaten anything since last night.

He pulled the barn door open all the way before stepping inside. His nose wrinkled at the smell of smoke, but it was familiar enough to be comforting—like coming back to the firehouse after a long day. You could smell the day's disaster, but you were still home.

"Laddin?"

No one answered, which was weird. He stepped farther into the barn and had a moment of remembered terror staring at the burn marks on the floor. He'd examined every single mark on his body from those fairies, and the memory of being pinned down while Laddin struggled alone to help him made violence burn in his blood. It was a visceral response that spiked his adrenaline and made him want to blow up the entire structure.

But he wasn't here to relive his personal trauma, he was here to find Laddin, and so he forced himself to look away. He wasn't going to think about it. He wasn't going to *remember* anything. He was going to find Laddin, and they were going to fuck each other senseless to put a good spin on a lousy day.

So where the hell was the guy?

He saw Laddin's suitcase closed up and ready for transport. It was right next to the closed van, and he knew for damn sure that Laddin had done that. When they'd left that morning, everything had been open, burned, and messed up. So Bruce mentally pieced things together.

Laddin had come in, closed up the van, and gotten his suitcase. But something had distracted him, grabbed him, or turned him into magical goo. Panic rose quick and hard in Bruce's body. And with the adrenaline already there, the change was quick and fast.

One moment he was a man looking around the barn, the next second he was on all fours as a wolf, sniffing for Laddin. Fortunately he found him quickly. The smell was so strong that his wolf mind wondered what was wrong with his human nose to have missed it. Either way, Bruce found Laddin huddled beside the front bumper of the van. He went straight for him and tried to burrow into his arms.

Except Laddin wasn't letting him in.

He was sitting curled in on himself, his arms wrapped around his legs and his head buried deep into his knees. He was a tight knot of compressed energy held so hard that he was vibrating with it. Not shaking, but actually vibrating with how hard he was gripping his own body.

And Bruce couldn't break in. He tried everything a wolf instinctively knew how to do to comfort someone. He nosed in, he blew his breath on Laddin's skin, and he licked what he could touch. It didn't help. That was how he knew that Laddin didn't need an animal—he needed a man.

Bruce shifted again and was pleased to realize he did it easily. Apparently all he had to do was think about what Laddin needed and bam, his body accommodated his wishes. So now he was on all fours, squatting beside Laddin, as he spoke in the gentlest tone he had.

"Hey, Laddin," he said. He didn't expect a reaction and wasn't surprised when there was no response. So he took a deep breath and started talking for real.

"My first multicar traffic accident was brutal. I suppose everyone's is, but this one was *bad*. I'd seen street pizza before, but this incident was something I still have nightmares about. It was January, on the freeway. Someone was driving too fast on black ice and plowed into someone else, who ran into a truck, and then everything went to hell after that. My partner had a pregnant woman, DOA. I was cleaning up her husband, who wasn't going to make it either, but I had to try. And everywhere you looked, all you could see was disaster."

He paused to steady his breath. He didn't want to remember this but knew that Laddin needed to hear it.

"In any accident, all we think about is finding the victim, stabilizing the bleeder while watching for fire, and getting them ready for transport. That's it. Find, stabilize, transport. The sounds, the smells, and the noise—it's all chaos. We put one foot in front of the other until it's done. We don't think about it, we do our jobs."

He leaned back against the van bumper, blowing out the memories as he relaxed his body.

"And then it's done. We're back in the firehouse and no one's talking or we're talking obsessively.

Depends on the person. Me, I'm quiet. Then I'd find the nearest girl and I'd plow into her as fast and as furious as I can. But that only takes a guy so far. Eventually you have a moment when it's just you and your thoughts and suddenly you're back there again. And this time you can't shove it away. You smell it again, breathe it again, and the feel…." He shuddered. "I scooped gray matter off the pavement as we lifted his body onto a gurney. He was still breathing because the body does amazing things at times, but we all knew where it was going. We did our job and moved on." He swallowed as the memory rolled through him.

Then he looked at Laddin, who had lifted his head off his arms. His dark eyes were barely visible in the shadows, but he was watching Bruce. And he was listening.

"I scooped part of a man's brain off concrete, and it still haunts me." He leaned back against the wheel of the van. "What you went through today was worse. A thousand times worse. And I'll bet you never trained for that."

Laddin lifted his head. "There hasn't been time," he said softly.

Bruce shrugged. "I'm not sure you can train for murderous fairies, anyway."

Laddin let that hang in the air for a while. Eventually he relaxed his grip on his legs and set his chin on his knees. "I keep thinking this is like the rabbits, only it's so much worse."

Bruce frowned. "You've fought Monty Python killer rabbits?"

Laddin's lips curved into a ghost of smile. "No. Normal, everyday kind of bunnies living out their lives in the woods."

"And they attacked?" Bruce couldn't picture it.

"No. They were normal rabbits." He blew out a breath. "I ate them. We were running as a pack, doing something. I smelled them, dug around until they came hopping out, and then I...."

Ate them. Right. What the hell was he supposed to say about that? "Wolves will be wolves?"

Laddin shrugged. "Something like that. The thing is, I wasn't really popular as a kid." He held up his weird hand. "It was hard to play ball well with this. I managed okay and I had friends, but for baseball or basketball, I couldn't be as good as the other guys. Even video games had extra challenges."

And boys that age were all about sports. "No good at soccer?" He wouldn't have needed good hands for that.

"Not good enough, and believe me, I tried. I never made it onto any high school sports teams."

That was weird because Laddin seemed all about the pack. Unless.... "That's why you keep talking about the pack. About how you love running around as wolves. It's your team sport."

Laddin nodded. "It's the best. Sometimes, there's a goal—find something, hunt something, I don't know. But we're all together, part of a pack even though we're doing separate things."

A team. And when a team worked well, there was nothing better. "A good firehouse is like that too. It works whether we're fighting fires or hanging out eating barbeque." But how did the rabbits fit in?

"I never had that as a kid. Not after peewee football ended. It was just my mom and me, and sometimes my grandmother." He rolled his shoulders back and lifted up off his knees enough to look at Bruce. "Except for my mom's rabbits in her lab. I would go there after school

and she'd let me play with them. When I was really little,
I used to fall asleep in a pen with three or four of them
hopping around. And when I grew older, I would talk to
them. If Mama was busy, I'd tell them about my home-
work, I'd practice my speeches." He closed his eyes. "I
told them I was gay before I told Mama."

The rabbits had been his friends, his confidantes,
and his pack. Lab animals who probably had a doomed
life, but Laddin hadn't cared. They were there for him
when his mother was too busy. "Then you ate wild rabbits as a wolf?"

"Yeah." He looked up, his expression haunted.
"Bruce, they tasted fantastic."

What a mind-fuck that had to be. "Finding it hard
to reconcile the two? Childhood bunnies with—"

"Romping through the woods with my pack and
eating whatever hopped into view. Yeah."

"That sucks."

"Yeah. And then today I was nearly killed by pixies. Cute little fairies that are on cereal boxes and children's books. Those fuckers nearly did me in."

And in a pretty awful way.

Laddin closed his eyes. "I can't wrap my mind
around it." He dropped his forehead onto his arms
again. "And now I can't go outside because I'll see the
field. I'll look out there and—"

"Remember?"

Laddin's answer was a shudder. Bruce could relate.
He was very grateful to have his back turned to that circle of doom where he'd been pinned down. He wasn't
looking at it, but he sure as hell knew it was there.

Bruce pulled up everything he knew about Laddin.
They'd talked a little, shared about their before-were-
wolf jobs and lives.

"You're an explosives expert, right? I bet your work area was meticulous. Everything in its place, everything under control."

Laddin rolled his head until he was looking at Bruce. "Yeah. It's demolitions. Careless people get killed. Disorganized people lose body parts."

"We're taught the same thing in the fire academy. Everything in its place. Everyone doing their job. Protocol, procedure."

He stroked Laddin's cheek. It wasn't something he thought deeply about. He just wanted to touch the guy more than shoulder to shoulder. So he caressed the hard angles and rough five-o'clock shadow, then let his thumb roll over the man's lips. He felt the fullness of it and the texture. Soft. Rough. Wet.

His dick jumped in hunger.

"It all goes to shit in the field," Bruce said. "Not the protocols, of course, though that sometimes happens too. I mean the logic, the organization. The whole fucking system sometimes. We scramble to do what needs to be done, and after it's over, we put it back together. Hoses where they belong. Equipment cleaned and reset. Supplies refilled, bandages restocked, and everything in its place."

Laddin exhaled. "I worked on movies. If something went to shit, it was because someone fucked up. The demolitions were under control, the actors were only pretending to get blown to hell. And we didn't have to put shit back together because I made sure it didn't break in the first place."

Bruce nodded. He understood because he recognized the appeal of adrenaline even when your life was exploding around your ears. "Today wasn't a movie. No one had anything under control. And just like the bunnies, you both loved it and hated everything about it. Because it was messy, and you felt alive."

"I fucking loved eating those rabbits. I want to do it again."

"And you hate that about yourself too."

"Yeah." He lifted up off his arms. "What do I do?"

Bruce shrugged. He had no answers. "I'll answer that if you tell me how I can find the damned demon and save the world."

Laddin's lips curved. "I haven't a clue."

"Right back at you."

They waited a moment, their eyes connecting as Bruce's body heated and swelled to an uncomfortable degree.

"Bruce?"

"Yeah?"

"I hate this barn. Want to go back to our room and fuck?"

"Hell yeah."

"Then we'll save the world, okay?"

"Sure." Bruce grinned, belatedly remembering something. "I brought sandwiches too. Want to eat first?"

Laddin appeared to consider that, then nodded. "Sure. Thanks."

"My pleasure."

Laddin grinned. "Nah. That'll come afterwards."

Bruce rolled his eyes. "Promises, promises. You better put your dick—"

"Where your mouth is."

Bruce laughed—he straight-out laughed at the joke, which wasn't a joke at all because he sure as hell intended to do just that. So he held out his hand, and

Laddin took it. They hauled each other upright and headed around the van.

Laddin tensed as he stepped into the sunlight, and Bruce thought it was because he was looking out at the field. And maybe it was.

Or maybe it was something else. Laddin gestured at him, and his voice was weary and teasing at the same time. "Dude, will you put your pants back on? I mean I love the sight, but what if Lady Kinstead wanders by?"

What? Oh yeah. His sweatpants had fallen off when he'd shifted to wolf. But rather than grab the discarded garment, he pushed the joke, hoping to get Laddin to smile. "I don't know. Is she into threesomes?" He really was joking. He wasn't the least bit interested in sharing Laddin with anyone, much less his strange many-greats grandmother.

"Wulfric will cut off your balls for thinking that about his mother."

Oh right. "I guess I'll put on my pants."

"Good idea."

"Then you can take them off me when we're in our room."

And there it was. Laddin's smile. "Or maybe I'll rub one out while you strip for me."

Now there was an interesting idea.

Chapter 18

PRETTY ISN'T PERFECT

THEY'D JUST made it to their bedroom door when Nero walked down the hall. For such a big guy, he moved pretty fast, but even so, Bruce could see the weariness in his walk, not to mention the livid bruise that still covered half his face.

"Bruce," Nero said, "Wulfric wants to talk to you. That bedroom." He pointed to the room down the hall.

Laddin stiffened. "About what?" His tone rang with hostile challenge.

"About whatever the fuck he wants. He's the boss." Nero didn't like being questioned, and his tone made that absolutely clear. But Laddin didn't back down. He was exhausted, reeling, and could barely stand on his feet, but he was ready to fight Nero for Bruce.

And didn't that warm Bruce's heart? And cock.

But he couldn't let Laddin commit career suicide either, so he squeezed the guy's arm. "I wanted to check on Wulfric's wounds anyway."

"He doesn't have any wounds," Nero said. "The cleric healed him."

"Then why's he still in bed?" Bruce asked. If he knew anything about men of action, it was that healed leaders didn't hide in a bedroom away from central command. That told him that something wasn't going well for Wulfric.

To his credit, Nero didn't bluster. Instead his expression grew taut with worry. "Yeah. So go check him out, will you?" His eyes hardened on Laddin. "And you, get some rest. You're so strung out, you've forgotten that you're not in charge."

Laddin flushed at the hit but didn't back down. "I haven't signed on for the full tour, you know," he said grumpily.

"But you are on through the next full moon, *puppy*. So I suggest you get your ass to bed."

Bruce wanted to help Laddin out. The guy was defending him, after all. But Wulf, Inc. was a quasimilitary organization. Laddin needed to understand chain of command if he was going to work inside its ranks, and Bruce wouldn't do him any favors by interfering with that lesson. Though he did give Laddin a smile.

"I'll be fine. And he's right—you're dead on your feet."

Laddin gave in because he was smart enough to realize he wasn't going to win, but he still shot Nero an angry look. Then he turned back to Bruce. "Fine. Check out Wulfric, but don't take too long. I'm still your trainer, and we've got things to work out."

"Roger that," Bruce answered. There was nothing like being the new guy who got ordered around by everybody. He even knew that Laddin was doing it out of concern, but it had been a long time since he'd been

the probie everybody pushed around. He hadn't liked
it then, and he didn't appreciate it now, but he knew
enough to let it go, so he headed toward Wulfric's room.

What he saw when he stepped into the bedroom
stopped him cold. If this was what Nero called "healed,"
then Wulf, Inc. was in desperate need of medical personnel. And people with eyes.

Wulfric lay on his bed, barely moving. His long
legs stretched out beneath a thin blanket, his sunken
chest barely moved, and his face still looked as if it had
been used as a basketball in an NBA game.

Then Nero stepped into the room and suddenly
Bruce's vision went wonky. Superimposed over that
very ill man on the bed was the exact same guy, only
healthy and vibrant. His eyes sparkled, his skin looked
golden brown, and his face was movie-worthy for
rugged man-of-adventure roles. And it was all a total
illusion.

"This is Bruce Collier," Nero said. "He helped us
get you into the house. Feel free to beat the crap out of
him for me if you like. I can make you something better
for lunch while you do it. Want a steak?" He gestured to
the uneaten sandwich on a tray by the bed.

Bruce stared at Nero and realized the man didn't
see the truth beneath the illusion. Wulfric wasn't up to
beating up an egg, much less a man. And he couldn't
eat a sandwich, steak, or anything that required chew-
ing. His face was too swollen for that.

"No, thanks," Wulfric said, his voice weak. "I'm
not hungry."

Nero frowned. "You don't sound so good. Are you
sure you're okay?"

"I'm doing fine—"

"But I could use some bone broth," Bruce interrupted. "Or a smoothie. Even a sports drink would be great. And bring a straw, please. It's the only way I can get it down." He flashed Nero a weak smile. "It's been a hard couple days, and my stomach is still feeling unsettled."

Nero gave him a hard glare, but Bruce didn't flinch. Then, because he was feeling pissy, he added an extra kicker.

"Laddin will never forgive you if you let me pass out from low blood sugar. And unless I miss my guess, you really need to make nice with the only paramedic around."

He watched the muscle in Nero's jaw twitch. The man didn't like taking orders from anyone, but he didn't argue, especially when Wulfric chimed in.

"That sounds delicious. Would you mind getting one for me too?"

Nero might tell Bruce to go get his own fucking drink, but he wouldn't say that to Wulfric. So he gave his boss a clipped nod and stepped out. Bruce thought he'd slam the bedroom door, but he wasn't that petty. Nero probably knew something was off with Wulfric, but he didn't want to call out the mystical head of Wulf, Inc.

Bruce didn't have that problem. He stepped closer to the bed and peered at the man's bloody face. "You're a mess, and they can't clean it unless they can see it."

Wulfric's gaze shifted to Bruce. "I thought you might be able to see through the glamour."

"The what?"

"Fairy glamour. It puts out an illusion that most people can't see through."

Oh right. Nero had mentioned that when they'd first arrived in the barn. They'd done something then to dispel the illusion, but obviously it had worn off because no one but Bruce could see the truth.

"So even magical people can't see through it?" Bruce asked. Laddin had said that paranormal folks could see fairies, so a powerful werewolf like Nero should have been able to see through a fairy glamour.

Wulfric's lip twitched up. "I see your brother isn't the only smart one in the family. Let's just say that this is an extra-strong glamour."

That explained why Nero couldn't see through it, but not why Wulfric felt he had to keep up the illusion in the first place. Thinking he might as well get started, Bruce went into the bathroom and filled a basin with water. The first step was to clean out the wounds. Then he'd see what mess was underneath.

"I thought that cleric woman healed you," he said as he came out with washcloth and basin. There was a basic first-aid kit by the bed, but it was nearly empty. He'd have to send someone for the full med kit, if there even was one.

"She did, but all magic requires belief," Wulfric answered. "You should remember that."

He would. "She looked like someone who believed."

"She does. I don't."

Bruce paused just before dabbing at Wulfric's face. "You don't believe in magic?"

"Not really."

"Aren't you over two hundred years old? And a werewolf who uses a fairy glamour?"

Again, the guy's lips twitched. "Irony is one of the few joys left to me." And while Bruce stared at him, Wulfric's shoulder lifted in a weak shrug. "They believe, and so the glamour gets stronger when they're here. They want me healed, so her spell worked to keep me alive."

"But you don't want any of it?" He'd met many people who didn't care if they saw tomorrow, usually the severely depressed and the elderly. He supposed a two-hundred-year-old guy would count as elderly, though the body he saw—even the injured one— looked to be around thirty years old. If it wasn't for the swollen, damaged face, he'd seem as vital as anyone, even if he was on the thin side.

"I don't believe in any of it. There's a difference."

Not one that Bruce could understand, so he focused instead on what he did know. He rinsed out the washcloth and held it up. "This could hurt a bit." Or a lot.

"If I can use a fairy glamour, I can dull pain."

Really? "I thought you didn't believe in it."

The guy's eyes flashed with humor. "I believe in the hydrocodone I took an hour ago."

Now that was something Bruce understood. He started cleaning out Wulfric's wounds. He was as gentle as he could be, but the guy's face needed a plastic surgeon. "I don't usually work on this end," he said. "I'm the 'scoop them up and get them to a hospital' guy."

"And now you're the werewolf who eats a fairy apple so he can save the world."

Bruce didn't even blink. "There's lots of irony there too, if you care to look."

"I am. Believe me, I am."

Well, wasn't that cryptic? "Care to explain how I'm going to do that?"

"You're the one who ate the apple. Don't you know?"

Bruce shook his head. "All I've got is a bunch of murderous fairies telling me I'm going to save them."

"My mother says it too. About you saving the world."

Great. "I just came here to help my brother."

"He's the one guy who doesn't need it."

"Yeah, I've already figured that out, but thanks for poking at the wound anyway." He dabbed hard on a crusted-over abrasion. Wulfric didn't so much as blink.

"Tit for tat," the man answered. And when Bruce shot him a confused look, he smiled. "You're poking at my wounds."

Right. Banter. He was trading quips with a two-hundred-year-old werewolf who didn't believe in magic. Could his life get any weirder? "You really need a doctor. And a plastic surgeon."

"My mother will make me pretty again once this is done."

"And if it gets infected?"

Wulfric stretched to the bedside table and pulled open a drawer. There were pill bottles in there. A quick scan showed them to be heavy-hitter antibiotics and the hydrocodone.

Bruce nodded. "What about other pains? Bones? Joints? Are you having any trouble breathing? Heart palpitations?" He ran through the standard litany. Wulfric shook his head for each one. "Are you lying to me?"

"Would it matter if I was?"

"To me? Not in the least. To you, if you suddenly keel over from sepsis? Yeah, probably." Or maybe not, given that Wulfric didn't seem to care if he lived or died.

"I'm not lying. It takes too much effort."

"Says the guy with the fairy glamour."

"That was put on me years ago. I couldn't take it down if I tried."

That explained the hero worship Bruce heard in everyone's voice whenever they mentioned Wulfric. Bruce kept working on the wounds. He stopped when Nero came in with a couple of bowls of broth, two smoothies, and some sports drinks. And one straw.

Nero set everything down on the edge of the bed, his gaze turning sharp the moment he saw the bloody water in the basin and the antibiotic cream that Bruce had been using.

"You're a fucking asshole, you know that, Wulfric?"

The superimposed image was back, and it showed a healthy Wulfric grinning. "I do try."

Nero looked at Bruce. "He going to live?"

"Probably. But he needs to be watched closely. He ought to be in a hospital."

"They can't see through the fairy shit."

Right. That did cause a problem.

"I've survived for two hundred years. I'm not going to keel over now."

Even though he might want to. That was the message underneath the guy's words, and Bruce didn't have a way to address that. He wasn't the touchy-feely type. That was why he'd become a paramedic. He routinely rolled out lies like *You'll be fine. The doctors are the best. Your wife is fine and will see you at the hospital.*

He'd long since stopped looking to find out if what he'd said was true. He didn't check up on patients after the hand-off, and he sure as hell wasn't hanging around to learn that the wife hadn't made it after all.

Nero, however, took the words at face value. He grunted in approval and shoved a straw into the bone broth. "Drink." Then, when Wulfric gingerly held it to his mouth, Nero continued, "I can't believe I offered to make you a steak."

"I know," Wulfric agreed. "I gave up meat decades ago."

"Bullshit," Nero countered, and Bruce had no idea which was true.

It didn't matter. He focused on debriding the wounds, then applied the cream and gently laid gauze over the injuries. All through the process, Nero watched them both with heavy eyes, and the superimposed glamour stayed strong.

Bruce had finished putting everything away when Wulfric asked him a question. "So what are you going to do?" he asked. "About finding the demon and saving the world."

Bruce turned back. He didn't have a fucking clue. "You're the one with fairy magic. You tell me."

He thought Wulfric would treat it as a joke—that was what he'd done with just about everything so far. Instead, the man narrowed his eyes. Beneath his lowered lids, his blue eyes seemed to blaze. And well beneath the glamour, a kind of shimmer happened. It was like his blood suddenly started to glow.

While Bruce was still blinking to clear his vision, the sight disappeared.

"What did the prince tell you?" Wulfric asked.

"That I would be *more*."

"*Be* more? Or *have* more?"

Bruce had to think back, but he thought he remembered the exact words. "Have more."

Wulfric grunted. "There you go."

Bruce almost said something caustic, but Nero beat him to it. "Use your words, Wulfric. Not all of us have two hundred years of experience to understand code from the 1800s."

"Be thankful for that," Wulfric said. Then he took a deep breath. "The apple gave you power. Think of it like electricity. You have a store of it inside you now. Like a big battery."

Great. That wasn't disturbing at all. "What do I do with it?"

Wulfric rolled his eyes. "You create a light bulb."

"A light bulb?"

"Yes. One that will save the world."

"And how do I do that?"

Wulfric shrugged. "I can't tell you that. You have to figure it out."

"A light bulb."

"Make it a big one, because that demon is growing stronger every day."

Great. "Any other helpful advice?" He invested his words with as much sarcasm as he could manage.

"Yeah. Drink the smoothie. You're running on empty, and I'm lactose intolerant."

Nero was right. The guy was an asshole. "Me too," Bruce said. Then he grabbed the sports drink and chugged.

Chapter 19

WHEN SUPERHEROES TAKE OFF THEIR CAPES

LADDIN THUMBED off his phone and let his hand, phone, and entire body drop onto the mattress. It had been an hour since Nero had taken Bruce to see Wulfric, and that was too long. Didn't they see that the man was doing everything he could to help out? And under extraordinary circumstances too. He'd become a werewolf, been attacked by two sets of fairies, gotten handed the responsibility for saving the world, and now had to report to Wulfric as if he were a schoolboy being sent to the principal.

It took all of Laddin's self-control not to storm into Wulfric's room and chew him and Nero out. The only thing that stopped him was the knowledge that it wouldn't help Bruce one bit. The man had to find his own way with the higher-ups. But still, it pissed Laddin off.

So he'd grabbed all the distraction techniques he could think of. He'd taken his shower, organized his suitcase from the mess it had been, stopped by the kitchen, and even phoned Captain M to give his report and express his opinion on Bruce loud and clear—that he was a good guy and would be a great asset to Wulf, Inc. if they would stop treating him like a traitor. She hadn't been any more impressed by his assessment than Nero had been.

So now all he could do was lie on the bed and stew—

The door opened and Bruce tiptoed in.

"Do you seriously think I'm asleep?" Laddin asked. "What happened? Are you all right?"

Bruce stepped into the light. He looked a little wild around the eyes but otherwise okay. "I'm fine. Why aren't you sleeping?"

Laddin sat up. "Because I was worried about you. What did Wulfric want?"

"Medical attention. He's got a fairy glamour that makes him look good even though he's at death's door."

"He's dying?" Laddin asked, alarm shooting through him. Wulfric was the cornerstone of Wulf, Inc. Sure, he rarely interfered with the day-to-day activities, but he was the one who guided the company, who said what was and wasn't important, and who.... "Is that why everyone adores him? Because of the fairy glamour?"

"Probably. Because honestly, he's kind of an ass." Bruce dropped down on the edge of the bed. "He says I have to make a light bulb."

"Incandescent, fluorescent, halogen, or LED?"

Bruce laughed and the tension in his shoulders eased with the sound. "Metaphorical. He says I've got fairy electricity inside me. I have to create a light bulb that uses it."

"Oh. Got any ideas on how to do that?"

"Nope."

Laddin sat up and faced Bruce. "Well, I've been thinking—"

"Of course you have—"

"Shut up and listen. You've been going nonstop. One of us has to process, and I'm the most organized thinker here."

"You are?" Bruce challenged.

Laddin rolled his eyes. "Please. I'm the most organized person everywhere."

Bruce tilted his head. "Really??"

"Let's say unfolded socks make me insane."

"Good to know."

"So, listen. You've eaten the apple and the cherry, and everybody says you'll find the demon."

"By Thursday."

"Two days from now. Awesome." Not. "You've got this fairy electricity inside you, and you've got to figure out how to create a light bulb."

"You're repeating me."

"Because I'm wired. I had a triple espresso while I waited for you."

Bruce perked up. "They have an espresso machine here?"

"Focus. Why don't you build your light bulb at the lake where everyone says the demon is? We've been running around behind the scenes here, but we need to be on the front lines. You have to use your juice to—"

"Shine a light on the demon. Got it." He pushed to his feet. "So let's get me some espresso, and then we can head out to Lake Wacka Wacka."

"That's not its name."

"It's what Nero calls it."

"Nero can't remember names for shit. It took him three weeks to call me anything but Mr. Happy."

Bruce smiled. "You are chronically perky."

"God bless caffeine. And before you go in search of that espresso, I have to tell you something. We can't go to the lake right now."

"Why not?"

"Remember those phantom kangaroos that smashed Nero's face?"

"Not really."

"Doesn't matter. Captain M told me they're back… with reinforcements. They're being ridden by Haunchies."

"By what?"

"Some Wisconsin thing. They're little people whose goal is to cut everyone down to their size. So they're smashing equipment and slicing up people's legs."

Bruce frowned as he looked out the window. "They'll need paramedics."

"Not you. You have to build your light bulb."

"I don't know how to build a freaking light bulb." He sighed, and Laddin could see the frustration that chewed away at his confidence. Bruce wanted to help. Hell, the man wanted to save the world, but he hadn't the foggiest idea how.

"One step at a time. How do you usually figure things out?"

"YouTube video."

"This isn't going to be on the internet."

"Yeah, I figured." He blew out a breath. "I'm a hands-on kind of guy. I usually work things out by doing them."

"So do something. Anything."

Bruce stared at him, his hands lax by his side. As the seconds ticked by, his forehead furrowed, his breath shortened, and his hands slowly tightened into fists.

Laddin waited until he couldn't take it anymore. "What are you doing?"

"Trying to see the demon."

Laddin could already tell it wasn't working. A moment later Bruce flopped backward on the bed with a groan. "We are so totally screwed."

"You've barely started," Laddin countered. "You can't give up now."

"I've shot my one wad. I've got no other ideas. And if we can't go snooping around Lake Wacka Wacka right now, then I've only got my fallback position, so to speak."

There was a wryness in his tone that Laddin didn't understand. He crawled up on the bed to lie next to Bruce. "What position is that?"

Bruce rolled his head to look straight at Laddin. "Whenever I get stuck, whenever I can't see my way through a problem…."

"Yes? You do what?"

"I find the nearest willing girl and do her. Any way I can. It clears my head and I figure things out."

"You can't possibly have been that studly in school."

Bruce's mouth curved up into a devastatingly handsome smile.

"Okay, you probably were."

"A gentleman never tells."

Laddin snorted. "Something tells me you told everyone in the firehouse."

Bruce's expression sobered. "No, I didn't," he said softly. "It was bad enough I was using the girls for my own ends. I didn't need to humiliate them in the process."

So even in his sexcapade years, Bruce had been a gentleman. "My mistake."

Then, suddenly, the man's cocky grin was back. "The girls were the ones who told everyone. I neither confirmed nor denied."

Laddin snorted to cover the hurt he felt. He didn't like thinking about Bruce's playboy ways, especially when it involved him banging every girl he came across. Fortunately, they had a world to save, so he suppressed his personal problems and focused on Bruce's.

"Not that I object to an orgasm to clear one's head—hell, it was how I got through French class—but I'm fresh out of horny girls right now and—mmph!"

The kiss was fast and delicious. It had just the right level of need mixed with playfulness. Bruce's tongue pressed in, danced with Laddin's, then pulled back.

"Whatever gave you the idea I was talking about girls?"

"The fact that you said 'girl.'"

"I was talking about my past. This is my right here, right now."

Laddin frowned, unable to dance away from the question. "So you've accepted it? That you're into men?"

Bruce shrugged. "I'm not a deep thinker. I let Josh do that." He immediately rolled on top of Laddin and pressed his thick cock against Laddin's. "I want you. And it's a bit hard for me to think about demons when we're in a bed together with the door shut."

"You do realize everyone will hear us anyway?"

That gave Bruce a moment's pause; then he shrugged. "We'll tell them I was doing exactly what Bitter... you know who... told me to do."

Laddin winced. "He told you to have sex with me?"

Bruce's grin was wide. "He told me the sex would be fantastic. And since we can't go to the lake now that slasher kangaroos are running around...."

"You want to clear your mind and experiment with your powers."

Bruce's expression took on a serious cast. "You okay with that?"

Laddin's body was definitely okay with that. He was already thick, and his hips ground upward against Bruce's. But he didn't say anything, and when he thought Bruce would simply take the invitation, the man did the exact opposite. He pulled back and looked into Laddin's eyes.

"You gotta tell me this is okay."

"Fuck buddies again?"

"It worked last time."

It had. But…. "I know you better now."

Bruce's eyes widened and he nearly leaped off the bed. In the split second before he turned his face away, Laddin saw his expression of hurt, as if he'd taken Laddin's words completely the wrong way.

"Wait!" Laddin grabbed Bruce but lost hold when the man jerked away.

"It's okay," Bruce said, his words rushed. "It's not the time. If I need to jerk off, I can do it myself in the bathroom or something."

"Bruce. Damn it, slow down!" The guy was heading out the door to leave, but Laddin didn't let him. He grabbed hold of Bruce's chin and jerked him back until they were face-to-face. "You are going to calm down and talk to me. Right now."

"Good God," Bruce said with an exaggerated eye roll. "You don't have to go all Oprah on me. If you don't want to fuck, we don't have to—"

This time Laddin was the one cutting off his words with a kiss. Only his kiss was aggressive. He thrust his tongue straight into Bruce's mouth and made him shut up. He felt the man's shock in his sudden stillness. And then, when Laddin gripped the back of his head, Bruce pushed him up against a wall and kissed him back.

Their tongues dueled—in his mouth, in Bruce's mouth, back and forth as they ground together. But this wasn't a passionate kiss. It was an expression of anger and frustration and need, not passion—and certainly not love, though God knew no one had said that word yet.

When Bruce finally let up, they were forehead to forehead, and their breaths came out in harsh panting, Laddin finally managed to speak.

"I know you better now," Laddin said. "I *like* you more. I like you a lot. And the meaningless sex stuff isn't meaningless to me anymore."

Bruce took a moment to process that. Then, when he spoke, there was a raspy tone to his voice. "It's been one day. One fucking day. You don't know me at all."

Really? "Seems like longer."

Bruce grunted in response, so Laddin elaborated.

"It seems like you've saved my life twice, been given an impossible task, and spent the whole time trying to do right by your brother."

Bruce pushed back and ran a hand through his hair. "What do you want from me, Laddin?"

Laddin straightened his shirt and moved away from the wall. He knew Bruce wouldn't accept any touch right then, but that didn't stop him from holding out his hand. And when he spoke, he thought about his words and prayed they were the right ones. "I don't want anything *from* you. I want to help you."

"I don't know how to save the world."

"I know."

"I just wanted a break, you know? I just wanted…."

"Okay."

Bruce stilled; then he turned back to Laddin. "What?"

"I said okay. We can fuck."

"Don't do me any favors or anything." Bruce's tone was angry.

Laddin gave him a lopsided smile. "I've had a hard-on for you since the moment we met." Then his gaze slid to the floor. "I just wanted you to want me." He lifted his gaze again as he struggled for the words. "I mean, you saved everyone. You're a superhero that way. I wanted to be more than some random guy in the crowd."

Bruce stared at him, his expression torn between tender and horrified. "You did not just call me a superhero."

"I'm pretty sure I did."

Bruce fell back against the dresser. "I thought you—out of everyone—were paying attention."

"I was. What did I miss?"

"That I'm a monster who beat the crap out of my little brother. A lot. That I've fucked tons of women I didn't respect and couldn't care less about. That I ate fairy fruit so that I could get powerful. Don't you get it, Laddin? I'm the monster, not Josh. My father guessed wrong. It wasn't ever Josh. It was me the whole fucking time. I'm the monster."

He really believed that. After everything he did to help people, he still thought of himself as a monster. "That's a whole lot of guilt you're carrying around. I can't remember ever meeting a more remorseful monster in my life. And in the few weeks I've been with Wulf, Inc., I've met a few."

Bruce lifted his chin and shot Laddin a glare. "Saying sorry doesn't excuse what I did. Ask Josh."

"I don't care about what you did, Bruce. I care about who you are now. And nothing I've seen says you're a monster."

Bruce didn't say a word. He stayed hunched against the dresser with his gaze on the floor, the picture of misery. He hated himself at a really deep level. He despised who he'd been as a kid, felt like he could never make up for his mistakes, and flat-out believed the bullshit his father had spewed for years.

"I'd really like to beat the crap out your father," Laddin muttered.

"I've thought that a thousand times."

"Then why haven't you? You're bigger than him, even without the werewolf or fairy stuff. You could probably put him on the ground by the time you were eighteen."

"Sixteen."

"So why didn't you?"

"Because it would kill my mother. Because he was paying for Josh's education, and I didn't want Ivy to come home from war and find a broken family."

"Because you made sure everyone got out without destroying your mother or committing murder."

Bruce shrugged. "My dad had his good moments too. He came to my games, he protected Ivy from asshole boyfriends. I think he really loves my mother. It was just with Josh that he was crazy."

"And Josh got out."

"Yeah."

"Sounds like you were protecting them all. Sounds like you were a kid with a fucked-up father and you did the best you could."

Bruce raised his head. "You're forgetting one important part. I liked it. I liked beating up my brother."

"Who doesn't? Especially after having a forced vasectomy. I'd be pissed and whaling on anything I could too." He stepped forward and set his hand on Bruce's chest. The man flinched, but he didn't draw back, and in time, he inhaled deep enough that Laddin's hand could slide across the muscled contours. "I think you're a pretty amazing guy. But what I think doesn't make any difference. You've got to like who *you* are before anything I say will sink in." He pressed his lips to Bruce's hard jaw, then whispered his next words. "You have to *love* yourself before my love will make a difference."

Bruce blew out a long, slow breath. That was good, because Laddin had feared that the guy would run at the first mention of the L-word. Instead, he pressed a tender kiss to Laddin's mouth. "I've hated myself for a really long time, Laddin. I don't think there's any love left in there."

"You sure about that? I mean, we know you love this, right?" Laddin stroked his hand across Bruce's chest again, using a nail to cut across that hard nipple.

Bruce gasped and his dick twitched where it lay heavy against Laddin's thigh. "That's not the same thing, and you know it."

"I do, but we've got to start somewhere, right?" He rolled his hips so that his cock rubbed against Bruce's, and they gasped together. "Tell me one thing," he said as he pushed off Bruce's sweatpants, allowing Bruce's thick, ruddy cock to thrust up between them. "Tell me that it's me you want to fuck, and not some random guy you saved from the fairies."

Bruce caught Laddin's mouth with his. He gripped Laddin's shoulder and angled his mouth so that the play between their tongues was fast. It made Laddin's breath catch and his dick pulse with need. And then Bruce ripped his mouth away.

"It's you, Laddin," he said. "It's definitely you."

Laddin grinned. "Then let's clear your head." He grabbed Bruce's arm and whipped him hard toward the bed. He couldn't have done it if Bruce was unwilling, but the guy practically flew onto the mattress. When he finished bouncing, he gripped Laddin's sweats and jerked them down too. Laddin's cock leaped forward, wet and so eager it hurt.

But when Laddin went to join Bruce on the bed, Bruce held up his hand. "Stay right there," he ordered.

Laddin froze. "What? Why?"

"Because I want to show you that it's you I want. No one else." Then, while Laddin was still standing there with his heart beating so fast, Bruce climbed off the bed, got down on his knees, and wrapped Laddin's cock in his big hand.

Pleasure zapped through Laddin's body, and he hissed at the sensation. Then Bruce put his glorious mouth on Laddin and sucked him right in. He knew what to do. He stroked and squeezed in the right tempo, and he used his tongue to drive the need higher. Laddin lost control of his body as he thrust into Bruce's mouth. His hips jerked and his belly tightened. And when the moment came, he dove straight into the whiteout, sensation, pleasure, and need colliding until there was nothing but bliss.

Pure, ecstatic bliss.

The first thing Laddin saw when he came back to himself was Bruce, still on his knees, grinning like he'd been given a bonus prize. Laddin blinked because—to be honest—he hadn't seen a lover look like that. Not after giving so well without receiving anything in return.

"You okay there, Bruce?" Laddin asked, surprised by how breathless he felt.

"I've never gotten a guy off before. You looked amazing."

"I…. That's because… I mean… it was amazing. *You* were amazing." He put a hand to his mouth, mortified by his stammer.

Bruce pulled the hand away and they kissed. Bruce's mouth was hard, and his tongue thrust deep. His cock was there between them, thick and ruddy, and suddenly Laddin wasn't interested in standing anymore. So he pulled Bruce to the bed.

"Want to learn how to top?"

"Yes." No hesitation. No restraint.

Laddin grinned. "Good. Because I want to teach you. Stay right there." Now he was the one doing the ordering as he pulled the condom and lube from his bag. Then he taught Bruce what to do. He explained things as clearly and precisely as he would a new kid in demolitions—only he was the one about to get blown apart.

He lay back on the bed, facing Bruce, and let the man find the angle and the rhythm. He let Bruce see his lust and his need, even as he felt the burn cut through him. Bruce thrust his magnificent cock in so deep that Laddin couldn't stop squirming, thrusting his own cock uselessly into the air. And he watched in wonder as Bruce's body flexed above him. Bruce's chiseled face tightened, and his hard abdominals moved in a glorious display—into Laddin, deeper, harder—while Bruce's eyes took on a laser focus and his mouth pulled back into a grin.

And Laddin watched while his heart stuttered and his body pulsed.

Raw male power in the act of possession. It was so beautiful, it tore him apart.

He watched, and he was ridden.

And when Bruce finally exploded inside him, Laddin blew apart too. And he fell in love.

Chapter 20

DON'T WORRY, BE HAPPY

BRUCE WOKE to a ringtone that played "Don't Worry, Be Happy." What was even funnier was the way Laddin rolled over, grabbed the phone, and answered with a very crisp "Yes, Captain!"

Bruce was still rubbing the sleep out of his eyes when Laddin leaped out of bed and gestured for him to do the same. "We'll leave in ten minutes. Will you inform Nero, or should I?" And then he finished with "Yes, ma'am."

He hung up the phone while Bruce was pulling on his sweats. He definitely needed to get some real clothes. But at least he had his boots, muck- and cheese-covered though they may be. "What's up?" he asked as Laddin started grabbing his own clothes.

"The kangaroo pack has been dispersed. We're heading in, even though it's nearly dark."

Bruce looked out the window, and sure enough, dusk was starting to gather on the horizon. "I don't know how much I'll be able to see," he murmured.

"Your fairy sight should kick in. My guess is that you won't need real light. In fact, you might be better off without it."

Good point. "I guess we'll see what happens."

Laddin finished lacing his sneakers. Then he looked up, but not exactly into Bruce's eyes. "So, um, did you get any clarity?"

From the sex, he meant. Had their roll in the hay helped him sort out his life? Hell no, but he didn't regret it for a moment. "It cleared out the cobwebs," he finally said. "Which gives room for inspiration to strike, right?"

"Right." Laddin turned away. There was a tightness in his body that Bruce didn't like. It could be because they were headed into the spooky dead zone known as Lake Wacka Wacka. Or was it something else?

"Laddin—"

"Listen closely. It hasn't hit the news yet because no one wants to talk about it, but there's this huge depressive cloud around the lake. It's really intense. The normals are sobbing uncontrollably—there have been three suicides and dozens who just left because they couldn't take it anymore—and even our crew is being overcome by it. That's why we cycle people in and out fast."

"Because they get depressed?"

"Suicidally depressed. You can laugh at me all you want, but I'm there to keep the cheerful going. One positive thought can counter a hundred dark ones."

That really wasn't his experience, but Bruce didn't argue. Laddin was acting very intense right now—the exact opposite of his usual upbeat self—and Bruce wasn't one to challenge a superior officer until he understood the situation.

But when Laddin didn't keep speaking, Bruce scrambled to fill the silence. "Uh… yes, sir!"

Laddin rolled his eyes. "I don't need you to salute me. I need you to not laugh when I tell you to—"

"Don't worry, be happy?"

Laddin frowned. "Yes. That."

"I wasn't laughing. Certainly not at you." He frowned. "Did I miss something or do something? You're acting very…."

"What?"

"Commander-in-chief?" That wasn't the right description, but he couldn't find the right words just then.

"Because I am your trainer. I am your commander-in-chief."

Neither of them looked at the bed. They hadn't exactly been acting like an officer/recruit a few hours ago. And the fact that they both were avoiding the view was suddenly really obvious.

Laddin addressed it first. That was no big surprise, since the guy tended to fill awkward silences.

"I don't know how to act right now. I've never been in charge of an op, and I've never had to train a new recruit. Hell, before a couple of months ago, the worst thing I had to do was yell at actors to get the hell out of the blast radius." He took a breath. "I don't know what to say to you, and I told the captain we'd be out the door in…." He looked at his watch. "Now."

"How about 'We'll talk later'? Then we can take our time and really figure it out."

Laddin blinked, then nodded. "I can do that." He hesitated; then his voice rose in clear doubt. "Can you?"

"I can." He hoped. He strongly suspected Laddin wanted to talk about feelings, and that really wasn't his strong suit. But for Laddin, he'd try.

"Deal." But Laddin didn't move. "One more question before we go."

"Yes?"

"Was it spectacular?"

"What?"

"You said that the fairy said that after you ate the apple…."

"That the sex would be off the charts?"

"Yeah." Pause. "Was it?"

Bruce grinned. "And off the next chart after that." He winked at Laddin. "Thanks."

"My pleasure." He paused at the door. "I'm going to want details, you know. Very clear, very specific details."

Bruce chuckled as they went out into the hallway, but his laugh faded immediately. His brother and Nero stood waiting for them, both leaning against the wall, their arms folded and their expressions dour. It was disturbing how much their poses mirrored each other. Especially since Bruce could remember a time, before things went bad, when Josh used to echo Bruce's poses.

Then Nero straightened and held up his car keys, but he didn't hand them over. Instead, he spoke sternly, and Bruce listened closely, knowing that this was a mission briefing and people who enjoyed breathing really ought to pay attention.

"I texted the way to the lake to your phone. Don't deviate from it, because there are crazies everywhere, as well as the press. Stratos and Wiz will meet you at the checkpoint. Get in, find the fucktard demon, then call me. Don't engage. It's dangerous and you're not trained."

"I know," Laddin said. "Captain M already told me."

"And did she tell you about the depression effect? It's real—"

"Yes." Laddin held out his hands for the keys. "We're just there to look around."

Nero grimaced. "I should go instead—"

"You've been there often enough," Laddin interrupted. "You're already growling at people, and you weren't exactly Mr. Sunshine before."

Nero accepted the statement with a grumpy kind of grace. Then he dropped the keys into Laddin's hand. "Hold on to your sunshine." He looked at Bruce. "And don't eat any more fruit."

Bruce nodded while Laddin headed into the kitchen. "No need," he called. "I made sandwiches yesterday."

Of course he had. Laddin was a planner, and that was always handy among first responders. And rare. Bruce grabbed the bag of food with a grin of thanks, only to be stopped by his brother.

Josh was suddenly standing between him and the exit. His expression was closed down, his arms still folded, and his mouth pressed into a tight, angry line. Bruce braced himself internally. He really didn't want to take one of his brother's verbal jabs right now, and he sure as hell didn't need it as he headed into whatever was at Lake Wacka Wacka, but he didn't appear to have a say in the matter. So he stood still and waited.

Eventually Laddin got impatient. "Josh, either spit it out or get out of our way."

Josh's gaze flicked briefly to Laddin, then back to Bruce. Then he spoke in a surly tone reminiscent of when he was twelve. "Don't die. I'm not done with you yet."

Wow. That was more of an admission of affection than he'd had from Josh in years, and it took him a moment to process it. And then, rather than respond with the grace of an adult, he, too, regressed to twelve-year-old communication. He grunted and shrugged. And then he stood there like an idiot trying to find a way to speak.

Again, it was Laddin who was too impatient to let them flounder. He grabbed Bruce's arm and hauled him to the front door.

"Hug it out tomorrow. Let's go save the world now, okay?"

Then Bruce and Josh responded in perfect stereo: "Okay." The similarities in their voice and intonation made it sound like they were in perfect harmony, absolute accord.

It was weird and special, and for the first time in years, Bruce looked at his brother with real hope in his heart. Maybe, just maybe, they could find their way back to being brothers again.

Then he turned and headed toward the barn. Meanwhile, Nero called out one last reminder. "If you find something, call me! Don't engage on your own!"

Bruce held his tongue as they got into the car and reversed out of the barn. He waited in silence as Laddin pulled up the directions on his phone and passed it to him. Bruce had no problem playing navigator, but he was appalled by the length of time it would take to get to the lake, and that pushed him to voice his objection out loud.

"He's being ridiculous if he thinks we have time to wait for him to get to us. It'll take us an hour to get there."

"I know," Laddin said, his voice grim.

"If we have a chance to take out this demon, I'm taking it. We can't afford to let it disappear again."

"I know."

"And if Nero is any type of leader, he would know that too."

"He is."

Bruce looked at Laddin, seeing the tight set to his shoulders and his hard grip on the steering wheel. *WTF?* "Care to explain what's going on with you? The only time I've seen you this stressed was when your life was in danger. Or mine."

Laddin cut a hard look at Bruce, then blew out a breath before focusing back on the road. "My guess is that he's given Wiz detailed instructions on what to do. Wiz is the only werewolf who has magic, and he's as experienced as Nero. Stratos is a newbie like me, but she's got some special woo-woo of her own. Don't ask me what, because I don't know. Those two keep their secrets close to the chest."

Okay, that made sense. He'd have to meet this Wiz and Stratos to judge how well he could work with them, but he had no problem handing off the dangerous part to the more experienced fighters. He'd had enough danger from the pixies to last a lifetime.

"So that explains the mission parameters. Now tell me what's going on with you."

Laddin didn't answer, but his jaw clenched hard enough that his neck bulged.

"If you're supposed to be the sunshine and light person, you're not doing a good job right now."

"I know!" he huffed. Then he visibly relaxed his hands on the steering wheel.

Bruce waited, watching as Laddin drove hard and dangerously fast on the country road, as if he was trying to outrun something. But the only thing following them was the full moon.

Oh shit. The *full moon.* He wouldn't have put it together if Laddin hadn't also glanced—repeatedly—out the window at the bright orb.

"Um… you're a moon werewolf, aren't you? You said I wasn't but that you—"

"Yes."

"So what happens to you?"

"I rampage around killing rabbits. No people so far."

"So far?"

Laddin shrugged as he gestured ahead. "Everything's wonky out there." He again took a deep breath and relaxed his hands. Then he also shot a hard glance at the moon. "Here's what I know. During a full moon, everything feels more intense. Feelings, hungers, desires."

"Desires?" Bruce echoed as he put the pieces together. "Desires like…."

"Like love." He shot Bruce another look, this one filled with confusion. "With you. It's intense and real and—"

"And it's only been two days."

"I know."

"It can't be real, Laddin. We're just…." What? Just getting to know each other? True, but in that time, they'd saved each other's lives and had conversations he'd never have with his closest friends. He'd talked about his father, Josh, and the fucked-up way he was raised. That wasn't something he spilled to anyone, but he'd felt like Laddin knew it all before he spoke. The guy saw through his bullshit to the stuff underneath. So he'd talked, and once the words were shared, he felt closer to Laddin than he did with his own family or anyone at the firehouse.

But while he was thinking how it might be the L word, Laddin was busy reiterating their previous arrangement.

"Just friends. A quick fuck to release the tension. *I know.*"

"That's not what I meant," Bruce said, though he sure as hell didn't know what he *did* mean.

Laddin wasn't waiting. "Look, what I feel is just that. My feelings. The moon doesn't give me new emotions, it simply accentuates the ones I have. So yes, I feel love for you. And lust. Like over-the-moon kind of lust."

"No pun intended."

Laddin flashed a grin, but it didn't last long. "I kind of like that part."

Yeah, Bruce did too. "But what does that mean?"

"Hell if I know. I'm telling you that my emotions are really intense right now. I didn't realize it until I stepped outside and saw the moon." He took a deep breath. "But that could be a good thing."

That was Laddin, always looking on the bright side. But that wasn't Bruce. "Intense feelings, as we're walking into a zone of depression while looking for a demon? Tell me how that's a good thing."

"Because assuming we're still good and that you're not freaked-out by this—"

"I'm not." And he wasn't. Or he hoped he wasn't. It was new and hard to process quickly.

"Then I can focus on the good parts of love. The warm feelings and the sexy times."

"You find it easy to search for a demon while sporting a boner?"

"It's better than thinking about slitting my wrists. Look, we need me to stay upbeat while everything around us is telling us to give up. I can do that by thinking about you. About how I feel about you and what we just did, and what we're going to do when we get back. That kind of stuff."

"Because love is upbeat."

"Yes, it is. Look, we've all had heartbreaks, me included. But this part of love is easy for me. It's the fun
part. And no matter how you feel about me—good, bad,
or indifferent—I still feel good about you."

Bruce blew out a breath. "That's got to be the most
civilized thing I've ever heard. About feelings." So
why wasn't it settling right with him? "You really don't
care how I feel about you?"

"Of course I care! I'm praying you want to keep
fucking me every spare moment you get. And I hope
we can make something of this in the future. But for
right now, I'm settling into loving you." He glanced
over. "Assuming that's okay with you."

"How could that *not* be okay with me?"

Laddin shrugged. "People get weird when the L
word shows up."

Fair statement. And in truth, he was a little weirded
out, but only because this conversation was so mature.
He couldn't remember a clear discussion of feelings that
wasn't muddled, tearful, or nearly violent. But he could
meet Laddin on an equally logical plane. "If you're okay
with me not being ready to say it back, then I'm okay
with you feeling whatever it is you're feeling."

Laddin released a sigh. "You can't even say the word."

"Love. That you feel love. For me." God, that was
hard to say. The words came out stilted and a little angry. Damn it, what right did Laddin have to throw love
into the middle of a mission to find a demon? But that
was the problem with people as openhearted as Laddin.
They felt things and let them spill over everywhere.

"Why are you angry?" Laddin asked, his voice low.

Good question. "I'm not angry, I'm…." He didn't
know what. "I feel bad for you." Then, to cover, he gestured ahead. "Take a right at the stop sign."

Laddin followed the direction, then continued with their conversation. "You feel bad for a guy who is in love with you." His voice was deadpan, but anger throbbed in the air.

Why did he have to keep saying that word? It made Bruce twitch every time. "You know about my past. You know that I've been a shit to every lover I've ever had, and that's a long list. You know how I treated my own brother. Hell, you even know how fucked-up I am over all of it."

"Yeah. So?"

"So, I've been an asshole my entire life. And I may be trying to make up for it now, but I'm still an asshole. And no amount of love from you is going to change that." Bruce slumped in his seat and delivered the final blow. "Falling in love with someone you want to change is never going to work."

"I don't want to change you. I think you're fine the way you are."

Bruce shook his head. It was all he could do in the face of such willful blindness.

While he turned to stare moodily out at the full moon, Laddin pressed him with questions he didn't want to explore. "You think you're a monster, right?"

"I said asshole." Though monster fit.

"And did you think of yourself that way before coming to Wisconsin?"

Of course he had. Or had he? He'd happily slept with girl after girl. At least he'd been honest with every one of them. As for his relationship with Josh, it was complicated and confused.

He suddenly realized that he'd never actually thought of himself as a monster until recently. Sure, he'd been a jerk and a bastard, but he'd never thought

"monster" until he'd eaten the fairy fruit and it had
opened his eyes to a world full of them.

He turned to gape at Laddin. "You think this is because of that fairy asshole?"

Laddin shook his head. "No, I think it's the demon's field. I think it takes normal bits of guilt and
magnifies them into words like *monster*. Look deep,
Bruce. Do you really think that badly of yourself?"

Yes.

No!

Maybe?

Bruce rubbed a hand over his face. "This magic
stuff is fucked-up."

"Yes, it is." Then he flashed Bruce a grin. "But it
keeps us on our toes, right?"

"And buried in cheese."

Laddin shuddered. "Let's not go there right now,
okay?"

"Okay." They lapsed into silence for a bit while
Bruce fed Laddin more directions. There was more traffic here. Press vans and cops. No one stopped them yet,
but that would come soon enough. "What does all this
mean?" Bruce asked, not really expecting an answer.

"It means you need to remember that you're not a
monster."

"I've been an asshole at times for sure. But you're
right—I'm not a monster." Saying it aloud helped so-
lidify it in his mind.

"And I love you."

Bruce winced, but he tried to take it in without
arguing. As he did, the tension inside him eased—and
the part that kept insisting he was a monster dimmed.
It didn't go away, but it wasn't front and center in his
thoughts anymore.

With that realization came understanding. "You're using positive thought to fight the depressive field."

Laddin nodded. "Effective, isn't it?"

Yes. But that made him wonder, were Laddin's feelings real? Or was he latching on to love as a way to fight depression? Was everything they'd just discussed a tactic to be used in the field and nothing more?

Shit, now he was more confused than ever. But they'd run out of time to discuss things, since the next turn brought them to the first checkpoint. It was time to stop thinking about feelings and start looking for the demon that was ending the world.

Chapter 21

HOW MANY FAIRYLANDS ARE THERE?

LADDIN PULLED up to the first checkpoint and forced himself to smile at the guard. He handed over his ID and waited while Stratos came out to meet them. Her hair was tied back into a short ponytail and her eyes had a haggard drag to them, but she smiled and tossed Bruce his Wulf, Inc. ID dog tags as she climbed into the back seat of the car.

"Don't lose that," she said. "Wiz used the last of his magic last night to make them for you. They'll even stay on you if you go wolf."

Laddin watched Bruce stare at the tags, then swallow. It was like he was stuffing all extraneous thoughts and feelings into a mental box labeled *Later* so he could deal with the problem at hand.

Laddin respected that. Not many people could be that tidy, but Bruce knew how to prioritize even something as immediate as emotions. A moment later he put the tags over his head and tucked them under his T-shirt.

"Where's Wiz?" Laddin asked.

"Waiting at the last checkpoint." Then, before Laddin could ask, she held up a hand. "We're taking a break from each other."

He wasn't surprised. Even back at headquarters, the two bickered all the time. They argued about everything—from who was supposed to grab the whiteboard markers all the way through complex magical theory. He could barely remember a time they weren't at each other's throats. And it must be even worse this close to the lake. Unfortunately, right now, they needed Wiz. He was the only experienced field operator among them.

"Stratos—" he said.

"He thinks he knows everything."

"That's because he often does." Wiz was Sheldon, Doctor Strange, and Sherlock Holmes all wrapped together in one handsome, arrogant package.

"I know that!" Stratos said. "Still, that doesn't mean I'm going to let him get away with acting like he's all that."

"Even when he is?"

Stratos growled low and deep in her chest. "Just shut up and drive. We'll pick him up soon enough. See if you can stand him."

She slumped back into her seat, but Laddin was watching her reflection in the rearview mirror. Her body was tired and her expression bleak. She was not the firecracker of a woman he knew, the one who had once ruled the *WOW* gaming circuit as much for her attitude as her skills. "How long have you been in this zone?"

"Since well before you got here." She looked at Bruce. "You going to solve all our problems?"

Bruce flashed a cocky grin. "Absolutely not. You've got way too many issues for me to fix."

"Great," Stratos muttered. "Another guy who thinks he's funny."

They were both fronting. Laddin could tell Bruce was acting cocky to cover up how shaken he was by the L-word discussion. Stratos was doing much the same, resorting to her angry persona rather than admit she was afraid. They all were.

That left him to infuse some sunshine and light into the discussion or watch his teammates self-destruct.

"What do you call cheese that isn't yours?"

His teammates stared at him like he'd lost his mind.

"Nacho cheese." Only he pronounced it *not yo' cheese.*

Dead silence. Then Bruce twisted in his seat. "Did you seriously just make a bad cheese joke?"

He shrugged. "Tough crowd."

"Don't you mean, tough cheese?"

Now it was Laddin's turn to stare. "What?"

"Tough cheese. You know, like tough nugget. Or tough love. Or, I don't know, tough noogies. Don't they say that in LA?"

"Never. But then, we don't have murderous cheese like you do in the Midwest."

Stratos lost her temper. "Have you both lost your minds? You're supposed to be looking for the world-ending demon! And the expression is *tough nut to crack*!"

Bruce and Laddin looked at each other, then shook their heads. "No, it's cheese," Laddin said.

"Definitely cheese. That's way more dangerous than nuts. Especially in Wisconsin."

She gaped at them, and they grinned back. Laddin would have held the pose longer, but they were approaching the second checkpoint. As he pulled the car to a stop, he heard her grumble, "Crazy. The world's fate is in the hands of crazy people." But there was a lightness in her tone that hadn't been there before, and when he glanced back through the rearview mirror, her lips were curved in a slight smile. A very slight one, but it was something.

It disappeared the second Wiz jumped into the car as they crossed through the gate.

"You were supposed to meet us at the third checkpoint," she snapped.

"Change of plans. Park wherever you can. We're getting out here."

"What? Why?"

He turned dark eyes toward her, but his voice filled the car. "Because something strange is going on, and it starts before the third checkpoint. Don't ask me what it is. I'm still thinking, but my guess is it's some sort of fairy shit. Nothing else can confuse my brain like the damned fae."

No one spoke for at least a minute. Laddin was busy finding a stretch of ground to park on. The others, presumably, were noticing how the road stretched ahead for maybe a half mile, then ended in a gray haze, like thick smoke. Only it had flashes of color that fuzzed out his brain. Whatever was ahead, it was too chaotic for him to make sense of. And he wasn't alone. He caught a glimpse of a pair of confused-looking reporters stumbling down the road toward them. One carried a mic, the other gripped a camera, but neither seemed able to function. They rambled forward, wearing shell-shocked expressions. A moment later, others followed—some in National Guard uniforms; some wore lab coats and carried laptops. No one spoke, and they all looked like they were escaping the apocalypse.

That was when Bruce started cursing. It was soft and low, but the sound filled the inside of the car with frustration.

"What?" Laddin pressed. "What do you see?"

Bruce didn't seem to want to answer, but Laddin wasn't going to let him get away with it. They needed information and they needed it now.

"We're going in there," Laddin said clearly. "And we need to know what you see."

Bruce shot him a heavy stare filled with dread. "Fireworks."

Laddin was so horrified, he couldn't speak. But neither Stratos nor Wiz knew anything about what had happened.

Wiz spoke first, his voice commanding. "Is that a joke?"

Stratos answered. "They don't look like they're joking, but I can't see anything but smoke."

Laddin shook his head. "We're not. He's not." He squinted as he looked forward. "I can hear some booms and see the smoke, but nothing else."

Then Bruce jerked his arm forward to point into the haze. "I see people down. I count six, but there could be a lot more." His expression tightened as his gaze kept moving, looking everywhere at once but never landing anywhere. "I think they're tied down like I was."

"So how do we get them out?"

Bruce put his hand on the car door even though Laddin was still easing the car forward, trying to get as close to the smoke as possible. "One at a time, that's how."

"Wait!" Wiz exclaimed. "Fairies are unpredictable, and they're dangerous. We need a plan."

Like they didn't know that already. Meanwhile, Bruce started issuing orders. "You three get the people out. I'll handle the fairies."

"Hell no!" Laddin snapped.

"Why you?" Wiz asked, his voice sharp.

"Because I've got experience with them."

Wiz reared back. "Since when? You're a puppy."

Laddin slammed the car into Park. "Since earlier today, when he offered up his firstborn child!"

Stratos's voice hitched slightly as she opened her door; then she looked at Wiz. "I don't think we've been getting the full action reports."

"We're werewolves," Wiz returned. "Nobody does the paperwork."

Laddin did the paperwork, but now wasn't the time to point that out, because Bruce was already heading for the haze. The firework booms were there, but not nearly as loud as they should have been, given the amount of smoke.

Bruce shot him a concerned look. "You okay?"

"Yeah. Sure." Just because he was walking into a repeat of last night's nightmare, that didn't mean a thing. But then he happened to look up. Or maybe it didn't just happen, because something was pulling at him. Something strong.

The moon.

But it wasn't the regular moon. There was a second one. A fairy moon that seemed to illuminate the smoke in a mesmerizing white glow. And deep inside him, his werewolf howled in hunger.

"Laddin?" Bruce asked, his voice heavy with worry.

"I'm good," Laddin lied. Except it wasn't a lie, because he had it under control, right? It was just a moon.

Or two moons. And though his werewolf itched to be free, Laddin was in control. "I'm fine," he repeated.

"Then let's get it done," Wiz said, his voice hard.

"You're getting the people out," Bruce said, "while I distract the pixies."

"No," Laddin said firmly. "We're all getting the people out, and then we're looking around for the demon. No negotiations, no interactions with the fairies. We don't have anything to bargain with, and they're busy anyway."

"They're exploding firecrackers on top of people," Bruce snapped. "People they've tied down with burning rope."

"What?" Stratos snapped. "Where? All I see is smoke."

Wiz squinted into the haze. "I can see it. Maybe. I don't know."

Laddin was beginning to understand. "These are fairies at work. Bruce sees them the best because he's a werewolf because he ate fairy fruit."

Wiz nodded. "Makes sense."

"Whatever," Bruce said as he moved forward.

Laddin rushed to keep pace with him while Stratos and Wiz followed. "No negotiating," Laddin said firmly. "No promises, no engagement. Get in and get out."

"And find that demon," Wiz ordered.

"Yeah," Bruce agreed. "In and out with the people. Find the demon. No problem." It wasn't going to be that easy, though. They all knew it, but that was the goal and maybe they'd get lucky. "And one more thing," he muttered darkly. "Don't worry. Be happy."

It came out as a command, but it was enough to make the others smile. Not Laddin, though. He was too busy fighting the call of two moons. It had been bad enough on the drive over, when he felt every-thing stronger. Love, lust, hunger, desire—all of it was ramped up. But now with two moons in the sky, he was desperate to tear through everything for the sheer joy of moving, of eating, and most especially of hunting. His nose twitched, and damn if he didn't smell something yummy. He didn't know what it was. There were too many humans, too much fairy smoke, but it would be interesting to taste.

Bruce made it to the edge of the haze. Laddin did as well, putting his hand up to feel a kind of barrier tingling against his palm. It wasn't strong enough to keep him out, but it was there.

"Right through here," he said to the others. Then he stepped through to what should have been a parking lot before the third checkpoint. What he saw instead was an open field filled with fairy lights and—

Bang! Boom! Roar! Squeal! Noise!

He'd heard the booms before, but they were nothing compared to what happened the moment he stepped into the smoke. Sound overcame him—a rolling wave of deafening nonsense all going off at once. He dropped to his knees and covered his ears. Wiz, too, collapsed in on himself the moment he crossed the threshold. The only one who remained unaffected was Stratos. She stood there, her eyes going back and forth as she shook her head.

"I don't see anything. It's just gray to me. Wiz!"

Wiz held up his hand to keep her back. Laddin was recovering too, thanks to Bruce's hand holding him strong. But it was Wiz who slowly stood up.

"We're inside the barrier. I think it's a fairy circle," he shouted. "You can't see anything?" he asked Stratos.

"No!"

He nodded as if that made sense. "You're immune to fairies. They can't hurt you, but then you can't see them either."

"Then let me go get the wounded." She pointed at the nearest body. "There's a man there." She squinted. "It's hard to see. Like I'm in a fog. But—"

"Go together!" Laddin said. He looked at Wiz. "She has to pull up the white ropes holding people down. They'll burn you. If she's immune to fairy magic, then she should do it."

"I'll guide her," Wiz said.

"You go left. We'll get the ones on the right," Bruce said.

Wiz and Stratos nodded and headed for the man stretched out on the ground. Bruce and Laddin, however, didn't get more than three steps before Erin Rodger-Dodger appeared in front of them.

"You have come, Windy Wolf! Take us to Fairyland now!"

"Fairyland! Fairyland! Fairyland!" Hundreds of dancing lights erupted into cheers. It was deafening. It was annoying. And it pissed off the wolf inside Laddin.

Meanwhile, Bruce straightened up to look at the pixie in confusion. "Isn't this Fairyland?"

She fell backward, as if she'd been tackled. But her words came through clearly enough.

"This is Earth Fairyland. Not Fairy Fairyland."

Oh hell. This was why they never negotiated with fairies—because their entire world made no sense at all. Bruce echoed the sentiment as he threw up his hands in disgust.

"I don't know the difference," he growled.

The entire field stilled. The chaotic fairy party went dead silent to stare at them. Which, as it turned out, was a good thing, because there was no interference as Wiz and Stratos carried two people out of the haze.

Erin Rodger-Dodger got to her feet. She dropped her hands to her knees and glared at them as if they were the enemy. Dozens of tiny glowing fairies hovered behind her. Oh shit, they were going to rush them.

"Wait!" Bruce called. "I want to help. Just explain. I thought you wanted to come here."

"We made this place! Why would we want to come where we already are?"

Good point.

"Um… how? How did you make this place?"

She rolled her eyes. "From your thoughts." When Bruce stared at her, she pointed at Laddin. "Think of something."

Laddin didn't have the wherewithal to think of anything specific. He was still battling the damned moon shining down on him, making him insane.

"He does not have enough power. Help him!" she ordered as she pointed at Bruce.

Bruce frowned. "How?"

"Give him your power!"

And finally Laddin understood. "You're a battery, right? What if you can give your power—your energy—to me?"

Bruce blew out a breath but nodded. "Okay. But how?"

Might as well take a stab in the dark. "Hold hands?"

"And then imagine my current going into you," Bruce finished, already grabbing hold of him. "Ready?"

"Yes." Okay, that was a total lie. His wolf was straining and coiling inside him. His thoughts were on the moon above, not the fairies around them. He had to focus, but there wasn't time as Bruce grabbed his hand.

It started out as a warm trickle of energy moving from palm to palm as they gripped hands. It was actually soothing, and Laddin started to relax. But the moment he did, the trickle became a flood. Power burst through his mind, scattering any illusion of control. His wolf surged forward, and before he could stop it, the wolf took all that power and gave it one single focus.

The moon.

"Yes!" Rodger-Dodger cried. She held up her hands as if to catch his thoughts, as did the fairies around her. They leaped up and grabbed something out of the air. It was pale white, and it glowed with an eerie beauty.

Moonlight.

And then all those fairies rushed together, holding their creamy white glow aloft. They leaped, they danced, and they threw the light together bit by bit. The tiny thing grew and grew until right there in the center of the fairy field was a huge, bright, beautiful moon.

The light of three moons now converged on Laddin. The one from Earth normal, the one from Earth Fairyland, and now this third one. Right there in front of him, so close he could touch it.

The transition from man to wolf was seamless. One second he was a man; the next he was a wolf who gloried in the incandescent light right before him. The moon!

He touched it. He leaped upon it. He howled out the wonder of it and reveled in the madness. And then everything else was forgotten.

Chapter 22

PUPPY PILE!

BRUCE WATCHED in fascination as the fairies gathered what appeared to be tiny ripples in the air. They caught it in their hands like children grabbing sand, and as the ripples spilled out between their fingertips, they reformed as light. Moonlight, he realized. But that was secondary to the beauty of what he was seeing.

Until Laddin started to howl.

It took him a moment to realize that Laddin had wolfed out, abandoning everything to leap onto the glowing orb the fairies were still building. Bruce stared, confused by what was happening until he heard Wiz scream at him.

"Stop making a moon! We're *werewolves*!"

He watched in dismay as Wiz, too, tore off his clothes in a movie-worthy display before transforming midleap into a wolf.

"Wiz!" Stratos screamed, true fear in her voice.

Bruce couldn't stop it. He'd given the power to Laddin, who had built the thought. He should have taken the time to think it through. He should have realized that the moon was on Laddin's mind. And now….

He watched in dismay as Wiz jumped onto the still-growing moon. The two wolves growled at each other, showing their teeth and bristling from nose to tail. Oh hell, they couldn't fight each other, they were allies! Except obviously they could.

Then another howl cut through the air.

Stratos. Already wolfed out, she looked a bit silly in a sports bra and boxers. She leaped up onto the moon as well, adding her fury to the already explosive stand-off between Laddin and Wiz.

Then Bruce felt it too. He wasn't sure why it took so long to drop into his brain. Maybe because his vision was filled with all the other stuff. But as the fairies put all their energies into creating a moon, the other things around them faded away. There were no more fireworks, no more chaos. Even the rope restraints on the people on the ground disappeared as the moonlight grew stronger and brighter. To Bruce's relief, the people slowly got to their feet and each headed out of the fairy circle.

The people were safe. Now he just had to find the demon.

But he couldn't focus. His entire vision was filled with that silvery glow. It called to him. He felt the pulse of the light. It sped up his blood and made his mouth pull back into a wolfish grin. Fur sprouted on his skin. He was shifting, and no matter how much he resisted, the pull of that moon was too strong. For others as well, because he heard howls, distant but coming closer.

The wolves on the moon heard it too, and they turned, bristling and sniffing as they prepared to leap. He couldn't lose them. He couldn't lose Laddin!

He stopped fighting the change. He wasn't going to win against it anyway, and at least as a wolf, he could run with Laddin. He didn't care about the others. He needed to stay with his mate.

His human mind twitched at that last word. A discordant clang that was quickly lost amid the pull of the moon. He dove into the change and emerged a full wolf. This time, when a howl sounded, he joined in. He didn't know that wolves had language, but in this form, he understood.

I'm here! I'm coming!

The others leaped off the moon and bolted hard for the distant howls. He joined in, using all his strength to catch up. It was wonderful, this power in his legs and the way the air flowed through his fur. He leaped over rocks, pivoted past dead brush, and when he took a misstep, he rolled and tumbled, head over tail, until he righted himself with a quick scramble.

He never stopped moving, and after one last furious burst of speed, he caught up to Laddin, almost tackling him. He was coming in from the side, and Laddin was tearing ahead. Or maybe not so far ahead, because when Bruce thought he was about to surprise his mate, Laddin turned and leaped. He caught Bruce around the haunches, and together they rolled in a joyous scramble of yips and licks.

Hello! Hello! I'm so happy!

Me too!

The sounds were all around them as bodies tumbled about in greeting. There was so much to smell, so much to learn.

Hello! Who are you? I'm friendly!

Then he caught another scent, another taste on his tongue.

Brother. Josh.

Only Josh wasn't returning the greeting. Not really. He was prancing slightly but not wagging his tail. His nose twitched, and when Bruce yipped in greeting, Josh didn't return it.

One by one, the other wolves caught the tension. They quieted and pulled back. And though everyone was breathing hard, they made no sound as they fell into line behind Josh.

These were Josh's friends. Josh's pack. And Bruce wasn't part of them.

Laddin was the only one who spoke. He stood like the third point of a triangle as he yipped twice, first at Josh then at Bruce.

What's up? he asked. What's wrong?

Bruce let his head dip. He wasn't part of their pack. He was the outsider to everyone but Laddin, and his own brother was the one holding the rest back. As a man, Bruce would have said something cutting to hide the pain. But as a wolf, he simply dropped on the ground and put his head on his paws in misery. He wasn't going to fight his brother. Despite the moonlight flooding his body with energy, he was tired of trying to belong. More than anything, he was sick of fighting with his brother.

So he didn't.

Laddin came forward and whined as he pressed his nose against Bruce's neck. Then he looked up at Josh and growled. That startled Bruce enough that he looked up in surprise. Laddin was fighting for him? Laddin was growling at Josh as if… as if….

As if Laddin was claiming Bruce no matter what the hell Josh thought. And the joy of that had him rolling to his side to lick Laddin. Wolfish licks conveyed so much, especially as Laddin returned the gesture. Affection. Love. Pack.

But then a sharp bark from Nero had them looking up.

Someone was coming. It was another wolf, walking with the slow precision of someone very old or very grand. Bruce barely gave him a second look because Josh was stepping forward. His nose was twitching and his tail was up.

Laddin let out a low yip. *What are you doing?*

Josh didn't respond beyond a quick flick of his ear. He came forward, his mouth open and his teeth very bright.

The wolf in Bruce wanted to back away. This was dangerous. Josh wasn't indicating friend or foe but just kept creeping forward. But the man inside Bruce's wolf kept his body still. He would not run from Josh. If Josh wanted to take his revenge now, then so be it.

But he wasn't going to be crawling on the ground either. He got up onto all fours, but he didn't run away. Still, he kept his head slightly lowered because he would not fight his brother.

Josh opened his mouth right in front of Bruce's face. All around them, the wolves were still. Bruce knew that Laddin was twitching in concern, but all he could see were Josh's very sharp teeth.

And then suddenly Josh's mouth narrowed… and he blew hard, straight into Bruce's nostrils.

Ew!

Hot, wet air went straight up his nose. Bruce flinched back, snorting and rubbing his nose in the dirt. That was gross!

All around him, the wolves yipped in laughter. Bruce felt himself bristle. They thought this was funny—

Then Josh tackled him—full wolf, full body—catching Bruce by surprise. He felt Josh's teeth on his neck, felt the scramble of claws at his belly, and he twisted to get away. He couldn't. Josh was big and fast, and Bruce didn't have the leverage.

He also wasn't getting hurt.

It took a moment for that realization to hit him. Josh wasn't coming in for the kill. He was playing with him. Every time Bruce tried to regain his footing, Josh was there, knocking him down, rolling around with him, and….

Licking him.

Hello, you big goober! Hello!

Bruce's human mind was still trying to make sense of what was happening, but his wolf mind knew just what to do. He yipped and wrestled, then yipped some more while more wolves, more bodies, joined the pile.

Hello! Welcome to the pack! Hello!

He greeted them all, and one by one, he put names to the scents. Nero, Wiz, Stratos. Bing, Yordan, and then Wulfric. That slow wolf, the one who joined them eventually—he was Wulfric, and he was as spry and happy as the rest of them.

Throughout it all, Bruce smelled Laddin. He kept track of Laddin. And he knew Laddin was the one at his side, the one who yipped the happiest, and the one who was, for Bruce, the beginning and the end, the first and the last, always in this pack.

His pack.

He had a pack now, and the joy of that filled him to bursting.

He howled with delight, and every single one of the wolves answered.

Hello!

Welcome!

Pack.

HE WOKE to the sound of a human female singing. It was a strange music—earthy and wild—and it called equally to wolf and man. There were words, but he didn't understand them. And yet just as he knew the meaning between a yip and yowl, he knew what was being said.

Wake up! Come greet me!

He did, coming awake in his human body, responding with words while others all around him murmured their greetings as well. Some came in the form of words, others in barks.

"Morning," he said, his voice thick.

Laddin said the same, though in Spanish, right next to his ear, because he and Laddin were entwined. The furry body on which they lay barked, and the two others at their feet—one human, one lupine—responded as well.

Bruce blinked the sleep out of his eyes to see the pack in a huge pile together. Not merely the eight he had names for, but more. The big wolf with the raspy yip, the white wolf who never said a word. The one who smelled of pepper, and the other whose fur curled like a poodle's and yet smelled like a grizzly bear. He knew them all by scent, even in their human form. And he was amazed at the size of the pack. There were twenty-two of them, plus the woman who walked daintily among them, teasing some with her toes and petting others regardless of whether they were wolf or human.

"Mother," Wulfric said in a dignified voice. "Please tell me you brought clothes with you."

Lady Kinstead paused as she turned to her son with an ethereal grace. "No. Why would I?"

"Because we're naked and in the middle of nowhere, Wisconsin."

"Speak for yourself," answered Stratos as she pushed to her feet and stretched. She still wore a sports bra and shorts, though they were tattered.

"Forget the clothes," Nero muttered as he sat up and rubbed his face. "Does she have a phone?"

"Why?" she asked, her brows drawn together in confusion.

From across Nero's lap, a large brown wolf straightened up and shook out his fur. Then there was a sudden center of cold air and a golden light before Josh appeared in his human body. "I've got one," he said as he pulled an iWatch face off the chain holding his dog tags. "Give me a sec to connect."

Bruce was torn between being impressed by his brother's foresight and wanting to mock the guy for being unable to go anywhere without his tech. But before he could say a word, Lady Kinstead stepped daintily between two wolves who apparently intended to stay in that form. She came right up beside Bruce, then dropped to one knee before him, putting them eye to eye. Then she asked her question.

"It's Thursday. Do you have the answer?"

It was Thursday? Already? Had they really been running for *two days?* Shit! And no, he did not have any answers. In desperation, his gaze landed on Laddin, who was looking at him with hope shining through his eyes. In fact, a quick glance around told him that everyone was looking at him expectantly. Even the wolves.

"I'm sorry—" he said, but Wulfric interrupted him.

"Start with the basics. You must have figured out your power. You made the moon, after all."

"Not me. I…." His gaze went back to Laddin. "Well, maybe. I mean, I figured out the light bulb."

Yordan sighed. "Not exactly rocket science."

Josh rounded on the guy with surprising ferocity. "Give him a minute. My brother may not think logically, but he does think."

"Hey!" Bruce said, a little insulted by the "not logically" part of that statement, but before he could voice it, Yordan grunted his acceptance.

"Instinct guy. I can get behind that."

"Everyone shut up!" Laddin snapped. "This isn't easy on him, and commentary from the peanut gallery only muddies the water."

"Mixed metaphor there, Laddie," Stratos said, but then she bit her lip at Laddin's glare.

And then everyone was looking at him again. Fortunately, Laddin grabbed his hand and his attention. "Don't look at them. Look at me. What did you figure out about the light bulb?"

"Not what. Who. It's you, Laddin. I'm the current, you're the light bulb. You made the moon, not me."

Laddin took a moment to absorb that. Then he shrugged. "Not one of my best ideas."

To the side, Bing rolled his shoulders as if unkinking his back, and his black hair flowed about his shoulders in a very cinematic display. "We did not eat any rabbits or deer. It was a successful run at a time when we all needed the break."

That was definitely true—except Bruce had failed at the one thing he was supposed to do. "I didn't see the demon. I don't know where it is."

Lady Kinstead stroked across his jaw. The touch was gentle, and there was no censure in her voice when she spoke. "Are you sure?" she asked. Though he didn't feel it in her tone, her question reverberated with judgment all through his body.

"No, I'm not sure!" he snapped. "I'm not sure of anything. And it doesn't help when you put the fate of the world on my shoulders and no one tells me the basics. It would have helped to know that there are two different Fairylands."

All around him, wolves and people straightened up in confusion. He saw looks shoot back and forth between them, but it was the wolf—now man—with the whispery voice who said what everyone else seemed to be thinking.

"There are two Fairylands?"

"Yes," Bruce huffed. "That's what Erin Rodger-Dodger said. That they made Earth Fairyland, but they want to go to Fairy Fairyland." He struggled to put meaning to what he'd seen before going wolf. "The pixies are Earth fairies, right? They take our thoughts and make moons and stuff. And Bitter you-know-who, the fairy prince, is from Fairy Fairyland. He doesn't have anything to do with what the pixies make."

He took a deep breath. "So there are two Fairylands, and nobody told me." It was a lame way to end his statement. The truth of the matter was that he'd been tasked with finding the demon, and he'd failed spectacularly. Except when he looked around, everyone was looking at him with shock and a little bit of excitement in their eyes.

"What?" Bruce asked. "What did I say?"

"We didn't know," Wulfric said, his voice low and his expression thoughtful. "Fairyland is so complicated.

I assumed that the pixies created another part of it, another realm, so to speak, in a vast land."

"No," Bruce said. "It's an entirely different place. Or dimension. That's what Erin said."

"Created from our thoughts," Laddin said in a bright voice. "It makes sense. The pixies use our thoughts to create Earth Fairyland, whereas Fairy Fairyland is—"

"Created from fairy thoughts," Josh said. "It's like the difference between Windows and Mac OS. The end products may look similar, but they're not the same at all."

Stratos nodded. "And they don't play well with each other."

Okay. So this was interesting, but it didn't solve the problem. They still didn't know where the demon was. Unless....

Bruce exhaled loudly, the realization hitting him broadside. Then he asked a question to everyone and no one in particular. "You guys searched everywhere for the demon, right? But who searched Fairyland?"

The man with the whisper voice answered. "A Fairy Queen."

"She could search Fairy Fairyland, but what about Earth Fairyland?"

Silence.

Bruce groaned. "Nobody asked a pixie?"

Nero shook his head. "They're not exactly easy to pin down."

"Find, pin down, or talk to," Yordan agreed. "In fact, they don't often talk to anyone except you, Sir Farts-a-Lot."

"He's Windy Wolf to the fireworks fairies," Laddin said.

Lady Kinstead smiled, and the expression was half-mad even as her touch across his cheek was tender. "So, young one, what do we do? How do we save the world?"

"We need to ask the pixies," he answered. "Either the regular fairies or the cheese ones."

Laddin pushed to his feet and looked around. "We're not near the tree where the cheese ones hang out. And the fairy circle was…."

Josh was looking down at his iWatch. "We're on the far side of the lake. Ground zero is over there." He waved to the east where, sure enough, Bruce could see the black edge of the lake and the dead trees that surrounded it.

It didn't matter. Bruce was pretty sure he could call them. After all, some things worked the same whether it was on a Mac or a PC. Clicking worked the same. So, calling out fairy names three times should bring them in an instant.

Then he glanced around at the nearly two dozen people and wolves sprawled on the ground. "I suggest all of you back away."

Most of them did. Wulfric was especially spry as he bounded to his feet and backed about fifty yards away. "I'll just confuse the issue," he said as he moved.

"As will I," echoed his mother as she joined him.

Josh pointed to a hedge that bordered a road. "I've got a support car coming with clothes from there."

"We're backing up," Whisper Guy said. "But we're not leaving you."

Everyone nodded, and Bruce was grateful for their support. Laddin, however, remained staunchly by his side, and when Bruce turned to say something, he held up his hand.

"I'm staying," he said firmly. "You're not negotiating with those crazies alone, so don't bother arguing."

Bruce grinned. "I was going to say thank you."

"Oh. Okay. You're welcome."

With a last look around, he took a deep breath and started to call out. Except when the moment came, he realized he couldn't exactly remember the full titles. "Oh shit," he cursed, but Laddin squeezed his arm.

"Grand Cheesy Fetid Feta and Dollarback Erin Rodger-Dodger, we call you. Fetid Feta. Erin Rodger-Dodger. Fetid Feta! Erin Rodger-Dodger!" The last was said with a note of command, and Bruce was pleased when the two fairies appeared before him.

Sadly, that feeling didn't last for long.

Chapter 23

NEGOTIATING WITH TODDLERS

THE GRAND Cheesy arrived while Laddin was calling Erin. The still-big fairy blinked into the space before them, midscream.

"Me!" He stomped his foot hard enough to shake the ground.

Then, while Laddin was drawing breath to call again, Erin Rodger-Dodger appeared. She took a moment to look around, spotted the Grand Cheesy, and pointed at him. "You!"

She didn't have the size or voice to match Fetid Feta, but when she stomped her foot, the ground trembled just as much. Then she rushed forward like a football player and banged into Cheesy's leg.

"You!" she repeated.

He looked around, clearly disoriented, but the moment he saw her, he stomped his foot again. "Me!"

She tumbled backward from the force of his stomp but then quickly regained her feet as she adjusted her hat as if she was tilting a Stetson across her brow. Then she threw something at him and a tiny firework exploded across his knees. The burst of bright red was impressive for such a tiny charge.

"You!"

"Stop that!" Bruce snapped, but the fairies were too involved with each other to notice. Each time they bellowed or stomped or exploded something, the impact seemed to grow.

"Feta! Erin!" Laddin tried to step between the two, but it didn't work. Worse, the next firework burned his legs, and he jumped back in pain.

Bruce caught him, of course. And one shared glance between the two of them was all they needed to make a decision. They needed to get the fairies' attention, and yelling wasn't working.

Laddin reached out at the exact same moment that Bruce grabbed his hand. The minute they connected palm to palm, warm current flowed straight from Bruce into Laddin. He was careful this time with his thoughts as he pictured both fairies silent and paying attention to him.

"Be quiet," he said. He didn't yell it, but the sound seemed to roll through the field.

Both fairies abruptly stopped.

Wow. Laddin looked at Bruce.

"Can you maybe send less power?"

Bruce nodded. "I'll try. Maybe try to draw a little less too."

"Got it." This was going to take a little experimentation. Meanwhile, he invested his next words with less force, more casualness. "So we'd like to talk to you, if that's okay."

Erin turned to him. "We hear you, Windy Wolf Rider."

Laddin frowned a moment, wondering at the label. Was that a reference to sex with—

"Not important," Bruce muttered.

Definitely not important. Embarrassing, yes. Important, no. "So…," he said as he looked at Bruce. Up until now, Bruce had taken the lead in the fairy negotiations. He was the one with the fairy power. But it was now flowing from Bruce to him and the pixies were looking at him, so he decided to take a stab at a solution.

"We're looking for the demon that fried the lake and is poisoning the ground. Do you know where he is?"

In unison, both fairies said, "Yes."

Laddin inhaled sharply, as did Bruce. In fact, he guessed that anyone within hearing distance took an excited breath.

"Will you take us there?"

In unison, both fairies said, "No."

Crap.

"Why not?" Laddin asked.

Erin lifted her chin. "He is very big." She glared at Fetid Feta. "Much bigger than you."

"We want to meet him anyway," Laddin pressed.

"And we didn't make him that size," Bruce added.

Erin stomped her foot. "Yes, you did!" Fortunately, her foot stomp didn't echo through the field. That was progress, but the way Fetid Feta bickered back at her was not.

"No," Feta said, pointing at Erin. "You made him big with power from them." He swept this finger at everyone in the field.

"You are big!" she snapped back. "With power from him!" She pointed at Bruce.

Wow, it was like trying to talk to toddlers. Or two spoiled actors. Laddin held up his hand and poured a little of Bruce's power into his words. "Answer my question," he said firmly. "How did the demon become so big?"

Both of them rolled their eyes. It would have been comical if they didn't so desperately need the information. Feta pointed at Bruce.

"You thought."

Erin pointed at herself. "And I made him bigger."

Feta pointed at Laddin. "You thought."

"And my friends made him bigger."

Then Feta pointed past them at Nero. "You thought."

"And we made him much bigger!"

Feta turned and pointed at Josh, who stood beside Nero. "You thought—"

"I got it!" Laddin interrupted before Feta pointed at everyone in turn. "Every human nearby thinks about the demon—"

"And he gets bigger!" both Feta and Erin said at once.

"Because that's what you do?" Bruce asked. "The Earth fairies take thoughts and make them into things. Like the moon and the—"

"Fireworks!"

"We do it too!" Feta cried. "We do it here." He pointed to the ground. "And there." He pointed to the distant bushes. "And over there." He pointed to the field to the right. "And—"

"We got it!" Laddin interrupted.

"But how does that make the demon bigger?" Bruce asked.

Laddin didn't wait for the fairies to answer. "Because everything we think creates their world, which—I

guess—bleeds over into our world. The demon origi-
nally came from a short story that the locals told. That's
how we know how to kill it. Because Josh read the story and told us."

Laddin looked back at Josh, but it was Wiz who
caught his attention. The man quietly pulled out a gun
from a tiny pocket on his dog tags. The guy was naked and the pocket was about the size of a quarter, but
he pulled out a pistol anyway and showed it to Laddin
before hiding it behind his back. It was the way the
townspeople had killed the demon in the short story—a
special bullet, right between the eyes.

Then Laddin looked back at Bruce, who was still
sorting through how the fairies worked. "They take our
thoughts and create things in Earth Fairyland."

"Which sometimes bleeds over into our world.
That's how they created a moon that was powerful
enough to affect the werewolves in our world."

Bruce rubbed a tired hand over his jaw. "I hated
fairy tales growing up."

That wasn't the point. Laddin focused again on
the fairies. "So the demon is in your Fairyland—Earth
Fairyland. We know he's very big, but we still want you
to take us to him."

"No." Again, both fairies spoke at once.

"Why not?" This time, Laddin and Bruce spoke at
once, which was weird and kind of cool.

"Because," Erin said as she pointed at the two
men. "You cannot go there."

"He must come here," Feta finished as he pointed
at the ground.

Laddin looked at Bruce, who nodded. "Then bring
him here."

"No!" Erin cried out. "You will make him bigger, and he is big enough."

"We won't make him bigger."

"Promise?" Feta asked.

"No!" That answer came from at least three people behind them. Laddin had no idea who, but he didn't need the reminder that promises were never easy with fairies.

"I promise that we don't want to make him bigger."

Erin wrinkled her nose. "That is not a promise, that is a wish. You don't wish him bigger, but he is getting huge anyway!"

Feta nodded. "Huger than huge."

"The hugest!"

Laddin interrupted before they got distracted again. "What if we made him smaller?"

Bruce leaned in. "What if we made him go away completely?"

Erin folded her arms in an angry pout. "All you do is make him bigger!"

Laddin looked at Bruce. "That's because we keep thinking of him. All of us do. We keep thinking and worrying, then the media spins story after story—"

"And he gets bigger," Bruce muttered. "But if we get him here…." His gaze hopped back to Wiz, the implication clear. If they got him back here, then Wiz could shoot the thing between the eyes. Problem solved.

Erin shook her head, her frown clear beneath her flower hat. "I will *not* bring him here. I will not bring him anywhere near you!"

"I will," Feta said, his voice smug. "I will bring him right here if you take me to Fairyland." He grinned as he lifted his head. "I want to be even bigger!"

Bruce sighed. "I told you. I can't take you to Fairy Fairyland. Only Bitt—" He abruptly changed his word, presumably because he didn't want to say Bitterroot's name out loud. "Only the fairy prince can do that, and he's already said no."

Feta folded his arms and lifted his chin in defiance. "And I told you, Smoked Gouda has said you will."

"Then bring the demon," Bruce said. "If Smoked Gouda is right, I will get you to Fairy Fairyland afterward."

Feta appeared to think about that. That had to be hard to do given that his brain was probably made up of mold.

"I swear I will do my best to convince the fairy prince to take you," Bruce added.

"Deal!" Feta clapped his hands. "I will bring the demon here. Then you will take me to Fairy Fairyland."

"No!" Erin said loudly.

It didn't matter, because Feta looked at everyone gathered there. "Think very hard!" he ordered. "Think of bringing the demon here for you to see."

They had no choice now. They had to roll with it for as long as they had the pixie's agreement. So Laddin thought as hard as he could. He thought about how Wisconsin was dying mile by growing mile, and he thought about ending that disaster once and for all. As did everyone else. A single glance around the field showed him every serious face, jaw tight with determination. But nothing happened until Bruce held out his hand. Laddin took it without conscious thought, but the moment their palms connected, he felt the power surge through him.

Bring the demon here, he thought.

And it came.

Chapter 24

GODZILLA NEEDS TO GET HAPPY

BRUCE HAD dressed as the Creature from the Black Lagoon once for a haunted house. That was what he expected to appear. Something a little more than man-sized and black with ickiness.

He'd gotten the icky part right.

First off, the thing was huge—larger than Godzilla—and it sprawled at the edge of the lake like Jabba the Hutt. There were eyes and definitely a maw, but beyond that all he saw was a boiling mass of anxiety. It made his hands sweat and his heart pound triple time. And the sound it made was like a hissing snake. Low, angry, and steadily building until he thought he would go crazy waiting for it to strike.

Someone screamed, and it was probably him. Then he heard the steady rapport of a gun. He whipped around to look.

It was Wiz with the pistol aimed straight up at… it. He emptied his entire clip at the thing.

Normally Bruce would have said it was too far away for a handgun. A bazooka might be too small to score a hit, but looking back at the—the living nightmare—he could see the impact right where it was supposed to go. Puffs of explosions dead center between the eyes. Over and over.

He waited for the thing to die. He prayed for it to shrink, melt, or whatever it would do. He'd be thrilled if it went *poof* in a burst of ashes, but nothing happened.

"Damn it!" Wiz cursed. "It's changed."

"What? Why?" Bruce demanded. Hadn't they said they knew how to kill it? That all Bruce had to do was find it and they'd take care of it?

Josh groaned from beside Wiz. "It's evolved beyond the story version. It can't be killed the same way."

Curses rolled through his mind, but he didn't have time to let his fury fly because a great deal was happening, and it was all bad. First rule of a firefighter—see what's happening and breathe. That was all he had to do.

He squinted at the monster as he forced himself to make steady inhales and exhales. He managed to sort out roiling tentacles and bubbling masses that swelled, burst, then collapsed back on themselves. Except it wasn't collapsing to the same size it was before. Now that he looked with narrowed eyes—and his mind wasn't busy screaming in terror—he could see little specks of yellow fairy lights all over the thing. They were the pixies, catching something, then pressing it into the demon... which made it grow bigger. In tiny increments, but there were a thousand of those little fairies, each adding a tiny bit over and over.

"You're making it bigger!" Erin screamed, and she was right.

Just like with the moon, the fairies were catching everyone's thoughts, their fears, their terror, and making it into more demon.

"Stop that!" Bruce snapped. "Stop them from adding to the thing!"

She glared at him. "It is what we do. We take what you think!"

"And make that," he realized. Oh God.

"Think happy thoughts!" Laddin bellowed. "Don't worry!"

Nice idea, but that wasn't going to work. Not with that demon towering over them.

Then it got worse. Someone cried out, not in fear but in warning. Bruce looked over, and pretty soon he found what they were screaming about.

Kangaroos—a whole herd of them hopping full tilt straight at them. And if he didn't miss his guess, they were being ridden by gnomes or leprechauns. Who the hell knew? He heard Josh curse and Nero moan, "Not again."

But then, from the opposite side of the herd, something else appeared—something dark and ghostly. It looked like a Dementor from the Harry Potter series, but someone bellowed, "Lich." And this time Erin stomped her foot hard enough to grab Bruce's attention.

"And now you bring its friends!" she screamed.

She was really pissed off, and Bruce couldn't blame her. Everything they'd done had made things worse. He looked around in panic, hoping to find some help. There were people far more experienced here than he was. Surely they knew what to do.

They did. They squared off with the kangaroos and the lich. They protected themselves and each other. But while they kept everyone alive, they did nothing to stop the demon-turned-swamp-megalith that was going to swallow them whole.

Then Laddin grabbed Bruce's hand and whipped him around so that they could face each other.

"Happy thoughts!" Laddin screamed. He jerked Bruce close enough so that he didn't have to bellow. "I love you."

Right. Happy thoughts. But a few choruses of the Barney theme song weren't going to save them. The demon was too big, and its friends were going to kill them all long before they figured out how to shrink it.

"Don't think!" Laddin ordered. Then he pressed his mouth hard to Bruce's. The kiss was rushed, and they clanged teeth. Before Bruce could adjust, Laddin pulled back. "Feel. Just feel!"

What he felt was crap-his-pants terror, but he didn't have any better ideas. "Er, yeah. I, uh, I love you too."

Laddin rolled his eyes, and Bruce couldn't really blame him. Talk about lame. Mouthing the words wasn't going to do it. He had to really put his thought, his power—

"You have to *feel it*!" Laddin said.

Right. He had to put his feelings into it. But he was feeling afraid! He was feeling like the world was ending and it was all his fault.

Laddin lifted their joined hands. "Light me up!"

Light him? Oh, right. Laddin was his light bulb. All he needed to do was push power into the guy's hands and Laddin would do the rest. Bruce exhaled in relief and pushed as much energy as he could through their matched palms.

He felt the flow of energy, he felt his shoulders relax, and he knew that he hadn't fucked up entirely, because Laddin would be able to fix things. Except it didn't work. He saw Laddin close his eyes. He watched as the guy inhaled, as if drawing in everything good about the world, and then exhaled a simple phrase.

"It's okay. Everything's okay."

Bruce felt the power of it. He felt his lips curve into a smile, but all around him the noise continued. The demon hissed, the people on the kangaroos whooped as they hopped around, destroying everything in their path, and someone screamed, "Disintegrate!" at the lich.

"Don't think about it," Laddin said, and Bruce didn't have to say a word. They both knew it was impossible to *not* think of what was going on around them.

So Laddin pressed his forehead to Bruce's. They were eye to eye, nose to nose, and when he spoke, the words felt like they were for Bruce alone. The nightmare to their right or the disasters going on all around them, melted into the background.

"I love you," Laddin said.

Bruce grimaced and tried to pull away. "That's not going to work. We need to sing something. 'Happy Birthday' or 'Good Vibrations.'" They were the only two songs he could think of right then.

"It's not working because you don't believe it," Laddin said. "Why don't you think I love you?"

Bruce took a moment to focus. Was Laddin really trying to have a serious conversation while evil kangaroos were dashing around? Apparently he was, because his expression was fierce and he wasn't letting Bruce look away.

"Because you're just saying that. It's not real."

Laddin glared at him. Then he abruptly flattened his hand on Bruce's chest. "Feel this, you idiot. It *is* real!"

Now that sounded like true emotion. Irritation and annoyance. Bruce heard it but then felt something else—a current of power feeding back to him through Laddin's palm. What energy he fed Laddin was coming back to him even stronger.

"I love you," Laddin said, conviction in his voice.

"Right," Bruce echoed. "You love me. And I love you." He threw that last part in, hoping it would do what was needed. But all he had to do was listen to know that the demon wasn't any smaller or quieter.

"You don't believe me," Laddin said, frustration clear in his tone. "Why can't you feel it?"

He did feel it—warmth, power, and affection. "We have to try something else."

Laddin shook his head. "This is the answer, but you have to believe it."

Bruce nodded, and he tried. He really wanted to believe, but he wasn't the kind of guy someone could love. He was the guy women fucked and the guy who ran into burning buildings for your kid. He was the one people hugged with tearful gratitude, then forgot five minutes later. And at night he was the guy who went home to an empty apartment in a crappy area of town.

He was the also the one who hurt his own brother when he was angry at his father. That wasn't someone to love. That was someone you thanked for saving your kid—on the lucky days he managed it—and then walked away from. He just lived. And that was the truth.

"I love you," Laddin repeated. "You think I'm bullshitting you, but this is it. It's real love. And do you know how I know that?"

Bruch shook his head.

"Because I want a future with you. I've been thinking about what we could do after this is all over." He took a breath. "I don't want work in the field."

Bruce felt his lips curve. Laddin's neat-freak side would make working in this kind of chaos impossible.

"I thought I wanted to go home back to my old life. I do, but I want you more, and you're here, not in LA. So I thought we could get a place in Michigan where I can work with Captain M and keep things in order for the field teams. They need someone who makes things tidy so they can do their jobs."

"You're perfect for that."

"Yeah," Laddin said, "I am. I like LA, but I'm tired of the fake stuff, you know? I want something real." He lifted his chin. "I want you."

Bruce huffed out a breath. It was too soon to be talking about things like this, and it certainly wasn't the place. But before he could say something stupid, Laddin tightened his hand into a claw on Bruce's chest. It dug in hard enough to make Bruce shut up.

"Listen to me!" Laddin ordered, and Bruce nodded. "I want to come home to something. To *someone*. And when I close my eyes and picture who I want to be with, it's you, Bruce." He paused a moment to see if his words were sinking in. They were. And more than that, Laddin was feeding the image straight to Bruce's heart. The current of energy from Laddin's palm was creating the picture in Bruce's mind.

"A two-story house with a backyard," Bruce said, giving words to the image Laddin was feeding him. "Right on the edge of the state park, so we can run as wolves if we want to."

Laddin smiled. "I get that you're a medic and a firefighter. You'll probably want to be jumping into fires when you're seventy."

Bruce snorted. "Maybe not seventy, but at least until I'm sixty-five." He sobered. "I'm good at it, Laddin."

"And we could use a good medic and someone who keeps his head around fires." There was a sudden explosion by the lich, and they both flinched. But Laddin wasn't letting anything stop him. "I don't even know what your favorite dish is, but I'd have it there waiting when you came home. I'd watch you eat it and smile like you do when you're so satisfied, you're bursting with it."

Bruce knew the smile he was referring to. The one that usually came after sex with Laddin. "It's lasagna. And I bet yours is amazing."

"It is. And do you know what else I think when I look at you?"

Bruce shook his head.

"Kids. I know you can't have them, but I still see them. A linebacker of a little boy with that dimple you have in your chin."

"That's a scar from a house fire."

Laddin smiled. "It's yours, and I like it. And when I look at our son, I see that on his chin."

"What about your dimples? And a really straight nose?" Laddin's dimples were on his butt, and they were cute. As for his nose, it was ruler straight, which was a far cry from Bruce's, which had been broken more times than he could count.

"It goes with my neatnik side."

"I'd teach him how to make a big mess in the backyard as we build a treehouse." He'd always wanted one of those.

"And I'll teach him how to clean up his room before we construct Lego bridges and blow them up with tiny bits of C-4."

Bruce blinked. "Seriously? You blew up your Legos?"

"Oh yeah!" Laddin looked like he was in the midst of a really good memory. But then he focused back on

Bruce. "This isn't infatuation, and I'm too old for endless rounds of fucking."

"You're a year younger than me!"

"Exactly. Which means it must be getting pretty boring for you too."

It had been. Until he'd met Laddin.

"It's what I want, Bruce. I want a life where you come home to me and little LB."

"Lyndon B. Johnson?"

"Laddin and Bruce. LB."

"Except your name is A-laddin. And no kid of mine—pretend or otherwise—is going to be mistaken for a politician." His expression softened. "How about Aaron? That was my grandfather's name, and he was a pretty cool guy."

Laddin grinned. "I like that."

"Yeah," Bruce said. "Me too." And by that he meant he liked the whole vision. The two-story house, the kid blowing up his toys in the backyard, and Laddin with his arms open wide when Bruce came home from work. "I like that a lot."

"I love you," Laddin said, and this time the words settled deep into Bruce's heart and soul.

"I love you too," Bruce said, the words a bare whisper because he was awestruck by the power of them. He was in love. Real love, with someone who loved him back. Someone who knew who he was deep inside and still wanted to build a home with him—who wanted to make a family with him. It made his knees weak with gratitude, with joy, but most of all, with love.

"I wish it was real," Bruce said.

"It is real," Laddin said. "Because we'll make it so."

"Yes," Bruce agreed. For Laddin, he'd make it work. "We'll adopt, right? No firstborn from us."

Laddin nodded, both aware of the fairy promise. "I don't need a baby from my body. I just need a child and someone to raise him with."

With that thought in mind, with the image of their family settling into his heart, Bruce pressed his mouth to Laddin's. It was meant to be a soft kiss—they were still in the middle of a battle, after all. But along with the love came passion. And so when he kissed Laddin, his mouth grew firm and hungry. Laddin was equally bold, equally demanding.

With every twist and thrust of their tongues, they loved each other. Completely, lustfully, and with their whole hearts. Heat built while the fairy power zipped between their bodies. It was lust, joy, and wonder, plus a myriad of other wonderful emotions mixed in. But most of all, it was love, newly found and shared between the two of them.

Eventually they had to stop kissing because they needed to breathe. When Bruce pulled back, he realized he couldn't hear hissing anymore. Then Laddin looked around and whispered, "Where'd it go?"

Bruce looked up. He saw blue sky, and he heard silence.

The demon was gone. The kangaroos and their riders were gone. Even the lich was nowhere to be seen. And while everyone else was looking around in dazed confusion, Erin clapped her hands in delight.

"You made it smaller!" she said in satisfaction.

Actually, Bruce was pretty sure they were both bigger, right then, which was embarrassing because they were both still naked from their romp as wolves.

"What the hell is that?" Wiz said from down by what had once been the edge of the lake.

"It's a baby!" Stratos said as she bent down to see. She didn't touch it, but just squatted down and stared.

Bruce and Laddin looked at each other, their eyes wide with shock. Bruce was the first to speak. "It can't be."

"I bet it is."

"But… it can't!"

"Yes, it can. The pixies made what we thought about—him." Laddin looked down at Erin. "Right? That's our baby?"

Erin nodded. "You had a very good thought."

"Yes, he did. We did!" Laddin said as he took off running down toward the edge of the lake.

Bruce watched him go, his mind refusing to move but his body quickly following anyway. But when he got to the edge of the lake, Lady Kinstead was there, and she knelt down to where Stratos refused to go. With gentle hands, she scooped up the child and wrapped him in her scarf. Laddin was at her side, looking the baby over with greedy eyes.

Then he looked up at Bruce and pointed to the child's face. "He has the dimple. Right there. Your dimple."

Lady Kinstead smiled. "And he has your eyes and nose," she said sweetly. Carefully, she offered the child to Laddin. "You have a beautiful son."

Laddin gathered the child. Someone had taught him how to hold a baby, because he quickly tucked it close. Then he looked up at Bruce. "We made a baby," he said, laughter in his voice. "Bruce, look!"

Bruce was looking, but his mind couldn't comprehend what he was seeing. "We were just talking," he murmured, even though he knew it was a lie. They'd been creating. They'd been forming a future with words, fairy magic, and love.

He stepped closer. He had to see. He needed to know if it was true.

Others were coming over as well. On two feet or four, they edged closer, but Laddin was holding the child as if it was the most precious gift in the world. Which, now that Bruce thought about it, it was.

"Hey, little Aaron. I'm your daddy," Laddin cooed. "Well, I'm Daddy Number One. Daddy Number Two is over there." He looked up. "Come on, Number Two, say hi to your son."

Josh had made it to Bruce's side. His face had a streak of mud across it, but that didn't dim his grin. "You have all the fairy magic in the world, and you make a baby with it? What, no power left over to give Uncle Josh a Ferrari?"

Bruce shot his brother a look. "You can't even drive a stick! What the hell would you do with a Ferrari?"

"Give the car to Uncle Nero," Nero said with a happy grumble. "Go on," he said, nudging Bruce's shoulder. "Go say hello to what you made."

It wasn't possible. It wasn't even logical. And yet Bruce stumbled forward, and as he stood there looking stupid, Laddin offered him the baby. He hadn't intended to take it, but he couldn't let the child fall, could he? The feeling of having little Aaron in his arms was perfect, and the little pink bow the baby's lips made as he sucked on his fist was even more perfect. Bruce didn't know what to think. He sure as hell couldn't be feeling this swell of love for a child that used to be a demon.

"It's not real," he murmured.

"Sure looks real," whispered the older man who—he now realized—couldn't speak above a whisper.

"Yeah," chuckled Josh. "Please say I can be there when you explain this to Mom."

"No!" Bruce said, his voice hard. "No parents. No others. Not yet." Not until he could wrap his own head around it. Then he looked at Laddin. "Did we really make a baby? Did we really make *our* baby?"

"Yes," an arrogant voice said. "Yes, you did. One born of love and magic. It's unusual, to be sure, but he is definitely your firstborn child."

It took Bruce a moment to recognize the voice—and then even longer to make himself look up from his child to see the fucking fairy prince standing there.

Bitterroot. And the asshole had said *firstborn child.*

The guy wasn't dressed in salad right now. Instead, he was tall, dark, and his black eyes glittered with excitement. Bitterroot brushed a butterfly off his shoulder and reached for the child.

Bruce pulled back the child, and Laddin stepped between them.

"Get back, you fairy bastard!" Laddin growled.

"It is my right," Bitterroot said firmly. "The child is mine by bargain of power. The very same power you used to create him."

"Oh, child," Lady Kinstead said, her voice ringing with dismay. "You didn't bargain away your baby, did you?" She looked at Wulfric. "Didn't we make a rule? No fairy deals? Didn't we?"

Wulfric nodded, but he didn't speak to her. Instead he turned to Bitterroot. "There must be—"

"I will not speak with Wulfric the Deceiver."

Wulfric pressed his lips together, dipped his chin, and took a step back. With him went Lady Kinstead, her expression infinitely sad. But even as he stepped back, Nero pressed forward.

"Come on, Bitterroot. What would you do with a magic demon child anyway?"

"This child will be cherished beyond anything you can imagine," Bitterroot snapped. "The bargain was made, the power used, and the child is *mine*!"

"No," Bruce said loudly. "Absolutely not. This is not my firstborn child. I didn't—we didn't give birth to him. We—" He didn't really know what they'd done, but it didn't seem to matter. He could see that in Bitterroot's face.

"Do not fight me on this," Bitterroot said, his voice heavy with menace. "You will not win."

"You can't have him—" Bruce said.

"We won't give him up—" Laddin said at the same moment.

Bitterroot squared his shoulders and raised his hands. The butterfly that had been dancing around his shoulder settled into his open palm. "You will die, and I will still have the child," he said. But before he could do more, Yordan rushed forward. His big hands were raised palm out, and his bullhorn-like voice echoed in the clearing.

"Whoa! Whoa! Whoa! Let's not go talking about dying, okay? We just finished with one demon, we don't need to go making another." He glanced over at Bruce. "No offense."

Bruce didn't even understand what the man was saying. He was too focused on finding a way out. How did they escape the fairy prince's bargain?

Meanwhile, Nero came to stand shoulder to shoulder with Yordan as they looked at Bitterroot.

"What would it take to leave the child alone?" Nero asked. "What do you want instead—"

"There is no instead," Bitterroot interrupted. "I need the child." Then his voice took on a softer note. "He will be cherished and adored above even myself.

You don't know what a human child means in Fairyland." He shook his head. "There is nothing else you can offer me."

"I won't—" Bruce argued, but Stratos cut him off.

"What about time?"

Everyone looked at her in confusion.

"You mean like visitation?" Yordan asked. "One weekend here, one weekend there?"

"I'm not giving up the rights to my child!" Bruce said.

"You already gave up your right to him when you ate the apple," Bitterroot countered.

Which was true. But he never expected to make a baby. And certainly not this way.

Stratos held up her hand as she focused on Bitterroot. "Look, we've just finished the mother of all battles. We don't even know if it worked. We don't know yet if Earth has been saved."

"It has," Bitterroot said, twisting his head enough so that he could flick his gaze to where Feta stood with Erin on his shoulder. "You have healed the land? No more poison in the water or the soil?"

"Yes, Fairy Prince," Feta said, worship in his tone.

"No, Fairy Prince," Erin said, her voice equally awed.

"What?" Bitterroot snapped. "Why no?"

"I mean there is no poison." She hopped on Feta's shoulder as she looked at Bruce and Laddin. "Their love is very strong. We were able to heal everything."

Bruce blew out a breath, and he wasn't the only one. Earth was safe. Wisconsin was healed. That was very good. But it didn't mean he was giving up Aaron.

"What I meant," Stratos said clearly, "was that we're still regrouping. Doesn't magic take a while in all those fairy stories? Aurora's curse didn't kick in until her sixteenth birthday. Rumpelstiltskin didn't show up in the delivery room. Give these guys some time before they have to think of giving up the baby. They're not even dressed yet."

Bitterroot folded his arms, his expression angry. "Do you think to find a way out by morning? You will not. The child will still be mine."

"Maybe so," Bing said. "But it is what humans do. We hold, we love, and we grieve. All these things take time."

"Yeah," Yordan added. "You're immortal. What is one more day to you?"

"I am not immortal," Bitterroot grumbled. "But I can be kind, though I do not think it will ease your pain." He took a breath. "In the morning, then. At dawn."

"At our tree!" Feta said with a bright voice. "We will host you at our tree!"

Bitterroot didn't even acknowledge the pixie. Instead, he looked at Laddin and Bruce. "Agreed?"

Neither Bruce nor Laddin spoke. Bruce didn't want to say yes to anything, but that was the problem, wasn't it? He'd agreed before. And while he was thinking of making a run for it, the fairy bastard made it worse.

"You cannot outrun me," he said with exaggerated patience. "Your power comes from me. So, do I take the child now? Or in the morning?"

Bruce looked at Laddin and saw agony reflected back to him. Agony, pain, and no hope whatsoever.

Bruce sighed. "In the morning."

Chapter 25

ANYBODY KNOW HOW
TO BURP A BABY?

LADDIN CARRIED the baby on the way back. They didn't say a word. Bruce was giving back-off vibes to anyone who came near, and Laddin was too busy holding a now fussy baby in his arms to talk to anyone, though Uncle Josh hovered nearby and winced at an angry cry.

"I bet he's hungry. I could eat a horse."

They all were. A werewolf romp always ended in a feast. Only they'd followed their romp with a battle, so food was weighing heavy on everyone's mind.

"There might be kangaroo meat back where we were," Nero said.

Josh cut him off. "No. Never. I'm not going to eat anything that tried to kill us."

"That's the exact opposite of the warrior code," Stratos countered. She dropped her voice to mimic a barrel-chested fighter. "We kill, we eat." Then she grunted twice for good measure.

"Didn't you kill a lich?"

She sighed. "That's twice I've battled that thing. If it comes back a third time, I want a badge or something."

"Lich Killer Queen?" Josh offered. He started improvising lyrics as they walked to the road Josh had indicated earlier. A support van was waiting in the distance. Hopefully it would have burgers for everyone. And bonus, he knew the van had emergency baby supplies.

Laddin looked to Bruce, but the guy was still bristling. His shoulders were hunched, his fists remained at the ready, and he kept sniffing like a wolf on the prowl. Laddin didn't blame him. He felt equally angry, equally protective. The problem was, everyone else was busy celebrating the win.

They'd defeated the demon. It didn't matter that the thing had been transmuted into a baby. It was no longer killing Lake Wacka Wacka, Wisconsin, or the world, and that called for teasing banter, a feast, and beers all around. It was only Laddin who felt like his world was ending. And maybe Bruce too. But everyone else was breathing a huge sigh of relief and looking for a place to celebrate.

Laddin pulled Aaron close to his chest so he could sing the child a lullaby his mother had taught him. It worked for a time. Aaron quieted and snuggled close while Laddin inhaled the smell of a new baby. His baby.

"Wiz and I will do a supplies run," Stratos said as she stepped near. "Who knew he has ten siblings and knows all about baby stuff?" She shrugged. "Plus, his Bag of Holding had clothes and money in it, so we can get going as soon as the Uber gets here."

"It's an infinite bag, right? Why not keep a motorcycle in it?" Josh asked.

"Because it's not a TARDIS," Wiz said.

"Well, obviously," Josh drawled. "A TARDIS would be way more useful right now."

"Thanks," Laddin said to Stratos, ignoring the others. She nodded in response, but her gaze landed on the baby.

"Look, I'm here to help," she said gently. "And I didn't hear everything that went down, but...." She took a breath as she raised her hand to touch Aaron's hair before pulling back. "Isn't he... you know... a demon?"

"No, he's not," Laddin denied, his voice forceful. Bruce reacted too. His head whipped around as he bared his teeth at Stratos. She threw up her hands and backed away.

"Okay, okay! I can see that you guys know what you're doing." But her voice implied the exact opposite. "I was just asking a question."

Wiz continued, his voice coldly matter-of-fact. "That same question is going to dog him his entire life."

"He's not a demon," Laddin repeated, but shit, the question wouldn't go away. He saw it on everyone's face, including Bruce's. And he felt it inside his own heart. He'd been right there. He knew exactly what had happened. His love, Bruce's love, and fairy magic had taken all their good thoughts and changed a manifestation of anxiety and pain—the demon—into a manifestation of love—Aaron. Good thoughts defeated bad ones by a thousand to one. Always. Assuming the feelings were real. Assuming the love was real. Assuming....

Laddin pressed his cheek to Aaron's and closed his eyes. There were so many doubts creeping into his head, and he knew if they were coming into his brain, they were crawling into Bruce's as well.

What he hadn't counted on was that the director of Wulf, Inc. would choose to add to those doubts. But there he was—a middle-aged man who was still hard-bodied despite his hangdog expression—waiting for them by the van. He spoke quietly to Stratos and Wiz and then gestured for Laddin and Bruce to step into his waiting limo.

Great.

Except Laddin wasn't going to step in until he got a few things first. Apparently he was the only one who knew that there was baby formula, diapers, and a couple of onesies in the support van. Why they'd been put there, he had no idea, but he was thankful for them.

He gently handed Aaron to Bruce so he could get the supplies. But even though the man took the baby quickly, Laddin was busy analyzing Bruce's expression. Had he been reluctant? Had he seen a grimace of distaste when Bruce took the child? Was he having second thoughts?

His own thoughts made him crazy, so it was a relief to mix the formula while Bruce diapered and clothed the child with deft fingers. Apparently paramedics practiced for this sort of thing. But when Laddin was about to hand Bruce the bottle, Bruce shook his head.

"You do it. I want to be able to shift if I need to."

"We're not going to be in any danger from the director."

Bruce arched a brow. "Are you sure?"

Laddin started to say, "Of course. He's on our side." But sides could change. And Laddin needed to be with Aaron in case things took a bad turn. "I hope I'm sure," Laddin finally said as he adjusted the baby in his arms and started feeding him.

Aaron took to the bottle immediately, growing less fussy now that he was eating. Then Bruce grabbed a few protein bars from the van, and together they walked to the director's limo, feeling as if they were heading for a firing squad.

Oh goody.

They climbed in without saying a word. The director was already seated where he could look straight at them. He spoke in a whisper—always—because he'd lost his voice in a battle with a vamp back when the bloodsuckers were the bad guys. Maybe that was why they were in a limo—for the quiet ride—because even though the guy whispered, Laddin heard every word.

"Start with what happened," the director whispered. He pointed at Laddin. "Go."

Laddin explained everything in detail—everything he remembered, felt, and believed. And most especially, he told the director that Aaron was a baby, not a demon, and anyone who had a problem with that could come talk to him.

The director listened with focused attention. He didn't question, didn't interrupt, and he sure as hell didn't give anything away.

After Laddin was finished, the director pointed at Bruce. "Your turn. Go."

Bruce pointed at Laddin. "What he said. One hundred percent."

The director's lips curved. "Nice try. Report."

Bruce blew out a breath, but he started talking. It was gratifying to hear Bruce echo Laddin's thoughts that Aaron had been created out of their love and fairy magic.

When Bruce was done, he fell silent. They all did. Then they watched as Aaron finished eating and Laddin had to adjust to burp him. Pat, pat, pat.

Nothing.

Shit. Wasn't the kid supposed to burp?

Pat, pat, pat.

Nothing.

Maybe he didn't need to burp. Laddin looked to Bruce, who shrugged in response.

Then the director sighed. "Give him here. You can't just pat. You have to rub his back too."

Come again?

The director huffed out a breath. "I'm going to show you two bachelors how to burp a baby. Come on. I've got three kids, and I always did the 2:00 a.m. feeding. I know how to do this."

Neither Laddin nor Bruce knew what to say to that, so Laddin passed over the baby, and they were suddenly getting a lesson in burping. Pat twice then rub. Pat, pat, rub.

Aaron burped on the second rub.

"There you go," the director whispered as he cuddled the child in his arms. "You'll figure it out. He'll probably let go into his diaper soon. That's how it was with my kids. Input, burp, output. Then sleep."

Bruce frowned. "So you believe us? You know—"

"That he's a real boy?"

Bruce nodded.

"Hell if I know. Magic can do some amazing things. It can also royally fuck you up. You boys up for both sides of that equation?"

Laddin nodded firmly—fiercely—and Bruce seemed to echo it.

"I'll need regular reports on the boy as he grows. He was created during a Wulf, Inc. operation, so according to the Accords, we're responsible for him. I'm going to need to keep a close eye on him."

"How close?" Bruce asked.

"Daily visits while he's little. Not because I need them but because I like kids. It's the teenagers who piss me off." Then he frowned, probably because Bruce was scowling. "Okay, weekly for the first three months. Then we can go to monthly. This is new territory here, boys. We've never had a demon turned adorable baby before." He abruptly stopped speaking and peered at the child's face. "Why does he have a scar on his chin?"

Bruce groaned as he fingered his own chin. "We did not give him my scar, did we?" he asked Laddin.

Laddin chuckled. "I think we did."

"*You* did that," Bruce accused. "But at least he got your nose."

He did, and Laddin felt another wave of love for the child.

"What are you going to do about the fairy prince?"

So much for that warm rush of love. All of a sudden, everything inside him clenched tight.

"The fairy prince is not lying," the director continued. "A human child is treated with reverence in Fairyland. He'd be cherished over there—"

"No." It took a moment for Laddin to realize that he'd been the one to say the word out loud. Sure, he'd been thinking it, but apparently he'd been thinking it so loudly that it tumbled out of his mouth. "I'm not giving up my baby to that prick."

"It is the law, though. You made a bargain." The director was looking at Bruce.

"We'll make another one."

"No!" Laddin said loudly. "We're done making fairy deals!"

The director grimaced. "You weren't supposed to make the first ones."

Laddin was about to argue, but Bruce cut him off with a wave of his hand. "Old news," Bruce said. "Do you know of any way to keep the child?"

Aaron was starting to smack his lips, and the director set his pinkie finger near the child's mouth. The baby rooted on that, opened his mouth, and started sucking on the director's fingertip.

"Definite human instincts," the director whispered.

And an unsanitary finger. But Laddin wasn't going to say that aloud. Meanwhile, Bruce was pressing for a solution.

"Anything you could do to help—"

"I can't," the director said with a sigh. "I can't break the Accords. It would mean war with Fairy, and nobody wants that."

"But—"

"The fairies are legalistic creatures. Letter of the deal and all that. That's how they usually screw people."

Laddin already knew that, and he was getting uncomfortable with Aaron going to sleep in the director's lap. That was his child and Bruce's. If anyone was going to cradle the boy while he slept, it would be one of them. So he scooted forward in his seat and gestured for the return of his child.

But the director didn't immediately hand him back. Instead he looked up, his eyes serious. "Are you sure you want him back?" he asked. There was a weight in his tone that meant so much more than the words themselves. But in case Laddin didn't understand, he pressed his point. "The more you bond now, the harder it will be tomorrow. If you want, I'll keep him for the night. I'll make sure he's—"

"No!" Laddin said, but to his shock, Bruce put a warning hand on Laddin's thigh.

"Hear him out," Bruce said softly.

Laddin didn't want to. Hell, he already knew what the guy was going to say. But he forced himself to sit still and listen, not because he wanted to hear what the man had to say but because Bruce obviously did. Then the director continued.

"If we can't find a way out, then the baby has to go to the prince. We can't go to war over this."

"I will—" Laddin said firmly.

"But I won't," the director countered. "You may be fierce, Laddin, but you can't take on all of Fairy on your own." He grimaced. "The whole of Wulf, Inc. couldn't either."

"So help us find a solution," Bruce said, much to Laddin's relief. Bruce was hoping for an answer, not a way out.

The director looked at Bruce. Then he took a long stare at Laddin. It was like he was weighing their resolve, testing their intent, or measuring their manliness. When it was done, Laddin didn't know if they'd passed or failed.

At least until Bruce held out his hands. "I want the baby," he said firmly.

"I do too," Laddin said.

The director nodded and gently passed the child back to Bruce, who cradled the sleeping baby in his lap.

"Okay," the director whispered. "You're committed to this path. To this child."

"His name is Aaron," Laddin said.

"Then let's figure out a way to keep Aaron away from the royal asshole."

THEY FAILED.

They went over everything with the director. Then, when they got to the pizza farm, they went over it again with Wulfric and his mother. The others listened and made good suggestions, but they didn't know the Accords like Wulfric and Lady Kinstead did. After all, they were the ones who had drafted it, and they had two centuries of experience with the fae.

No one could find a workaround. By midnight Laddin was exhausted. Bruce looked no better, but Lady Kinstead was the one to call it quits. She glided forward, pressed a kiss to the child's forehead, then another to Laddin's and then Bruce's.

"You should sleep now. Maybe it will look better after some rest."

"We have to keep trying," Laddin said, but Bruce shook his head.

"We've been at this for hours. Sometimes rest is the only way to find a solution."

Wulfric and the director nodded their agreement, but rather than leave, they smiled wearily at them.

"We'll keep trying," Wulfric said.

"Until the last moment," the director said. "We'll keep at it."

There wasn't any hope in their voices, but they were sincere in their words, and the others—Wiz, Stratos, Nero, and Uncle Josh—echoed them. Even Yordan and Bing had stuck around.

"Thanks," Laddin said to everyone. Then he and Bruce went to their room.

They set the sleeping Aaron in a crib that the B&B had provided, and then they held each other while looking down at the sleeping child.

Ten fingers, ten toes. Dimpled cheeks and chin. Long straight nose, and the hint of hair as dark as Laddin's, though it might lighten up to be the pale brown that Bruce had. Laddin had done the inventory at every diaper change. He'd smelled Aaron's baby fresh scent and felt the pull on his heart whenever the child had grabbed on to his finger and held tight.

He couldn't imagine losing the baby. Not now. Not when he was already so important to them both.

"What are we going to do?" Laddin whispered, agony in every word.

"I don't know," Bruce answered as he stroked his callused index finger across Aaron's cheek. "I can't believe this is happening. I have a child." He leaned his head against Laddin's. "We have a baby."

For a few more hours at least. And that brought him right back to the question at hand. What were they going to do?

"Tell me again," Bruce said as they stood beside the crib. "Tell me about that future you saw."

"We both saw it."

"Yeah, but tell it to me anyway."

"We'll get a two-story house near the state park behind the Wulf, Inc. mansion in Michigan. I'll still work for Captain M, and you'll—"

"I'll be a medic for someone. Probably Wulf, Inc., but firefighters are needed everywhere."

Wulf, Inc. really needed Bruce, but that wasn't important right then. "I've got the steady nine-to-five, and I love to cook. I'll be the one making lasagna for you when you come home."

"And I'm going to love every bite when I make it in the door, even if I have to microwave it."

Laddin mock shuddered. "You do not microwave lasagna."

"I'm not going to eat it cold."

Laddin smiled. "I'll keep a plate warm for you in the oven."

Bruce wrapped an arm around Laddin's back. "That sounds like heaven."

It did. Except that neither of them had mentioned Aaron, and Laddin couldn't keep the boy out of their story. "You're going to teach Aaron how to play ball, and I'm going to teach him how to blow up his toys."

Bruce snorted. "You're going to regret that, you know."

"Probably." Then he chuckled. "Definitely."

"And someday maybe we'll give Aaron a brother or a sister. We'll take them to baseball games—"

"And go running as wolves in the park."

Bruce waited a beat before asking, "What if Aaron isn't a werewolf? Or his brother or sister?"

Laddin shrugged. "Then we'll take turns running in the park. Or maybe they'll be able to do something else." He'd seen the files when he'd organized Captain M's filing cabinet. "Adoption of magical babies doesn't have the red tape normal adoption does. Magical orphans happen, and they need magical parents to raise them." He looked at Bruce. "You okay with that?"

"We turned a demon into a son. If I wasn't okay with that, I would have bailed back by the lake."

Laddin smiled. "I love you," he said, the words feeling like the most natural thing in the world.

"I love you too," Bruce returned. "And in case you're wondering, I'm in for the long haul. If you want. Even if things go south tomorrow morning—"

"They won't." Of course, that was a bold statement, given that neither of them had any idea how things were going to work out.

"But if they do, I want to try us anyway. You and me with a two-story house and lasagna. Kid or not, I want to give it a shot."

"Me too."

There it was—a commitment to each other, not just their son. And their kiss was, again, the most natural thing in the world. A kiss. Then another. And then Laddin whispered a question.

"So… you want to fool around before the 2:00 a.m. feeding?"

"Hell yes."

The move to the bed took no time at all. There was no space in the room anyway, so they both fell over onto the mattress. They were nearly silent as they undressed each other, and barely spoke above a whisper afterward. Aaron slept through it all as they took comfort in each other's caresses. And kisses. And hot, breathless orgasms.

And then they held each other and looked at the crib.

"That was weird," Bruce whispered. "Doing that with a baby in the room."

"Yeah," Laddin agreed. "Let's get separate rooms in the house."

"And a baby monitor."

"Deal."

They fell silent, and Laddin nearly slept. He was about to drift off when Bruce rolled over and fiddled with the clock. He was setting an alarm for their dawn meeting with Bitterroot. Except he didn't set it for before dawn. He set it for two hours earlier than that.

Given that it was well after midnight, they weren't going to have much time to sleep. Especially if Aaron woke in the middle of the night to be fed. But when Bruce saw him looking, he shrugged.

"I'm not giving up," Bruce whispered. "I'm leaving us enough time to come up with a solution."

Laddin didn't think two hours would be anywhere near enough time for that. They'd already been at it the entire day and had come up with nothing. But he didn't say that.

"If anyone can figure it out, it's you," he whispered.

"Me?" Bruce challenged. "Why am I so special?"

"Because you are," Laddin answered as he pulled Bruce close and shut his eyes. "You just are."

Bruce was silent a long time. Long enough that Laddin had thought he'd fallen asleep. But then he heard Bruce whisper words filled with awe. Awe, shock, and a strong dose of gratitude.

"I'm not a monster," he said. "I've fucked up, that's for sure, but I'm not a monster. I never was."

"No, you're not," Laddin agreed. "You're the man I love."

"Which makes me pretty okay, I guess," Bruce said. Then, after a long moment, "Which means you're pretty cool too."

"Yeah," Laddin agreed. "I am. We are." Then he pressed a kiss to Bruce's lips. And when they separated, he whispered the only words they needed. "I love you."

"I love you too."

They slept.

Chapter 26

BABY CHEESE FARTS

BRUCE WOKE with an idea.

He also awoke with a splitting headache and a crimp in his neck. The first was eased by turning off the alarm. The second was ignored because, damn it, he had an idea!

Laddin grumbled and the baby stirred, but Bruce's face must have shown his excitement, because Laddin abruptly sat up.

"What? What have you figured out?"

Bruce hesitated. "It's just a thought. It may be nothing."

"Don't go negative on me! We've seen how badly that affects the world. So, what have you figured out?"

Bruce didn't answer directly. He scrambled out of bed and headed for the bathroom. "Get dressed and—"

"I'll go to the kitchen and make a bottle. Aaron's probably getting hungry. Then we'll talk."

Bruce nodded and headed for the bathroom. His mind was racing the whole time, trying to work the angles, to figure out if his idea was possible. But right now he needed information, and that meant he had to talk to the higher-ups.

He stepped out of the bathroom and came up short. Wulfric was standing in the bedroom doorway.

"What have you got?" the man asked as he leaned against the wall. Damn, he looked half-dead beneath the fairy glamour. Bruce had forgotten he was still recovering from his near death a few days ago, but though he didn't look any worse than he had back then, he didn't look much better either.

Bruce waved him toward the bed. "Sit down before you keel over." But he was warmed that the guy had stayed awake, presumably trying to help work things out.

"The director's taking a shower. He'll be—"

"The fewer people who know about this, the better." Aaron was awake now and fussy. Bruce picked him up, marveling again at how strange life was. A week ago he'd been a bored firefighter with an emptiness in his life that he couldn't seem to fill. Not with endless girls, not with dangerous risks, and not with family. Then, after one visit from his brother, he suddenly had magic, a child, and—

Laddin walked in, and Bruce didn't even try to hide his sappy smile.

He had love, and that was the best magic of all.

Laddin sat in the rocking chair and held out his hands. "Give me Aaron, then start talking."

He did, but not to Wulfric and Laddin. As soon as Aaron was settled, Bruce lifted his head and called for the pixies.

"Erin Rodger-Dodger and Fetid Feta. Erin Rodger-Dodger and Fetid Feta. Erin Rodger-Dodger and Fetid Feta, I call you to come to me!"

"You named your baby after me!" Erin cried as she spun in a circle on her toe, right on the armrest of the rocking chair.

Laddin jerked, jostling the baby, who let out a cry of dismay. "It's okay, baby! You're going to have a wonderful life of magic!" Erin said as she pulled off her fairy hat and set it on Aaron's forehead. It slid right off. It was the size of a thumbnail, but that was okay because she caught it and put it back on her head.

Meanwhile, Fetid Feta appeared next to the bathroom, crossed his large arms, and glared at everyone in the room. "I should have a baby named after me! I'm the biggest!"

"We didn't—" Bruce protested, but Wulfric cut him off.

"Don't go there."

Right. "I need to ask you two some questions."

"Will it get us to Fairyland?" Feta asked.

"I don't know." That was a true statement. He focused on his first question. "Why do you appear like that? Like cheese?" he asked Feta.

"It was because of the man like you. The one who created the demon."

It took a moment for Bruce to follow that, but Laddin was already there. "The one who created the demon? You mean the one who wrote the short story that started this whole thing?"

Feta nodded. "He was like you." He pointed at Bruce. "He had a lot of magic, and he liked cheese."

"Like me?" Bruce asked. "He ate a fairy fruit?"

"So he could have a baby."

"Named after me!" Erin said as she spun around.

"Why do the cheese fairies play Angry Birds, then? Back when you first met Laddin at the tree?" They'd gone over every detail of the past few days, and that was a question he'd asked yesterday too.

"Because everyone likes Angry Birds!" Erin said. Then she launched into the air as if she'd been thrown from a slingshot and crashed on Feta's chest. He tumbled backward into the bathroom and they rolled around like in the game.

"Can't argue with that," Wulfric said. "I love that game."

So did Bruce, but he didn't have time to talk about video games. "But can you change your appearance? Can you look like something else?"

Erin sat up. "Why would we want to?"

"To get into Fairyland." Bruce pointed at Aaron. "Can you look like our baby?"

Both pixies stared at him for a moment. Then, abruptly, there were two more infants in the room—one the size of a handspan on the floor, the other nearly six foot tall as he lay half in and half out of the bathroom.

"No, no!" Bruce said as he jumped onto the bed to avoid getting kicked by Feta. "One baby, and exactly the same size."

Feta abruptly shrank down to the appropriate size, but Erin sat up as her regular self. "How will this get us into Fairyland?"

"I saw the cheese fairies combine, then split apart. I've seen them blow up and then reform. Hell, your guys went through my GI tract and came out as sparkly farts."

Feta grinned and his baby face said, "That was fun!"

Yeah. For them. "I am going to give a baby to the fairy prince. If you can meld into one baby that looks exactly like Aaron, then I will give you to him and he will take you to Fairy Fairyland."

Feta and Erin looked at each other, appearing to think hard. Meanwhile, Wulfric rubbed his hand over his face. "You would have to be an exact replica. You would have to feel magically like Aaron, not just look like him. And you would have to help us hide the real baby."

Bruce turned to Wulfric. "Could you help with that? Would the prince be able to see our child beneath your fairy glamour?"

"If he sees me, he can see the child."

"But he doesn't have to see you, right?"

Wulfric nodded. "I will hide your child. Mother can help with that, but this is really risky. If the prince finds out, he will come back for you."

"And he will find out," Laddin said. "The pixies can't keep up the charade forever."

Everyone looked at the two fairies who were slowly moving toward each other. Feta rolled over, his baby body aging to the size of a six-month- old. Erin dashed forward and back, as if she wanted to do it but then changed her mind.

"Is there a way to end the contract? To declare it done, with no one able to take retribution after it's over?"

"Maybe," Wulfric said, but he didn't look happy about it. "They'll add 'the Deceiver' at the end of your name. It'll end your dealings with the fairies once and for all. They won't work with you again." Bruce guessed that was what they'd done to Wulfric.

"I don't care," Laddin said emphatically. "I'll be happy if I never see them again."

"That's mean!" Erin and Feta said together.

"I don't mean you!" he rushed to say, though from the look on his face, he absolutely did. "Besides, you'll be in Fairy Fairyland like you want, right?"

"Fairyland," they both said together, in the same tone they'd use for *Nirvana* or *heaven* or *triple fudge chocolate cake with sprinkles*.

"So?" Bruce pressed the fairies. "Can you do it? Can you merge together to make a baby?"

Erin poked out her lips. "I can do it. You don't need him."

"I can do it," Feta said. It was weird hearing Feta's voice coming out of a kid. "You don't need her."

And right there, he saw the sticking point. Back when they'd first met, the cheese fairies had been fighting with Erin's fairies. They each believed that the other was preventing them from getting to Fairyland. It wasn't true, but they'd believed it. And so now they didn't like each other enough to go together.

Bruce crossed his arms and put on his sternest paternal voice. "You do this together or not at all. Smoked Gouda said that I was the one who got you to Fairyland."

"Us!" Feta cried. "Not them!"

"Together or not at all."

The two pixies looked at each other—one big, one small, and both pouting.

She pointed at Bruce. "You have to think very hard."

Feta pointed at Laddin. "You have to want it very much."

That wasn't a problem. Bruce crossed over and took Laddin's hand. The energy flowed between them easily, from him into Laddin and back again. It was even stronger than it had been by the lake.

Meanwhile, Laddin grinned up at him. "You're going to make a great dad," he said. Then he added with a mock-stern look, "Together or not at all."

Bruce grinned as he held up Laddin's hand. "Together," he echoed. "Or not at all."

Then they turned to look at the fairies. It was all up to them as Bruce began to concentrate. He wanted an exact replica of Aaron—one so perfect in every way that Bitterroot wouldn't be able to tell the difference.

Nothing happened.

At least, not at first. Both fairies were still pouting. But then—at the exact instant, as far as Bruce could see—they abruptly grinned. Erin spun around and cried, "Fireworks!"

Feta lifted up his chubby arms and cried, "Cheesy, cheesy!"

Suddenly there were sparkling lights everywhere, as well as the smell of every disgusting cheese in the world. Wulfric started to cough, Bruce struggled not to gag, and Laddin groaned.

"Keep picturing—"

"Aaron," Laddin said.

Fortunately it didn't last long. The cheeses all dove straight into Feta. The light fairies including Erin gathered into one large huddle, then turned en masse and rushed the fairy baby. It looked like they meant to topple him, but when they hit, they winked out of sight.

Suddenly there were no sparkling fairy lights anywhere. And no cheeses. Just Feta, sitting there grinning like an eight-month-old baby.

"To Fairyland!" he cried, the words echoing as if they had been spoken by a thousand tiny voices. And then he abruptly shrank down to infant size, becoming an exact copy of Aaron. At least, until the fairy baby farted. Smoke came out of his ass like what had come from Smoked Gouda, and the smell was rank.

"None of that!" Laddin snapped. "No cheese farts!"

The fairy baby pouted and crossed its arms.

"And no commentary," Bruce added. "You have to stay like a real baby."

"Then you have to think of us as a real baby!" the too-smart baby answered.

He could do that. Laddin's nod said the same thing.

It took a while to finish everything up. They had to feed, burp, and diaper Aaron before getting him settled with Wulfric. They had to dress and diaper the fairy baby, which wasn't as easy as it sounded. First, the child kept wanting to play. And for this baby, *play* meant peeing at inappropriate times and farting rancid smells before giggling like the pixies they were. If there hadn't been so much at stake, Bruce would have laughed. A lot. But he couldn't stop himself from thinking about what they were risking. As far as he could tell, Bitterroot was god-like in his abilities. Tricking him was like trying to trick Zeus. It was hard to do and the vengeance would be merciless and probably unending. He remembered the punishments meted out to Sisyphus and other uppity Greeks, and did not want to become a mythic cautionary tale.

But they were quickly running out of time and had no other options, so if he was going to have to roll a boulder up a hill for all of eternity like Sisyphus, then at least he'd know he'd given it his best shot.

"All in," Laddin said, kissing Bruce hard on the mouth. "No matter what."

Bruce nodded. Then he picked up the fairy baby and held it close. "This is our child. Don't think about it any other way."

Laddin nodded as he stroked fairy Aaron's cheek. "Our child." Then he wrinkled his nose. "You need to smell a lot better than that," he grumbled at the child.

"Then think of Aaron's smell," Bruce said, doing the same. "Remember it clearly."

Suddenly the room was filled with the scent of new baby. It was sweet, and it was definitely overpowering.

"A little less," Bruce said to the child. And then together, he and Laddin headed out of their bedroom.

They were met in the hall by all the members of their team and the director, who looked as sad as a man could look while still being dressed in a rumpled suit. Stratos was there too, appearing absolutely miserable, but no more than Yordan and Bing. Nero was grim, Wiz had lost his arrogant sneer, but it was Josh who stepped forward.

"Okay," he said with determination in his voice. "We're all here for you. What's the plan?"

Bruce blinked, unexpectedly overcome by the show of support, but it was Laddin who spoke. "There's no plan. We're …." He looked down at the baby. "We're giving him over."

"Bullshit," Josh said. Then he caught his brother's eye. "Do we fight? We need to know. Or are you running?"

Bruce shook his head. "No fight. And we're not running." He pulled the baby close to his chest. "We're giving him up." In his arms, fairy Aaron squirmed in happiness, but Bruce tightened his grip.

"You're handing him over?" Josh's voice was incredulous. "Just like that?"

"Yes," Bruce said. "Just like that."

Silence filled the room. It was so quiet they could hear fairy Aaron sucking on his fist like a vacuum cleaner. Bruce even tried to pull the tiny fist away, but it was suctioned in so hard that he had to give up or lose the image in his mind. This was baby Aaron. This was his son.

Nero touched Josh's arm, but his words were for Laddin and Bruce. "Maybe it's for the best."

"Don't say that!" Laddin snapped, but Bruce gripped Laddin's hand.

"Yes, it is," he said firmly. "We talked about this." And they had. They'd discussed how Laddin was going to be torn up and angry at giving up the child but that Bruce would be the mean one. He'd insist that the demon-turned-baby was too much for them to handle.

Laddin didn't say anything but turned his head away as if overcome with emotion, and damn it, the guy deserved an Oscar for the performance. Even though he knew it wasn't real, the sight cut at Bruce. He didn't like being at odds with Laddin, even when he really wasn't. And wow, wasn't that a measure of how far he'd fallen for the guy?

But they had a job to do, so he lifted his chin and headed for the door.

"Cut your losses, right?" Josh challenged before they'd gone two steps. "Do what you're told and damn the consequences because that's your style."

Was that what Josh thought of him? God, that was so wrong, it hurt to hear. It was even worse to see the rigid way Josh held himself and the angry clench of his jaw. Bruce had done everything he could to reconnect with Josh. He'd done everything to protect his little brother. And he'd never, ever cut and run when they were kids. He'd stuck it out, endured his father's "lessons" in how to fight, and he'd never complained about the bruises, cuts, or even the broken ribs that he blamed on football.

He'd never bailed in his entire life, but he had to make this look real. So even though it took every ounce of willpower he had, he forced himself to nod.

"Yes. That's my style."

Josh grunted. "Knew it." Then he backed away from door. "Go on, then. Let's go bail on your kid."

Bruce bristled. He wasn't bailing on his child. He was risking *everything* to save him. The only thing that stopped him from screaming that at his stupid brother was the fact that Laddin had taken his elbow and squeezed hard. "It'll be okay," he whispered.

The hell it would. He'd started this whole journey to reconnect with Josh. But now they were further apart than ever. Josh still thought he was an asshole. And a runaway father too!

"Come on," Laddin said loudly. "Let's get this over with."

Chapter 27

TO FAIRYLAND WE GO!

THEY MADE it to the oak tree by dawn. The silent procession stood in the middle of a fallow field, waiting. It was weird to go there and not see the cheese fairies, but then again, Bruce reminded himself, the pixies were here. Wrapped in his arms and smelling like day-old cheese.

"Wait!" whispered Laddin as he abruptly gripped Bruce's elbow. "What about the Earth? Aren't they supposed to do stuff on Earth? Are we about to kill—?"

"Don't worry," the fairy baby said in Erin's voice. "There are lots of us, and Earth will make more. She always does!"

"Shhh," Bruce said as he jostled the baby as if he were trying to settle it down. He glanced at Laddin, who nodded and blew out a relieved sigh. Bruce did too, because he hadn't even thought of the ramifications to Earth if all the pixies suddenly disappeared. He didn't understand exactly what the fairies did, but he

figured they had to have a purpose. He was glad that
he wasn't screwing things up again, even as he tried to
fix them.

Bruce and Laddin waited under the tree while the
others formed a semicircle behind them in a silent show
of support. Bruce couldn't feel more grateful, especially when the first rays of sunlight peeked over the horizon and Bitterroot appeared in a dramatic flash.

He didn't look like a salad fairy this time either.
No, he was man-size and wearing that pompous prince
outfit covered in butterflies that clung to the velvet.
Somehow that matched the arrogant cut to his jaw and
his upraised nose as he sniffed.

"What is that smell?"

Shit. Shit. Shit. This was not going to work.

Laddin sniffed loudly. "I think the baby needs a
diaper change."

"What have you been feeding the child?" Bitterroot gasped.

"Baby formula," Bruce said. "But, you know, it's
from Wisconsin, so it's heavy on the dairy."

The prince curled his lip. "It is good that I take the
child, then. Even I know that you must be careful feeding
dairy to a baby." He held out his hand. "Give it to me."

Laddin stiffened. "It's not an it! His name is Aaron!"

"No, it's not," Bitterroot countered. "My lady will
give him an appropriate name."

"Aaron is—"

Bruce interrupted before Laddin could go too far
in his "defending the baby" part. "Swear to me, Bitterroot. Swear that this child will be cherished, that he'll
be honored and protected. Swear it, Bitterroot, or—"

"There is no *or*," Bitterroot interrupted. "I have
sworn it already."

Laddin shook his head. "Not good enough."

Bitterroot sighed as he looked at them. "I swear it. This child will be honored and protected by myself and all my minions within Fairyland."

Bitterroot had minions? Lucky him. Meanwhile, a dirt-colored moth slipped out from beneath Bitterroot's hair and flew off into the morning air. The prince stared at it in confusion, clearly thinking something. Was it a tell? Were they about to be exposed?

Bruce rushed ahead, forcing his words out too loudly because he was trying to distract the prince. "How do I know you won't come back for something more? How do I know this is done for good?"

"Because that was our bargain. Your power for the child." Bitterroot held out his hands. "You are stalling. I told you this would be no easier in the morning."

"Swear it," Bruce said. "Swear this ends here."

Laddin spoke up. "And that you'll never do this to anyone else. This baby is the last child you grab."

"It is not a grab!" Bitterroot said, clearly offended. "It was a bargain—"

"Either way," Bruce countered.

Bitterroot blew out an annoyed breath. "Fine. The child will be cherished because he is more than enough to save my kingdom. I swear that I will barter for no other human child once I have this one and that our bargain will be complete. I also swear that I will bother you no more. You will not see me again unless you call my name. Now you will hand him over or I will have the legions of Fairy—"

"Stop with the threats!" Bruce snapped to cover his elation. They'd done it. They'd gotten the bastard to declare their deal done the moment the fairy Aaron was handed over. And as proof, a ruby-red butterfly detached from Bitterroot's sleeve and hovered in the air between them. "We'll do it. We'll hand him over."

Except now that the time had come, Bruce found it really hard to give the child up. Even though he knew it was the pixies, knew it wasn't his baby, handing anything over to the arrogant bastard went against everything he believed in. Laddin must have felt it too, because he crowded close as he stroked the baby's forehead.

"Will he be able to come back to Earth? You know, to visit?"

"Yes," Bitterroot said with clear impatience. "I will bring him back myself when he is ready."

Laddin's head snapped up. "And when will that be?"

"When it is time!" Bitterroot stomped forward, his frustration clearly outweighing his need to make them present the child like a gift to a king. "You do not need to know the details of a prince's education."

But Bruce really did want to know. And he wanted to ask a thousand more questions too, because when it came right down to it, he couldn't seem to make himself pass the child over. He couldn't give anything precious to that arrogant bastard, even knowing that it was the answer to all their problems and, more than that, the pixies wanted it.

"It's okay," Laddin said as he supported Bruce's arms. "We'll get through this."

Bruce didn't say anything. He couldn't. His throat was clogged shut and his feet wouldn't move. Laddin had to do it for him. Laddin had to be the strong one— the sane one—and do what had to be done.

"I hope this works out how you want," he whispered to the baby.

If there was an answer, Bruce didn't see it. Laddin lifted the child out of his arms and gave him to Bitterroot.

The prince held the child gently, and there was such elation in his face that Bruce truly believed a human child could save Bitterroot's kingdom. Except, of course, the baby wasn't a human child and Bitterroot had just promised not to do anything like this again. That meant the arrogant bastard was well and truly screwed.

There was real satisfaction in that. Assuming, of course, that they pulled this off.

"So we're done?" Bruce asked. "Well and truly done?"

"Yes," Bitterroot responded, his eyes still on the baby.

"Yes," whispered the director, who abruptly swept a net down over the red butterfly. While everyone watched, he muttered some words over the insect, making it freeze solid. Then, with steady fingers, he gently pulled out the butterfly and set it in a plastic container he'd brought with him.

"Tupperware?" Bitterroot gasped in horror. "You keep my bargains in Tupperware?" Apparently those little butterflies represented the prince's promises.

The director shrugged. "Actually, I think it's Glad. It was all we had on hand."

Bitterroot huffed out an annoyed breath. "I do not understand humans!"

Wasn't that the truth? Meanwhile, Laddin was offering up a small bag of supplies. "Um, did you want this? It's got formula and a diaper—"

"I will not put plastic on my child!" Bitterroot huffed, and damn if Bruce didn't stiffen at the *my child* part. "Only spun silk will touch his skin."

"In a diaper?" Laddin asked, his voice incredulous.

"Even so," Bitterroot announced, and then, in a flash, he was gone, along with the pixie baby.

Everyone stood still for a moment—a very long moment—as they looked around at one another. The same question was on everyone's face. Was it over? Was there anything more to do?

It was the director who answered as he tucked the frozen butterfly into his jacket pocket.

"All done," he said gravely. "You got him to swear that it was over. And thanks to this…" He held up another frozen insect. It was the brown moth. Bruce had no idea when he'd caught it. "…he's promised to cherish that child and not bargain for another one." He looked at Laddin. "Good call there getting him to say that."

Laddin nodded. Then he looked back toward the house. Bruce took his cue, and they started the long slog back to the house—though it was not so much a walk as a jog. They both wanted to make sure the real Aaron was safe and sound.

Josh trotted beside them, easily keeping pace. "So what was that that you gave the fairy asshole? A clone? Simulacrum? Doppelganger?"

Bruce frowned at his brother. "What makes you think it wasn't Aaron?" Hell, he'd choked up enough over the fake Aaron that he'd almost caught *himself* believing the lie.

"Please," Josh said. "This from the man who stalked me after a family dinner, took fairy fruit, and then turned himself into a werewolf, all so we could talk? You've never bailed on anything in your life. I didn't believe for a second that you'd let go of your own son."

Bruce stared at him, shock rolling through his system. "You knew? The whole time?"

"Of course I knew. I thought you'd get that when I said it was your style. It's *never* been your style."

"I know!"

"They why would you think I wouldn't know?"

It was a fair question, but honestly, he had no idea what his brother thought of him now. Certainly he knew what he thought when they were kids, and even a couple of days ago, when Josh said that Bruce ruined everything. But now?

He slowed to a stop to look at his brother. Josh mirrored his movement until they were standing face-to-face.

One by one, the others of their group stopped as well.

"Josh," Bruce said as he fumbled for words.

Laddin stepped up beside him and translated. "What that means is that he's so sorry for being a dick when you were kids, but your father made him do it and he was *a kid*. He even tried to protect you."

"I know," Josh said, his voice subdued.

"You know?"

"Yeah, of course I know. While you were off being interrogated, I called Ivy."

Their sister? "But—"

"She's not as stupid as she looks," Josh said.

"She looks like she's sharp," Bruce answered. "A sharpshooter, a sharp observer, and a really sharp Army nurse. They run the hospitals over there, you know."

Again, Josh rolled his eyes. "*I know*. That's what I said. She's smarter than she looks, and she looks like she's on the ball." He took a deep breath. "And she told me things about what Dad did to you. She knows about the vasectomy."

Bruce's head snapped up. "What? I never told her."

"You never told anyone, but she knew. And she said I was an idiot for not looking closer, but that I was forgiven because I'm the youngest and really not that bright."

Bruce snorted. That was Ivy for you, smarter than them both. So smart she'd apparently escaped their toxic home life unscathed. Or at least, less scathed.

But none of that excused all the shit he'd done to Josh over the years. "I'm sorry," he repeated. "Really damn sorry."

"Yeah, yeah, I know. And I'm sorry I blamed you all those years for my own inability to get off my ass and get on with my life." Josh looked at Nero, and then his gaze swept wide to include all of them. "I've got a purpose now. And I've got a new family—a family I love." He looked back to Bruce. "And we'd be thrilled if you could join us. You and my new nephew."

"I'd like that," Bruce said. "I'd like that a lot."

"Great!" Josh said as he hauled Bruce into a hug. Bruce returned it, suddenly blinking back tears. Josh seemed to be doing the same thing, because when they separated, they both ducked their heads as if something had flown into their eyes.

"And speaking of my new nephew," Josh said when they started back to the house. "Where exactly is he?"

"Wulfric's got him," the director whispered. When Bruce looked at him in surprise, he snorted. "Don't think that anything goes on with my people that I don't know about. And that includes my people's new baby boy." Then he looked at both Bruce and Laddin. "Now listen up. You both are going to take housing near the mansion in Michigan. It's right next to the state park and is an easy run to work." He pointed at Laddin.

"You're on duty with Captain M until I say different. She's been getting five times the work done since you were recruited, and I know that's you. So no more talk about going back to Hollywood. We need you, and now you have a magic baby that we need to protect."

Laddin tilted his head. "Tell me about this housing. Are we talking an apartment or—"

"They're townhomes."

"Two stories," Laddin exclaimed as he made a fist of joy. "Yes!"

Then the director turned back to Bruce. "I'd like you to stay on as our medic. You can rotate through the combat packs and pick the one you want. But if Nero okays it, I'd like you to stay on with him. The pack is based in the mansion, and that would allow you to go home to see the kid. We're completely understaffed, and we need advice on exactly what and how to get new people in."

Josh piped up. "We're revamping the recruitment policy because—"

"Yes, Josh, I heard you the first hundred times. And now you get to help your brother do that. If there's a better way to recruit new people, then find it and do it, because this little dance in Wisconsin doesn't feel like the end. It seems more like a shift from the beginning to the middle. There's more weird stuff coming, and we need to be prepared to deal with it." He paused a moment to look at them both. "Agreed?"

Josh snapped an "Agreed" like it was "Yes, sir!"

Bruce was slower as he watched his brother. When Josh looked back, Bruce said the words aloud. "I'd like that," he said. "Us working together."

"Then say 'agreed,' you idiot."

Bruce turned back to the director. "Yes, sir. Thank you, sir."

"Finally," the director said with a grin. "Someone who knows how to respond properly!" And then he didn't say anything at all, and no one else did either. Because walking slowly toward them were Wulfric and his mother… as well as an adorable bundle held tightly in Wulfric's arms.

Bruce looked at Laddin, whose face was split into a huge grin. A moment later they ran together toward their son.

Within minutes, Aaron—the real Aaron—was tucked safely into Bruce's arms. Laddin was fussing with the kid's clothing, making sure he was bundled up tight in the chilly morning air. And Uncle Josh came up beside them and started talking about all the chemistry-inspired practical jokes he was going to teach the boy.

Great. One parent teaching him explosives and an uncle teaching him chemistry. Good thing Bruce was a medic. He had the feeling they were going to need one at their house.

Their house. The idea was so wonderful that he had to share it. So he looked to Laddin. There were so many things he wanted to say, so many astonishing thoughts crowded into his brain, but none of them came through. All he could manage to utter were three little words, words Laddin spoke as well.

"I love you."

Epilogue

FAIRY FAIRYLAND IS NOT
WHAT IT USED TO BE

"THE TEMPERATURE in the dragon cages has been lowered five degrees. Is there any other way that I may serve you?"

Emma Davis (code name Mother) looked at the vaguely human-shaped fluff of light that had spoken to her and shook her head. "Nothing, minion. Thank you for your help." She knew that the sparkly lights were more like drones than real people, but she couldn't help treating them as living creatures.

"It is my pleasure to serve the Dragon Mother," the fluff said before it zipped away.

Emma considered calling it back. She was dying for someone to talk to, but conversing with a minion was like talking to Siri. Sure, it was fun for a bit, but eventually it got old.

She let it go, then walked down the line of cages, checking on her charges. They were all there, coiled around heated rocks and blinking jewel-bright eyes at her when she passed. She could talk to them too, and she sure as hell had in the past two months, since beginning her service to Bitterroot. Another ten and she'd be going home with her own dragon. Though what a werewolf like her was going to do with a dragon, she hadn't a clue. At least she had ten months to figure it out.

She was just admiring the blue dragon she called Beau because, well, he was a beauty, when Bitterroot came into the nursery. He appeared as he always did in this place—tall, dark, and arrogantly handsome. And damn if he didn't make her knees go weak when he smiled at her like a little boy with an ice cream treat.

"What have you got there?" she asked, referring to a bundle wrapped in silk that he carried in his arms.

"The salvation of my realm." Then, at her surprised look, he extended it to her. "Also, a present for you."

He was always giving her presents, some of them sweet, some of them downright silly, and a couple that were really bad ideas. The fae did not understand the human mind, that was for sure, but Bitterroot was trying, and for that she gave him a smile, all while bracing herself for whatever it was he held. It was roughly the size of a piglet and squirming, so she wondered if she was about to be both dragon and pig keeper.

Until she looked down and saw a human face. A human face on a baby.

"What is that?" she gasped.

"A human child. You said you wanted children, so I got you one."

"You what?" she cried, backing up against the dragon cages. "You can't go get a child the way you'd pick up a loaf of bread at the grocery store."

"I did not go to a grocery store!" Bitterroot said with indignation. "I had to barter very hard for this one. It was very expensive." Then he frowned down at the squirming bundle in his arms. "But I didn't think it would be so twisty. Or smell so bad."

Now that he mentioned it, there was a very foul scent coming from the bundle. And he was having a terrible time holding on to it. But her mind was still back on the fact that he had a *child*. And he thought he could give it to her!

"Are you serious?" she said, gaping at him. "You bartered? For a baby?"

"Yes," he said, irritation in his tone. "For you!" He offered her the squirming baby. "I don't understand your reaction—"

"No kidding! Who would give up their child?"

His expression sobered. "They didn't want to, but that was the arrangement. A firstborn child. Very standard."

She shook her head. "I don't care if it's the law, you give that child back! You can't go trading for children!"

His expression tightened and he shot her a furious glare. "You do not understand. I need a human child. My realm, my home—" He made an expansive gesture with his hand. "All of this will disappear unless I have one."

"I don't care!" she snapped back.

She would have said more. She would have said a lot more. But at that moment, Bitterroot lost control of the baby. It was squirming so much, he couldn't hold on, and it began to fall.

Emma dove forward to catch it. She might be horrified by what Bitterroot had done, but she wasn't going to let a child plummet to the ground. Thank God for werewolf reflexes. She caught it just before the infant brained itself on the floor.

Except what she caught didn't feel like a baby. It seemed to squirm and disintegrate right through the silk wrapping. She gasped, thinking she had hurt it. Then she thought it was deformed. Then she didn't know what she thought, because it started sprouting people—tiny people jumping out of it and running in all directions.

This was no baby—it was a piñata filled with tiny fairy creatures.

"It was a joke," she realized, completely appalled. "This was a stupid practical joke! How could you? I thought you'd dropped a baby!"

"If it is a joke," Bitterroot said, his voice low and angry, "then I am not its author."

She frowned. "What?" She pointed to the dozens of leaping, huddling, squealing creatures dashing around the place almost too fast for the eye to catch. "What are they?" And why did they smell like cheese?

Suddenly Bitterroot straightened up, his spine nearly cracking with the sudden tight cast to his entire body. "Earth sprites!" he hissed, revulsion in every word. "Pixies!"

It took a moment for her to process this. She'd seen many strange sights in Fairyland. Enough to make her seriously doubt her senses. But before her eyes were little girl fairies cavorting about screaming "whee!" And beside them were little boy… she didn't know what. But they smelled like cheese. Like really old, really rancid cheese. And all of them were growing.

As in *really* growing. Hand-size to knee-size to man-size and more. Thank God they'd all moved out of the nursery to start running around the outdoor grounds.

"They're getting huge," she murmured.

"In Fairyland, they will be as big as my house!" Bitterroot said as he scanned the area between the dragon nursery and his castle. "Or bigger," he whispered. His eyes were wide, and his jaw went slack with horror. And then he gripped the windowsill hard enough that his hands grew white.

"They told me it was their son! They deceived me!"

"Would that be the child's parents?"

"Yes!"

She folded her arms and grinned. "Good for them."

He whipped around and stared at her. "What did you say?"

"Good. For. Them." Then she looked out, watching the creatures dash around. The fairies seemed to be throwing fireworks everywhere, which exploded in colorful displays. And the others…. Well, they were forming a huge slingshot and were about to shoot something that looked like hard balls of cheese at the topmost spire on Bitterroot's castle. "Oh my," she breathed. "They're going to take down your castle."

"Not just my castle!" he exclaimed. "I need a human baby!"

"Well, what you got was…." She blinked. "What are they again?"

"Sprites!" he bellowed. "Pixies, imps! You have dozens of names for them." He rounded on her. "And they belong on Earth, not in Fairyland."

"Huh," she said as she leaned back against Beau's cage, laughter in her tone. "Well, I guess that sucks for you."

She ought to take this more seriously, because each pixie was now the size of a bus and was happily destroying everything in sight. The fireworks were getting larger by the second, and every boom shook the foundations.

"Are we safe in here?" she asked.

Bitterroot nodded, his expression grim. "I told you before that I reinforced the nursery. The entire realm can fall to ashes and we would still be safe in here."

Well, that was reassuring. "And the others in your realm?"

"The minions will dissolve and reform, as will everything else."

That was true. She had seen it happen more than once. He snapped his fingers and everything disintegrated in a fall of sparkly lights, only to reform as something else. Don't like the castle? How about a high-rise tower? Not into penthouse living? How about a beach house complete with an ocean and dolphins? Everything was constructed from Bitterroot's will.

Everything but her and—apparently—the pixies. And that made her happy enough to grin.

"Guess we're stuck in here for a while," she quipped as she pulled out a chair and sat down to watch the show. The cheese-like pixies released the slingshot and... wham! Dead shot right at the nearest spire. The tower crumpled to the ground as if it had been hit by a boulder.

She chuckled. "Are you going to remake it for them?"

"Why? They will just destroy it again."

That was likely. Especially since they were now aiming at the next tower, this one a little farther away.

"Hangnails and hobgoblins!" he suddenly spat.

"What?"

"I cannot take revenge on them." Then he closed his eyes in the first show of weakness from him she'd ever seen. "And I cannot bargain for another child."

"Good. You shouldn't be trading for babies like they're cans of beans."

He opened his eyes and stared at her. "You do not understand. I *need* a human child. It is the only way to save this place. To save all of it." His wave included everything.

She didn't care so much about the castle or its rapidly falling spires. But she did care about the nursery and the dragons. And, of course, herself.

"I don't understand," she said.

"Of course you don't. You have not tried to learn about me or the problems I face while you play with my pets."

"That's not true!" she said. But it was true. She'd come here so angry with him for forcing her into this situation that she'd turned her back on him the second she'd arrived. She'd focused on learning her job—how to take care of the baby dragons—and had steadfastly refused his invitations to dinner, for walks, for anything except what was absolutely required of her as a mother of dragons.

Except now she wondered just how much she had missed. What didn't she understand?

"Why do you need a human child?"

"It is the only way to preserve what I have here, but I have sworn not to get another child. I cannot go back to Earth and get one."

She nodded. "That's a good thing, Bitterroot. Humans shouldn't give up their babies."

"He would be a king in Fairyland!"

"He belongs with his human parents."

Bitterroot turned his attention back outside. The cheesy pixies were having trouble with the second spire. They'd only half destroyed it, so they were loading up again with what looked like triple the payload.

"It's the only thing that will save my home," he whispered.

"Well, you'll just have to find another way, instead of kidnapping somebody's child."

He nodded. "Such is the law. What I have sworn, I must obey."

"Good."

He turned to look at her, and his expression was calm, determined, and a little bit scary. Actually, it was more than a little scary. The way he looked at her had turned into an intense scrutiny or a desperate challenge. And she didn't like where either of those thoughts were leading her. Or him.

"Bitterroot…," she said, though she had no idea how to finish that sentence.

"You are a human woman," he said.

"Er, yes. Yes, I am."

"You can give birth to a human child," he stated. "In fact, you said you wanted one."

"Someday! I said someday. And with the right man." She straightened off her chair and started backing into the cage room. Except there was nowhere to go. Not with the dragon cages behind her and Pixie Armageddon outside. "Bitterroot, I'm not having your baby."

"I know," he said softly. "I am of Fairy, and I need a human child."

Oh shit. That sounded a lot worse.

"I'm not having a baby just so you can use it!"

He exhaled slowly and his expression turned cunning. "Well," he drawled in that really sexy, really annoying way he had. "I guess that means we have a lot to discuss."

"What?"

He gestured outside. "We cannot go out there until the sprites get bored and settle down."

She frowned. "How long will that be?"

He shrugged. "The last pixie invasion lasted a thousand years."

She swallowed. "That's a really long time." Good thing her contract was for only another ten months. But she didn't want to spend all that time locked inside with him. She'd go mad for sure and likely do something really, really stupid.

Meanwhile, Bitterroot grabbed a chair, flipped it around, and dropped it down in front of her. Then he sat and set his chin on his fist. It was a casual pose and one that never failed to freak her out, mainly because he was a pompous asshole of a fairy prince except in moments like this when he became casual. She knew it was a pose. He was mimicking something he'd seen on Earth. And yet, when she looked at him, she saw that his expression was defeated. Maybe even vulnerable.

"You really are in trouble, aren't you?" she asked.

His eyes grew hooded. If she had to guess, he was ashamed of his failure. "I will find an answer," he said stiffly. "I am the last living prince of this realm, grandchild of the human baby Eric, and protector of this *squeak*."

She winced at the strange sound. "This what?" she asked.

He started to answer again but then shook his head. That happened sometimes. There were words in the Fairy language that just sounded like mouse squeaks to her. Apparently whatever it was he protected was one of those words.

"So you're a big deal here," she said.

He dropped his chin back down on his fist. "Yes."

"And you need a baby to save all that."

"A human baby."

"And you think I'm going to give you one."

He looked up, and his eyes seemed to dance with merriment. It was a very fairy look, and it was mesmerizing.

"That isn't going to happen," she said. "You should know that."

He nodded. Then he glanced outside as the second tower tumbled to the ground with a rumble like thunder. When he turned back to her, that flash of vulnerability was gone. He straightened up on the chair and he faced her like the prince he was.

"Very well," he said calmly. "Then let us discuss exactly what will happen."

Epilogue 2

GRANDMA HAS A CONFESSION

AARON WAS getting heavy. The child liked to eat, that was for sure. Laddin set the bottle down on the table beside the rocking chair Ivy had given them and watched as Bruce unpacked another moving box and pulled out a gruesome head.

"What the he—heck—is this?" Bruce demanded as he dropped it back into the box. They both knew he'd been about to say *hell*, but they were trying to clean up their language in front of the child. It wasn't going so well for Bruce, and Laddin had already got enough quarters in the Curse Jar to buy a cheap espresso machine. He expected they'd have enough for an expensive one in another couple of months.

"That," Laddin said, "was my favorite prop from the very first movie I ever worked on."

"It's going to give Aaron nightmares." Bruce squinted at it. "It's going to give *me* nightmares!"

Laddin laughed. "Put it in the garage. I'll bring it out for Halloween."

"Not until he's a teenager. Gah, that thing is awful." Bruce picked up the box, holding it away from his face as if it were something more than a latex prop. Laddin was chuckling as he lifted Aaron to burp him.

After three months of parenthood, Laddin felt like he was finally getting the hang of having an infant. And to add to that miracle, the baby had slept six hours last night, so they were hoping for a repeat tonight. Laddin missed sleep, though he did enjoy lazing in bed with the baby between them as he and Bruce talked about how quickly their lives had changed.

They'd finally moved into the townhome at the edge of the state park. They'd both signed on to work full-time with Wulf, Inc. and were now creating a home for their tiny family of three. Official move-in day had been yesterday, so today was a lot of unpacking, and hopefully an initiation of their very own bedroom right across the hall from Aaron's nursery.

But only if the kid went to sleep soon, because honestly, Laddin was tired from working full-time while coordinating the move of his life from LA and Bruce's life from Indianapolis to right here, right now, in the largest home Laddin had ever had. Who knew Michigan real estate was so cheap?

"Look who I found outside," Bruce said as he came in from the garage.

Laddin looked up and gasped in true shock. "Mama? Nana?"

His mother rushed forward, with his grandmother a half step behind. They arrived in a wash of exotic perfume (his grandmother) and the slight antiseptic smell that always clung to his mother. And didn't that smell like home to him?

"Laddin! Sweetheart! Is this our little boy?" Mama cried.

For the first time in his life, the phrase *our little boy* didn't apply to him. The two women were cooing over Aaron, looking at his face and stroking his dark head of hair.

"Oooh, he's got your nose," his mother said.

"He's got your magic," his grandmother intoned, her eyes wide.

Over the women's heads, Laddin looked in alarm at Bruce. They couldn't tell his family about being werewolves or their magic or anything. Those were the rules, and Laddin was loathe to break them. It wasn't just about the consequence of sharing the magical secret. He didn't want to explain the whole demon thing, and honestly, the fewer people who knew about that, the better. In all respects, Aaron was a normal human boy.

Meanwhile, Bruce did his best to distract the women. "Let me take your coats."

"Mamma mia, I'm keeping mine on!" his mother cried. "Why do you live in such a cold place?"

"It's fifty degrees out, Mama. It's spring."

"In LA it's—"

"Smoggy and filled with traffic." Two things he did not miss from his old life.

His mother couldn't argue with that, and since she'd managed to take her grandchild right out of Laddin's arms and was now singing a Spanish lullaby to Aaron, whatever objection she might have had was lost.

Not so for his grandmother. She turned to both Laddin and Bruce and gave them an arch look. "We thought you were dead," she said in a stage whisper to Laddin.

"I called you."

"Your birthday was months ago. We didn't know what had happened to you."

Laddin spread his arms wide. "Nothing happened, Nana." He glanced at Bruce. "Except I fell in love."

"And got a baby."

Bruce came close as Laddin shrugged. A moment later Laddin was being supported against Bruce's side. It was a casual pose. There was no need to lean into Bruce, but he did anyway because he liked it, just as much as Bruce seemed to like holding him.

Mama finished her lullaby. Then she looked up at Bruce with a narrowed eye. "You going to marry my boy?"

Bruce flushed. "I asked him last week."

Laddin held up his hand and flashed the hardwood ring on his fourth finger. "I said yes."

Mama nodded in approval. "Good." Then she smiled. "I will put little Aaron to bed now, and then we will talk about how all this happened."

Laddin flashed Bruce an "I'm so sorry" look, but Bruce merely shrugged. It was a good thing they'd long since sorted out what story to give to family and friends.

Everyone waited as Mama climbed the stairs. She'd started up the lullaby again but kept interspersing the lyrics with cooing sounds. Laddin knew she was echoing Aaron's sounds. The boy had quite a repertoire of noises. He and Bruce had spent many evenings laughing together at the delightful sounds.

But the moment Mama was out of sight, Nana turned on them with sharp eyes and pointy nails. "How dare you!" she growled. "How dare you become a werewolf and not tell me!"

Laddin reared back in shock. "How do you know?"

"Because I can see it, child. On both of you." Her eyes narrowed when she peered at Bruce. "You're fairy-born, aren't you?"

"Um… yes, ma'am?"

"Harrumph." Then she grinned. "I was right about you, wasn't I, Laddy-boy? I knew you would change to magic in your twenty-eighth year, and I was right!"

"Yes, Nana, you were. But we can't tell—"

"I know, I know." Then she got a canny look in her eye. "But do you want to know about Aaron's future? I saw it in a dream—"

"No!" Laddin said, his voice hard. "Just because you were right about me, that doesn't mean I enjoyed twenty-eight years of speculation about my death."

Nana reared back, her expression hurt. "But I never said you'd die. It was a change to magic."

That was the truth. She'd never claimed he'd pass away. She said he'd have a complete change of life from one state to another. It was everyone else who'd assumed he'd kick the bucket.

Meanwhile, Bruce squeezed his arm and gestured them into the kitchen. It was the only room besides the nursery that was fully unpacked. "Let's get something to eat, okay? I'm starved, and the lasagna was a long time ago."

Laddin nodded as he grabbed the baby monitor. He wanted to be able to hear everything that went on upstairs too. He turned to his grandmother. "And then you can tell us why you're here."

Nana blew out a breath. "We wanted to see you, of course! And I wanted to tell you all about my dream—"

"No," Bruce said sternly. "No forecasting, no dreams, no stories. I know I just met you, ma'am, but I must insist on this. We do not need more drama around your great-grandson."

Nana pursed her lips. She hated being stopped from her drama, her stories, and most of all, her forecasting. But then her expression softened.

"I can see that you love him," she said, looking at Bruce and then back at Laddin.

"I do," Bruce said.

"And I do too," Laddin echoed.

"And the baby? Even though he's a magical child?" Her voice trailed away, and Laddin was appalled to realize she knew a great deal more than she was letting on.

"We adore our *son*," Laddin said.

Nana waited a dramatic moment. Her gaze was sharp, her mouth pursed. And then, with a happy clap, she giggled. "Then I'll tell you that I saw Aaron has a long and very happy life. As long as you two surround him with love—"

"*Nana!*" *Laddin cried. It was just like her to tell the* baby's fortune anyway, even though they didn't want it.

"—then all six of you will live happily ever after."

"Ma'am," Bruce began, admonishment in his tone, but Laddin cut him off.

"Six, Nana? What do you mean six?"

"Didn't I tell you?" She blinked wide and innocent eyes, as if she hadn't planned this from the beginning. "Aaron won't be your only magical child. There are three more in your future, and what an exciting future it will be!"

Laddin didn't know how to respond to that. He was too busy looking at Bruce and wondering if the guy was about to turn tail and run.

But all Bruce did was grin. And then he leaned back against the stove. "Six, huh?" he asked. "Is at least one of them a girl?"

"Yes! And she flies!" Nana said while Laddin let out a low groan.

"Don't encourage her."

"I don't think I can stop her," Bruce argued.

Wasn't that truth? Then Bruce held out his arm, and Laddin slipped easily into the space opened for him.

"You sure you want to hear this?" Laddin asked Bruce.

"Only if you do." Then he looked at Nana. "And only if it's good news and you swear to tell us and no one else. Especially not the kids."

Nana pursed out her lips and then she lifted her chin. "Will you tell me the truth about how you came to be a fairy werewolf? How you saved Wisconsin and ended up with a magical child?"

Laddin and Bruce shared a look, the question and answer clear within a few breaths. Then, together, they nodded.

"Very well," Laddin said. "It's a deal, but I expect you to keep your word."

"Of course," Nana said. "I agree." And then, to everyone's shock, a tiny little butterfly floated up from the sleeve of her coat and danced away—the same thing that happened when a fairy made a promise.

Holy moly, Laddin realized with shock. Nana was a fairy. That was how she knew all this stuff. His grandmother was a fairy!

She must have seen the shock on his face and realized that he'd seen the butterfly and knew the significance of it. But all she did was sit down at the kitchen table and gesture at Laddin.

"Make me some tea, please. And then tell me everything! Your mother's going to be at least an hour with that baby."

She was probably right. They could hear his mother talking to Aaron through the baby monitor. She said all sorts of things, but Laddin had grown up enjoying those talks. It was one of the most cherished memories he had of his childhood, that hour he and Mama used to spend every night talking about everything before bed.

Which meant that they had time, and Nana knew it.

So Bruce heated up the lasagna, Laddin brewed the tea, and together they talked with Nana. They told her the truth, and she, in turn, told them her predictions, all of which eventually came true.

It turned out that having a fairy grandmother was especially useful when raising four magical children.

Coming Fall 2021

Were-Geeks Save the Middle of Nowhere

Were-Geeks Save the World: Book Three

Into every generation is born a really scary relative. In this case, it's Walter Chen's aunt, who puts the spirit of a Chinese chaos god into his body. At first he doesn't notice because he's focused on shooting his indie film in Nowhere, Wisconsin, but pretty soon he's doing amazing kung fu. Cool!

Bing Zhi Hao was Walter's lead actor and best friend until he disappeared to become a werewolf and save the world. Now he's back and trying to make amends… except his shy roommate isn't quiet anymore. In fact, he's downright scary.

Bing figures out the demigod is taking over Walter—body, mind, and soul. Soon the man Bing loves will be gone and chaos incarnate will be born on earth. He has to convince Walter to fight off the possession and return to the man he was. But what can he offer a god to convince him to remain a man?

www.dreamspinnerpress.com

Chapter One

China

THERE ARE days so steeped in happiness that they are like the perfect ending to a well-loved series. It's Han and Leia kissing before Kylo Ren screwed up their happily ever after. It's saving the galaxy, recovering the lost treasure, and rescuing the princess all at once, and Walter Chen clutched every second to his heart, wishing he had the power to slow down time. Better yet, this wasn't a book or a movie. This was his real life, and he wanted to remember the details so he could savor them whenever his anxieties overwhelmed him.

Today was the booting ceremony as his manga comic began filming for television. Most series filmed in China had a ceremony to ask for blessings before shooting began. The production company, the stars, and the creators got together. Media was present, and everyone got to join in the celebration. He didn't even care that he was standing in the back of the soundstage, barely visible behind the lighting crew. He knew they thought he was an unimportant cog in the vast machine that was television.

It didn't matter, because he'd been the first cog. What had started as a fever dream, then drawn in desperate breaks from his barista job, was now about to become a television show, and he thanked everyone he met for their part in his good fortune.

"Yaz!" he said as his agent stomped up to him on her impossibly high heels. "Can you believe this?" He gestured expansively around the set.

"No, I can't!" she snapped. "It's un-freaking-believable, and I'm going to put a stop to it right now."

He blinked. She didn't sound giddy happy like he was. In fact, her brows were lowered as if he'd just killed her favorite purse Chihuahua, Louis. "Um, what?"

"Come with me," she said as she gripped his arm in a vise hold. "We're going to talk to the director right now."

Walter stumbled after her, doing his best not to sideswipe makeup artists, costume designers, or (God forbid) any of the on-camera talent. The female stars were so thin he was afraid he'd accidentally snap their bones. Then Yaz grabbed the director's arm and hauled him none too gently around.

"Did I or did I not negotiate for the creator to help with casting? Who plays what part is very important to Walter, and he has the right to give his input. He knows where the story is going. You don't."

DuYi blinked at her, understandably confused. He'd just finished toasting to the production's success for the eighth time. Her demands were completely at odds with the tone of the ceremony, and it was taking him a moment to adjust. "Miss Yaz," he said, "of course the creator was consulted. Did you get some champagne?"

"Really?" Yaz said as she pulled Walter forward. "Look around," she instructed Walter. "Did you choose any of these people? Did you?"

"No, I didn't, but it's—" He was going to say *not important*. Casting was a great deal more complicated than who would be the best actor to play the role. Especially in China—which was where this production was being filmed—actors were chosen because of political ties, fan engagement on the Asian version of Facebook, plus a zillion other factors. And honestly, Walter was too happy to want to argue over casting.

His agent didn't give him a choice. "No input. He hasn't been consulted on anything!"

The director frowned first at his empty champagne glass, then at Walter. "Who is this?" he asked.

And there it was, the deflation to his happy balloon that he'd been dreading. The director didn't even know who he was.

"This is Walter Chen." And when DuYi still didn't recognize him, Yaz snapped out in frustration, "The creator of *Winter Wolf's Reign*. The man who wrote the manga that you're taking to television!"

DuYi's eyes widened as he looked down at Walter. He blinked several times as if he couldn't believe that a short guy with glasses and ink stains on his fingers was the geek who could create something adored by a few million fans. "You're not Touko Chen."

Walter shook his head. "That's my cousin. He wrote the anime, but the original manga is mine." And then everyone stood there as they realized what had happened. Walter's agent had given him casting input, but that honor must have gone to his cousin by accident. Oops.

"Uh, well, um…," the director said, obviously sweating. "But you got the check, right? Those were sent to the right place."

Yaz rolled her eyes. "Of course we got paid. I made sure of that."

"Well, then, it's all good."

No, actually it wasn't all good. It would have been amazing to be part of the casting process, but since there'd been a screwup, Walter wasn't going to throw a wrench into things because he hadn't been sitting in the room when the decisions were made. He was about to say as much when Yaz started in on her I'm-shocked-and-appalled routine. She gasped, pitched her voice into a furious growl, and wasn't above pushing out a few tears as she demanded recompense for their error. It was one of the reasons she was a great agent.

She'd just gotten started with the "I am horrified that a director of your reputation—" when DuYi broke in.

"No, no! Of course we understand. Mr. Chen knows that he could not select the stars. That was explained to you, yes? That the principles were already selected. But of course you have been given the choice for the other parts. The remaining roles."

"What roles?" He already had the list of the actors and parts. Every one was assigned.

"Um, uh…." DuYi rubbed a hand over his forehead before he snapped his fingers. "Shan Ru, the drunken student who becomes a wolf. His role has not been assigned." He made an expansive gesture to where the kung fu actors were drinking and laughing together. "You may pick the man for that."

Yaz snorted. "He isn't important. He only has a few lines."

"But he is in almost every episode. He provides an excellent balance for the hero."

The guy was throwing him a bone, but what he didn't understand was that Walter was still writing the manga comic. If he liked any character, he would create a bigger role for the guy. Or if he hated anyone, it would be the simplest thing to kill him off. But he never got the chance to speak as Yaz narrowed her eyes at the group of fighters.

"They're stuntmen," she drawled. She sounded like she was calling them prancing clowns. Then she looked at him. "Walter's a martial artist too. He could probably do just as well. Plus he acts."

Walter absolutely did not act. He wrote, he drew, and he practiced a weird form of kung fu because his aunt paid for the lessons. That did not make him a stuntman by any stretch of the imagination. And so he was about to say when DuYi clapped his hands with a cheerful grin.

"Excellent! Walter will work out with the men. He can tell me who will play the drunken student tomorrow." Then he sauntered off, speaking rapid Chinese to the clutch of fighters.

Meanwhile, Walter clutched Yaz in panic. "I can't fight with them! They'll kick my ass."

"Nonsense," she said as she patted his arm. "Just throw a few kicks and look critical. This is about appearing to be good instead of actually—"

"Getting my ass kicked by real martial artists?"

She frowned at him. "Well, yeah. Don't get your ass kicked. I'm going to squeeze out more money from them for screwing up with the casting." Then she gave him a quick wink before sauntering off toward the lead producer.

Which left Walter standing there as a costume girl came up and handed him a gi while making gestures toward a back area of the soundstage covered with mats. As he looked, the stuntmen were en masse pulling off their street clothes. Some of them were obviously unhappy with the change. They hadn't planned on working out on the day of the booting ceremony, but DuYi had ordered them to, and now they looked at Walter with expressions ranging from annoyed to gleefully evil.

Oh hell. Because the pissed-off guys really would kick his ass. Fortunately, he'd learned early how to deal with bullies. It wasn't a foolproof tactic, but it might work here. He hoped.

He wasn't a great martial artist, but he was a kick-ass comic. He'd learned young that if he looked funny while doing stuff, people would laugh. And laughing people—even if they were laughing at him—didn't usually beat him up.

So that was his plan. He'd spent a lot of time learning moves that looked ridiculous and still managed to get him out of trouble. He'd suffer a few bruises along the way, but that was better than the pummeling that could happen. So with a weak smile, he found the bathroom and changed. And then he stepped onto the mat to face a dozen guys who really were not impressed with his lack of muscles, size, or general intimidation factor.

"Um, hi, guys. Look, this wasn't my idea. DuYi just thought we could, you know, hang out a bit."

Silence. Either they didn't understand English or they didn't care.

"Um, well, okay. But I've had some champagne, so I don't know how good I'll be." He mimed drinking and gestured over to the main area. And again, no one cracked a smile. Hell. These guys were major hardasses. "Okay. So what are we, um, going to do?"

A big guy stepped forward and greeted him with a quick bow. "We begin with throws," he said in English.

"Okay. Hi, my name is Walter." He held out his hand to shake.

"I am Kong." And wasn't that a really obvious name for the man? He had anvil-sized hands and shoulders a broad as some beds. And he took Walter's hand in his and, instead of the warm handshake Walter had expected, bent his knees and threw Walter across the floor.

Oh yippee. It was going to be one of *those* sessions. Fortunately he knew how to roll into the throw such that he landed without too much damage. He did so now, coming back to his feet with an aw-shucks smile.

"You got me there. Nice throw." He searched their faces, looking for someone who showed that he understood English. No one gave him the least clue. The next guy approached. He was not as big as Kong, but his hands were just as strong. He bowed, introduced himself as Teng, and also threw Walter across the mat.

This time he'd been ready. He even managed to defend against the first grip, but Teng was fast and switched tactics midgrip. Walter went flying, this time toward the cardio equipment. He barely managed to avoid braining himself on the elliptical machine.

"Ha ha. Nice throw," he said as he rolled to his feet. What these guys didn't realize was that he was memorizing every single one of their names. He doubted he had any real casting control, but anyone who was an asshole just to be an ass here was not getting his vote for a part. It was the only revenge he had, and he gleefully embraced it as he got tossed from one side of the soundstage to the other.

Some were nicer than others about it. Some were downright cruel. And though Walter might have successfully defended himself against a few, he chose not to make the effort. Instead, he poured on the drunken stumble. It was the only way for him to save face—by claiming he was drunk—plus, it gave him to hope they'd start laughing.

They did, some with more cruelty than others. And he kept memorizing their names while he stumbled "accidentally" into the cardio machines, the fake trees of the set, and even one of the makeup tables.

He was getting pretty beaten up. His ribs already ached with bruises, not to mention his legs. And he wondered just how long it was going to take until they got tired of this. He sure as hell was. So this time he drunk stumbled into one of the fake trees of the set. It had hard pointy branches, and he let his gi get caught while he twisted and fumbled to escape. He put his best comic confusion into the work, and sure enough, Kong's laughter boomed across the soundstage. Walter had already guessed that the guy was the leader, and pretty soon everyone else was chortling too. All except for one guy. He was built differently than the rest, and Walter had noticed him earlier. He was the one man who never introduced himself, who watched everything with dark serious eyes, and who now stepped up to unhook Walter's gi.

"You are free now," he said in slow, careful English.

He was, but Walter exaggerated his movements just enough that he was caught again, much to the hilarity of his audience. Excellent. Except the guy standing next to him didn't break a smile. He leaned into the problem and gently disentangled Walter again.

"Now—"

Walter swayed, catching himself again.

"Please stand still."

He did and was unhooked.

"Now you are free—"

He raised his arms too far and caught his sleeve this time. To the side, everyone was holding their sides with laughter. Everyone except the man with the dark, serious face who stood patiently beside him, unhooking him while watching everything closely as if he were trying to save Walter from further embarrassment.

Walter actually felt bad for the guy because he was working so hard to keep him free and Walter was purposely messing up his work. But it kept the tormenters off of him. So in a way to make amends, he held out his hand.

"Hello. My name is Walter." Then he tensed, ready to be thrown across the room now that his gi was free.

But the man didn't throw him, though he could have easily tossed him halfway across the room. "Hello. My name is Bing. Please, I wish you to teach me." He spoke the last part in an undertone loud enough for Walter to hear, but none other.

Naturally Walter reared back with an embarrassed laugh that wasn't fully faked. He had no idea what this guy's deal was. Too bad too, because Bing flashed him a smile that was camera-ready gorgeous. High cheekbones, cute dimples, and a steady gaze that suggested honesty. Walter didn't trust it, of course. He'd learned young that actors were good at their trade. They could fake sincerity better than anyone. And so he snorted as pretended to reel into the tree again. "Bing? Like a

Bing cherry? I'm sure there a joke there, but I'm too drunk to think of one."

"No matter," Bing said with a shrug. "They have thought of many." He glanced over at the others, who were losing interest now that Walter wasn't falling on his ass anymore.

Poor guy. It seemed he'd been a butt of a few jokes too. Walter could relate. Now that he was standing still for a bit, he could feel the ache building in his body. He stopped himself just short of groaning. He was going to pay hard for today's "workout." In the meantime, Bing looked up at the others and spoke rapidly in Chinese.

Kong frowned but shrugged, then waved at Walter. "Bye-bye, Walter," he said in a singsong voice. "Come back anytime."

Jerk. It was clearly an invitation to get his ass kicked again, but he was supposed to be a drunk American too stupid to know subtext. So he just smiled and waved as the others wandered away. It didn't take long until everyone else had left the work out area. There were still people in the other corners of the set, mostly the construction crew painting something. Walter could smell the paint if not see the people wielding the brushes.

He waited long enough for the fighters to leave. Strangely, it was Kong who remained the longest, his gaze heavy on Bing, who simply stood there like a Chinese man of mystery. It was cliché, but Bing personified it to a tee, and eventually Kong shook his head and disappeared.

Walter waited a breath, then a second, and then he finally exhaled in relief. The head tormentor was gone.

Bing noted it and patted Walter's arm. "Kong can be kind, but his father has disciplined most of it out."

Walter plopped down on the mat. "One of those dads. I have one too, but he gave up on me young. My two older brothers got most of the heat." They also got the coveted medical degree whereas all Walter had ever wanted to do was draw comics. That was him, the comic genius/disappointment.

"Kong's father is the grand master who trained all of us, but he makes sure that Kong is the very best."

Kong wasn't the best person. That, obviously, was Bing, who dared be kind to the stupid American. "Kong is old enough to be responsible for his own actions."

Bing smiled. "In China, we can never escape our parents."

"In America, we can run very far away and sometimes they forget about us."

Bing smiled, and they shared a moment of connection. It was really nice given that the past hour had been about smiling through an ass-kicking. But as the seconds ticked by, Walter realized that Bing was just standing there waiting. The guy probably had better things to do than babysit a lost American. Hell, given his looks, he probably had a dozen more fun things to do with better-looking people. "If you have to leave, I'll be fine. My agent is around here somewhere." Assuming Yaz hadn't forgotten him.

"I am waiting in hopes you will teach me," Bing responded.

Walter laughed. "Teach you what? You guys are way better than I am."

Bing waited a moment to answer. In fact, he waited an uncomfortably long moment with his steady gaze dark on Walter. And then he squatted down beside Walter. "I do not believe you are less talented than us. And you are certainly well trained, though not in our type of kung fu."

"I'm trained in monkey kung fu. It's all my aunt would pay for."

"A fine discipline."

Wow. The guy sounded like he meant it.

"But what you did here," Bing continued. "That did not come from your teachers. That you figured out on your own, and so I wish to learn it from you."

Walter leaned back. "I… um…." Just how perceptive was this guy? Just how much had he figured out?

Bing extended his hand. "Will you teach me?"

"Teach you what?"

"How to fall as if drunk. How to land on your face without hurting your nose. How to land against the wall with such noise and yet stand up without bruises."

"Oh, there are bruises," he said. "Believe me."

Bing nodded. "Will you teach me?" His expression was so earnest that Walter knew he was going to give in. It was disconcerting, really, because the guy was so gorgeous, and yet so simple in his approach. Everything was spoken clearly without any subversion, without a shift of the eye or body. None of the usual tells of someone who was distracted or lying. It was as if he were exactly as he appeared—a gorgeous guy with singular focus who sincerely wanted to learn. From Walter.

It was flattering to be the focus of such a man. And a little bewildering to a guy who was used to being discounted.

"I can show you what I do," Walter finally said. "It's not that hard."

So he began to teach while Bing earnestly mimicked. They worked for hours, flowing in and out of patterns of movement. He adjusted how Bing walked, landed, even stood. And in the end…

It didn't work.

Bing couldn't fake being drunk. He couldn't even credibly fake a stumble. It was impossible for him to smoothly fall as if he'd been off-balance. The man didn't have any comic timing. Not in his body, and not in his language either. He was earnest. He was kind. And he never failed to give Walter the respect usually reserved for heads of state or religious icons. It was like being treated as Ghandi or Mother Theresa, and after a couple hours of it, Walter had to punch Bing in the shoulder.

"Dude, I just made a joke. Crack a smile, will you?"

Bing turned and gave him a brilliantly warm smile. One that showed off his dimples, that made the light catch his eyes just right, and had little Walter perking up with interest. And then a second later, the smile was gone, replaced by Bing's habitual mask of respect.

"Um, wow. That was…." Sudden. Weird. Unsettling. "You were so happy there for a second, and then it was gone."

"I am happy," Bing said quietly. "I am sorry I am such a bad student."

Walter bristled immediately. "You weren't a bad student. You listened, you tried, you—"

"I can't do it like you do. It does not look real."

That was true. No sense in denying it. "I don't think you're a comic actor, Bing. With practice, you could learn this so that most people wouldn't see that you were faking, but it isn't natural for you. You're the brooding intense guy, not the comic relief. That's good, by the way. Means you're a leading man not the supporting character with the weird face." If Walter was every going to make it in movies—which was not on his list of wants—then he'd be the guy with the awkward body that brought in the laughs but never, ever got laid.

Bing nodded, his gaze downcast. "It doesn't matter. I am not likely to get a role anyway."

Damn it, Walter wanted to help him, but the role of Shan Yu required someone who was naturally funny. Someone who could appear drunk but still fight. Someone who wasn't quite as good as the hero—physically or morally—but was appealing nonetheless. It required a comic actor or someone who was so stiff as to be made a laughingstock. The role could go either way, but Bing would be a disaster at both.

"I'm sorry," Walter said gently.

"One day, maybe."

Walter smiled. "Yeah. Sure." But he knew that good roles were hard to come by, and no way would Bing just walk into a dark, mysterious character role. That required connections and money. If he had to guess, Bing had neither.

Meanwhile, Bing surged gracefully to his feet. When he extended his hand, Walter gripped it and allowed himself to be pulled upright. "Do you wish to change? We have a bathing area—"

"God, yes. We Americans don't smell nearly as pretty as you." Then honesty forced him to adjust, because there were absolutely great-smelling men in America. He just wasn't one of them. "I would love a shower." Bing, on the other hand, smelled fantastic. How was it that even his sweat smelled sexy?

Bing smiled, and this time the look was natural and easy. "This way."

He led Walter into a basic shower area, and both of them stripped down before stepping into the stalls.

Walter tried to be respectful. Hell, he tried to be completely private with his lust. But Bing was beautiful. He had a sculpted torso, rippling muscles, and a golden tan that made Walter's mouth water. His hair was dark, his smile genuine, and the way he moved filled Walter's head with such desires.

Better yet, he caught Bing looking back. Walter didn't have a physique like a god—not like Bing did—but he was muscular and not too chubby. And while Bing wrapped a robe around his body to hide himself, Walter covered himself with a heavy towel and then a robe, both knotted to hide his erection. Bing noticed, of course. The man seemed to be hyperaware of the smallest movements, or he had been when they'd been training together. He had to know that Walter was interested. More than interested. Walter was practically dripping with desire.

They headed together for the shower stalls. They walked side by side, and when Bing took a quick darting look at Walter, the side expression was so beautiful that Walter stumbled. Right there and not on purpose, Walter's knee buckled just enough to throw off his balance.

Bing caught him. Of course he did. He was that fast, that smooth. And while they stood there practically nose to nose, Walter took the risk.

With a slow, deliberate movement, he pulled himself higher on Bing's body and pressed his mouth to Bing's.

The kiss was slow and sweet. He didn't fumble like usual but pushed his tongue between Bing's teeth and teased him there. He ducked in and out, he murmured a low sound of appreciation, and he gripped Bing's shoulders hard enough that he could feel the play of the man's muscles.

He felt Bing's breath catch. He knew it when Bing opened his mouth and angled his head. And he practically sang in ecstasy when Bing's tongue darted forward to play back.

Yes, yes, yes!

Walter's blood surged and his erection stiffened painfully. He got his weight under him, and he began moving Bing behind the curtain toward the shower wall. They were going to do such things to one another—

"No!"

Bing tore himself away from Walter's face. He scrambled sideways on the wall, and though his breath heaved, his word had been spoken in a desperate whisper. And then repeated even quieter.

"No."

It took a moment for Walter to adjust. His robe had fallen open and the towel had unwound to drop onto the tiled floor. He was standing there painfully erect while the man of his dreams appeared to be holding on to the wall for support.

Well, that didn't seem right.

He took a moment to steady his breath. Then he straightened as best he could, though his erection was still straining forward like a Bing-seeking missile. "Um, okay," he said. "Did you… um… need something?"

Like maybe a condom? A statement of devotion? A medical report? Anything that would suggest they could pick up again where they'd left off?

Walter knew that wasn't going to happen. He could see it on Bing's face. But part of him—the hard and horny part—was still holding out hope.

"I am sorry, Walter," Bing said stiffly. "There has been… misunderstanding."

Yeah, so he gathered.

"I… I date girls," Bing said. Then he blew out a breath. "I am not gay."

Walter almost said, "Are you sure?" Because for one, people could be into both girls and guys. But even more than that, Walter knew kisses, and his gaydar was pretty good. No one kissed like Bing had without being into it. And if that were true, then Bing was at least bisexual, or whatever term he wanted.

But he didn't say any of that. Whatever the truth of Bing's sexuality was, he had said no, and there was no point in trying to logic anyone into bed. It never worked, and even if he could manage to get Bing into bed, there would clearly be regrets in the morning.

So Walter backed away. "My mistake," he said, hating the desperate rasp to his voice. "I was confused. My bad."

He hadn't been confused. Hell, he was pretty sure Bing was the one who was in denial here. But again, there was no point in using logic. Bing would face his sexuality when he was ready. Walter just prayed he was around when Bing finally decided to explore. In the meantime, he needed a shower.

A cold shower.

He backed out of Bing's stall and headed to the next one. He flipped the water on to icy, and he forced himself under it. And when he was finally out and dressed—while Bing was still in the shower—he called Yaz, who was apparently still in discussions with the producer and director. She hadn't abandoned him and wanted him to join her in the conference room when he was ready.

"And hey," she said just before hanging up, "did you decide on who's going to play Shan Yu?"

Walter smiled. He knew just the person. "Kong will make a great buffoon. Give him the role."

"Great—"

"And there's another character I want to lay in right now."

Typical for Yaz, she didn't miss a bit. "Sure thing. Who?"

Walter lowered his voice. He didn't want anyone else hearing what he was about to say. "There someone who's going to be important next season. Someone we need to lay in now."

"Okay. Who is it?"

"He's named Red Wolf. And I'm giving Bing Zhi-Hao the role. Can you make sure that happens?"

"Red Wolf. Bing. Got it."

Walter nodded, hoping Yaz was sober enough to get it done. She probably was, but he intended to join her just to be sure. "Five minutes and I'll meet you up there."

Then he quickly finished dressing and called to the shower. The water was still running, but he was sure that Bing would hear him.

"My apologies, Bing, but I must rejoin my agent. I wish you the best of luck. I hope that next time I am in China, we will be able to work out together again." He kept his voice polite, professional, and without any of the longing he felt inside.

The water abruptly shut off. "Yes, Walter. That is my hope as well."

The words were polite, the tone completely professional. But would the man step out from behind the curtain and say something else? Better yet, would he do anything else? Like grab Walter and drag him into the hot, wet shower?

Walter waited, his heart pounding in his throat. God, how he hoped….

The shower kicked back on. No Bing. No sudden illicit sex in the back of a soundstage. Walter was being dismissed.

Not a surprise, and yet disappointment gripped Walter like a vise. But he could work with that. Especially since he intended to pour all of his hunger into creating the role of Red Wolf. If he couldn't give Bing the kind of hot sex they both craved, then he would give him the role of a lifetime.

That would work out for Bing, at least. And Walter would get to fantasize about his hot Asian god and call it work.

KATHY LYONS is the wild, adventurous half of USA Today best selling author Jade Lee. A lover of all things fantastical, Kathy spent much of her childhood in Narnia, Middle Earth, Amber, and Earthsea, just to name a few. "There is nothing I adore more than to turn around on an ordinary day and experience something magical. It happens all the time in real life and in my books." Her love of comedy came later as she began to see the ridiculousness in life.

Winner of several industry awards including the Prism—Best of the Best, the Romantic Times Reviewers' Choice Award, and Fresh Fiction's Steamiest Read, Kathy has published over sixty romance novels and is still going strong.

Her hobbies include racquetball, rollerblading, and TV/movie watching with her husband. She's a big fan of the Big Bang Theory (even though it's over), and her favorite movie is The Avengers because she loves everything created by Joss Whedon. And she'd love to share all things geek with you in person at any of her many appearances. She's usually found at the loudest table in the coffee shop or next to the dessert bar. To keep up with all things Lyons/Lee, sign up for her newsletter at www.KathyLyons.com. You'll get early peeks, fresh news, chances to meet her in person, plus prizes and geeky gifts.

Facebook: KathyLyonsBooks,
Twitter: @KathyLyonsAuth
Instagram: KathyLyonsAuthor

Read how it all began in

WERE-GEEKS
SAVE THE WORLD
BOOK ONE

WERE-
GEEKS
SAVE
WISCONSIN

KATHY LYONS

Were-Geeks Save the World: Book One

When badass werewolves battling supernatural evil realize they need tech support, they recruit a group of geeks with hilarious—and romantic—results.

Chemist Josh Collier is having a blast at a comic book convention when he gets the shock of his life—he's a werewolf! WTF? Before he can howl, he's whisked away to a secret lair by Nero, a hot guy dressed as a Roman centurion. Josh's former life is over, and his genius is needed at Wulf, Inc.

Nero has no interest in babysitting a trainee were-geek when he'd rather be killing the demon that wiped out his entire pack. While Josh analyzes the monster's weapon, wild passion ignites between him and Nero.

With destiny and their pack in the balance, can they survive the demon out to destroy Wisconsin?

www.dreamspinnerpress.com